CW01499564

BLACK SHUCK BOOKS

presents

THE COMPLEAT
VALENTINE

being the combined edition of

THE NINE DEATHS
OF DR VALENTINE

THE HAMMER
OF DR VALENTINE

and

THE LAST TEMPTATION
OF DR VALENTINE

written by

MR JOHN LLEWELLYN PROBERT

The Compleat Valentine

John Llewellyn Probert

BLACK
SHUCK
BOOKS

« When the whole story is known
the world will never forget it.»

Edward Valentine, MD, FRCS

Black Shuck Books
www.blackshuckbooks.co.uk

The Compleat Valentine
first published in 2018 by Black Shuck Books
this edition first published in 2019 by Black Shuck Books

The Nine Deaths of Dr Valentine
first published by Spectral Press, 2012

The Hammer of Dr Valentine
first published by Spectral Press, 2014

The Last Temptation of Dr Valentine
first published by Black Shuck Books, 2018

All content © John Llewellyn Probert 2018
Cover and interior layout © WHITEspace, 2019

978-1-913038-01-4

The Nine Deaths of
Dr Valentine

Dedicated to the memory of Vincent Price

1

The man's body was a writhing ball of fire.

Suspended a hundred feet above the river Avon by the chain that had been wound around his neck, the wriggling form bucked and twisted as it hung from the Clifton Suspension Bridge in the absolute blackness of the early March morning, creating a fiery inferno that could be seen for miles.

It wasn't long before somebody noticed it.

An hour later, and despite their best efforts, by the time local police and fire crews had hoisted the by-then lifeless smoking body back up onto the bridge, the press had already arrived on the scene.

Detective Inspector Jeffrey Longdon ran a hand through thinning hair and regarded the collection of television cameras and hastily-dressed anchor-people behind the police barrier with disdain. Behind him, the charred corpse was being loaded into an ambulance. *At least they managed to do it before Sky news turned up*, he thought with a hint of pride, before remembering that Sky didn't have a Bristol office and tended to be late for everything that happened in the area anyway. He ordered his men to keep the bridge closed until sunrise when forensics could give the place a thorough going over.

"Commuters from Leigh Woods aren't going to be happy, sir," said Sergeant Jenny Newham as a photographer with a particularly bad case of body odour tried to sneak past the barricade. She gave him the wagging finger treatment, and when that didn't work, employed the tried and tested upraised palm in his spotty face, which did the trick. "They all use the Clifton Suspension Bridge to get into Bristol."

"Fuck 'em," said Longdon, reaching for his cigarettes and realising his wife had hidden the packet again to help him in his attempts to give up. He took one of Newham's and borrowed her lighter as well. "Them and their gas-guzzling four by fours can get to work the long way down through the gorge. It's not going to hurt them." He took a deep drag and felt dizzy, forgetting that his sergeant's Gauloises contained about ten times the nicotine he was used to. He focused on his watch to try and stop his head from spinning.

"Sun won't be up for another hour, sir," Jenny said. "Do you want to wait for forensics to start work?"

Longdon shook his head and coughed before taking another drag. "Have they managed to wake Patterson up yet?"

"The pathologist?" She nodded. "Apparently he's on his way in."

"Good," said Longdon as they made their way back to the car. "I want to know everything about our victim. Not just what he died of. I want to know how old he was, what he was wearing, and if Patterson can manage it I even want to know what he had for tea."

~

"A hearty meal of fish, potatoes and some kind of green

vegetable. Could be cabbage, possibly broccoli. Difficult to tell because of the gastric digestion of the soft parts. All that acid, you see." Dr Richard Patterson MBBS, FRCPath put the dead man's stomach back down. As he laid it on the porcelain dissection slab it made a squelching sound and some of the contents he had just been describing leaked out. Longdon rolled his eyes while Jenny stifled a gag. "But of course what you want to know is *how* he died."

"If it's not too much trouble, Richard," Longdon knew his pathology colleague was a bit of a performer and he liked to humour him as best he could, but it had been a long day so far and it was still only eleven AM.

"Well, the burns, obviously," said Patterson, indicating the blackened eviscerated corpse on the table. "They pretty much cover his entire body. And the costume he was wearing wouldn't have helped."

Longdon raised an eyebrow at that. "Costume?"

Patterson nodded vigorously. "Oh yes." He tapped the charred skin of the man's right forearm with a scalpel handle and was rewarded with an unpleasant cracking sound. "This isn't normal eschar. Your chap was dressed up in some sort of costume, head to toe, so that when he was set alight it melted into his skin as well as setting it on fire." Patterson grimaced. "Very messy. And very painful too, I should imagine."

"Head to toe you say?" Longdon wanted to get that straight. "You mean his head was covered?"

"Exactly," said Patterson. "Some sort of all-over body thing. You know, like a diving suit. I've sent a sample off to forensics but they may be a while because they'll have to sort out what is skin and what isn't, which is never very easy."

"Well as soon as you find out let me know," said Longdon, looking around the post-mortem room and wondering what kind of person enjoyed spending most of their working day in such a place. "Any idea if it could have been suicide?" he asked.

Patterson sniffed. "You'd have a better idea of that than me, Inspector. I suppose it's conceivable that he got himself dressed up, wound a chain around his own neck, soaked himself in petrol and jumped off the Clifton Suspension Bridge but it's all a bit elaborate for someone who wanted to do themselves in."

"Elaborate and bloody impractical," said Longdon, turning to leave. "No, this isn't a suicide, and it wasn't an accident either." He pointed at the blackened thing on the dissecting table. "I want a full report on that on my desk before lunchtime, not that I'm planning on eating anything after the morning I've had."

~

"Nothing from Missing Persons yet, sir," said Jenny once they were back in the inspector's office.

"Bloody typical," said Longdon, going straight over to check the coffee machine, which proved to be empty, as did the tin beside it he kept the coffee in. "Does someone keep coming in here and pinching my Hot Lava Java?" he said, snapping the lid shut.

"No idea, sir," said the sergeant with a smile. "But I do know you finished the last of the other packet on Friday before we left."

"So I bloody did," said Longdon, suddenly remembering. His eyes strayed to the half-empty jar of Nescafe by the kettle. He pondered the possibility for a whole ten seconds before shaking his head. "Anything from dental records yet?"

"Nothing there either, sir. According to Dr Patterson, the teeth that aren't melted are in excellent condition so there may not be a dentist with any record of him."

"So he took care of himself," said Longdon, "whoever he was." He sat down behind his desk and pondered whether or not to ring the Chief Inspector yet.

"You know what he'll say, sir," said Jenny.

"How did you know what I was thinking?" Longdon asked with the hint of smile.

"Because you're a born worrier." she said, returning it, "and talking to the Chief Inspector is the next thing on the list to worry about."

"Enough with the shrewd remarks, Sergeant," said Longdon, "let's just keep our fingers crossed that's all we have to worry about for now."

2

Dr Evan Pritchard made a point of getting home early that evening.

It hadn't mattered that his last patient of the day had wanted to talk and talk, the persistent symptoms of her neuroses still failing to be controlled, either by behavioural therapy or by the drugs he had prescribed for her. Eventually he had found it necessary to curtail their already over-running session, and Mrs Violet Twelvetrees had not been impressed by his excuse for having to practically manhandle her out of his private rooms. Pritchard had thought it was a very good excuse, partly because he considered a wedding anniversary to be a perfectly plausible reason why a man should want to get home, and secondly because, while he had constructed occasionally ludicrous falsities to get him away from more bothersome patients in the past, this one was actually true.

Which was why he was surprised when he got home to find the house in darkness.

"Miranda?"

There was no reply. *Strange*, he thought. Perhaps she was late home herself, but that made no sense. His wife hadn't worked for several years now, not since he had gained his consultant post, and it was hardly likely that she would have forgotten what the date was. He switched on the kitchen light and draped his jacket on the back of a chair. He was about to go upstairs when he saw the note that had been left on the pine kitchen table. The lilac paper (Miranda's favourite) had been folded once and his Christian name scribbled in purple ink (another of Miranda's little eccentricities) on one side. He opened it and read the message within aloud.

"Darling, don't worry, I haven't forgotten about tonight, especially not after last year." Last year was still a bit of a sore point, not least because he had not just forgotten their anniversary, but had been at a conference in Vienna when he should have been at home with her. "I just thought it would be more fun if we did something a little different, so I'm waiting for you. But not here. If it's gone 5.30—" Evan looked up at the clock to see it was closer to six "—then the chauffeur should be waiting outside to take you for a little ride, and at the end of it you'll find me, and an extra special surprise. So what are you waiting for? Lots of love, M."

Pritchard folded the note back up and put it in his pocket, frowning as he did so. It was definitely his wife's handwriting, but the style was unlike anything she had said to him for several years now. He allowed himself a wry grin. Perhaps she was trying to rekindle old passions, and if that was the case he had no objection at all. Outside, a car horn blew. He pulled on his jacket and grabbed his overcoat, just in case they ended up somewhere chilly. His grin broadened as he remembered the time in Paris when they'd ended up having an impromptu assignation by the Seine on a chilly March night just like this one.

He climbed into the back of the waiting limousine and

was surprised to find another lilac note waiting for him. *Enjoy the ride, my darling*, said more of that elegant purple script, *and when the car reaches its destination, just follow the trail to find me!* Pritchard tucked that note away too and settled back as the car drifted through the Bristol streets. The driver was hidden behind smoked glass, not that Pritchard felt like conversation anyway, but he wouldn't have minded at least a clue as to where he was going and how long it might take to get there.

The journey turned out to be shorter than he was expecting. The car pulled onto the side of the road and the door was opened. Pritchard stepped out to find himself on an area of grassy parkland he recognised as part of the Bristol Downs. From where he stood by the roadside, stretching away and around the shadowy outline of a clump of conifers, led an avenue of candles that had been placed in glass containers to prevent the wind from blowing out their flames.

Well, she's gone to an awful lot of trouble, I must say, thought Pritchard, wondering if Miranda had perhaps caused some disaster and had needed to create an elaborate apology for it. Still, it certainly made a change from their usual arguments. As the car drove away he made his way along the avenue of flickering lights, stumbling a little on the uneven ground.

When he rounded the conifer trees his mouth dropped open in astonishment. He hadn't been sure what to expect, and while he had been trying to guess what this improvised path might be leading to, he was still taken aback by what he saw.

At first Pritchard thought he was looking at a giant

inflatable horse floating in the air. Then, as he came closer, he realised it was a hot air balloon, and that it was not a horse but a unicorn. The wicker basket was made for one man, or two at a very tight squeeze. Stapled to the front was another lilac note.

All you have to do is get in, my darling, it said. *I've prepared a very special surprise for us and all you have to do is let the very clever controls on this lovely balloon guide you there.*

Pritchard looked up to see an arrangement of electronic devices fixed to the frame a couple of feet below the brightly burning gas jets. The balloon itself was filled with air and ready to ascend. He took another look at the note and raised an eyebrow. Miranda had been known to do crazy things like this, but that had been years ago, when they'd first met. All the same, he was intrigued, and not a little excited, by the prospect of what might happen next, and so he buttoned up his jacket and climbed in.

Without warning the guy ropes came free from their attachments, presumably triggered by some device that had been activated by his climbing into the basket. Pritchard marvelled: what remarkable things they could make nowadays! He gripped the edge of the basket as it began to ascend.

Soon he was floating over Bristol. He saw the Clifton Suspension Bridge and the Avon Gorge way beneath, the headlights of cars travelling along either side of it tiny pinpricks of light in the darkness. Then he was heading over Clifton itself and towards Bristol City Centre. He passed over the university and as he headed down Park Street he realised the balloon was beginning to descend.

It's a funny way to get to the Sheraton Hotel, he thought, that being the obvious destination to meet up for a romantic evening.

But the balloon didn't head towards the hotel. Instead the electronic devices hummed and burred, and Pritchard's journey took an abrupt right turn toward the imposing four storey, neo-Georgian building that stood close to Bristol Cathedral and took up one whole side of the area locally known as College Green. Pritchard knew it was the Bristol Council House, the building that acted as the city's seat of government. What he wasn't expecting was for the balloon to halt its progress just above the building at the end nearest the street.

Pritchard looked over. Just below him stood one of the two golden unicorn statues that were positioned on the roof at either end of the long curving building. He waited for a moment for the balloon to move on but it stayed put. He shook the basket in case something had got stuck. What on earth was he supposed to do here?

Two students crossing the green waved at him. He was tempted to shout for help but felt so acutely embarrassed that all he could do was wave back.

As soon as he raised his hand he felt something give way beneath him, as the bottom of the basket opened and Pritchard fell through. The cheerful expressions on the passing students' faces turned to ones of horror as they watched the man who had just waved to them hang onto the side of the basket for dear life, his legs flailing beneath him. What they didn't see was the row of spikes that emerged from the basket's border that caused him to release his grip.

Pritchard fell no more than three feet. Unfortunately his fall was broken by the horn of the gilded unicorn beneath him, which penetrated his spine and passed through his body to emerge from his chest. Despite his injury his body continued to twitch as the unicorn onto which it had been skewered gradually turned a dark shade of scarlet, but by the time anyone managed to get to him he had long since stopped moving altogether.

3

"So you're saying that a unicorn-shaped balloon carried this man over the council building, dropped him onto a two-foot-long spike belonging to another unicorn and then flew away again?"

The student, whose name was Steven Cope, nodded in response to DI Longdon's question.

The inspector turned to Cope's girlfriend Helen. "And that's what you saw as well?" he asked. The girl nodded in agreement and pulled her coat tighter around her. The air on College Green had turned very chilly. "And at no point," he persisted, "did either of you see who pushed him out?"

"No-one pushed him out," said Helen.

"What do you mean?" asked Jenny, who was busy taking notes.

"There was no-one else up there with him," said Cope. "Or if there was they must have been a midget. That basket was tiny. Anyway, if there was they would have fallen out with him."

"Because the bottom of the basket actually opened so he fell through it?" Longdon sneered. "I've never heard anything so ridiculous in my life."

"Well, to be honest, I had never *seen* anything so ridiculous," said Cope. "The balloon wasn't even travelling in the direction the wind was blowing. None of it made sense."

Longdon leaned close to him. "And how much have you had to drink tonight?" he asked.

Cope was defensive. "Couple of pints at the pub," he said, and then looked at his watch. "And they should have worn off well before now."

It was close to three in the morning. A healthy crowd of onlookers and reporters, including Sky News this time, had arrived within minutes of the first mobile phone footage going up on YouTube. They had come to record, broadcast and just generally stare and point at the body of Dr Evan Pritchard as it was inexpertly removed from its gilded murder weapon. And so thus it was that Dr Pritchard's lifeless body was brought down to earth, albeit with the occasional wobble and scrape along the brickwork of the Council House. They were just loading him into the ambulance when a taxi pulled up and a glamorous but exceedingly distressed-looking middle-aged lady got out. She exchanged words with one of the officers at the police cordon, who brought her over to Longdon and Jenny just as they were dismissing the two students.

"Sorry to bother you sir," said the officer, "but this lady says she knew the deceased."

"Well that's a charming way to put it," the woman snapped, her eyes blazing. "I'm his wife."

Longdon looked at Jenny. "I wasn't aware we'd released any details to the public," he said.

"That hardly matters when something like this is all over the bloody television." Miranda Pritchard looked up at the bloodstained unicorn. "I recognised him as soon as the damn thing came on the news."

"Even upside down and bent backwards?" Jenny couldn't help but say.

Miranda glared at her. "Obviously you're not married or you wouldn't be surprised that one can sometimes come home to find one's husband in that kind of position, stark staring drunk and moaning about his job or his colleagues or some bloody patient he's been having trouble with. God knows I used to find him like that often enough."

Jenny resisted the urge to smirk as she said, "And the reason you didn't report him missing this evening was...?"

Miranda's face reddened. "I was with... a friend," she said.

"For a night of television watching, obviously," said Longdon.

"You're bloody rude, Inspector," spat Miranda.

"And *you're* holding up our investigation, madam," he replied with no less vehemence. "We'll need to see you at the station tomorrow for questioning of course, but while you're here perhaps you could explain these?" He held out a handful of crumpled lilac notes. "They were in his pocket. Apart from his wallet and keys they were all he had on him."

But Miranda was no longer listening. She was staring, speechless, at the slips of paper.

"Well?" said Longdon. "Did you write these?"

Mrs Pritchard nodded slowly. When she spoke next her voice was little more than a dry croak. "Yes," she said, before looking at the detective with tears in her eyes, "I wrote them. But over two years ago."

"You mean he kept them all this time?" said Jenny.

Miranda shook her head. "I wrote them," she said. "But not for him."

"For another... friend?" said Longdon.

"Yes, Inspector," said Miranda, the tears flowing now. "For another friend. Happy now?"

"We'll take a full statement from you tomorrow," said Jenny, who called over the officer who had brought Miranda across. "You'd best get some rest."

As the sobbing woman was led away Longdon lit his first cigarette of the day.

"You're not happy are you?" said Jenny.

Longdon exhaled loudly and looked up at the unicorn. The fire brigade had a ladder up to it now and someone was trying to clean all the blood off.

"This city has just seen two elaborately planned murders in two days," he said. "If you want me to go further I'd add 'unnecessarily complicated' and 'ridiculous' to the description but that's strictly off the record. And I'm sure you don't need to ask me if I think they're linked. No, Sergeant Newham, I am not happy, I am not happy at all." Longdon threw his cigarette down and trod on it. "The only thing I'm hoping at the moment is that it's over."

4

If DI Longdon hated one thing more than being in charge of morning briefings, it was conducting them after he'd had no sleep the night before.

Sergeant Newham had done him the inestimable service of popping into the Starbucks on the corner beforehand to get him a couple of double espressos. He accepted the tiny paper cups with a grunt before doing his best to give her a warm smile. She was a good girl and was doing a hell of a good job putting up with him in what the press was already beginning to call 'The Death Plunge Murders'.

'Police Baffled!' said one tabloid, a phrase Longdon thought had gone out in the nineteen-fifties.

'Police No Further in Bristol Death Probe,' said the Telegraph, which was honest without being unkind.

'Is This What We Pay Our Taxes For!!!' the Daily Mail had screamed while guiding its readers to pages two through five for the in-depth story of the Bristol police force's catalogue of blunders and mistakes over the last five years. *No doubt guaranteed fact-free*, thought Longdon, and put together with the sole intention of getting the wrong sort of people's blood boiling. Not that any of that mattered. There was a murderer at large and he needed results. He knocked back both coffees, got to his feet and called for order.

The assembled officers stopped chatting and

regarded Longdon with respect. He knew it was really because they were all relieved they weren't standing where he was, in charge of a murder case that already had national press coverage and absolutely no leads.

"Ladies and gentlemen," he said, "thank you for coming." There were a few appreciative chuckles at that. "As you know, for the moment the Chief Inspector has allowed me to remain responsible for this case. Whether that's because he thinks I'm the best man for the job or the most disposable member of staff to carry the can when this all goes tits up I have no idea, but that doesn't matter." He turned to the pinboard behind him that summarised the information they had so far. "What does matter is that we need to find whoever's responsible for these murders before he – or she – does it again."

A young man with thinning sandy hair in the front row raised his hand and identified himself as Detective Sergeant David Kinsey. "Are we sure the murders are connected, sir?" he asked.

Longdon shrugged. "To be honest, no. The mode of death in each case was different but outlandish enough in both to conceivably be the work of the same person. Our psychologist Dr Diana Weston—" Longdon pointed to a smartly dressed young woman with dark hair pulled into a tight bun and spectacles that were much too large for her small face "—is working hard putting together a profile of the killer's thought processes based on what we have found so far. I understand she isn't quite ready to present her findings yet." The girl shook her head and looked down at the bulging file on her lap. "But I'm sure she will at the earliest opportunity. Now, if there are no further questions," Longdon turned back to the board. "The first victim was discovered two nights ago hanging from Clifton Suspension Bridge in a state of immolation."

The door banged open. Longdon rolled his eyes at the interruption and was about to release a barrage of abuse at the interloper until he realised it was the pathologist.

"Ah, the good Dr Patterson," he said. "I hope you've got some information of use to us."

Richard Patterson waved the manila file he was holding at Longdon. "I've got the post-mortem findings on our late Dr Pritchard," he said. "He died of massive blood loss caused by puncture of the aorta and inferior vena cava by a heavy metal object thrust through his back just to the left of his first lumbar vertebra."

"Nothing surprising there, then," said Longdon. "But I was rather hoping you might have unearthed a bit more about our first victim."

Patterson looked confused. "Haven't you seen my report?" he said.

Longdon shook his head. "I only know what you told me the other morning in the autopsy room," he said.

"But I sent you an email! I was here until God knows what time last night typing it."

"Which probably explains why I haven't read it yet, seeing as I was unexpectedly called to our impaled friend at the Bristol Council House," said Longdon, aware that this exchange was being watched keenly by his assembled team. A couple of them at the back even appeared to be taking notes.

"Well, you might want to read it when you have a minute," said Patterson, turning to go.

"Just a minute, doctor." Longdon could sense all eyes were on him. "In case you hadn't noticed, we are having a morning briefing here. Anything you might have to say could help us with the case. I'd very much appreciate it if you could summarise what you've found for us now."

"You might want to read what I've said yourself before releasing it to your men," said Patterson. "It's a bit odd."

Longdon knew he was going to start shouting in a minute. "I'm sure it can't be much more 'odd' than what we've already had to deal with, Doctor," he said. "So if you would be so kind?"

Patterson cleared his throat, looked at his shoes as if pondering something for a moment and then said, "Well, if you insist. As you know, the man's body was completely covered in full-thickness burns, and you may remember I mentioned to you that he seemed to be wearing some sort of suit." Longdon nodded. "Well, I sent samples off to the laboratory and they confirmed that what they received was a mixture of skin, rubber, and something else which they eventually concluded was the charred remains of synthetic hair fibres. Black ones. These were all over his body except for his face, where the rubber was of a different consistency." Patterson took a deep breath and looked at the sea of faces watching him. "The design and the rubber used were of a make commonly associated with certain brands of fancy dress outfit, and therefore, from the consistency and distribution of the synthetic hairs, it would seem that when the victim died he was most likely wearing a gorilla suit."

Longdon eventually broke the silence that ensued. "A gorilla suit?"

Patterson nodded. "Combining their findings with mine, our victim was probably wearing the gorilla suit when he had petrol poured all over him. The chain was then put around his neck, after which he was set on fire and pushed off the Clifton Suspension Bridge."

If Patterson had been a performer in a play he could not have got a better reaction from his audience. Hardened veterans and newcomers alike shifted uncomfortably in their seats at his calm clinical description.

"And do we have any further clues as to his identity?" Longdon asked.

Patterson shrugged. "No fingerprints, no distinguishing marks, not even eye colour to go on," he said. "Even the inside of his mouth was so badly scorched that quite a few of his teeth had either been dislodged or had melted, so comparison with dental records is proving difficult as well." The pathologist glanced at the room full of thoroughly uncomfortable police officers before turning back to Longdon. "Can I go now, please?"

Longdon nodded and turned back to his team. "Now you all know as much as I do," he said. "So far this lunatic has murdered a respected psychiatrist and an unidentifiable other, in both cases using means so far removed from what one might grudgingly describe as normal murder that we can only assume that he's clever." He looked at Dr Weston, who nodded. "And resourceful." She nodded again. "And, as you have no doubt already guessed, my major concern is whether or not he has any more planned. Well, I want us to be ready for him. Get out there and don't rest until you've found something that can either lead us to him or give us an idea of what he might be planning next. I don't want to be reading tomorrow about another poor bastard who's been bumped off in the kind of way you should only see in a Road Runner cartoon."

5

"Martin, where are you going?"

Dr Martin Davies closed the front door and looked back down the corridor of his lovely home to where his wife Wendy was looking at him admonishingly. He cursed to himself. It didn't look as if he was going to get to see Tracy this morning after all.

"I just thought I'd pop into the hospital and—"

He wasn't allowed to finish his sentence.

"Martin," said his wife, advancing on him with the spatula she had been using to cook the kids' scrambled eggs. "What day is it?

"Saturday," he said, trying hard not to avert his eyes from hers.

"And what," she said in a voice that was so quiet so as not to disturb the children and yet at the same time was positively terrifying, "did you promise Jemima and Jocasta you were going to do today?"

Now Martin had to think. He was sure he had promised to take his two daughters somewhere, but hadn't that been last weekend? Or the next one? From the look on Wendy's face it was obviously this one. He looked at his wife. Her black hair was tousled and she was wearing her favourite weekend grey leggings that were wearing out. She had that black T-shirt on that made her breasts stand out in a way he never let her know for fear she might stop wearing it. Even when she was mad at him she was beautiful, perhaps even more so. Perhaps it was time to call it a day with Tracy, he thought. He tried to stop thinking about both women and remember what he was supposed to have promised the girls.

It was Jocasta, his seven-year-old, who saved him. From behind the closed kitchen door she called, "When's daddy taking us to the zoo?"

"I knew that," said Martin in a tone of voice that patently betrayed him as not having had a clue.

Wendy was inches from him now, and raised the spatula so it was almost touching his nose. "You know what I ought to do with this, don't you?" she said. Martin could only nod. "And the only thing that's stopping me is that I know you'd like it too much."

He didn't know what to do and so he kissed the tip of her nose. Wendy giggled.

"You're a bloody naughty man, Martin Davies, wanting to go to that place which owns you body and bloody soul for most of the week." Martin was about to make his excuses but she held up a hand. "I know, you just want to go and make sure your patients are all right and believe me, I think it's admirable that a paediatrician should show such concern for his children there. But how about showing a bit of dedication to your children *here*. You know, your *actual* children? The ones I gave birth to after you spent some not inconsiderable time—"

Martin shushed her and pointed over Wendy's shoulder. Jemima had opened the kitchen door. His nine-year-old was standing there with her arms folded.

"Daddy," she said. "Jocasta keeps wanting to know when we're going."

"Just as soon as you've washed your hands and got your coat on," said Martin, looking at his wife, "isn't that right, Mummy?"

"That's right," said Wendy, "and just as soon as Daddy gets his coat on and gets the car out of the garage." She looked back at him. "Isn't that right, Daddy?"

A quarter of an hour later, and with the two girls safely secured in the backseat of his Lexus, Martin Davies was headed for Bristol Zoo.

~

The car park was almost full by the time they got there, even though it was only a little after half past nine. Martin cursed his forgetfulness as he did his best to squeeze between a Land Rover and a minibus that asked if several feet could be left next to it to allow disabled passengers to alight. *They never need all that and besides, we'll probably be around and finished before they get back*, Martin figured, letting the girls out and ensuring the car was locked.

"Can we go and see the squiggly things, Daddy?" said Jocasta, pointing at a sign that had been erected near the entrance.

Quite why his youngest daughter had developed such a fascination for invertebrates, and in particular the kinds of creatures that would make Wendy scream and which Martin himself would prefer not to get too close to, was anyone's guess. He looked at the poster displayed prominently next to the entry turnstiles. 'Today's Special Attraction!' it said in bubbly day-glo lettering, followed by, in the kind of shaky shimmery scary font Martin thought had gone out of fashion in the nineteen-seventies, 'The Creepy Crawly Creature Feature!' Coiled around the words were rather intimidating-looking cartoon depictions of centipedes, spiders and scorpions, all of which appeared to be attacking the words that were advertising them. At the bottom of the poster, in the far-more-friendly day-glo letters again, were the words 'Presented by Everyone's Friend, Captain Clowney!'

"Please!" said Jocasta, in the way only a seven-year-old girl who knows how to get her own way with her father is capable of. "And it's with Captain Clowney! Please please please!"

Martin had heard great things about Captain Clowney from Jocasta following the last time Wendy had taken them along to one of his zoo shows, allowing Martin to spend another couple of exhausting but rewarding hours with Tracy. That time it had been about monkeys. Or was it penguins? Anyway, trust Wendy to get lucky with something vaguely acceptable and for him to end up with the chamber of horrors.

"Do you want to go and see all the creepy crawlies as well?" he asked Jemima, who nodded enthusiastically.

"I don't like some of the things on that poster," she said. "But I do like Captain Clowney. He knows a lot about animals."

"All right then," said Martin, handing over his credit card to pay the admission price and asking for tickets to Captain Clowney's Creepy Crawly Creature Feature as well. The girl behind the booth tore off several strips of paper which she handed to him before activating the button that allowed the three of them through the turnstile. Martin just had time to glance at the poster again and note that the performance was scheduled for lunchtime before they were through. He looked up to see Jocasta already heading for the gift shop and a whole world of plush animals that she most definitely did not need any more of.

"Come back here, Jocasta," he said and then, when he beheld her glum face, "there'll be plenty of time for that later. Besides, how do you know Captain Clowney might not have cuddly centipedes and scorpions for sale at his show?"

"You can't cuddle a scorpion, silly," said Jocasta, the gift shop already forgotten as Martin set off with Jemima holding his left hand and Jocasta his right for a leisurely tour of the animal enclosures.

They took in their favourites (the lions and tigers for Jemima, the monkeys and vultures for Jocasta, who had liked the singing ones in Disney's *The Jungle Book*) and stopped for crisps and Coke. It was surprisingly sunny for the time of year and they sat outside the cafeteria, the girls slurping noisily from their drinks bottles. Martin wished they sold something a bit stronger than just lemonade as he realised the time was edging ever closer to Captain Clowney's Hell On Earth for People Who Frankly Didn't Like Creepy Crawlies One Little Bit. Martin had never really considered himself to be such a person, but he did jump when he saw any spider larger than a fifty pence piece. And anything that buzzed near him would be frantically swatted away for fear that it was a wasp, even when it wasn't the season for them.

He sat and watched a line of ants rescue fragments of

a crushed fruit pastille from beneath their seat. That was the size of insect he was comfortable with, and he had a feeling – a horrible, gut-churning feeling – that the Captain Clowney show was going to be one of those things that featured audience interaction. Which always meant the dads. Which meant he might get dragged up in front of everybody where the frank and utter terror of having some hideous wriggling thing waved in front of his face or put on his shoulder would be so obvious to everyone that he would never be able to set foot in the hospital again in case any of his staff had been in the audience.

"Are you all right, Daddy?" said Jemima, putting down her empty crisp packet.

"I'm fine, my love," said Martin, realising that he was sweating. He took out his handkerchief and mopped his face. "It's just a bit warm out here, that's all."

"No it isn't!" said Jocasta. "It's cold. Can we go and see the creepies now?"

Martin looked at his watch. Twenty minutes to go. "I suppose we could go and find where it is and get some seats," he said, getting to his feet with some difficulty as his legs seemed to have turned to water. He wobbled a bit and Jemima took his hand.

"Oh, Daddy, stop being silly!" she said as the two girls guided him past signs pointing to where Captain Clowney would soon be waiting.

The Insect House was a self-contained building the size of the cafeteria they had just left and was, to Martin's relief, situated just five minutes' walk away. Martin peered up at the massive anthropomorphic beetle that smiled down at him from above the entrance and felt a twinge of dread deep within his soul. On either side of the sheet plastic swing doors were signs announcing the special show at twelve that would be admission by ticket only.

"Come *on*, Daddy!" said Jocasta, oblivious to Martin's obvious reluctance to go in. The two girls pulled him through the swing doors where a chubby girl in a green shirt took their tickets.

"If you go in and through the door to your right you'll find there's plenty of room inside," she said with a smile. "Sometimes it's good to be early."

Martin didn't want to be early. He didn't want to be there at all, he now realised. But there was no turning back. All he could do was hope and pray that he didn't get singled out for any audience participation. Maybe if they sat at the back and kept quiet—

"Can we sit at the front, Daddy?" said Jocasta the minute she saw him edging to the back of the auditorium. "Please! I won't be able to see *anything* from up there."

The room in which they found themselves looked like a small lecture theatre, with the back half being taken up with rows of banked seating that had been arranged on scaffolding. At the front was a brightly lit performance area whose yellow papier maché contours had presumably been constructed to resemble the arid dunes of the desert.

It was only when Martin had made sure his daughters were settled and he had sat down that he saw the throne.

It was placed dead centre at the very back of the stage,

and was the only feature other than the desertscape. Quite why it was there, or what part it might play in the proceedings, Martin wasn't sure, and it was only when he squinted to focus on it that a shiver scuttled along his back bone.

It was in the shape of a giant golden scorpion.

The backrest formed the curling tail, the massive stinger poised as if to pierce the skull of whoever might dare to sit on the rich velvet upholstery. The arms ended in open claws, pointing upward, the red leather lining of each presumably indicating that the unfortunate victim was meant to rest their arms in the claws themselves. Eight gilt legs emerged evenly from the seat. From its place at the back of the stage the scorpion throne probably looked very regal and very imposing.

To Martin it looked terrifying. In fact, the only thing more terrifying than the throne itself was the fact that it was enclosed on all four sides by transparent perspex, forming a cubicle with a door at the front.

Martin looked around him. The place was beginning to fill up, mainly with families, but there were a few large, almost uncontrollable, parties of under-tens with just one or two adults to stop them from running hither and thither, spilling the drinks and snacks he was sure he had seen a sign forbidding the bringing in of, and trying to solve the insurmountable problem of who wanted to sit with whom.

"How much longer, Daddy?" said Jocasta.

Martin looked at his watch and another wave of fear flooded over him. "Just five minutes, my love," he said, squeezing her hand more for his comfort than for hers.

She pulled his head close and whispered, "Don't worry, Daddy. It'll all be over in a bit."

Martin smiled at his perceptive daughter and was just about to tell his two girls just how much he loved them both when the house lights went down and a frivolous voice boomed over the loudspeakers.

"Who's it time for?"

"Captain Clowney!" responded those in the audience who had obviously been to one of these before, Martin's children included.

"He can't hear you," said the voice. "Who's it time for?"

Again the response, so raucous and shrill this time that it bordered on the hysterical.

"Well, here he comes!" It was all the excuse the children in the auditorium needed to scream and shout, stamp their feet, drop their drinks and generally make a mess of themselves at the altar of the man who came bounding on to the stage from the left.

Martin had never liked clowns. Even as a child the one reason he hadn't wanted to go to the circus with his parents was because of the so-called funny men. If they were so silly and friendly and happy, he had reasoned, why did they need to paint their smiles on? Somehow he had gone from that to deciding it was because they'd forgotten how to really smile and had to remind themselves by looking in the mirror at the painted one before they came out onto the stage.

If ordinary circus clowns scared Martin, Captain Clowney was a new experience in terror. Possibly the most disconcerting thing of all was that he was dressed all in white, like some sort of demented antiseptic entertainer on a high risk diseases ward. His white jumpsuit and boots were almost hidden by the ankle length white cloak he wore, a flamboyant garment that had been decorated with glittery crescent moons, stars and tiny ringed planets. His face was white as well, with his lips and eyes encircled with the kind of rouge that made Martin think of a badly painted ventriloquist's dummy. But the worst was the hair – a huge fluffy shock of ginger that had been scattered with glitter and teased through the holes in the headgear the captain was wearing so that it looked as if his head was exploding through his cap.

"Good morning, boys and girls!" he said. His voice was vaguely effeminate or possibly deliberately campy, and betrayed a hint of an American accent.

The response to his greeting was deafening.

"And who am I?"

There was another grating outburst as the assembled youthful throng chanted his name.

"That's right," said Captain Clowney, before adding with a big wink, "and mums and dads in the audience can just call me George."

Martin groaned and then found himself laughing at the joke, if only because he needed something – anything – to help relieve the tension.

"And what are we going to see today?" Captain Clowney asked.

"Creepy crawlies!" the children responded in the kind of singsong monotone that always creeped Martin out, suggesting as it did the presence of some kind of infantile hive mind.

"That's right," said the clown, holding up his hands and wiggling his fingers while making scary noises. "Creepy crawlies. Would you like to see one now?" The audience response was as predictable as it was loud. "Good. Well in that case what I want you to do is help me call my good friend Natasha onto the stage because she's helping me look after all the creatures we're going to be seeing today."

Natasha was the girl who had taken their tickets on the way in. She climbed onto the stage still dressed in her regulation uniform, but now she was carrying a plastic box the size and shape of a large tupperware container. She placed it on the small green baize-topped folding table Captain Clowney brought centre stage. Martin could see things moving in it. Now he was *really* wishing they hadn't sat in the front row.

"Let's start with something really wriggly!" said the Captain, taking what looked like a pair of baby salad tongs from one of the pockets of his cloak and lifting the lid of the glass box.

Martin recoiled as a squirming centipede was taken out of the container. Its body was as thick as his thumb and as long as his outstretched hand. The room was thrown into such a state of hush that he swore he could hear the creature's mandibles clicking against the device that held it.

"You won't find this in your garden at home," said Captain Clowney as the thing continued to wriggle. "It's from Brazil." He paused and looked around the room to ensure he had everyone's attention before continuing. "And it's very, very *poisonous!*"

If nothing else, Martin was impressed with this man's ability to turn a room full of restless anticipant children into one in which a pin dropping in the back row could have been detected. But wasn't it a bit irresponsible playing with something like that with youngsters present? Martin turned round and could see from the worried looks of some of the parents that they must be thinking the same thing.

"Before any of you get worried, perhaps I should say that my friend Natasha has reassured me that this little fellow has had all the poison taken out of him before today's performance," said the Captain. The collective adult sigh of relief was almost palpable. "Of course if I were to drop him he might scuttle up someone's trouser leg!"

The clown pretend-fumbled the angry-looking creature to a few accompanying audience gasps before returning it to the case.

More examples followed, all seemingly selected for their ability to inspire terror rather than for any real attempt at education, although Captain Clowney was sure to mention the country of origin and of course the dangerousness of the succession of giant beetles, hissing cockroaches and oversized locusts which followed. Some respite from the grotesques was provided when a tank featuring moon moths was brought in and one little girl from the audience had one settle on her finger after it had been treated to a dab of pheromone by the Captain. Then came the part Martin had been dreading.

"For our next demonstration we need a volunteer." Captain Clowney waved away the forest of infantile hands which immediately went up. "No. This time I need an adult volunteer," he said, his eyes scanning the audience. "One of you mums or dads who are feeling particularly brave, who fancy showing their kids that there's nothing to fear from one of the most terrifying creatures that lives in the desert!"

Martin could feel Jocasta poking him in the thigh but he kept his hands by his sides. *Let some other poor bugger get shown up*, he thought. *I'm not going anywhere near that stage.*

"We need someone to be the Scorpion King!" said Captain Clowney, indicating the throne Martin had seen earlier. *And there's no way at all that I'm going near that*, he thought to himself as the captain added, "Or Scorpion Queen, of course. Now, who is prepared to come out here and show everyone what they're made of?"

Hands were being tentatively raised now, but the Captain didn't seem to be too taken with the choices on offer. He teased at plumes of his copper hair as he looked around the room. Martin tried hard to shrink in his chair as the clown's gaze swept along the front row...

...and came to rest on Martin.

"You, sir!" said the Captain, holding out a white-gloved hand.

Martin shook his head, but the Captain was insistent.

"Oh come now, sir! Surely you wouldn't want to pass up an opportunity to be the Scorpion King in front of your lovely daughters and all the other boys and girls and ladies and gentlemen here?"

"Go *on*, Daddy!" said Jemima, her nine-year-old voice already tinged with embarrassment at her father's reticence. Behind him, Martin could feel the relief from those already lowering their hands, safe in the knowledge that someone else had been picked to go up on stage.

"Come on, my dear fellow," said the clown, who now seemed less funny than ever, "we mustn't keep everybody waiting, must we?"

Martin got up, even though his feet weren't too keen on the idea. He followed the Captain to the perspex box. The clown made a show of reaching into his voluminous cloak, from which he produced a gold key. He held it up to the audience.

"The key to the kingdom!" he said, unlocking the door and opening it to allow Martin to gain access. "Now, if the king would be so kind as to take his place upon his throne." Martin turned to look at the audience, at Jocasta and Jemima, so proud of their daddy for whatever doubtless embarrassing stunt he was about to be subjected to, and realised he had no choice but to sit on that horrible-looking chair.

"Arms in the rests, please," said the Captain, indicating the leather-lined open claws. "We need to have our king looking regal."

Was it Martin's imagination or was there now more than a hint of menace in the clown's voice? He shifted uncomfortably on the chair before grudgingly placing his wrists between the golden scorpion's pincers. Martin knew he was shaking but he was trying his damnedest not to show it front of everybody.

When the pincers clicked shut he yelped.

"Goodness me, goodness me," said Captain Clowney

to the audience. "It would seem our pretender to the throne is a little distressed at what I have done." He turned to Martin. "Let me just reassure him and all of you that it is merely for his personal safety, and for the safety of any of the harmless little creatures that may soon be finding their way into the Scorpion King's domain." Martin was terrified now but he didn't dare back out and face being a laughing stock in front of his children. Captain Clowney ignored him and went back to addressing the audience.

"Every ruler must undergo a test. Every king must earn his crown. So it was in the days of ancient Egypt when this rite was performed on young princes before they could ascend to rule after their fathers had died. The ancient Egyptians had a name for it." Captain Clowney paused for maximum dramatic effect. Martin was on the verge of demanding to be released but the clown was too quick for him. "They called it 'The Trial of the Scorpion'!"

There was an intake of breath from the audience. Some children were so close to the edge of their seats that one in the back row actually fell off.

"But just to reassure everyone, not least our young prince here," said the Captain, "the scorpions I'm going to place in here are absolutely harmless and cannot even sting. This is just a bit of fun to show you the kind of thing they used to do in the *olden days*."

When he said those last couple of words Captain Clowney gave Dr Martin Davies such a look of sheer hatred that Martin actually drew in breath to scream. He was only stopped by the Captain saying "When you've had enough, just yell and I'll let you out."

Then the Captain locked the door.

"Another mere precaution, ladies and gentlemen," he said. "The zoo would be most displeased with me if they were to lose any of their prize specimens and I myself would be mortified if any were to go missing."

Martin struggled. He could hardly move. What's more he could no longer hear what the clown was saying. Perhaps the box he was in was soundproof. The white figure waved his arms around dramatically before pointing above him. Martin looked up to see an open pipe. The mad bastard wasn't really going to drop scorpions on Martin's head, was he? Not in front of everyone, not at a kid's matinee show.

He felt something land lightly on his forehead. It tickled, then it scratched.

Then it stung.

Outside the clown kept talking and gesturing as Martin felt the spot that had been pricked suddenly become numb. The numbness spread from his temple, over his ear, down the side of his face and into his throat with such rapidity that by the time his brain had told his mouth to scream he couldn't.

Another something fell past his face and landed on his knee.

Martin couldn't move his head now, but out of the corner of his eye he could see a black scuttling shape that was trying to gain purchase on his worn jeans, trying with the two heavy pincers it had in front of its body. It didn't take long for the creature to get frustrated, and then raised its tail, the bulging black stinger poised to strike.

Pain like Martin had never known flooded his knee and spread rapidly up to his groin. His left leg kicked out involuntarily as more scorpions landed on it. Outside it looked as if Captain Clowney was encouraging the children to cheer at the braveness of the volunteer. The pain was everywhere now, little pinpricks of hell that were numbing and then burning his shoulders, his back, his hands.

He could even feel them crawling on his face.

He strained to look down and saw that the floor was now a sea of writhing darkness. Some of the creatures were starting to climb up the insides of his trouser legs. What had gone wrong? Had they brought the wrong scorpions along? Had that girl Natasha made a mistake?

No.

That wasn't it at all, Martin thought as he stared through watering eyes at the figure that was still cavorting gaily before the crowd. He thought he had recognised that voice, heavily disguised though it was, but had dismissed the idea as being impossible. But now, as he had no option but to watch the man who had disguised himself as Captain Clowney present Martin's death to an audience of under-tens, he suddenly realised who it was who had locked him in here to be submitted to a long, slow and painful death in front of his own children.

And he realised he was doomed.

Through his now swiftly darkening vision he watched the man he had never thought he would see again give a final flourish of his cape before leaving the stage. The clown had probably told the audience he would be back in a moment to release his captive, but Martin knew he would be making good his escape.

It took a minute before anyone else realised what was wrong, and that was only because the sites of the multiple stings Martin had endured were beginning to swell in such a way that his face had suddenly taken on the appearance of a puffy, reddened meringue. Natasha took the key they had all seen Captain Clowney use and fitted it into the lock of the perspex cubicle.

It didn't work.

Now the children were screaming and security guards were hammering on the specially reinforced plastic. As his consciousness began to fade all Martin could do was say that he was sorry, sorry to Wendy for cheating on her, sorry to his children for not spending any time with them, and sorry to the man who had imprisoned him in here for what Martin and the others had done all those years ago.

6

"You say you'd known him for a couple of years?"

A tearful Natasha nodded as there was a crash from behind them. Longdon turned to see two of his officers struggling with the body of the recently deceased Martin Davies.

"Sorry, sir," said Sergeant Newham. "We're having a bit of trouble getting him out."

"Yes I can see that," said Longdon as he watched his men trying unsuccessfully to pull the doctor's dead, swollen body through the doorway to the cubicle. After the room had been cleared and the police called, the fifty-seven scorpions they had found in the cubicle with the late doctor had been anaesthetised and taken away by the zoo's veterinarian to ensure that they hadn't been harmed.

Removing Dr Davies himself, however, was proving to be a more difficult matter.

"It's because he's so puffed up," said the sergeant.

"Well, get someone to take the bloody perspex apart, then," said Longdon irritably, before turning his attention back to Natasha. "And you say you had no idea he was going to do this?"

The girl shook her head. "He said he was going to do some kind of routine with that throne, but nothing like this. I don't even know where he got the scorpions from."

Longdon frowned. "What do you mean?" he said. "Don't they belong to the zoo?"

Natasha blew her nose and wiped her eyes again. "No. We've got a couple of Asian forest scorpions because they're quite big and black and look scary, but their venom isn't all that dangerous." She glanced at the box behind them and at the police force's increasingly clumsy efforts to extricate the oedematous body of Dr Davies. "We don't have anything that could do something like that."

"So we have someone who didn't just plan this murder but brought along his own scorpions as well," said Longdon.

"And probably painted them," said Natasha.

"I beg your pardon?"

"Most poisonous scorpions live in the desert," Natasha explained, "so they tend to be yellow or orange to blend in. I'm not an expert but if he wanted to kill someone he'd have used something like that."

"Jesus Christ," said Longdon. Behind him the efforts of the Bristol police force finally met with success, and at last the body of Dr Davies was laid upon a trolley.

"He's going to droop over the sides a bit what with all that swelling," said one of the paramedics who were there to wheel him out. "Maybe we'd better put a couple of blankets over him."

"Yes, I think that would be a good idea," said Longdon, close to the point of exasperation. He looked around him. "Where's that bloody personnel officer?"

"Here, inspector," said a short bearded man whose badge proclaimed him to be Jim Burrows from the zoo's Human Resources department.

"Right, Mr Burrows," said Longdon, pointing to the

wobbling trolley behind him, "perhaps you can tell me how the man who did that managed to pass all your no doubt rigorous security and child protection checks?"

Burrows shrugged. "Captain Clowney has an impeccable record, Inspector. He's been putting on shows here for a few years now, once or twice a month. He's become quite a favourite with the children."

Longdon failed to be convinced. "Presumably you have all his details on file?" he asked. "Real name, date of birth, contact address and so on?"

Burrows looked incensed. "Of course, Inspector. We're very careful indeed about who we employ here. All I can say is that there was nothing in his police check that suggested he was anything other than the most trustworthy of individuals."

"Well, just make sure you have all his records forwarded to my office," Longdon said before shouting across the room to his colleague. "Sergeant!" Jenny Newham looked up from supervising the removal and tagging of the perspex chamber as evidence. "When you've finished here, go and find out if those scorpions they took out of here were painted will you?"

Jenny looked confused. "Sir?"

Longdon ignored her as he swallowed hard and went to interview Davies' family.

~

By the time they got back to the station Longdon and Newham had had more than their fill of distraught relatives, irate zoo officials and unscrupulous members of the press keen to discover what gory horrors the

Bristol Killer ("They're not just bastards, they're unimaginative ones too," Longdon had quipped as he moved the latest pile of dailies off his desk) had managed to come up with this time.

"Richard Patterson's in your office," the desk sergeant said to Longdon as he entered. "Says he's got some information for you."

"Let's hope it's a bit more useful than 'He was stung to death by scorpions'," said Longdon.

"Painted scorpions, sir," said Sergeant Newham with a winsome smile.

"Of course, Sergeant." Longdon could still see the horrified expression on the zoo officials' faces. Every scorpion that had been recovered from on and around the body of Dr Martin Davies had died within an hour of being taken away. Something about the toxicity of the paint they had been dipped in to give them such a black colour.

"Probably made them mad as well," Natasha had said. "No wonder they stung him so much." Apparently the RSPCA were going to be involved, and the zoo officials were not impressed when Longdon told them that was the least of his concerns. The two reporters who overheard his words, however, loved it, and scuttled off immediately to start constructing the next day's headline, which would no doubt be along the lines of 'Blundering Detective Animal Hater As Well'. In the end they concentrated on the distress of Dr Davies' family in the light of his having been stung over three hundred times by a room full of lethal scorpions.

"What do you want now, Richard?"

The pathologist was sitting beside Longdon's desk. The coffee pot in the corner was bubbling away.

"I hope you don't mind but I took the liberty of putting some on" said the doctor. "I have a couple of things I need to talk to you about."

Longdon pushed back his desk chair and flopped into it. Jenny stayed standing in the corner.

"I cannot possibly let a lady stand," said Patterson, getting to his feet and letting the Sergeant have the chair. The pathologist perched on the desk, which creaked ominously.

"Well?" said Longdon after a suitable pause.

Patterson waved a thin manila document at him. "We have an ID on our first victim," he said. "An Andrew Wells, not of this parish, which is why it took us a little while to track him down. He works in Buckinghamshire, where his wife filed a missing person's report on him last week."

"I don't suppose he was *Dr* Andrew Wells, was he?" said Longdon, already expecting the answer.

"No," said Patterson who, scarcely missing a beat, then added, "he was *Mr* Andrew Wells, a Consultant in charge of a local hospital Accident and Emergency department. Apparently he'd worked there for seven years."

"Three deaths, three doctors," said Longdon, leaning back in his chair and staring at the ceiling.

"I wonder what the hell they did to upset someone so badly?" said Jenny.

"More importantly," said Longdon, realising that if he leaned any further back his chair might fall over, "we need to find out if anyone else might have upset our killer as well. Get every single scrap of information you can about these three doctors and find out what it is that links them."

"Yes sir," said Jenny.

Longdon shooed her out of the room. "Now, Sergeant!"

Jenny Newham closed the door with a bang as she left.

"You shouldn't shout at her," said Patterson. "She's a good girl, and she obviously thinks the world of you."

"Then she isn't a very good judge of that sort of thing, is she?" said Longdon, trying to conceal the grin Patterson's comment had provoked. He looked at the bubbling coffee machine. "Was that all you had for me?"

"Not exactly." Patterson got up off the desk and poured them a mug each. "The other thing isn't exactly factual. In fact, I'm not really sure what to call it."

Longdon tried to take a sip but the coffee was too hot. "Richard, what are you going on about?"

There was a pause as Patterson seemed to be trying to decide whether he should speak up or not. Eventually he said, "It's not just the fact that they're all doctors that links these killings."

"What do you mean?"

Patterson sat down and waited for Longdon to follow suit before continuing.

"Do you watch horror films, Inspector?"

It might not have been the last thing Longdon had been expecting Patterson to say but it was close. "No," he replied, "never really been my thing, and certainly not the kinds of films that the press have been likening all this business to. When I was a kid I watched some Hammer films, but this *Saw* thing they keep comparing the murders to doesn't sound like the kind of fare anyone sane should really be watching. And what is it about calling all this horror stuff after things you'd find in a toolbox? Anyway – why?" Longdon narrowed his eyes. "Are you a fan?"

"Oh good Lord, no!" Patterson rolled his eyes. "It's my daughter, actually. She loves the things. Can't watch enough of them. No idea what the appeal is myself but there we are. Anyway, it was after you rang me to do the autopsy on this latest killing that she pointed it out."

"Pointed what out?"

Patterson opened his briefcase and took out an A4 printout of a garish movie poster. Longdon looked at the face of the man depicted on it and didn't think he had ever seen so many different shades of red.

"I don't have the facilities at home, but fortunately Vice has just invested in a new colour laser printer so I ran this off down there," said the pathologist, turning it round so Longdon could get a better look at it.

"*Edgar Allan Poe's immortal masterpiece of the macabre 'The Masque of the Red Death'*," Longdon read aloud before looking up at Patterson. "And this is important because...?"

Patterson made himself comfortable. "Because in Roger Corman's 1964 film *The Masque of the Red Death* the character of Prince Prospero, played by Vincent Price—" Patterson tapped the face on the poster "—organises a party where the character of Alfredo, played by Patrick Magee, gets suspended in the air while wearing a gorilla suit. Which is then set on fire."

Longdon waited for Patterson to continue and then realised the pathologist was waiting for him to make the connection. "Like Dr Wells," he said.

"*Mr* Wells," Patterson corrected. "Surgical consultant, you see. They can get very upset if you don't get their title right. But yes – exactly like Andrew Wells."

Longdon took a swig of his coffee which thankfully was at last comfortable to drink. Where was Patterson going with this? "And this piece of random information helps us how, exactly?" he said.

Patterson took another sheet of paper from his briefcase.

"*Love means never having to say you're ugly.*" Longdon read that tag-line out loud again before looking at the picture of a rotting skull-faced cadaver about to kiss a beautiful woman.

"In *The Abominable Dr Phibes* the character of Dr Phibes, played by Vincent Price—" again Patterson tapped the poster in case Longdon wasn't getting the idea "—engineers the deaths of a number of doctors, and of particular interest here is the death afforded the character of Dr Whitcombe, played by Maurice Kaufman."

Longdon looked up at Patterson. "I don't suppose he's dropped out of a balloon, is he?"

The pathologist shook his head. "He's impaled on a brass unicorn head, Inspector."

"Like our Dr Pritchard?"

Patterson nodded. "Like our Dr Pritchard."

Another poster came out of the briefcase, this time of a woman's bleeding eye with a spider crawling across it.

"I'm not even going to read what that says," said Longdon, unable to bring himself to quote the poster's tagline of *Flesh Crawls! Blood Curdles! Phibes Lives!*

"In the sequel to *The Abominable Dr Phibes*," Patterson continued, ignoring his colleague, "rather unimaginatively titled *Dr Phibes Rises Again*, the character of Dr Phibes, yet again played by Vincent Price, causes the character of an archaeologist played by Keith Buckley to be stung to death by the same creatures that killed our Dr Davies while trapped in a throne that is itself fashioned in the shape of a giant golden scorpion."

"Oh bloody hell," said Longdon, putting his head in his hands.

"Bloody hell indeed, Inspector," replied the pathologist.

"And I suppose there are other films in which this actor kills people?"

Patterson nodded. "Apparently so, quite a lot of them in fact, which really puts the pressure on your Sergeant Newham to find out what the connection is between the victims so far, or the press might find they're going to have stories for the rest of this month."

"More likely this year," Longdon groaned, stretching his arms. "So what am I supposed to do now? Call in a film critic?"

Patterson tapped the *Abominable Dr Phibes* poster again. "It might not hurt to at least get a book on these films so we can get some idea of what the killer might have in store next."

"All right," said Longdon. "I don't suppose your daughter fancies coming in to help?"

Patterson shook his head and smiled. "She's away at university, following in the footsteps of her father. I wouldn't want her to be involved in this anyway and I certainly wouldn't want it to interrupt her education. I'm sure you'll be able to find someone locally who knows about these sorts of films. Although I'd suggest you make your inquiries discreet. There are a lot of very odd people around who like these kinds of things."

7

"Dr Parsons? I think Mrs Fudgsin's bowels have had a good result from that enema."

Lorraine Parsons dropped her cigarette and trod the burning ember into the tarmac, extinguishing it with a hiss. She turned to see the rotund face of practice nurse Garry Bellamy peering anxiously around the fire exit door. She knew that no-one, not even staff, was supposed to go through it 'except in cases of emergency', at least according to the practice's annual interminable lecture from that prig of a fire safety officer. Still, Garry wasn't going to tell anyone, not after what she had caught him doing with some of the items on the proctoscopy tray last month.

"All right, Garry," she said, following him back inside. "If you're happy with what she's managed to do, send her on her way with one more sachet. But tell her she's absolutely not to have more than half of it at a time, otherwise it'll be her husband they'll be carting off to casualty with shock, instead of his wife with a simple case of constipation."

"All right, Doctor." Garry sniffed and pointed to the door to Lorraine's consulting room. "Your husband's on the phone. He said he'd wait."

And you'd better not have told him why he's had to wait, thought Lorraine as Garry shuffled away, *or else a few other people might find out what you get up to when you think there's nobody else here.*

"Hello, Gareth," she said once she had the surgery door closed.

The voice on the other end of the line didn't sound happy.

"Look," she said. "I can't do it. You know I've got this bloody thing to attend this afternoon. You'll just have to take Davinia to the Pony Prom yourself. No, I don't know what the hell a Pony Prom is either. Your daughter has probably got entirely the wrong end of the stick. After all," she said with a sigh, "she does take after you in so many ways. Yes, I love you too." She put down the phone, sending away the husband she didn't really love at all and the daughter she was coming to despise for her slow-witted ways, and looked at her watch. It was nearly one o'clock, which meant that with any luck her surgery hours were over for the day. A quick phone call to Martha her receptionist confirmed it, and after she had filed away her patients' notes from her morning consultations she turned her attention to the letter she had been sent through the post three weeks ago.

"Lavenham Productions would like to take great pleasure in cordially inviting you to participate in their reality television programme 'This Civil Life'. We are dedicated to reproducing, for one afternoon only, a famous period in history in a village of local importance. In order to increase the verisimilitude we are looking for professional people who would be willing to play the roles they do in everyday life now, but in an historic context. Consequently, lawyers, farmers, shop owners and others in your area have all been contacted in the hope that they will be willing to participate in this exciting project. Your cooperation and involvement in 'This Civil Life' would be greatly appreciated and, as we have already pre-sold the programme to a commercial broadcasting channel, we will be able to show our gratitude with a financial reimbursement for your time, which you may either donate to the charity of your choice or do with what you wish."

Below that was her name and the details of the not inconsiderable sum of money to be paid into her bank account should she be willing to take part. Lorraine looked at the figure again and went over the numbers in her head for the umpteenth time. The money Lavenham Productions was willing to pay should be just enough to cover the gambling debts she had accrued on the Thursday afternoons when Gareth had thought she was doing her special learning difficulties charity clinic in Bristol. In fact, she had been at the racetrack trying to win back the money that should have gone on their summer holiday last year. Thank God Gareth had no idea how she'd lost all that money. But never mind, she thought with a smile as she tucked the letter into her bag, if one afternoon of reality TV could pay for it all then why not? And it wasn't as if Gareth watched any of that kind of stuff, so it was hardly likely she'd be found out.

The sun was breaking through the clouds as she got into her car and set off into the wilds of the Somerset countryside. March was starting off nicely, she thought, as she put on her sunglasses and turned up the stereo, and it was about to get even better.

She followed the map that had come with the letter, grateful that she had remembered to bring it as she was taken down ever more minor roads after leaving the M5. Eventually, as her car was scraping its way along the hedgerows of a single track, macadam-paved lane, and Lorraine was dreading to think what the loose chippings were doing to the emerald green paintwork, and assuming she must have taken a wrong turn, the road suddenly turned a corner and widened.

And she found herself three hundred years in the past.

The town square into which she drove was large, and the ground had been matted with straw, presumably to cover up any road markings as well as to add to the authentic feel they were obviously trying to reproduce. There were people everywhere, many of them in period dress. A man in a very un-seventeenth century long-sleeved shirt bearing the stovepipe-hatted logo of the production company came running over waving a clipboard. Once she had wound the window down she could hear what he was saying.

"I'm afraid this route is closed today," he shouted over the noise of whatever it was a team of carpenters were constructing in the middle of the square, "we're filming, you see."

"I know," said Lorraine, showing him the letter. "I think I'm supposed to be a part of it."

The young man's apologetic expression broadened to a smile. "Dr Parsons! Thank you so much for coming! We weren't sure if you were going to be able to make it. Andy Deacon – pleased to meet you."

"Well, I did ring to confirm," she said, shaking his outstretched hand.

Andy nodded. "Even so, we know that doctors can get

unexpectedly called away. It's wonderful you've been able to make the time for our little production."

Lorraine eyed her presumed co-stars as they milled about. "It doesn't look that little to me," she said.

"By comparison with some of the things I've worked on," he said with a smile. "But you're right. They've really done a marvellous job with very limited resources here."

"Don't you mean *you* have?" she narrowed her eyes.

"Oh I've just been hired for the day as a production assistant," he said, looking behind him, "which is a shame really as this all looks such fun I wish I was on it for longer. Anyway, I'll show you where you can park your car and then we'll get you into costume and makeup."

The village (Lorraine still hadn't seen a name and the film company's map had simply marked it as 'Location') was so tiny that once she had, with Andy's help, negotiated her car slowly across the square and out the other side, she found herself past the tiny crop of buildings and turning left into a field where there were numerous other vehicles and a number of tents.

"All set up this morning," said Andy with a grin. "I'm always amazed at how quickly all these things come together. You wouldn't believe that at six o'clock none of this was here, would you?"

"So have you all been working on this somewhere else, then?" said Lorraine as they got out of her car.

Andy shrugged. "Not exactly. Independent production company, you see. We just get the phone call and turn up, a bit like you. I've worked with a few people on here before, but most of them I don't recognise.

Apparently they want everything done by teatime which is why there's such a rush on. The money's phenomenal, though, so I'm not complaining."

Lorraine slammed the car door and locked it. "Which reminds me," she said, "when exactly do I—"

"Get paid?" Andy smiled. "It'll all be done by a bank transfer in a couple of days. Unless of course you'd prefer some other method?"

Lorraine shook her head. Thank goodness she had opened that private bank account that Gareth knew nothing about. The fact that it was several thousand pounds in the red now just made it all the more appropriate for the money to go straight in there.

She was still thinking about what a shot in the arm this was going to be to her finances as Andy led her across the field towards one of the smaller tents.

"We'll get you into costume first and then sort out your makeup," he said.

"What period in history are we actually doing?" she asked.

Andy stopped. With the expression on his face she might have just told him she thought she was supposed to be on a cookery show. "You mean they haven't told you?"

Lorraine shook her head. "I just know the title 'This Civil Life' but they didn't tell me anything else."

"Oh my goodness, I'm sorry." They were nearly at the tent now as Andy turned round to point back to the village. "For one afternoon we are turning that collection of mouldy old buildings into a seventeenth century village. The English civil war, you see?"

Lorraine nodded as realisation dawned. That explained the plethora of peasant costumes she had seen on the way in. "But what about the people who actually live in the place?" she said. "Have you sent them all away for the afternoon?"

Andy grinned. "All part of the magic of television," he said. "When the team arrived this morning there were a couple of tumbledown old farm buildings that hadn't been used in donkey's years. You'd be amazed what can be achieved with a few backdrops and some standing set scenery borrowed from the Pinewood backlot."

Lorraine squinted at the village in the afternoon sunlight. It was obvious now, of course. She had actually just driven through a set, and it had only been her expectations and assumptions that had led her to believe anything else. She smiled. "That's very impressive, you know," she said.

Andy did a little bow. "Nothing to do with me," he said. "Well, not much, but thank you anyway. Now come and meet Melissa."

Melissa was tall, had a shock of pink frizzy hair and a suspiciously deep voice. She got Lorraine to stand next to a full length mirror, stroked her chin, hummed and hawed and then took three scruffy looking dresses off a rack of the things that all looked the same as far as the doctor was concerned. She held each one up next to Lorraine while conducting a running conversation with herself.

"Too Kate Winslet," she said of the first, shaking her head and throwing it on a chair "and my God, you don't want to be likened to her do you? I mean, fifteen years ago, okay, but now that look is *so* out of date. Mind you, so is Meg Ryan." Now she was holding up the second dress. "I don't know why they've given me these to work with," she said with an exaggerated sigh. "I mean this isn't supposed to be *Sleepless in Somerset*, it's supposed to be real life. Let's try the third." Lorraine didn't like any of them but at least the third had a bit more to it. Melissa pursed her lips, "Hmmm. This one makes you look a little bit Rachel Weisz, especially if they use a soft focus camera on you, which of course they won't. Oh well." She handed Lorraine the dress. "Try it on and we'll see how it looks."

The only place to get changed was behind the rack of dresses, and Lorraine managed it in record time. Melissa seemed happy enough and passed her on to the next tent, where a grumpy makeup artist called George made her hair look awful and added a couple of skin blemishes.

"They all had them in those days," he said when she protested about him trying to add a wart with hair coming out of it. Once he realised she'd be tugging it off as soon as she was away from there he gave up and sent her outside where Andy introduced her to Malcolm, who was a solicitor from Cheltenham and had been dressed up to look like something out of an Arthur Miller play.

"Are you excited?" he asked as they made their way back over to the mostly fabricated buildings. "I was delighted when I got the letter." It turned out he belonged to one of those historical re-enactment societies, which was apparently how quite a few of the people there had been recruited.

"Happy?" Andy asked once the two of them were back

in the town square. Malcolm gave a delighted nod but Lorraine wasn't quite so sure.

"What am I supposed to do exactly?" she asked.

"Just play along," said Andy. "There's sort of a script to get things going and some of the people here are genuine actors, so all you have to do is react to what's going on."

Lorraine looked up at the wooden pole that had been erected in the middle of the square. "What's that for?" she asked.

"You'll see," said the production assistant. "I've been sworn to secrecy or else I don't get paid. The producer wants real reactions so he doesn't want anyone knowing too much."

In that case, the only reactions he's going to get from me are confusion and looking increasingly pissed off, Lorraine thought. Then she remembered the money and made herself calm down. But something else was bothering her. As she looked around she realised what it was.

"Where are the cameras?" she asked Andy just as he was leaving.

He gave her a big smile and pointed to the windows of various houses. "All concealed in there," he said, "so you don't have any distractions at all."

"I've got some lines." Malcolm was so excited he couldn't help but blurt out the words.

"Yes Malcolm, you have," said Andy, "but no telling Lorraine what they are, remember? Otherwise your historical society doesn't get that donation it's been promised." Malcolm looked suitably told off as Lorraine marvelled at how the production company had obviously managed to get what they wanted by offering financial reimbursement in all manner of ways. Andy looked around. "Right," he said. "I think we're about ready to go. I had a word with everyone else while you were getting ready. Our main star is offstage at the moment but once I'm out of here the cameras will start rolling so we'll be needing you to just be yourselves."

"Be ourselves how?" Malcolm asked.

"Just talk about the weather or how you got here," was the reply. "You know, just general chit-chat. You'll know once the show has begun."

I'm more interested in knowing when it's over, thought Lorraine, although she guessed that would be obvious enough when the time came. She tried to make small talk with Malcolm as Andy dashed off behind the scenes, but the man already bored her, it was getting cold, her dress itched and she was keen to get the whole thing over with.

She didn't have to wait long.

"Bring forth that sorceress condemned to burn!"

The voice, whose deep booming tones carried over the mumbling crowd, came from beneath the arch in the far left hand corner of the square. Everyone turned to see who had spoken, and Lorraine had to stand on tiptoe to be able to see the man to whom the voice belonged.

He was of medium height, but the black stovepipe hat he wore made him look taller. His garb was period perfect and the black cloak he wore swirled about him as he walked. As he reached the centre of the square through the parted crowd the voice boomed again.

"I say for a second time: where is the witch who by her foul deeds has committed herself to be cleansed by the purifying flames?"

There was a pause before Malcolm, still standing next to her, jumped in realisation.

"Oh my goodness, that's me," he whispered to her, before calling out to the sinister man in black, "I have her here, good my Lord."

"Then bring her to me that I might set eyes upon this evil harpy." His blue eyes glittered with a gleeful malevolence. *Whoever he is, he's bloody good*, thought Lorraine, wondering who it was who was destined to be subjected to his melodramatic overtures. As she did so she became aware that the crowd had separated itself from her as Malcolm had linked his arm in hers.

"Don't worry," he whispered. "Just play along. All part of the show."

"Me? What, no, get off!" Lorraine spluttered, but it was no use. Besides, if she spoiled it all there was a chance no-one would get paid and then she'd be in all sorts of trouble.

"Before me, my good man! Now, if you please!"

As meekly as she knew how, which admittedly wasn't very meekly at all, Lorraine allowed herself to be brought before the witchfinder, who made a point of keeping his distance from the accused. When she was pushed to her knees she offered some resistance, but then she remembered she was wearing the costume department's rags so it didn't matter if they got messed up.

"Well, young lady," the black-clad man said. "Have you anything to say for yourself?"

There was a nudge behind her from Malcolm. What on earth was she supposed to say? And then she remembered. Be yourself, she had been told.

"I am a doctor, your worship," she said, hoping that was how one addressed a seventeenth century witchfinder.

"A doctor!" That seemed to amuse him. "A doctor, she says!" Now he was addressing the crowd. "A woman healing the sick? In this day and age? I ask you, men and women of this village – have you ever heard of anything more absurd in your entire lives?"

There were lots of cries of "No!" and a few more worrying shouts of "Burn her!" as the crowd started to get into the spirit of the thing.

"I have healed the sick, sir," said Lorraine, also getting into the swing of it, "on many occasions, and with some success I might add."

"Coincidence, luck, or worse..." The witchfinder raised his voice for maximum effect at this point. "The work of the Devil! And of the Devil's own! And I see this particular servant of Satan does not even try to defend herself but willingly admits to her evil practices! For her there can only be one absolution!"

There were more cries from the increasingly enthusiastic crowd now, and for the first time Lorraine felt a pang of worry. She looked round and breathed a sigh of relief that she couldn't see a stake anywhere that she could be tied to.

When the crowd had died down the witchfinder spoke again.

"I therefore have no alternative but to pass sentence. The path of the righteous can be difficult, and we who do God's work perform it sometimes with the heaviest of hearts. Yet I say that to save this woman's soul she must undergo absolution by burning."

Lorraine could feel hands grabbing her now and she realised she couldn't move. She struggled and cried out as the witchfinder called for something called 'the frame'.

"Don't worry," Malcolm whispered to her as she was dragged forward. "They wanted to have a fire here but health and safety wouldn't let them. I heard them talking about it this morning."

Well, that's a relief, thought Lorraine as she allowed herself to be dragged to the centre of the square where a wooden construct that resembled a telegraph pole had been erected. It had to be at least twenty feet high. Were they proposing to tie her to that? And if so, why had they made it so high?

There was movement from the other side of the square. The crowd parted again as four men approached, carrying what looked to Lorraine like a ladder, about the same length as the pole. When they laid it on the ground she could see there were loops at one end for her hands and feet. Still held in a vice-like grip, she was turned to face the crowd.

"Mistress Lorraine Parsons," said the witchfinder from behind her, "you have been found guilty of the most heinous crime of witchcraft, of encouraging others to place trust in you and in claiming to have abilities which you did not possess."

Lorraine frowned. That sounded a bit odd. Shouldn't he have said 'do not possess?'

"For that I order that you be lashed to the frame, raised up and then lowered into the purifying flames so that all might see your just retribution at the hands of the Lord."

As he spoke Lorraine felt herself being lifted up and set down on the wooden frame. She struggled as they slid the loops of hemp over her wrists and ankles, not just because the frame was bloody uncomfortable but because she was starting to get scared.

But not as scared as she was when the witchfinder came round to face her.

He had kept his distance before but now there he was, right in front of her, an evil smile on his lips and malevolence in his eyes. However, neither of those was what struck a greater fear into her heart than she had ever known.

She recognised him.

It had been many years and he looked older, but she recognised him.

A man she had thought was dead.

"I will pray for you," he said, not looking as if he meant a word of it, and as they began to raise her up Lorraine realised that she wasn't going to be leaving this place alive.

That was when she started screaming.

"See how the guilty party now pleads for her life!" the witchfinder crowed as Lorraine was hoisted up. The crowd was now so worked up that it was impossible for her to make herself heard. "Secure the ropes!" he commanded, and within a few short moments Lorraine was twenty feet above them, lashed to the wood, cold, afraid, and already reduced to gibbering in terror. It was therefore unsurprising that the crowd ignored her as the witchfinder once again commanded their attention.

"This... *woman* has been found guilty of one of the

vilest of crimes," he said, "and it is only meet and right that she be justly punished for it." Suddenly his voice changed and became far less theatrical. Suddenly it was just the man who was playing the role who was speaking to them and the effect was more than a little disorientating. "Unfortunately, ladies and gentlemen, due to the various mandates and regulations placed upon us by health and safety we have been denied permission to build a suitable pyre in the town square to ensure this witch is properly punished." He spoke with such a lightness of tone that some members of the crowd actually laughed, and there were a couple of joking cries of "Shame!"

"But other arrangements have been made," he continued. "As I am sure many of you are aware, one of the other methods of punishing a witch was to subject her to the humiliation of the ducking stool, and while we do not have exactly the device they would have used back then, we do have the means to lower our accused into a large quantity of water!"

The crowd parted for a third time as a large circular tank was pushed into the town square, covered with a thick tarpaulin.

Up high on her perch, still cold and scared, Lorraine had heard what the man had said and was almost at the point of crying tears of relief. It was all a show! Of course it was! And that man – she must have been mistaken! Besides, there was no way he could have been who she had thought he was. And now all they were going to do was dunk her in some water and let her go. She looked up at the sky. *Thank God*, she thought, *and if I get out of here I*

*promise I'm never going to gamble again. I'm going to go back
to Gareth and Davinia and be a proper mum and never cause my
family any more trouble.*

There was a creak. The ladder to which Lorraine was
tied had been fixed at the lower end so that as the tension
on the ropes holding the top end close to the pole was
loosened, Lorraine was lowered face-first towards the
ground, and towards the tank that had been positioned
beneath her.

It's just water, she kept telling herself as the tarpaulin
loomed nearer, *it's just water and these loops aren't too tight.
Once I'm down I'll be able to get out.*

She was halfway towards it when the witchfinder
pulled the tarpaulin away. Lorraine breathed another
sigh of relief as she saw the water. She had been worried
for a moment that it might be filled with something else
– spikes or poisonous creatures.

It was only when she was very close that she noticed
how the sunlight shimmered unnaturally on the liquid's
surface, and that the lining of the tank seemed to be
made of glass.

By then of course it was too late. The acid in the vat
was so powerful that by the time it had eaten through her
bonds it had already eaten through her face, and by the
time anyone had managed to find something the acid
didn't corrode to pull her out with, Lorraine Parsons was
long gone.

And so was the witchfinder.

8

"So you're telling me that this man dissolved a girl in acid in front of forty witnesses and no-one can come up with a description of him?"

Longdon had known when the call came through that it was another one. After all, who else was going to be responsible for a hideous murder in a non-existent village filled with locals dressed as peasants and built by a hired-for-the-day crew who knew nothing more about the project than the numerous shell-shocked individuals they had interviewed so far?

"I think it's what he was wearing, sir," said Newham as the last of the ambulances took more than its safe quota of emotionally traumatised witnesses to the local hospital. "All they remember is the hat, the beard and that weird hairstyle he had."

"Which, according to that costume lady Melissa, is dead on mid-seventeenth century," said Longdon, frowning. "Did she seem a little bit odd to you?"

"They're film people, sir," said Newham. "They're all a bit odd."

"I suppose you're right," said Longdon as he glanced over to see two of his men getting dangerously close to the acid vat. "For God's sake, keep away from that until the disposal team arrives, can't you?" he shouted. "We've already got five members of the general public who need treating for acid burns. I don't want any of you lot turning up in their wake. It'll make us look even stupider than we already do."

"At least we've got an ID on the victim sir," said Newham, consulting her notebook. "Good thing that lawyer chap asked her what her name was."

Longdon nodded. It hadn't surprised him one little bit that it was another doctor. "How are we coming along with establishing a connection between these people?" he asked.

"Believe it or not, there are a number of links between the other three," said Jenny, flipping back a few pages. "The medical community's smaller than you think, and because of the way the training works, they'd all been around a whole load of different hospitals before settling down in their permanent jobs."

"Well, maybe this one will help us narrow it down. Even if we do we've still got four people dead and we're no closer to knowing what this lunatic might do next." Longdon rubbed his eyes.

"The smell of that tank getting to you, sir?" said Newham.

Longdon shook his head. "Been burning the midnight oil, Sergeant. I never thought I'd be subjecting myself to a non-stop diet of old horror films for the sake of a case but at the moment I have a stack of DVDs that reaches to the ceiling to get through."

Newham's phone bleeped and she flipped it open. "Well, at least we might be able to save you a few headaches," she said with a smile. "We've managed to dig up a local film critic who claims he knows all about the films of Vincent Price."

"Have you told him why we want to speak to him?" said Longdon as they headed for the car.

"No sir," said Newham. "I thought that would be best coming from you."

~

His name was Stanley Sanders. His hair was white, his velvet jacket was burgundy, and his age had to be well past bus pass qualification. He sat in Longdon's office with his hands clasped neatly on the desk as he was sworn to secrecy.

"It's vital for the case we're investigating at the moment, you see, sir," said Newham as she got him to sign all the appropriate forms.

"You mean the one that's all over the papers?" said Sanders in the kind of tired, aloof tones that made Longdon immediately feel sorry for any film-maker who had ended up under his critical eye. Jenny said that it was. "So you're asking me to keep quiet about what everyone in the country probably already knows?"

Longdon rolled his eyes. Why couldn't they have found some bright young thing who knew about this stuff? Preferably female, with a sunny disposition and a figure that could knock him into the middle of next week. He stopped his somewhat noirish daydreaming and regarded the slightly odd looking man in front of him.

"What we are about to tell you isn't common knowledge, sir," he explained. "And so far it's just theory. That's why we need your expert help."

"If you say so, Inspector," came the reply. "But I warn you now – my knowledge of film has lapsed somewhat since I left the paper. In fact I'd be hard pushed to remember anything past 1980."

Longdon frowned at Jenny, who shrugged. "I'm sure that will be fine, sir." He proceeded to explain the events in the case so far. Sanders looked alternately shocked, intrigued and impressed as Longdon listed the deaths and the suspected inspiration behind them. Eventually he came to the latest, which he described in the kind of detail that had Mr Sanders reaching for the scented handkerchief in his pocket.

"That'll be *Witchfinder General*, then," said the ex-movie critic with a cough. "Quite a classic if I say so myself. The scene he's decided to reproduce is the one where Vincent Price, playing Matthew Hopkins, engineers the death of one of the accused village girls by a method that is probably completely historically inaccurate but which certainly made for a dramatic scene in the movie. Of course, your girl was dissolved in acid, which might also be a nod to 1953's *House of Wax*, or possibly *Scream and Scream Again*, made fourteen years later."

"That's all very helpful, sir," said Longdon. "But what we really need to know is – how many films are there where Vincent Price kills people?"

There was a pause while Sanders counted on his fingers, paused, shook his head, started counting again and then eventually said, "I'm not sure – maybe thirty or so?" As Longdon and his sergeant looked horrified he added, "but of course that's not including the films in which Vincent Price stars and people are killed by people other than him, such as your first murder. If it's based on the one from Corman's *Masque of the Red Death*, Vincent Price doesn't actually do the killing in that particular instance."

Longdon soon began to regret asking Stanley to go on, as what he had anticipated as a short chat began to evolve into a two hour lecture on horror films. Eventually he was relieved when the Chief Inspector rang, which was something he never thought he would find himself admitting to. He picked up the receiver and consulted his notes while Jenny escorted Stanley out.

"Yes sir," he said, doing his best to placate his already irritated-sounding senior officer, "we do seem to be fairly sure that it's the same killer in each of these cases." He winced at the next question. "No sir, I'm afraid we aren't any closer to identifying him." He looked at the notes he had made while Stanley had been talking. "We're working on the theory that whoever he is he's been setting this up for years. The name of the man who had the affair with Mrs Pritchard, the real name of Captain Clowney, and the name of the individual who hired everyone for the reality film shoot we have noted down as Henry Jarrod, Anton Phibes and Edward Lionheart respectively, all of whom I am now reliably informed are characters played in films by the actor Vincent Price." He paused to allow the Chief Inspector to speak. "That's right sir – Vincent Price. An actor, sir, in horror films. Old ones. Apparently the deaths all mimic his films, too. Yes, I know it sounds very far-fetched, sir. Yes sir, absolutely ridiculous – I agree, sir. But to be honest, it's the only lead we have, and according to our expert... A local film critic, sir. It just seemed to be a good idea to..."

Longdon realised there was little point in continuing as the voice on the other end of the line became a tirade. Sergeant Newham walked back in just as Longdon was putting down the receiver.

"Bad news, sir?" she asked

"Well, his Lordship isn't happy," said Longdon, "and I can't say I blame him. Four deaths and the only thing linking them a bunch of films they don't even show on late night television anymore." He pointed at his hastily scribbled notes. "Do you know how many films there are where Vincent Price murders someone?" Jenny shook her head. "Thirty. And there's usually more than one murder per film." He put his head in his hands. "God knows how many more there are going to be before this is finished."

"Probably five more at the most, sir," said Jenny, passing him the piece of paper she had brought in. Longdon rubbed his eyes and stared at the paper. "It's the link we've been looking for," she continued. "Putting Lorraine Parsons into the equation clinched it but it took me a while to check all the facts. And type it out so it was easy for you to read."

Longdon ignored her smile as he looked at the name at the top of the page.

"Victoria Valentine," he read.

Jenny nodded. "They were all involved in her case. She was an eleven-year- old girl dragged out of the river following a car accident. She was close to death when they brought her to the hospital, and as far as I can tell it was a hopeless case even though they all did their best – casualty officers, surgical team, anaesthetists – apparently one of them was a GP who happened to be at the scene of the accident. Of course most of them were junior staff who moved and ended up training in different specialties, but that's the only case that links the victims."

Longdon read through the list of names. "So that leaves us with Christopher Skilbeck, Jasper Morgan, David Sparkes, Geoffrey Marsden and Caroline Conrad."

Jenny frowned, took the list off him and looked at it again. "Sorry, sir, my mistake," she said as she handed it back. "I said there might be five more potential victims but in fact there are only four. Dr Conrad died last year. Misadventure."

Longdon raised an eyebrow. "Nothing suspicious, then?"

"Well, now that you mention it..." The sergeant looked uneasy. "She was a nerve specialist and had been plagued for years herself with chronic back pain. In fact, she'd volunteered to be a guinea pig for some kind of electronic spinal implant. Anyway, when they found her it had somehow malfunctioned and she'd received a massive electric shock to her spine."

Longdon groaned. "Oh God, it's *The Tingler*."

"The verdict was that she must have somehow tried to boost the signal from the implant and ended up killing herself."

"No," said Longdon, "it's *The Tingler*. Vincent Price discovers this creature that can crush your spine when you're afraid. According to our Mr Sanders you had to scream to dislodge it. I don't supposed she was gagged when they found her?"

Jenny shrugged. "No idea, sir. Shall I find out?"

Longdon shook his head. "No, never mind. I think we can safely up the body count to five. All we're missing is a suspect. What about the family of this little girl?"

"Well that's where it gets interesting," said Jenny.

"Oh *good*," said Longdon as sarcastically as he could manage. "This has been *such* a dull case so far."

"The man driving the car was Edward Valentine, who was the chief surgeon at the hospital they took her to. He knew all the staff who treated her. Well, he *would* have known them."

"What do you mean?"

"Edward Valentine's body was never found," said Jenny. "It was assumed he drowned in the wreck and his body was washed out to sea. We're very close to the Bristol Channel here, sir."

"I am aware of that, sergeant," he said irritably, "living in Bristol and everything."

"Sorry, sir. Anyway, they never found him and there was no other family. It was all very sad, actually."

"And the story's not exactly getting any brighter, is it?" said Longdon, handing the sheet back to her. "Get every one of these people on the phone, tell them their lives are quite probably in danger, and that we are making arrangements for them to be taken to a safe house until we find out who's doing this."

"Already taken care of, sir," the sergeant replied. "Where exactly are we going to take them?"

"No bloody idea at the moment," said Longdon. "But well done for sorting all that."

Jenny smiled. "You were talking to Mr Sanders for quite a long time."

"I bloody was as well," said Longdon, looking at his pencilled scribblings. "By the way," he said. "Do any of these men keep poodles?"

Jenny looked confused. "No sir, why?"

"Oh, just something Mr Sanders mentioned," said Longdon with a shudder. "So have we had any responses yet?"

"The only one we know anything about is Dr Sparkes, who's on holiday in the South of France."

Longdon breathed a sigh of relief. "Well he should be safe enough down there," he said.

"I'm not sure, sir," said Jenny. "Apparently he was meant to be back at work a week ago. He hasn't been seen since he set off for a tour of the wine-producing areas."

Longdon's face fell in resignation. "So he's probably nailed inside a barrel somewhere, then," he said.

"Sir?"

Longdon tapped his notes. "*Tower of London* – a remake, apparently. Or possibly *Theatre of Blood*. Either way it's all to do with Richard III bumping off the Duke of Clarence by drowning him in a vat of wine."

"Well, I suppose we could keep our fingers crossed that he's just lost," she said as she went back to the list. "Otherwise we've left messages with Dr Skilbeck and Mr Marsden, who was the surgeon in charge of the case. Mrs Morgan told us that her husband Jasper retired a year ago and now spends much of his time wandering around the country putting together a book on old churches, which is what he's doing at the moment."

"Any idea where he might be?"

"Somewhere in Wales I think, sir, but exactly where not even his wife knows."

Longdon stared at the list of films before him, filled with murder, mutilation and suffering. Surely whoever was doing this wouldn't have the nerve to kill someone in a church, would they?

"In that case, Sergeant, as you so aptly put it, let's keep our fingers crossed that he's all right."

9

"How simply marvellous!"

Jasper Morgan clapped his hands and crowed with delight as he regarded the stained glass design in the church's east window. How unexpected to find such a beautiful rendition in such an out of the way spot!

"It is a very good example of its type, isn't it?" said the vicar. "We're so proud of it here that it's always a pleasure to be able to 'show it off' as it were, especially to someone who knows a little about these matters. Such individuals are, I can assure you, few and far between."

Morgan nodded with enthusiasm before turning round to behold the rest of the church of St Valentine. "I must admit I'd been hoping I might be allowed a private personal tour of this particular building," he said, "but, in all confidence, my dear fellow, I had heard from some of the locals that the vicar wasn't the most co-operative of sorts!"

The vicar gave him an extra-wide smile. "They may well have been referring to the last curate of this parish," he said. "I've only just very recently arrived, and when I learned of your visiting the area it seemed somehow appropriate that you should be the first to receive a guided tour from my good self."

"Appropriate?" Morgan frowned as the vicar put his arm around his shoulders and led him down the aisle.

"Why, yes, indeed," the vicar continued. "My dear

chap, an enthusiast for church design who, in his autumn years, is thinking of devoting some of his well-earned retirement to the composition of a tome on the very subject? What more appropriate an individual could there be?"

They had reached the end of the aisle. Morgan was about to examine the font when he felt himself being turned round.

"You can get a much better view of the window from back here," the vicar said.

It was true. From here, with the afternoon sunlight filtering through the greens and reds, it was possible to behold the true majesty in the depiction of Saint Valentine performing the act that had apparently led to his sanctification.

"You know what he's doing to the little girl?"

Morgan glanced at his companion and then back to the glass. "I remember reading it somewhere," he said, hesitating, "but I'd appreciate it if you could refresh my memory."

"Of course," said the vicar. He pointed to the kneeling child. "The story goes that Valentine, while under house arrest, was asked to cure the sight of the judge's blind daughter, which he duly did, resulting in the conversion of much of the judge's household to the faith." He sighed. "It must have been wonderful to have been able to save a little girl like that. Our Lord does move in mysterious ways. Of course," he continued with a little laugh, "it did often end quite badly for His servants. I believe Saint Valentine suffered a fate considered at the time to be an appropriate punishment for his alleged 'miracle'."

The vicar looked at Morgan as if prompting him. All Jasper could do was nod and reply, "Of course, of course."

"I hope you would not consider it too forward of me if I were to perhaps remind you of that as well?" said the vicar after allowing a suitable period of time to pass, during which Dr Morgan resolutely failed to provide the information himself.

"Please do," said the doctor. He had produced a small notebook from his knapsack and was now taking out a pencil. The vicar left him to his scribbling and proceeded back up the aisle.

"Some stories say that he was stabbed to death by a drunken mob, others that he was run through with a spear and then dragged through the streets tied to the tail of a horse."

"Tail...of...a...horse," Morgan mouthed the words as he wrote them down while the vicar allowed him to catch up.

"Oh yes. Then there is the story of his being beheaded. I believe they used to do that to quite a lot of saints."

"It did rather put a stop to what they were up to, didn't it?" said Morgan with a childlike chuckle.

"I suppose so," said the vicar, nearing the choir stalls. "As far as I am aware there are, however, no stories of his being drowned, burned alive, or being force fed his own children." He stepped behind the pulpit, and disappeared.

"Did they really do that?" said Morgan, looking aghast.

The vicar's voice carried on from where he was momentarily hidden. "Oh, you wouldn't believe some of the punishments that have been meted out to the guilty over the years, Dr Morgan, you really wouldn't. Anyway, I am reliably informed that the true means of St Valentine's martyrdom was by a device similar to this one here."

With that the vicar returned, wheeling a complicated-looking contraption into the aisle. It consisted of a metal framework on four wheels, from the top of which protruded two long runners that extended far beyond the device itself.

"What on earth is that?" said Morgan, fascinated. He tucked away his notebook and rushed forward to examine it.

"Medieval technology," said the vicar with a grin. "Don't touch it – it's very old, and very fragile. Of course there's no way of proving that this is the actual device that was used and I very much doubt it was, but it certainly dates from the time and—" here he gave Morgan a big smile "—it *is* fun to pretend."

"Oh yes it *is*!" said the doctor, taking out his camera. He was about to press the button and then stopped. "I presume it's all right if I..."

The vicar nodded. "Of course, my dear fellow, of course! Take as many pictures as you like, and of the window as well if you wish."

Dr Morgan was allowed his amusement for ten minutes before he was interrupted.

"Do you know," said the vicar, "I've just had an idea."

"What's that, then?" said Morgan, now back down at the atrium and taking pictures of the frankly uninteresting font.

"What if I were to take a picture of you pretending to succumb to this old thing here?" The vicar gave the framework a very gentle pat. "So you could be seen to be suffering the martyrdom of St Valentine – in the Church of St Valentine?"

The doctor's glee at the idea was almost matched by his companion's. "I say, would you? I mean, would you mind?"

"Well, it's not every day we have someone like you in here so I don't see why we shouldn't make a special effort," the vicar replied, looking around him. "Now, we need something for you to sit in." His eyes roamed the church for a moment before settling on an ornate-looking chair near the choir stalls. "That should do nicely," he said.

He picked the chair up and set it carefully at the head of the aisle, facing away from the altar. "This is where the bishop sits when he comes to offer his benediction," he said, lowering his voice to a whisper. "But if you promise not to tell anyone, then neither will I."

Morgan was barely able to contain his excitement. "Cross my heart and hope to die," he said.

"Indeed," said the vicar, adjusting the cushion before Morgan sat down. "Now, Saint Valentine would of course have been restrained," his eyes began to search the building again.

"What about those pretend manacles over there?" Morgan said, pointing to a nearby anti-slavery exhibition that had apparently been put together by a local school. A set of rusty-looking chains hung next to brightly illustrated poems about torture and repression.

"Well spotted!" The vicar crossed the aisle and picked them up. They rattled as he did so. "Looks like someone managed to find the real thing," he said. "They're a bit dusty – I hope that's not going to be a problem?"

"Not at all," said Morgan. "It'll add to the authenticity, and that will add to the chances of my book selling."

"Of course," said the vicar, clamping Morgan's wrists to the arms of the chair. The key was even rustier, and grated in the locks as he turned it. "Comfy?"

"It's a bit tight," the doctor replied, "but that's okay. It's only for a moment, after all."

"We need to keep your head still as well," said his companion. "Partly for authenticity but mostly for your own safety." He attached a leather strap that ran under Morgan's chin and behind his ears. It achieved the job admirably. "And now we're almost ready to begin!"

The vicar wheeled the device round so that it was facing the now helpless doctor and proceeded to arrange the runners so that they were propped either side of his head. "And can you guess what goes on here?" he asked.

Morgan would have shaken his head if he'd been able to. Instead he croaked a muffled "No."

The vicar reached behind the near-most pew and picked up a tiny trolley to which had been affixed two steel daggers. He placed the little vehicle on the runners and ran it back as far away from Morgan as the metal rails would allow.

"Ideally they should be red hot," he said as he attached the trolley bearing the blades to a heavy spring at the end of the frame, "but we can't have everything. Now, what should actually happen is this: the little trolley is released and it runs along these rails, and then the knives put out your eyes."

"Put out my eyes?" mumbled Jasper.

"Exactly," the vicar nodded, "and not just that. The force imparted to the blades by the spring at the back here means that in actuality they wouldn't just blind you; they would be driven through the back of your skull and into the chair itself."

"The bishop wouldn't be pleased," said Morgan, trying to laugh. "And that's how St Valentine was martyred, is it?"

The vicar's expression changed as he came closer and leaned over the helpless doctor. "No," he said. "Not at all, actually."

The doctor eyed the steel spring-loaded knife blades and then looked back at the vicar. "I beg your pardon?"

"You know, I really must give you credit for living up – or rather, down – to my expectations, Jasper," said the black clad figure, much more coldly now. "I suspected you would be as lazy and incompetent a researcher of church history as you were an anaesthetist, and it would seem I have been proven correct."

"What on earth do you mean?" Morgan coughed against the neck restraint and tried to struggle, but it was too tight.

"I mean that you have no idea who St Valentine was, do you? Just like in the old days, you intended to rely on someone else telling you all you needed to know so you could struggle on without actually having the faintest clue what you were doing. Well, this time, that has backfired." Now there was barely concealed anger in his tone. As he leaned close to his prisoner his voice was barely a whisper. "You don't recognise me, do you?"

The doctor tried to shake his head.

"No," said the vicar, removing his upper row of fake teeth. "It's amazing what a false overbite, a pair of glasses, and of course ten years of utter agony can do to alter the appearance of someone you used to know so well."

The penny had dropped now. Morgan stared in shock as he mouthed his captor's name.

"Yes," said the man who had imprisoned him, "It's me. It is Edward Valentine, returned from the grave to claim his just revenge. Tell me – have you ever seen a film called *Theatre of Blood*?" Morgan shook his head. "That's a pity. It's a very good film. Of course you're not going to get the chance to see it now, or anything else for that matter. So I suppose it's just as well that I summarised every one of its quite outrageous and horrible murders as part of that poppycock I was making up about the fate of that poor saint." He paused, returning to the device he had attached to Morgan's chair. "Every murder except one, that it." He stroked the button that would release the spring. "You're about to be blinded, Dr Morgan, but before I release the knives I feel I ought to tell you that you're not the first to receive such a dramatic method of punishment. I do, however, feel that you are the one that's most going to upset the christening that's due in here in about half an hour."

"For God's sake, Valentine!" Morgan pleaded, trying hard to turn his face away from the trajectory of the shining steel. "There was no way we could save her! We all tried! We all did our best! It was a hopeless case! Please! Please! For God's sake!"

"Not for *God's* sake, Dr Morgan," said the man in black. "For mine."

His thumb came down on the button.

10

"And that is why there are only two of you left."

Longdon regarded the shocked expressions of the two men sitting in front of him in the station's interview room. It had been the only place available for him to talk to them when they had been brought in, and their concern that they had both been apprehended regarding some unknown misdemeanour had quickly turned to horror as Longdon recounted the series of deaths that had occurred over the last few days.

"And are you seriously suggesting that Edward Valentine is responsible for all of this?" Geoffrey Marsden must have been close to sixty but he wore it well. The few streaks of grey in his hair matched his eyes, and while he was obviously shaken, his stoic expression betrayed the fact that he had witnessed horror many times during his long career.

"We think so, sir," said Longdon. "For a start, Dr Valentine's body was never found. Second, it's impossible to think of anyone else who could bear such a grudge against such a disparate group of people."

"If what you say is true, then why haven't you caught him yet?" demanded Christopher Skilbeck. He had been Marsden's junior ten years ago, but was now a consultant surgeon himself and had been dragged down from Nottingham. The rotund little man was sweating and his black suit looked rumpled.

"Well, for a start, the only pictures we have of him are ten years old," said Longdon. "Plus, he seems to have managed to get close enough to his victims without them recognising him that we suspect his appearance has either radically altered, or he has become something of a master of disguise."

"Either that or they just weren't expecting someone long dead to turn up and try to kill them," said Marsden. "At least we're forewarned."

"And under protection, sir," said Longdon. "Until all of this has blown over."

"What does that mean?" Skilbeck fidgeted in his chair. "I've got patients to see."

"We appreciate that you both have, sir." said Longdon, "but neither of you are going to be of much use to your patients dead, so if you'll just bear with us, then hopefully we can prevent that from happening."

There was a pause as that sank in.

"How exactly do you propose to prevent us from being killed?" said Marsden. "We aren't going to have to go to some dreadful safe house are we?" Both he and Skilbeck paled at the mention of the word.

"All our safe houses are full at the moment, sir," said Longdon, their disdain not lost on him. "So our only alternative was to keep you in the cells here." He paused again for effect and for the joy of seeing their faces. "But fortunately one of our staff has volunteered his own home." He held up his hands. "Now, before you start complaining I should explain that it's Dr Richard Patterson, our pathologist, and the only reason I've agreed is that apparently he's got some huge old rambling place in the country south of here, so there should be plenty of room and little chance that anyone should be able to find out where you are. As well as that, you'll both be assigned police protection."

"Where is this place?" said Skilbeck.

"Probably best if you don't know the details, sir," said Longdon. "One text message to a wife or a mistress and for all we know our Dr Valentine will have picked it up and will be on his way there."

"And even with police protection you think he's still a threat to us?" said Marsden.

Longdon leaned over the table separating him from the two men. "Have you not been listening to what I've been saying? This is a man who has managed to get a man stung to death by scorpions in front of a class full of children. Who has put together an entire seventeenth century village filled with volunteers in front of whom he then dissolved a woman in acid. In the last seven days he has flung someone off the Clifton Suspension Bridge, impaled someone on the roof of the Bristol Council House, and popped over to Wales to spear one of your former anaesthetic colleagues through his eye sockets while he sat manacled to a bishop's chair. So in answer to your question: yes – no matter what we do, I will still very much consider this man to be a threat."

Marsden and Skilbeck exchanged fearful glances.

"Well if you put it like that..." said Marsden, shifting in his seat.

"I do," said Longdon as Jenny Newham entered the room. "Now, if you would both be good enough to go with the sergeant, she will arrange transport for you.

Your families have already been informed of the situation and they know you are under our protection, so you needn't worry."

The two men waited in the corridor while Longdon gave Jenny some final instructions.

"And if you see Richard, tell him thank you, will you?" he said.

"Well, when I last saw him I got the impression you didn't give him much choice," said Jenny with a grin.

"That's his own bloody fault for offering in the first place. I know he just wanted to brag about having a big house and he never thought we'd take him up on it, but that's his problem." Longdon got out of the chair and stretched. "Who've we got assigned to protect Lord and Lady Precious out there?"

Jenny pretended to think for a moment. "We've got Shenley and Standen there until 10.30 this evening, then I think you'll find it's you and me."

"Always drawing the short bloody straw," said Longdon with a sigh.

"Is that you or me, sir?" said Jenny as he followed her out.

"Now, you start being cheeky and you might find yourself reassigned to something a bit less glamorous," said Longdon with a smile. "I'll see you tonight. When absolutely nothing is going to happen, right?"

Jenny gave him the firmest of nods. "Right."

They were, of course, to be proved wrong.

Patterson's house was hidden deep within the wilds of Somerset. Despite that, and an evening that kept threatening rain, Jenny Newham was only five minutes late for her shift. She parked her blue Mini in front of the rambling gothic building, which was nothing more than a black silhouette against the charcoal clouds gathering overhead, and knocked as hard as she could on the heavy oak door.

It was opened almost immediately by a man she recognised as DS Michael Shenley. A grin crossed his freckled face as he realised who it was.

"So," he said, "you found it, then?"

Jenny returned his smile as she went inside. "It was a bit of a maze getting here," she said. "Thank God for SatNav."

If the outside of the building had been imposing, the inside was almost overwhelming. A huge entrance hall boasted an ornate staircase running up the left hand wall and leading to the upper floor. The rest of the wall space was taken up with suits of armour, antique swords, and other items of medieval weaponry. A door to the right led into the lounge.

"Do you think Patterson caught this himself?" Jenny tapped the stuffed grizzly bear that was positioned near the front door. It didn't growl and instead made a rather hollow sound.

"No idea," said Shenley. "But we haven't seen him this evening. Otherwise I would have asked him. He rang earlier, though. Apparently he's stuck doing a couple of post-mortems, otherwise he'd be here."

"Not more victims?" said Jenny.

Shenley shook his head. "Nothing to do with this case as far as I'm aware." He glanced upstairs. "Our two little boys are sleeping like babies."

Jenny snorted. "It's a bit early for bedtime, isn't it? What have they been doing?"

Shenley led her into the vast room to the right, where on a table near the huge bay window were lying two empty bottles of J&B whiskey and two glasses. "The same thing doctors always do when they get bored," he said, pointing at the detritus that had been left by Messrs Marsden and Skilbeck. "I'm not sure how happy Patterson's going to be about them raiding his drinks cabinet."

Jenny looked around the room, marvelling at the huge open fireplace opposite the door, the rich fabric of the curtains that hung over the windows both front and rear, and the book-lined walls. "He's pretty comfortable in here, isn't he?"

"We haven't had much of a chance to look round," said a voice from the door.

Jenny turned to see the wiry figure of DS Vince Standen. "We've been too busy looking after our increasingly pissed-up charges," he said, "at least until a couple of hours ago when they finally dragged themselves off upstairs. Since then we've been alternating patrolling the grounds and checking all the doors and windows."

"It's been all quiet," said Shenley, handing her the paperwork and making to leave. "Hope your night's the same." He paused by the lounge door. "Where's your colleague, by the way?"

"Oh, he's more lost than I was," said Jenny with a grin. "I called him on the radio before I came inside. He should be here in about half an hour."

"Well, if you're sure?" Shenley gave her a look of concern.

"I'll be fine," she replied, taking out her gun and waving it, "and besides, they've given me this awful thing to help defend myself with. Now off you go."

The first thing Jenny did once they were gone was tidy up the whiskey bottles. She wouldn't have been able to help herself anyway, but the thought of Richard Patterson turning up and going crazy about his plundered alcohol supply meant that hopefully she had managed to avert at least one crisis this evening.

Next, she went to check on her charges.

The staircase was carpeted in thick scarlet-coloured pile and Jenny's boots made no sound on the heavy fabric as she made her way upstairs, past paintings of people who didn't resemble her pathologist colleague in the slightest. She made a mental note to ask him about them when he finally turned up.

A walnut-panelled corridor led away from the landing, with rooms either side. The first one was lushly furnished but unoccupied. The second revealed the heavily sleeping form of one of her charges. His black hair identified him as Christopher Skilbeck, as did the fairly capacious clothes that had been strewn across the intricately woven Persian carpet.

Next door was much the same, only here the heavily sedated individual hidden beneath the sheets had streaks of grey in his hair, and a tweed jacket that had been clumsily hung on a bedpost before Geoffrey Marsden had retired for the evening. Jenny shut the door behind her. There was one other room on the corridor, which Jenny checked for security. This was also unoccupied and was presumably used by Patterson as a viewing room, as the only items of furniture were an ornately carved straight-backed chair which was positioned four feet before the widescreen television set that took up the entire left hand corner. Both the screen and the room were currently in darkness. Jenny crossed the room and drew back the curtains to make a cursory inspection of the window, which had been bolted shut. It must have been a trick of the light, because as she looked through the glass at the countryside beyond, it almost looked as if there were bars on the outside.

She was on her way back downstairs when the front door opened. She smiled, expecting to see Longdon, and her face fell when she realised it wasn't him.

"I very much hope that face isn't for me!" said Patterson, shrugging off his overcoat and hanging it on the grizzly's muzzle.

Jenny apologised. "It's just I was expecting it to be DI Longdon," she explained. "He still isn't here yet."

"Probably got lost," said Patterson going into the lounge and rubbing his hands. "The roads around here can be a bit interminable. Would you like a drink?"

"Not while I'm on duty," she reminded him.

"No, no, of course not. Silly of me." Patterson went to

the Victorian-looking globe by the window and flipped up the lid to reveal his drinks cabinet. He eyed it with disbelief. "Have they really drunk all of my scotch?" he said.

Jenny shrugged. "Apparently so," she said.

"Bloody surgeons," said Patterson, pouring himself a gin from a nearly full bottle of Hendricks and squirting in a few drops of tonic. He paused before taking a mouthful. "Can I get you something else? Tea or coffee?"

"Maybe later – thanks," said Jenny as the pathologist took another sip from the glass.

"Very well, but do let me know if you get thirsty," he said. "How are our guests doing? Have you had a look at them yet?"

"Sleeping soundly," Jenny replied. "I don't think we're going to hear a peep out of them all night."

"Good stuff," Patterson took another sip. "So all we have to worry about is our Dr Valentine getting in here and murdering us in some ludicrous and unimaginable way."

"Not us," said Jenny, "them. He's only bumping off the people he wants revenge on."

"Yes, of course," said Patterson, putting the glass down. "Well, if you'll excuse me I have a few things to do before I turn in. You're sure I can't get you anything?"

Jenny shook her head. "I'll be fine, thanks. I'll just wait here until Longdon arrives."

"Very well," he said with a smile. "Don't be alarmed by any banging around you hear upstairs – it'll just be me."

"I'll check anyway if you don't mind," said Jenny. "Any banging around might just be our suspect killing the men we're supposed to be protecting, and that wouldn't look good for anyone."

"You've got a point there," said Patterson, making for the stairs. "Maybe I'll bump into you in a bit."

Jenny smiled and checked her watch. Longdon should have been here by now. Presumably he was still stuck on the back roads of Somerset somewhere. She closed the drinks cabinet lid and then looked around the room. She'd already checked upstairs, and Patterson would raise the alarm if anything happened up there now, so in order to keep herself busy she decided to check the outside of the house.

She was careful to leave the door on the latch and took the torch from the boot of her car. The wind was picking up as Jenny made her way back to the front of the house and proceeded to make a circuit of the outside of the building. The windows at the back were securely shut.

As Jenny tugged on the back door handle she felt a slight spatter of rain, accompanied by a flash of lightning. She waited for the inevitable thunder clap that would follow so she could get an idea of how far away the storm might be, but none came. A few more drops of rain fell, followed by another flash of white light, and this time Jenny realised that the light wasn't due to an electric storm at all.

It was coming from one of the upstairs windows.

By the time she had made her way back round to the front of the house, Jenny had worked out that the light was coming from the empty room that she had last looked in – the one with nothing in it but the TV. Patterson was probably watching something before going to bed, but she knew she needed to check on it anyway.

When she got back inside the house the lights were off.

Jenny flicked the switch by the door but nothing happened. *Great*, she thought, *a power failure on a night like tonight*. She used the torch beam to find the stairs and climbed halfway up before calling out.

"Dr Patterson? Are you all right up there?"

There was no reply.

"Richard?" Jenny began to climb the stairs once more, but more cautiously now. The flickering white light came again, this time from the landing. Everything was just suspicious enough that by the time she reached the first floor Jenny had decided she was going to have to wake up the two men she had been sent there to protect, regardless of how drunk or hungover they might be.

The flickering light was coming from the room at the far end. The door was only open a fraction, but the rest of the house was in such darkness that the light was conspicuous. Jenny called Patterson's name again and when yet again there was no reply, she knocked on the door to Christopher Skilbeck's room and went in.

The surgeon was still asleep, the glow from Jenny's torch picking out his motionless form beneath the blankets. Jenny coughed loudly to try to wake him, even though she knew it was unlikely he would hear her.

"Mr. Skilbeck?" she said, coming closer. "Mr Skilbeck, I'm sorry to have to disturb you but for safety's sake it's probably best if we have you awake just for now."

The figure in the bed did not move.

Jenny was almost over him now, and as the torch beam played over his body Jenny thought he was breathing remarkably lightly for a man drunk to the point of being comatose. In fact it didn't look as if he was breathing at all.

"Sir?" Jenny reached out a hand to shake the man's shoulder. Nothing. "Mr Skilbeck," she said, pulling back the blankets, "I'm sorry about this but I'm going to have to—"

She was cut off in mid-sentence by what she saw beneath the bedsheet. Christopher Skilbeck's head was lying on the white pillow, but the body below it was all wrong. It was too thin and too tall to be that of the man she had seen in Longdon's office.

Then she saw the pool of blood where Skilbeck's head had been surgically stitched to the other body's neck.

Jenny stifled a scream and threw back the covers completely. In the swaying beam of the torch held in her shaking hand she saw that the head and right arm of Mr Christopher Skilbeck had been stitched to what looked like the body of Mr Geoffrey Marsden.

Jenny spun round and flashed the torch around the room. She released the breath she had been holding when she was satisfied that there was no-one else in there with her. Then, as quietly as she could, she tiptoed next door, where she found Mr Marsden's missing head and arm had been stitched onto the squatter torso of Mr Skilbeck in the same way.

The killer wasn't here, either.

A muffled cry came from the room at the end of the corridor; the one with the flickering light. Jenny drew her gun and called out.

"Police! I'm warning you now – I'm armed and there's backup on the way. The best thing you can do now is give yourself up."

Silence.

"Richard," she said, "are you okay?"

Still silence.

Again Jenny thought about going back downstairs to radio for backup, but her overriding concern was that Patterson might have caught Valentine in the act. He might be in that room now, being subjected to some form of hideous electric shock treatment that was killing him while she was standing here dithering.

Her mind made up, she crept up to the door of the last room on the right and nudged it open.

The television was on.

She didn't really register what was playing on the screen. It looked like some film about medieval times, with the villain having trapped the helpless hero beneath some huge swinging torture instrument that was threatening to cut him in half. That was all she saw before her attention was drawn to the chair.

Someone was sitting in it.

No, some *thing* was sitting in it.

The tiny, still figure was no bigger than a child, and as Jenny crept closer she realised that was what it was. A little girl, pigtails tied with blue ribbon, brightly polished shoes on feet that couldn't quite reach the floor. As good as gold and as still as the grave, sitting patiently while the film on the television screen came to an end.

Jenny checked there was no-one behind her, and then spoke.

"I don't want to scare you," she said. "But my name's Jenny and I'm a police officer. I need you to come with me."

As she reached the chair Jenny felt her legs turn to water as she realised her words were falling on deaf ears. Dead ears, in fact. As dead as the rest of the beautifully dressed, well preserved, mummified corpse of a little girl that had been propped up in the chair to watch a film on which the credits were now rolling and which starred...

"Vincent Price, of course," said a cold voice from behind her.

Jenny Newham turned to see a figure silhouetted in the open doorway. As it took a step forward she realised who it was. And she also suddenly understood why it had been arranged for the last two victims to come here.

"You're not Dr Patterson at all, are you?" she said, pointing the gun at the man who seemed to have grown several inches taller since she had last seen him.

"On the contrary, my dear young lady, I am," he replied, taking another step into the room, "or at least I have been for the last ten years. The man who was Richard Patterson before that suffered a rather unfortunate accident that left his place on a training scheme in forensic pathology free. But yes, before that I was, and indeed still am, Dr Edward Valentine. Or rather, *Mr.* Edward Valentine, at your service."

He gave a little bow while keeping his eyes on the gun.

Jenny glanced at the thing in the chair. "Then that... that... child is..."

"Victoria?" Now Valentine was looking over Jenny's shoulder and addressing the corpse of the child directly.

"Has the film finished?" He looked back at Jenny. *"The Pit and the Pendulum* is one of her favourites, you know. In fact, I believe I told Detective Inspector Longdon that at one point. You know, I can't tell you how many times we watched some of these before..." His voice tailed off as he looked behind Jenny again. "If the film's finished then it's bedtime, as well you know," he said to the withered lifeless figure in the chair. "You won't object if I put her to bed, will you?" Now he was addressing Jenny again. "It's just that she does get a little grumpy if I let her stay up too late."

Jenny trained the gun on him. "You're under arrest, Dr Valentine," she said, "and you're going to come downstairs with me where we're both going to wait until DI Longdon gets here."

"Oh, I don't think he'll be here for some time," said Valentine with a chuckle. "The directions I gave him should have taken him a good twenty miles in the opposite direction, and I do so hope he resorts to his SatNav so the false postcode I gave him can be put to good use. I'm sure he'll get here eventually—" and now his voice was cold again "—but before he does I have plans for you, young lady. You don't really think I had only just arrived home when I pretended to, do you?" He gave Jenny a wicked smile and then looked behind her once again. "Victoria, stop that!"

This last sentence was barked out loudly and so abruptly that Jenny couldn't help glancing behind her. That was all the time Valentine needed to wrest the gun from her and clamp the chloroform-soaked cloth over her mouth and nose. She fought for only a few seconds before darkness descended.

12

It was close to midnight when Longdon finally got to Patterson's house, his SatNav switched off and his temper frayed after having got directions from a pub on the verge of a lock-in over in Clevedon. The petrified-looking landlord had relaxed a little, and become far more co-operative, once Longdon had explained that the police business he was on was not the closing down of small rural public houses. In fact, once Longdon had ordered a pint and one for the landlord as well, the man had gone so far as to draw a map to Patterson's house.

"At least I think that's where you want to go, sir," he said, scratching his stubbly jowls. "It's the only place around here that fits that description. Mind you, even if it is owned by a doctor, that still don't rightly explain the weird building jobs they've had over there the last couple of months."

Longdon didn't really have time for chit-chat but something in the publican's tone made him want to know more. "How on earth would you know?" he asked.

"Small part of the world, sir," came the reply. "We all know each other's business around here."

Longdon nodded. That part was true enough. "What kind of building jobs?" he asked.

The landlord looked around and then became more conspiratorial. "Well, it's all a bit strange, sir, if you ask me. My wife's second cousin, Les, well he had to deliver all this metalwork that he said looked as if it would be more at home in some kind of ancient museum."

Longdon's interest dropped. So that was all the man meant. "You mean suits of armour, swords, that kind of thing?"

The landlord nodded. "But that's not all. He had to pick something up from the Avonmouth ferry. Came over from Spain apparently." The man leaned in closer and Longdon was surprised he couldn't smell booze. "He says it was the biggest blade he'd ever seen, shaped like a crescent moon and of a size that could cut a man in half." Suddenly he seemed embarrassed by his outburst. "Well," he said, more soberly, "it could if it was connected up to all the other stuff he picked up as well. Like some huge pendulum, apparently."

Longdon was out the door and into his car before the landlord even realised he had gone. As he crossed beneath the motorway, stopping regularly to examine the pencil-drawn map, Longdon was scarcely able to believe what his instincts were telling him. Patterson had been with them for years. *But not more than ten years*, he reminded himself, *in fact only just less than five*. Where had he been before that? Had the man who had performed all the post-mortems on people actually killed people himself, even Dr Richard Patterson, or had he somehow assumed the man's identity at some point before coming to Bristol? Even with the stringent checks available, Longdon knew all too well how easy it was to falsify paperwork, forge certificates and, if one so wished, take on another identity entirely. All you needed to be was resourceful, wealthy, and very, very clever. Dr Edward

Valentine had been all three. And, thought Longdon with a shiver as he drove as fast as he could down the pitch-dark country roads, he probably still was.

~

The house was in darkness when Longdon arrived. Hammering on the front door yielded nothing in the way of a response, and the heavy oak was too robust to force, so instead Longdon resorted to an inspection of the ground floor windows. The front of the house appeared impregnable. It was when he went round the back that he saw, about thirty feet away from the main building, set back in the house's capacious grounds, what looked like a stone temple.

A stone temple with light seeping from beneath its double doors.

Longdon took one final look at the house before deciding that if he was going to get any answers and, indeed, save any lives tonight, it was probably going to be over there.

The ground was soft underfoot and Longdon took care to tread carefully in case traps had been set. He doubted it, however, as he had a feeling that he was meant to see what was inside the imposing stone building he was now approaching.

The doors were made of iron and the right hand one swung open at his touch. Longdon found himself facing a pair of heavy black curtains, which he parted tentatively. Beyond was a scene that could easily have been lifted from any of the films Longdon had been watching over the last couple of days.

Along each wall, set at regular intervals, were torches of flickering flame. At the far end lay Sergeant Jenny Newham, manacled to a slab of grey stone, the heavy pendulum the landlord had mentioned poised fifteen feet above her ready to begin its descent, the curved steel blade so highly polished that it reflected the orange light from the torches like a mirror. Longdon breathed a sigh of relief when he saw that she was unharmed, then drew back in horror when he saw the grotesque tableaux of burned and mutilated figures that had been arranged in standing positions around her prostrate form.

"Welcome, Detective Inspector!"

The voice came from the shadows in the far left hand corner. A voice not entirely unlike Richard Patterson's, but the tone was far more confident, flamboyant, theatrical.

"Patterson?" Longdon squinted but it was impossible to see who was speaking.

"I must confess," the voice continued, "I was starting to get a little concerned that you might not get here in time. Imagine that! Spend ten years constructing the greatest story Vincent Price never starred in and then have the climax ruined by the incompetence of the police force. Although I suppose I should thank you, really."

Now a figure stepped from the darkness, a figure Longdon recognised all too well.

"I see you're not that surprised to see me, Detective Inspector."

"No, Dr Valentine," said Longdon. "I am not, although I admit I'm surprised you're not wearing a cape and some theatrical makeup."

Valentine tutted. "Too over the top, my dear Inspector. I do have to make good my escape shortly and I should hate to trip over an unwieldy cloak. We real-life villains do sadly have to make some concessions to reality, hence the simple black suit you see me in. Much better for remaining unobtrusive. Oh, and it's *Mr* Valentine, by the way. I believe I already mentioned how particular we surgeons are about such things. "

"None of that matters," said Longdon. "You're not going to get five miles without every available police unit on your tail. You may as well give up now."

"May I, Inspector?" Valentine smirked. "How very... *television* of you. Surely you realise by now that individuals such as myself always have an escape plan?" As he spoke he fingered the heavy lever next to his right hand. "Now, I suggest you stay right where you are or I may be forced to begin my recreation of Roger Corman's *The Pit and the Pendulum* prematurely."

Longdon considered rushing him but Valentine was too far away.

"Just keep still, Inspector," said Valentine, "and no-one will get hurt. Well, no-one *else*."

"Are you all right, Jenny?" Longdon called.

"Fine, sir," came the muffled reply. "Just a bit... you know."

"She's unharmed, and hopefully she's going to stay that way," said Valentine, taking a step forward to the first of the hideous figures. "You know, one of the advantages of being the pathologist on the case where you yourself are perpetrating the murders is that it is so much easier to get hold of the bodies afterwards." He tapped the blackened corpse on the cheek, causing it to wobble precariously. "Did you like my Alfredo? Poor old Andrew Wells, thinking he was off to a fancy dress party in his honour and instead finding himself swinging over the Avon Gorge."

"He wasn't your first, though," said Longdon, "was he?"

"Quite right, Inspector," Valentine replied. "That was, as you so cleverly worked out, Caroline Conrad. In fact, it was she who gave me the idea. When I was trying to decide how best to punish those who failed my Victoria I learned of her spinal implant. How delicious it would be, I thought, if she were shocked to death through it, just like in *The Tingler*. That film, I am sure you are aware, was made in black and white." He looked again at the charred remains of Andrew Wells, and then at the rest of the macabre tableaux. "But from there I decided that if the rest were to die, they should die in colour."

He moved to the second mutilated figure, the one with a gaping wound in its abdomen. "And so Dr Pritchard was despatched by the unicorn from *The Abominable Dr Phibes*. My God, his wife was *boring*, but it was necessary to strike up an illicit relationship with her in order for his demise to be achieved. Similarly, with Dr Davies, I had to spend interminable months under that clown makeup entertaining tedious children twice a week in order to recreate the scorpion death from *Dr Phibes Rises Again*."

He moved from the puffy, embalmed figure of Martin Davies to an empty chair. "But probably my proudest achievement was Lorraine Parsons. Can you imagine it?

An entire scene from *Witchfinder General* recreated just for her! And she never realised it, or had the opportunity to appreciate it. And the burning by acid instead of flame was a masterstroke, don't you think?"

Longdon stayed quiet, not wanting to do or say anything that might endanger Jenny Newham's life.

"After that, Jasper Morgan was a bit of an anticlimax." He indicated the slumped corpse of an elderly man no longer in possession of his eyes. "But I had to have a scene from *Theatre of Blood* in my repertoire and it seemed the most appropriate. And finally..." Valentine's guide to the dead came to an end with the two people Longdon recognised as being the men he was supposed to be guarding this evening. "I realise I'm pushing things a little bit here, but in the original 1958 version of *The Fly* a scientist has his head and right arm exchanged with that of the title insect. Naturally I couldn't do that, but swapping these two gentlemen's appendages in a similar manner seemed a most appropriate way to deal with both of them at the same time."

Valentine surveyed his tableaux with pride, then he moved back to the heavy lever that operated the pendulum mechanism. "And now," he said, "for our finale."

"Before you go any further," said Longdon. "Could I just ask one thing?"

Valentine pondered for a moment, his fingertips resting on the lever. "Go on."

"Why?"

"I beg your pardon?"

Longdon gestured to everything around him while

edging forward as surreptitiously as he could. "Why all this? Why such an elaborate way of dealing with the people you blamed for the death of your little girl? Why not just shoot the lot of them and be done with it?"

Valentine shook his head. "If only you could hear yourself, Inspector. *Shoot* them? The people who took my reason for living away from me? Who failed miserably to keep her alive for even a few moments once she was on the operating table? My dear Inspector, it is not for *them* that I have spent the last ten years planning and scheming, but for her, for my Victoria." There was the hint of a tear in his eye now. "When the whole story is known the world will never forget it. They will never forget the mad surgeon and the horrible way he murdered nine of his colleagues, but most of all they will never forget why I did it. They will never forget *her*. And that, Inspector, is why I have done all this. So that she will live on, in the minds of everyone who hears this horrific story. Then perhaps I can finally bury her."

"Her memory, you mean?" said Longdon, still moving closer.

"No, Inspector," said Valentine, wheeling out the figure he had hidden behind the bodies of Andrew Wells and Evan Pritchard, "I mean my Victoria. She is going to watch as her story – *our* story – comes to an end."

Valentine reached out, and pulled the lever. There was a grating of gears and the sound of heavy machinery being put into operation high in the building. Slowly, the heavy pendulum blade swung to the right, rising higher and higher until it was almost parallel with the ground. Then it stopped, hanging suspended in space.

"I do expect you to escape, you know," he said, addressing Jenny as well. "Otherwise it would hardly be a fitting end to the story, a story that would have no-one to tell it if at least one of you did not survive. However, I'm sure you will appreciate that I need to escape too—" he looked above him into the rafters "—and I thought this marvellous contraption the most appropriate way of killing... a little time?"

With that he pushed the lever forward and the pendulum began to swing, the distance between the blade and the helpless girl diminishing every time it passed above her body. Longdon rushed forward and began to grapple with the manacles that held her in place.

"My colleagues have the keys, Inspector," said Valentine. "But you're going to have to be quick."

Longdon turned to see Valentine taking one of the torches from its sconce and applying the flame to the already burnt form of what was left of Andrew Wells. Then he moved from victim to victim, setting them alight. They caught fire so rapidly it was clear they had been coated in something flammable.

"All that embalming fluid," explained Valentine as he moved to the corpses of Skilbeck and Marsden. "It works beautifully, as you can see. I think you'd better hurry."

Figuring that Valentine wouldn't have hidden the keys on the first corpse, Longdon instead ran to the ones at the other end that were only just beginning to catch light. He searched the pockets of Geoffrey Marsden and shook the corpse for good measure before moving onto Skilbeck.

"Getting warmer, Inspector," said Valentine with a

chuckle as he made his way to the door. He pointed to the mummified corpse of his daughter, just beginning to char from its proximity to Wells' body. "I shall leave what is left of Victoria to watch over you. She always did enjoy a good ending."

And with that he was gone. Longdon was searching Martin Davies' corpse now, all the while batting at the flames which were beginning to spread across the floor. Nothing.

"Sir!" came Jenny's voice from behind the flames. "It's almost—"

"I know! I know!" Longdon risked a brief glance behind him to see that the blade was almost touching her. The corpses of Evan Pritchard and Andrew Wells were now so ablaze that all Longdon could do was kick at them helplessly. He'd lied! Valentine had lied! There were no keys here, none at all. He'd searched every victim, every one except...

Longdon turned to look at the empty chair intended to represent the absent body of Lorraine Parsons. *Oh, very clever*, he thought, giving it a kick. The chair fell over to reveal a set of tiny silver keys taped to the underside.

"Sir, I—"

"Coming, Newham, I'm coming!"

As fast as he could Longdon tore off the tape and ran to his helpless partner. The blade swung across once more and as he undid her ankles he could see that the next stroke would make contact. Her wrists were trickier and as he struggled with the final manacle the blade swept across her. She screamed as it slashed open her shirt, leaving a nasty gash on her belly. Then she was free and off the slab before the pendulum could continue its inexorable descent.

"You okay?" Longdon asked as supported her.

"Fine," said Jenny, her hand over her wound. "At least, I think so."

Longdon looked around them but there was no sign of Valentine. The walls of the building behind them were now a livid, flaming scarlet. They were about to get back to the car to radio for help when the roof fell in with a crash. Longdon paused. As well as the sound of destruction he could hear something else, above and beyond the noise of the collapsing building.

"Can you hear that?" he said to his colleague.

Jenny shook her head.

"Listen," he said. "I could swear someone's playing music."

Jenny concentrated and then, eventually, she nodded.

"Isn't that 'Somewhere Over the Rainbow', sir?" she said.

Longdon nodded and gave an exasperated sigh. Something told him the manhunt that would ensue after this would lead nowhere. Despite the very best efforts of everyone involved, this was one case that was going to remain open.

They weren't going to catch Dr... no... *Mr* Edward Valentine.

But the man in the raven-shaped hot air balloon that was currently soaring towards the horizon could have told them that.

The End

The Nine Films of Dr Valentine

Hello my friends. It's that time again. Time to decide whether or not you wish to leave the story you have just read and close the book, hopefully with a warm feeling of having been properly entertained, or whether you want to know a little bit more about the influences and thought processes behind the construction of this latest volume of mine.

It's been customary in my previous books to provide, at this point, a few snippets of background information for those interested in how a particular project might have come together. For a change, and because of the significant influence of horror films on this particular story, I thought that this time it might also be rather fun to provide my thoughts on the movies that are referenced in the text. So here we go. Presented here with the blessing of my publisher, and for your delectation and above all entertainment, are my reviews of some very special films, altogether with the usual ragbag of reminiscences and autobiographical bits and pieces that are my way of writing about all this stuff without having to do a proper book about it. For a change, I am going to reassure the casual reader who for some reason is looking at this bit before reading the novella that precedes it, that this afterword isn't loaded with any more spoilers to the story *The Nine Deaths of Dr Valentine* than a youth mis-spent watching the films that influenced it.

The Tingler (1959)

Just prior to writing these notes I finished reading William Castle's autobiography, *Step Right Up – I'm Gonna Scare the Pants Off America!* I've always admired Mr Castle, not least because he always seemed to be having so much fun entertaining his audiences. The projects for which he is most remembered today also benefited from his presence, usually at the beginning, sometimes at the end, and occasionally at some point in the middle, introducing the 'Fright Break' (would audiences stay to see the nerve-shredding climax of *Homicidal*, or would they chicken out, collect a ticket refund, and have to spend the rest of the running time cowering in 'Coward's Corner'?) or the 'Punishment Poll' (thumbs up or thumbs down for the evil *Mr Sardonicus*). As I hope you can tell from my introduction to this afterword (and from the introductions and notes in my other books if you've been kind enough to buy them), there's a little bit of William Castle in me, although I have yet to include any gimmicks in my books. But there's still time.

The gimmick in *The Tingler*, Castle's follow-up to *House on Haunted Hill* (which had also starred Vincent Price) was called 'Percepto' (the name dreamt up by his secretary at the time) and involved cinema seats being wired with tiny electric motors to give audience members a shock at the appropriate moment. The gimmick came after the writing of the film's screenplay, although it would not be difficult to assume it was the other way around.

Vincent Price plays Dr Warren Chapin, a pathologist,

who has noticed that his post mortem examinations of executed patients show that their spines have been partly crushed. He does the horror movie scientist thing of combining that with another probably totally unrelated observation (the tingling of one's spine during fear) and comes up with his theory of the Tingler, a creature that only materialises at moments of extreme fear and can crush your vertebrae if you don't scream. But how is Price to demonstrate this neither scientific nor reasonable theory? Why, via entirely non-scientific and non-reasonable methods, of course! As chance would have it, Vincent's married to horrible man-eating Patricia Cutts in one of those for-the-money arrangements beloved of pulp 1950s scientists. Vincent and Patricia hate each other, which allows screenwriter Robb White to include some more of the deliciously nasty husband-wife banter that graced *House on Haunted Hill* as well. It also gives Vincent a reason to drug her, pretend to shoot her, and then take an X-Ray of her spine. Behold! A massive centipede-lobster thing appears to be clinging on to her vertebrae! Never mind that this makes no sense as she's unconscious when the X-Ray is taken, and should in fact be dead as she hasn't had a chance to scream - we now know the Tingler exists!

Vincent has become friendly with Olly (Philip Coolidge) who runs the local cinema. Olly has a deaf-mute wife whom he wants to kill so he can have money as well, but without the (presumably sign-languaged) ill-feeling. He achieves this in one of the film's standout scenes that epitomises Castle's approach to the horror genre. Veering between silly (a hairy hand holding an axe) and properly unsettling (a bath full of blood from which a hand emerges) Olly gets the desired effect and takes his wife's dead body round to Vincent's house, as Price gave her a sedative earlier in the evening. Olly explains that it may have worked a bit too well. Vincent promptly performs a post mortem and behold! From behind a curtain, and all in silhouette, he produces from the lady's spine a massive rubber wobbly thing with lots of little legs. It tries to bite him on the arm so he locks it in a steel box. Patricia, who has now come round and is a bit upset about the whole drugging and shooting incident, decides to get her own back by drugging Price in return and then setting the Tingler loose. The titular monster is actually rather endearing, wobbling along on the carpet, propelled more by that rather fine wire-like appendage tied to its head than by its tiny legs. In fact, if the viewer were not 100% convinced that the Tingler is real, one might also think it was being dragged along.

Vincent is saved and determines to be rid of the rubbery fiend. He takes it to the cinema, where it gets out and terrifies the audience on screen while at the same time enabling Mr Castle to indulge in a bit of actual bottom-buzzing tomfoolery with his real audience. Thankfully it's caught, put back into Olly's dead wife (I think) and Vincent makes a phone call, presumably to tell the police about Olly's crime or possibly to tell William Castle that he's not going to be in any more of these.

The Tingler is absolutely daft and absolutely bags of fun. It took me a little while to realise that I wanted a Tingler-related murder in my Vincent Price tribute, but once the film had come to mind the idea of shocking someone to death through their spinal column just had to be included. I would dearly love to have been in a cinema that had been wired for Percepto and I think that sort of gimmick just adds to the entertainment experience that a certain sort of horror should be. Perhaps one day one of my books could have tiny invisible pads to give the reader a shock on appropriate pages?

Step right up...

Tower of London (1962)

Here we have a remake of the 1939 Rowland V Lee film of the same name that starred Basil Rathbone and Boris Karloff. Roger Corman's 1962 version was apparently shot in black and white against his and producer-brother Gene Corman's wishes, and watching the film it's easy to see why they weren't happy, as Daniel Haller's sets look as superb as anything from AIP's then-current Poe cycle, and the costumes look as if they deserve the benefit of colour as well.

When his father Edward IV dies, Richard (Vincent Price) decides that he would rather like to be King and if a little bit of murder and torture is required then that's not going to stop him. He's haunted throughout the film by the ghosts of those whom he has killed who keep telling him where he's going to die. He eventually meets his end in an extremely economically filmed version of 1485's Battle of Bosworth field, which consists of Price gurning in a helmet superimposed over footage pinched from the 1939 version and a map of England put together by someone who has no geographical knowledge of the country whatsoever. The only part of the film where things really come together is Price's descent into the castle torture chambers, where the whipped body of Sandra Knight is on display in a pillory prior to her meeting her death on the rack. Otherwise it's a surprisingly horror-free affair, and the overall movie is rather patchy and dull considering its pedigree, and it does suffer immensely from the lack of colour. The 1939 version is much better, and oddly enough also features Vincent Price, this time in the role of the Duke of Clarence. It's interesting to compare his portrayal of Richard here with the rather more camped-up version in *Theatre of Blood*. *Tower of London* is very much a footnote in the Corman-Price canon, but I needed a death that was French, and drowning in wine seemed as good a way to end one's days in that country as any, so *Tower of London* gets a reference in *The Nine Deaths of Dr Valentine*.

The Abominable Dr Phibes (1971)

"Nine killed you, nine shall die! Nine eternities in doom!"

Dr Anton Phibes is determined to revenge himself on the medical team he believes to be responsible for the death of his wife in the car accident that also mutilated him to such a degree that his head now resembles little more than a grotty scarred skull. Being rich, brilliant and insane, and possessing PhDs in theology and music amongst others, it's therefore entirely reasonable that when Phibes isn't out and about killing doctors and nurses in the style of the ten biblical plagues visited upon Egypt, he's back at his lavish house playing his organ while surrounded by life-size clockwork jazz musicians and a beautiful girl called Vulnavia.

The Abominable Dr Phibes is a wonderful, crazy, eccentric, stylish horror film. The story was put together by novice writers James Whiton and William Goldstein and apparently originally had an ending that climaxed at Wembley Stadium. A couple of rewrites and the intervention of producer Louis M Heyward and director Robert Fuest later, and the scene was set for one of the classics of the genre to be born. But it's not just the central idea, Fuest's direction or Vincent Price's performance that makes *Phibes* the success that it is. Brian Eatwell's sets are splendidly decadent, and achieved on a low budget that only occasionally shows. Basil Kirchin's weird jazz score emphasises the other-worldliness of what's happening on screen, and even though there were apparently a few problems over the music (with John Gale being brought in to write the memorable Vulnavia theme) what remains in the film works very well indeed. The tax breaks afforded AIP by filming in England meant that a veritable cornucopia of eccentric British acting talent could be drawn upon, including mad Welshman Hugh Griffith, mad Englishman Terry-Thomas, and mad Scotsman John Laurie, not to mention Peter Jeffrey, John Cater, Aubrey Woods, Peter Gilmore and of course the lovely Caroline Munro, who has to play dead for the entire film.

Depriving Price of the ability to speak may have

seemed like a terrible mistake but instead it allows him to act the role using a variety of expressions as well as making him seem more like the victim of the terrible accident that ruined his face and killed his wife. The film is by no means a comedy but it's certainly horror as light entertainment, and its catalogue of creative deaths (a clockwork frog mask bursts a man's head, another chap is drained of blood while watching naughty films, and of course one poor chap gets impaled on the horn of a brass unicorn) are as amusing as they are horrible. The 1920s setting contributes to the film's unique look and rather than having Phibes escape, which is how the original script ended, it's something of a masterstroke to have him simply disappear and at the same time be the final part of his own plan by having embalmed himself. I still have no idea who Vulnavia is supposed to be, and the fact that she ends up dissolved by acid intended for head surgeon Joseph Cotton's son doesn't stop her from appearing in the sequel, albeit played by a different actress. In fact, despite the fact that the film didn't really leave much in the way of hooks for a sequel, its huge success meant that one appeared the following year. It actually took me a few years to catch up with *The Abominable Dr Phibes* and it remains one of my favourites. As a lad, one of the things I used to do in quiet moments (as well as putting together imaginary Amicus anthology movies using tales from the *Pan Book of Horror Stories*) was try to think of other outrageous themed deaths that someone like Dr Phibes might use to exact revenge. It's taken over thirty years but I'm delighted that in the end I managed to come up with this one.

Dr Phibes Rises Again (1972)

Dr Phibes Rises Again was, in fact, the second horror film the little JLP ever saw, at the tender age of nine, on a Friday night at around 11pm. I'd read about the first film in my Alan Frank *Horror Films* book and marvelled at the full page colour picture from it in Denis Gifford's *A Pictorial History of Horror Movies*. I think there was a picture of Phibes in Arabian regalia with the Vulnavia of the moment, Vally Kemp, in the *TV Times* of that week as well. I also remember being thrilled by the prologue sequence that summarises its predecessor in a couple of minutes before cracking on with the story of Phibes' house having been destroyed in the three years since he embalmed himself with Victoria in the basement. This time he's looking for the River of Life, but his arch-enemy Biederbeck has pinched the map that shows its location and set off for Egypt on his own mission as his supply of life-prolonging elixir is running a bit low. Understandably a bit perturbed at this, Phibes sets off in pursuit, bumping off all who get in his way in a variety of creative and unpleasant ways. Hugh Griffith is back, still mad and still Welsh, but instead of playing a rabbi he's one of Biederbeck's chums who ends up sealed inside a giant gin bottle. John Thaw, pre-*Sweeney*, is torn to pieces by an eagle and, in the most memorable and disturbing murder for my younger self, Keith Buckley ends up stung to death by scorpions after being trapped in a scorpion throne. It's probably not surprising, then, that this was the death I wanted to include in Dr Valentine as it's the one that made the greatest impression on me when I first saw this film. It all ends badly for everyone expect Phibes, who gets to drift off down the river he's been searching for, his beloved Victoria on the boat with him, to the strains of 'Somewhere Over the Rainbow' (which is why it's in my book as well). Apparently there was going to be a third film, entitled *Phibes Resurrectus*, reports of the pre-production of which were announced in *House of Hammer* magazine a couple of years later but sadly it never came to anything.

Dr Phibes Rises Again is almost as good as its predecessor, but not quite, because the idea at its centre isn't quite as ingenious or as creative. The film is, however, still worth ninety minutes of anyone's time. As well as Price and Griffith, cast members Peter Jeffrey and John Cater (as the law) returned, as did Terry-Thomas, and composer John Gale was also brought back and allowed to write music for the entire film this time. It's a great score – lush, witty, and full of Eastern promise. I can highly recommend the CD, which has to be one of the few albums I am aware of that provides alternative track titles in Latin. There should be more of that kind of thing.

Witchfinder General (1967)

And here we have the third horror film that little JLP ever saw. In fact he was perhaps a bit *too* little to cope with all of it and went to bed about an hour in, once his parents had got back from the pub. "They shot him," my mum told me the next morning when I asked how the character of Matthew Hopkins, the eponymous witchfinder played by Vincent Price, met his end. It was a few years later before I was able to discover for myself that before he gets shot by Nicky Henson, he's hacked to bits by a vengeful and unhinged Ian Ogilvy after Ogilvy's wife Hilary Dwyer has been tortured to insanity.

And so we come to the genesis of the book you are holding in your hands. I started writing in 2002 and almost straight away had the idea for a Vincent Price tribute that would involve someone killing people in the style of films in which Price had starred. I knew it would be longer than the standard short story length but also realised that at the time I lacked the ability to do it justice. At the very first Alt Fiction meet in Derby that I went to I mentioned the idea to several writer friends, including Gary Fry, Gary McMahon and Allan Ashley, all of whom said I should do it. But still I lacked the confidence. Strangely enough, as well as being the project I didn't think I could write, it also became the project I most wanted to do, and on the kind of grim and lonely nights that I just don't have anymore my thoughts would turn to just how I might put my Vincent Price project together.

And it always began with the police discovering a hacked up body in the dungeon of a castle. In fact, I think it was meant to be Raglan Castle as my story at that time was going to be set in Wales (I can now see my parents reading this and shaking their heads at the glory this story could have been). For some strange reason I was never able to get much further, and even my notebook from a couple of years ago has 'What Price Horror?' scribbled in it as a possible title and then a list of Vincent

Price films I intended to reference, including *The Haunted Palace* and *Tales of Terror*, neither of which made it into the final version. All it took in the end was a boot up the backside from Simon Marshall-Jones, who told me I had to get on and write it. For me, there's almost nothing better than a ridiculously tight deadline to get me to pull my finger out and deliver the goods, which I really hope I have done with this. Certainly it's the most enjoyable project I've ever worked on, and it's turned out far better than the ideas I had for it ten years ago. So there you have it – you have just read the longest story I will probably ever have in gestation. I think it was worth it, and I really hope you do, too, and if you have had a fraction of the fun reading the story as I had writing it then it was worth taking all that time over it.

The Fly (1958)

The first horror film I ever saw.

From those Technicolor widescreen beginnings (actually pan and scan because it was on ATV at 10.30pm on a Friday night) began my long love of the horror genre, which has lasted to this day, kept me sane when all about me has been doing its best to drive me to distraction, found me a career, given me reasons to always smile in the face of adversity, found me the love of my life, and been the single most influential factor in making me the person I am today. I like to think that's a good thing.

But back to *The Fly*. Let's see if I can write a bit more about this than I did about *Witchfinder General*. Kurt

Neumann's film is remarkably faithful to the George Langelaan novella, which I then sought out after watching the movie and found to my delight that it could be obtained from the local Woolworths in *The Second Pan Book of Horror Stories*. You can't do that these days, mainly because both the store and the book series have gone the way of all flesh. Although speaking of flesh I was delighted to see Mr Langelaan's story reprinted in Robinson's *The Mammoth Book of Body Horror* recently. Denis Gifford's horror movie book for children *Monsters of the Movies* (do they even do horror movie books for children these days?) had a still from *Return of the Fly* next to his write up of this film so I was a bit disappointed when David Hedison's creature was finally revealed, but otherwise I thrilled to this tale of matter transmission and the monster produced by mistake. Despite having read about the so-called 'hilarious' ending I actually found the tiny man trapped in the spider's web the most terrifying bit of the film. I went to bed that night scared but exhilarated, and I couldn't wait to watch the *Dr Phibes* film that was on next week. I've cheated a little bit in the way I've included this film here as a method of death from a Vincent Price film, but I just couldn't leave it out. And now you know why.

The Pit and the Pendulum (1961)

My parents have never been horror fans, although my mum in particular is a fan of such classics as Alfred Hitchcock's *Psycho* and Clint Eastwood's *High Plains*

Drifter – in my belief one of the very finest horror westerns ever made. Even so, because they courted in the Wales of the 1960s they ended up seeing a fair number of horror pictures at the cinema, and when I was a child they regaled me with tales of having seen Oliver Reed in *Curse of the Werewolf*, Hammer's *The Gorgon*, and Vincent Price in *The Pit and the Pendulum*. When I eventually managed to watch Roger Corman's adaptation of the Edgar Allan Poe short story I realised why it had made such an impression on them.

For its day, Corman's film is a triumph of inspired matte paintings, clever writing on Richard Matheson's part, a decent Les Baxter score, but above and beyond all that a terrific central performance by Vincent Price. While it's not as good as some of the later Poe pictures (especially *Masque of the Red Death*, more of which in a bit) the last twenty minutes is a gothic triumph, managing to combine Price at his most lip-smackingly evil, a massive torture device, and Barbara Steele, barefoot, beautiful and distressed, being locked up in an iron maiden, forever. It was rare for a film of this period to end on quite such a shocking note but Corman knew that if you've got the imploring eyes of a poor imprisoned Barbara Steele to make use of, you really can't fade out on anything else.

The first hour or so of the film does suffer a bit in being simply preparation for the big reveal at the climax, but on the whole it's not bad, with the usual sumptuous sets and photography. But it's the pendulum that made such an impression on sixties audiences, (including my parents) and that was why I wanted to feature it in the climax of the book. In fact, I originally planned to go even further over the top and have a room full of pendulums (pendula?) all swinging at different speeds, and if you tried to stop one it would set the others going faster. I got a bit bogged down in the mathematics of how to get everything to eventually stop, and once I realised I was scribbling the equations of simple harmonic motion from my A Level physics days, I knew I should really just go back and get on with the story.

The Masque of the Red Death (1964)

It's probably not surprising that Dr Valentine chose more than one Roger Corman Poe picture among the instruments of his revenge as they're all really rather splendid, and *The Masque of the Red Death* is surprisingly good for what amounts to the sixth in a series (not counting *The Haunted Palace*). A shift to England to take advantage of the Eady Levy and some of the acting talent, and the gaining of Nicolas Roeg as director of photography and David Lee as composer all help to make Masque one of the most lush, colourful, stylish and consistently watchable movies of the Poe cycle.

In medieval Europe Prince Prospero (Vincent Price) and his upper class chums, associates and hangers-on are holed up in his lavish castle, while outside the inhabitants of the surrounding barren forest are plagued with the Red Death. These include freckly Jane Asher, her father Nigel Green and boyfriend David Weston. All three are brought to Prospero's castle for amusement but only Jane is allowed to have a bath. Juliana (Hazel Court) isn't pleased as she suspects Prospero may be eyeing up Jane as a potential Juliana replacement and soon discovers that branding herself with an inverted cross and being subjected to another of Corman's psychedelic dream sequences (this time with a green filter) aren't enough to save her from being pecked to death.

Prospero, meanwhile, has, with his friend Alfredo (Patrick Magee), been busy getting them both involved in another Edgar Allan Poe story, 'Hop-Toad'. Alfredo gives Esmeralda, the tiny dancer, a good slap for knocking over his twentieth goblet of wine of the night and thus incurs the hatred of the titular jester (Skip Martin) who then tricks Alfredo into wearing the gorilla suit in which he comes to a fiery end. It's a testament to the skill of writers Charles Beaumont, and R Wright Campbell in particular, as it was apparently he who was responsible for incorporating the 'Hop Toad' story into the climax, that it seems like such a seamless part of the film.

The Red Death gets into the castle (of course) and in one of the finest climaxes of the Corman Poe cycle it spreads through the building as its victims enact a grim dance of death to David Lee's relentless, morbid music. Price's Prospero is its final victim, sweating blood and gibbering in fear after having been chased through Daniel Haller's beautiful sets before the Red Death goes to join all his extremely colourful friends for a bit of a stroll under the end title captions.

Of all the Corman Poe movies this is the one I can watch again and again, and I used the writing of these notes as yet another excuse. I wanted a visually arresting murder to start the story of Dr Valentine's revenge, and having someone hanging from one of Bristol's most famous landmarks was the obvious way to go, especially as the death of Alfredo would also perplex the police as to quite why anyone would end up meeting such a horrible death wearing a gorilla suit.

Theatre of Blood (1973)

It was around Christmas time in the late 1970s and the BBC was about to show, for the first time on British television, a film I couldn't find any reference to in either Denis Gifford's *A Pictorial History of Horror Movies* or Alan Frank's *Monsters and Vampires*. *Halliwell's Film Guide* at least mentioned it, grudgingly giving it one star out of four, which is admittedly one star more than many of the horror films he deigned to include in the second edition of his seminal volume. But it starred Vincent Price, and the caption in the *Radio Times* ("Someone is murdering theatre critics – in increasingly gruesome ways") was enough to encourage my pre-teen self to stay up and watch a film that would eventually become a lifelong favourite of mine. I say eventually because even being the precocious fellow I was, ten years of age was still a little bit too young to fully appreciate the delicious confectionery of horror presented to me on that initial screening. In fact, it was only a couple of years later, when I caught it on the tail end of a season of BBC2 horror double bills, that I truly began to appreciate what a wonderful piece of work it was.

Put together by a bunch of people who had very little to do with horror films usually (I believe composer Michael J Lewis had to be convinced because he didn't want to do a horror film at all), I think *Theatre of Blood* actually benefits from this, especially in having, in director Douglas Hickox, someone who was much more at home shooting brutal crime dramas than witty Shakespearean revelry. As a result, Hickox let the actors get on with the acting and concentrated on making sure the murders were as gory and as horrible as possible. An article in the UK adults-only fold-out horror magazine *Monster Mag* at the time of its release stated that *Theatre of Blood* had more violence in its hundred plus minutes than the entirety of World War II, and while that's going a bit too far, the 1973 production was extremely violent for its time, particularly when compared to the kind of movies still being made by Hammer (*Frankenstein and the Monster From Hell*) and Amicus (*From Beyond the Grave*) at the time.

Someone is indeed murdering theatre critics in London. Michael Hordern gets slashed to death by an assortment of vagrants and ne'er-do-wells in a grim and grotty warehouse, with Hickox making sure there's a nice big see-through plastic sheet present for all the blood to splash against as we wonder what on earth is going on. Dennis Price gets stabbed through the guts and dragged along a gravel path tied to the tail of a horse. The Gods of the Movies are rarely kind, but this was pretty much Dennis Price's final role, and after all the rubbish he'd been in over the previous couple of years it's nice that he was able to appear in something really good to go out on. Arthur Lowe gets his head cut off in a scene that, for me, is where *Theatre of Blood* begins to show its true colours. Up until then it's all been a bit grim, but the surgery scene is played for pure comedy, and Michael J Lewis' music compliments it perfectly. In fact it all works so beautifully (including Brigid Erin-Bates' collapsing maid as a coda) that it pretty much resets the feel of the film. After that Harry Andrews' lecherous Trevor Dickman (ouch!) getting his come-uppance (sorry) at the hands of a bulbous-nosed Shylock and a sexy Portia is almost as funny despite the smoking heart gouged from his chest that Price ends up holding. Likewise Robert Coote's drowning in wine ("I wonder if he'll travel well?") is a perfect balance of humour and horror, and it's only when we get to Coral Browne's electrocution that we're back in the realm of the properly nasty, even though she's been despatched by Price in an Afro. Robert Morley's death by being force-fed his own poodles was the only death colleagues of mine at work could remember when they had their memories jogged about the film, and the film just has to end in flames because absolutely nothing else will do.

Theatre of Blood is a film I have seen more times than I can possibly count, and I've listened to it even more, having made a C120 cassette tape of it on that second television showing. That tape was played so many times in the Probert family home that even now my parents can recite some of the dialogue, and my brother (who was six at the time) can still recognise the title music. As I have alluded to in my acknowledgements at the end of this book, it's one of a select group of films that actually made my childhood a better place, and were I to meet any of screenwriter Anthony Greville-Bell, director Douglas Hickox and most of all composer Michael J Lewis I honestly don't think I'd be able to stop shaking their hands.

I've probably come to the end of my piece on this and I still haven't mentioned the best ever fencing duel in cinema that involves trampolines, vaulting horses and ropes; *Barbarella's* Milo O'Shea and the mighty Eric Sykes as the law; Diana Dors ("Don't keep me waiting you naughty man!") as Jack Hawkins' naughty wife; Ian Hendry doing his best to provide a link between the set pieces and getting the last line; some excellent London locations apparently used by necessity because the budget didn't reach to any studio work; Diana Rigg giving her all and having the time of her life as Lionheart's daughter; and last but absolutely, totally and utterly not least at all, Vincent Price. No-one else could have played Edward Kendal Sheridan Lionheart, the great actor-producer modelled on Sir Donald Wolfit and others of his ilk, with quite the same gusto, wit, skill, melancholy and style as this marvellous actor who, despite the terrible punishments (Lionheart's own word) he metes out to the people who humiliated him, is smiling all the time at the audience who loved him so much. It's impossible for me to actually say how much I love *Theatre of Blood*, and Price's performance in it, but I really hope the book you hold in your hands goes some little way towards expressing it.

And Finally...

This was another book that was tremendous fun to write, and I hope you enjoyed it even a tiny bit as much as I did putting it together. If you live in or around Bristol I also hope you appreciated the nod to some of the locations, and if not, perhaps you might consider your next holiday here to see them for yourselves? I suspect that line isn't going to get this book approved by the Bristol tourist board (the rest of the book probably won't) but all I can do is try.

Where has Dr Valentine gone? One can only assume his balloon made it over the Bristol Channel, possibly into Wales (I can see my parents crossing their fingers now that will turn out to be the case). Perhaps *Dr Valentine Rises Again* could detail his quest for the River of Life over there, although he probably won't have much luck with the Usk. Sequels are funny things and right now I can think of a dozen different things that the good (or rather, very bad) doctor could get up to, but time will tell. If I do write a sequel, however, I will want the book to be equipped with electro-buzzers, ghost viewers which you have to wear to be able to read the twist, and a big plastic skeleton that flies out of the book at you close to the end.

Until the next time, I thank you. Take care of yourselves, be nice to each other, and I will see you all soon.

John Llewellyn Probert
High up in a balloon somewhere
Somerset
May 2012

Acknowledgements

Firstly I must express my gratitude to Mr. Simon Marshall-Jones for saying yes to a project that has been on my mind for years. Thanks, Simon, for getting me to finally sit down and write the thing - it was every bit as much fun as I thought it might be and if I could I'd do it all over again.

Secondly, this book would not exist without the artistic endeavours of a group of individuals who helped to stimulate my imagination, thrill me, entertain me, and most important of all keep me sane when I was growing up. I've already dedicated this book to Vincent Price, but my inestimable thanks and appreciation are also due to the other creative personnel responsible for the films *Theatre of Blood* and *The Abominable Dr Phibes*, namely Robert Fuest, Douglas Hickox, Anthony Greville-Bell, John Kohn & Stanley Mann, Louis M. Heyward, Michael J. Lewis (of Aberystwyth!) and James Whiton & William Goldstein. Thanks chaps - you really did all change my life for the better, and I cannot begin to tell you how much the movies you created mean to me.

Finally my thanks, as always, go to Kathleen, Lady Probert, who not only had to put up with me reading the entire text of this book aloud to her and acting out many of the scenes, but also had to endure my various Vincent Price impersonations as each of the characters from the films referenced in the text. Thanks, Kate. I don't know what I've done to deserve you, but it must have been something very good indeed.

The Hammer
of Dr Valentine

The Hammer of Dr Valentine is respectfully dedicated to all those highly talented and skilled men and women who helped make the productions of Hammer Films such fabulous entertainments.

And especially,

Peter Cushing and Christopher Lee

Because, gentlemen, you really were the best.

1

The man's body flew into the air.

It is not easy to fling a sixteen stone man from a cliff top into a Welsh valley, and the considerable velocity necessary to perform this feat had been attained by the use of the catapult into which the man had been secured. The device had been fashioned from heavy oak, and its spring-loaded mechanism employed the very finest high tensile British steel, just to ensure there were no mistakes.

No-one saw the body land in the valley below.

This was intentional, which is why this complex and dangerous procedure was being performed at night. Behind the stark outline of the catapult, itself only partly concealed by the surrounding foliage, the towers of Castell Coch stood impassive, their silhouettes black against the deepest blue of the night sky.

Prior to his release into the air, four guide ropes of woven steel had been run through the man's clothes. These extended from the catapult to the ground below. It was intended that the flying, and very much still-living, victim land in a very specific place, namely onto the point of the heavy gold cross that had been obtained with some difficulty from a local cathedral, and set into the ground of the valley below at a precise angle.

Following that had come the moment of truth.

The lever was depressed, the spring mechanism

released, and the sometimes-screaming, sometimes-pleading projectile was launched into the chill of the Welsh night.

The landing was perfect.

Even from a distance it was possible to see, with the aid of a pair of opera glasses, that the uppermost point of the cross had pierced its intended victim between the shoulder blades, or scapulae, as the perpetrator of this ghastly crime much preferred to call them. The blood-smeared tip emerged from the man's chest, and he hung there for a moment, gurgling amidst the gore, before his legs stopped twitching and all was still.

The man responsible for this was the same man who had supervised the removal of the cross from St David's Cathedral while posing as a high-ranking member of the clergy. He had also arranged for the design and construction of the catapult in Zurich, and its subsequent transportation to the UK under more secrecy than even MI5 was capable of. The man who had calculated the angle of trajectory, the arc of velocity and, most important, the speed at which a sixteen stone man needed to be travelling in order for the enormous crucifix to run him through, looked over the cliff's edge. He nodded with satisfaction to the beautiful girl beside him, the one who had lured the unsuspecting victim to this isolated spot, clad in the pink chiffon dress she was still wearing. The scene in the valley below looked very similar to the one from the film that had inspired it, right down to the black cape with the red satin lining that the victim had been forced to wear before being placed in the catapult.

Yes, he thought. That should get their attention.
That should get their attention very nicely.

2

"An Evening of Ancient Egyptian Splendour and Excitement!"

Margaret Upchurch, Mags to her (admittedly very few) friends, looked at the elaborate lettering on the gilt-edged invitation card for a third time, and wondered if she was doing the right thing. On the maroon velveteen quilt of her hotel room's double bed lay the elaborate costume that had accompanied both the invitation card and the details of the booking that had been made for her for that evening. Fancy dress really wasn't her thing, but if Professor Fuchs, whoever he was, wanted to hold a press conference at the British Museum to herald the return of his latest expedition, and have everyone attending dressed up in period costume to satisfy some peculiar kink of his, who was she to argue?

Mags grinned to herself. Oh yes, she was definitely going, if only to prove a point to those bastards who ran the British Museum, the ones who had tried to ban her from the place after that story she had written detailing their use of unpaid illegal immigrants as cleaners. It had all proved to be unfounded, of course, but the paper hadn't minded that – her story had helped to pick up a slow news day. Besides, it had been her first turn for that particular rag since all the business with that lunatic doctor a couple of years back. And, she thought to herself, with any luck there'd be at least a few pieces of juicy gossip at the post-conference party that should allow her to put together something the public would lap up, if only about how their money was going to waste on ridiculous endeavours like this one. Of course she had no idea if the expedition had been funded with public money, and in all likelihood it probably hadn't, but she saw no reason why she shouldn't hint at it in her article.

She held up the dress that had been sent to her. The size was perfect, and she nodded with approval. Someone had evidently done their homework. It was a bit revealing, though. Too much midriff and a fair old bit of cleavage would be on show, but at thirty one Mags prided herself on her looks having very much helped to get her to where she was today, and with any luck it would help loosen the tongues of any men who would be too busy staring at her tits to realise they'd dropped themselves in it, quote-wise.

At least the skirt was floor-length, she thought as she tugged it on. The shoes didn't seem exactly period, though – surely the ancient Egyptians didn't go in for strappy gold buckles and high heels? Not that she minded – they were a damned sight more elegant than whatever flat-soled sandal-things people probably wore back then. She slipped them on, again noting that they were a perfect fit. Whoever had organised this really had taken care of everything.

The phone in her room rang and she answered it, spoke four words and replaced the receiver.

Right down to the taxi to take her there, she thought, with approval.

~

The female taxi driver was just a little younger than she was. Why Mags found this vaguely disconcerting she couldn't say, but it was most likely because she suddenly felt very odd sitting in a car being driven by a normally-dressed attractive young girl while feeling as if she was on the way to a do for drag queens.

"It's a fancy dress party," she felt moved to explain. She clutched at the bejewelled headdress she had found it necessary to take off so she could get into the car, and awaited the driver's reply.

The girl said nothing, but Mags was sure her brown eyes held a knowing glint as she checked out Mags' reflection in her rear-view mirror.

Mags shut up after that.

London is always busy, but the traffic that Tuesday evening was especially bad. It was well past the time she was meant to get there when Mags was eventually deposited on the pavement outside what she assumed must be the British Museum. She showed her disdain to the driver by neglecting to give a tip, and it was only once the girl had driven away that she realised she wasn't in front of the building's main entrance in Great Russell Street at all, but some godforsaken side road round the back.

She was about to start walking when a nearby door opened.

The man standing in the doorway was in silhouette but he appeared to be wearing the uniform of a British Museum security guard, and that was good enough for her.

"Can you help me, please?" she said, fluttering her

eyelashes but keeping her voice firm. For some reason most of the men she knew seemed to prefer it when her voice had a harder edge. She held out the invitation. "I'm supposed to be at this. I know I'm late but the bloody cab driver decided to take the long way round."

The man stepped into the light and now she could see that he was a little older than she had first thought. His hair was concealed beneath the black cap, of course, but the streaks of grey in his sideburns lent him an edge of sophistication that was only augmented by his voice when he spoke.

"Ah yes," he said, once he had read the proffered card, "yes of course. Do come in. You are expected."

Mags followed him through the doorway, wondering how such a well-spoken man might have ended up in such a dead end job.

Perhaps there was even a story in it.

"Have you been working here long?" she asked as she followed him down what looked like a service corridor, if the walls of whitewashed breeze-block and intermittent dull fluorescent strip lighting were anything to go by.

"Not long," came the reply from in front of her. The man didn't turn round. "But these days you have to take jobs where you find them, don't you agree?"

"I suppose so." Mags didn't really care. Her feet were starting to hurt and she needed a drink. "So what did you do – before this, I mean?"

"I've been out of work for a couple of years," he said as they took a left turn, "but I've managed to find ways of occupying myself. Nevertheless, I'm sure you can appreciate how relieved I am to be here this evening."

"But you had a job before that?" Mags was nothing if not persistent. After all, she had made a career from it.

"Oh yes," said the man with the lovely voice, "but unfortunately it was all taken away from me."

"How?" Mags knew she was getting ahead of herself, but if it turned out to be interesting she could always ask him to go back over anything juicy.

The man paused, and turned around, allowing her to see the sadness in his eyes. "An accident," he said. "A death."

"Of a loved one, that much is obvious," said Mags, hoping she was sounding more sympathetic to his ears than to hers. "Was it someone close?"

The man had moved off again now, and she had to struggle to keep up with him. "My daughter," he said as they came out of the grim little tunnel and into what looked like the museum proper. Colourful murals depicting life in ancient Egypt adorned the walls, while at regular intervals glass cases on plinths housed tiny artefacts that looked like ragged pieces of junk shop tat, but which were probably priceless.

"That's awful," said Mags in her 'sympathy at the loss of a child' voice she had honed to perfection when she was working on a kidnapping story a few years ago. "What happened?" Before she could stop herself she added, "Was it medical malpractice?" Those always made wonderful sob stories.

Again the man paused, his face this time still turned away from her. "It's not really any of your business," he said, "but as a matter of fact, yes. It was a medical misdemeanour that led to her demise."

Mags thanked whoever or whatever it was that had caused her to be late. If she played her cards right she might be able to bag herself a thousand words of copy without having to go to this stupid Egyptian thing at all.

"That's terrible," she said, as they passed a man-sized statue of Anubis that had seen better days. This time she made sure to add a little quaver to her sympathetic tone. "But doctors can be real sons of bitches sometimes – arrogant, conceited, completely full of themselves. They think they're God when in fact they have absolutely no idea what they're doing."

The man stopped again and turned to face her. Ahead Mags could hear music, laughter, the tinkle of glasses. She hoped she would be able to get everything she wanted out of this bloke before they reached the party.

"I had no idea you were a member of the medical profession," he said.

Mags laughed like a harpy at that, forgetting for an instant what had happened to the man she was talking to. "I'm not a doctor!" she said.

"In that case you must forgive me," The man turned away and started walking again, towards the sounds of merrymaking. "For a moment I was under the mistaken impression that you knew what you were talking about."

Mags frowned. Whoever he might have been in the past, this jumped-up bloody security guard had no right to talk to her like that!

"Just a minute," she said, chasing after him. "I'll have you know that I'm a journalist, and a couple of years ago I covered a story for one of the national dailies about quite possibly the most insane member of 'the medical profession' this country has ever seen!"

Her outburst seemed to have little effect on her companion. "We have arrived at your destination, Miss Upchurch," the security guard said, opening a white side door between two mummy cases. He indicated she should step inside. Before she did so he added, "Please accept my apologies for any remarks I may have made that might have upset you. I do hope that what I have just said doesn't spoil your evening, and that you don't leave tonight feeling too crushed."

Mags paid little attention. She had heard that kind of thing before, too many times for it to have any effect on her. The laughter and chatting was very loud now, almost abnormally so, and she pointedly ignored the security guard as she stepped into the room.

The large, white, empty room.

At first Mags thought that the chamber in which she found herself had to be a vestibule, a conduit to the party proper. But the solid walls on every side of her told her that was not so.

She took two steps forward, and switched off the reel-to-reel tape recorder that was playing on the small square table in front of her.

Any noise that suggested a party might be taking place ceased. Now, all Mags could hear was the sounds of her own rapid breathing, and the click of her heels on the white tiled floor as she took another step forward.

The room wasn't quite empty.

There was something on the far wall. Lots of things, in fact. Some were in black and white, others were in colour. Some were pasted onto the wall, others held in place with drawing pins.

Newspaper headlines, magazine covers, columns and clippings, all meticulously cut out and pieced together.

All about the same thing.

Mags recognised her contribution to the makeshift mural, but it would have been difficult not to. Placed centrally, and outlined in bright red marker pen, was a piece entitled "Doctor Death – The Mad Medic Who Slew His Own Kind".

She was reaching out to touch the print when there was a voice from behind her.

"I was never Doctor Death, you know."

Mags turned. The security officer was standing in the doorway, but now he looked very different. The cap was gone, and his uniform had been substituted for an expensive-looking dinner suit. The black cloak with its red satin lining was the crowning extravagance, yet somehow it didn't look out of place on him.

The man radiated authority, and for the first time in many years Mags felt intimidated. She could feel her heart pounding as she did her best to stammer some kind of a reply.

"W-w-weren't you?" she said.

The man tutted. "Goodness me, no. If you had done your research properly you would have known that." He held out his arms and flicked his wrists with a flourish, causing the cloak to fall back over his shoulders. "Vincent Price played, rather indirectly, a character called Doctor Death in the 1974 film *Madhouse*. As I just said, if you had done your research properly for that...story that is pinned up there, you would have known that. Just as you would have known that *Madhouse*, a film considerably inferior to his wonderful *Theatre of Blood*, was not one of the inspirations I drew on to exact my revenge."

Mags was filled with a mixture of dread and excitement as she realised who she was talking to. She had hoped to get a good story tonight, but she had never dreamed she might be getting such an exclusive.

She drew herself up to her most statuesque, pleased she had put the headdress on when she had exited the taxi as it gave her extra height. She pushed out her quite respectable bosom, and imagined that she really was a queen of Egypt, just to give herself a bit of extra confidence. "You're Dr Edward Valentine," she said.

It was a statement, not a question. The man in the doorway nodded in response as he looked her up and down.

"I have to admit I did a splendid job estimating your measurements for that costume," Dr Valentine said. "It's such a shame your written work was never as presentable as you."

"If my story was that bad, tell me where I went wrong." Mags was always ready to take advantage of a situation, and she was delighted to realise that being faced by a flamboyant psychotic serial killer hadn't dampened her ardour one bit. "Give me your own, personal side of things. The story only Dr Valentine himself could tell. That would be something I could sell to the highest bidder. And let me assure you I know people who would be willing to bid very highly indeed. We could both end up very rich."

"I suppose we could." Valentine seemed uninterested as he rubbed his palms together. "The problem with the kind of reporting you do, Miss Upchurch – it is Miss, isn't it?" Mags nodded. "Yes, I thought it would have to be. The problem with your type is that the truth is never enough. It has to be embellished, exaggerated, turned into a story to thrill and chill, to be, by turns, both worrying and reassuring, and most of all, to give the public what disreputable publications like the ones pinned on that wall there mistakenly believe the public want."

"Not mistakenly," said Mags, jerking a thumb behind her. "Do you have any idea how many copies we sold of that story of mine?"

Valentine shook his head. "I don't have *any* idea, Miss Upchurch, I have an *exact* idea. Which brings me to why you are here today."

Mags' eyes brightened. "You mean you really want me to tell your story?"

There was a long pause before Valentine gave his reply.

"Not exactly," he said eventually, before permitting himself the faintest of smiles. "What I really want, is for you to be a part of the next one."

It took a moment for that to sink in.

"What do you mean?" Now the confidence had drained from Mags' voice, to be replaced by quivering uncertainty.

"Exactly what I said," Valentine replied as he adjusted something on the inside of the door. "Now, it takes around four minutes to read that prattling barrage of nonsense you called a newspaper story, so that is how long I intend to give you to try to escape this place. I would wish you luck, but as you can probably understand, that's hardly the point. And as I mentioned beforehand, I hope this little experience won't leave you feeling too crushed."

And with that he was gone, closing the door behind him.

Mags ran after him and rattled the handle. She expected it to be locked, and so she was surprised when it turned easily and the door opened.

It also set the timer mechanism ticking that Dr Valentine had attached to the handle.

Mags looked at the counter, which now showed there were less than four minutes left until... what? Was there a bomb in here? Surely not in the British Museum? Even Valentine wouldn't be insane enough or even capable of destroying a major British landmark.

If, of course, that was in fact where she was.

Mags remembered being dropped off in that unfamiliar back street, of the long walk down those grim corridors to this room. She stepped out into the passageway. The mummy cases that flanked the doorway were still there, but now they looked less convincing than they had when she had passed them before. Now they looked more like props for a television show.

Or a film.

Oh, God.

The methods by which Valentine had taken revenge on those doctors came back to her vividly, horribly.

She looked at the costume she was wearing, at the newspaper clippings behind her, at the fake mummy cases, and wondered what he had planned.

She didn't have to wait long.

The timer was still counting down, but already the walls were starting to creak around her, the fake murals starting to crack, the fake statuary beginning to wobble. There was a rumble from above. Mags looked up and coughed as plaster dust from the gaping rent in the ceiling caught in her throat.

She ran back the way she had come, but now the door to the exit corridor had all but vanished, a white outline flush with the wall that surrounded it the only evidence there had been a door there in the first place. She looked around her, realising now that there was no other way out, and that Dr Valentine had never intended for her to escape.

She hammered on the door in rage, in fury, and finally in desperation, screaming for help even though she knew no-one could hear her, no-one who would come to her aid, anyway. Back in the room papered with clippings the timer reached zero while Mags crouched, hands over her head, waiting for the inevitable blast.

She had time to scream just once as the ceiling cracked in half. Then the roof of the building caved in and she wasn't aware of anything anymore.

3

When the telephone rings between two and three in the morning, it can only ever be to convey bad news.

It took some time for John Spalding to register that the jangling noise wasn't part of the dream he was having. His thoughts were still very fuzzy as he turned on his bedside lamp and picked up the receiver. On the other end of the line a voice claimed they were Detective Inspector someone-or-other, asked him to confirm his identity, and then explained that he was needed to identify a body. Now.

"I beg your pardon?" Spalding struggled out of the sheets and sat on the side of the bed. On the nightstand, just next to the brand new reissue of Lotte Eisner's *The Haunted Screen* that he had agreed to review for *The Observer*, the misty red display of the clock read 2.27am.

A body. Now. At the mortuary.

"I'm sorry, but I'm a film journalist," Spalding explained, still trying and failing to wake up. "I don't do deaths unless it's someone famous." He sat up, instantly wide awake at the sudden thought. "*Is* it someone famous?" he asked.

"It's someone you knew," said the voice, "and you're the only one of her close personal contacts who's answering the phone at this hour so I need you to come here now, please."

It took Spalding thirty minutes to get there. Despite

its reputation as a never-sleeping metropolis, London was dead silent, and the black cab had no problem getting him across the city.

"What the bloody hell do you want to come here at this time of night for?" the driver asked him as the car pulled up to the rear of the hospital. Three police cars were already gathered there.

"Your guess is as good as mine," Spalding replied as he got out. He watched the man drive away before turning to face the gaunt concrete of the building before him.

He was greeted by a uniformed police officer, who led him through a pair of flopping plastic swing doors and down a corridor that was so poorly lit Spalding could barely see where he was going. He was ushered into a bare room where two men sat at a table littered with empty coffee cups. He presumed that the tarnished black telephone sat in the middle had been the one used to call him.

"Mr John Spalding?" A balding man, who more resembled an ageing wrestler in a mustard-coloured trenchcoat than a policeman, rose to greet him. Spalding recognised the voice. "I'm DI Derek Martinus. We spoke on the phone." He indicated the rumpled man next to him. "This is Dr Manners, he's our forensic pathologist. He'll take you to see her."

Spalding frowned. "Who?"

The DI and the pathologist exchanged glances.

"Perhaps you'd better take a seat," Martinus offered.

Spalding brushed imaginary debris from the cheap grey plastic chair before sitting down. It was as uncomfortable as it looked.

"As I said on the phone," the DI explained, "I'm sorry

to have had to drag you down here, but yours was the only number on her mobile that we could get an answer from."

"She?" Spalding hardly knew any women, at least not to the degree that he'd be called down here under such circumstances.

"A friend of yours, or at the very least a colleague." Martinus' face was grim as he told Spalding the story. "At eleven o'clock this evening we received a call to come to Montague Place. It's near the British Museum, just off Russell Square. When we arrived we found something strange. Something very strange indeed."

"Well you're certainly good at building suspense, Inspector." Spalding felt a tinge of irritation. "So who exactly did you find?"

Martinus paused before coming out with his revelation. "We believe the body to be that of Margaret Upchurch," he said, "a young lady who is in the same line of work as yourself, I believe?"

Spalding was no longer listening. The last time he had seen Mags she had been slinking out of his bedroom, but not before telling him what a lovely time she had had, and how they must meet up again sometime.

Mags was dead?

"It's true she didn't have any surviving close family," Spalding said, his voice shaking a little now, "and to be honest I have no idea if anyone related to her lives in London."

Martinus nodded. "You understand my predicament then, sir?"

Spalding agreed. "It's been nearly two years, but I'm

sure she can't have changed too much in that time. I shouldn't have any problem identifying her if that's what you need."

Martinus and the doctor exchanged glances.

"Well, there is a bit of a problem there, sir," said the policeman.

Spalding wondered why the DI was acting so shiftily. "Go on."

Martinus seemed almost embarrassed. Good God, Spalding thought, Mags hadn't bitten off more than she could chew, had she? She had always been a bit of a fan of the rough stuff but he didn't think she would ever get herself properly hurt.

"When we found her, her body was..." Martinus paused again.

Well go on! Spalding was getting impatient now. *Her body was what? Dressed in kinky getup? Twisted into an obscene position? In several pieces with messages carved into the flesh?*

"Her body was... covered with bandages."

Spalding let out a sigh of relief. "You mean she was found outside a hospital?"

Martinus shook his head. "No sir. I mean we found her lying in the street, covered in bandages. She'd been wrapped in them from head to toe, with just a space for the eyes. Of course by the time we found her the blood had soaked through in quite a few places. The blood from the injuries she'd sustained."

Spalding suddenly wished he smoked again. *Christ, Mags. What did you get yourself into?*

"What kind of injuries?"

Martinus scratched his head. "Well as far as we can

tell she was inside the building we found her near when it collapsed. Forensics are going through everything now, but it looks as if the whole lot came down on top of her, crushing every bone in her body." Martinus looked to the pathologist for confirmation. He was rewarded with a brisk nod. "Then someone... someone..."

Spalding tapped the desk. "Presumably I am actually going to see her in a minute, Inspector, so you may as well just tell me."

Martinus nodded. "Thank you," he said. "I never was good at breaking news gently." He took a deep breath before continuing. "For some reason someone dragged Miss Upchurch out of the rubble, wrapped her entire body in bandages, and then left her in the street to be found. In fact for all we know the person who did it was the same one who tipped us off."

Spalding shrugged. "Maybe whoever wrapped her up was trying to save her?"

Martinus paused for a moment before he answered that one.

"No sir. We don't think they were trying to save her. Quite the reverse, in fact."

Spalding looked from one man to the other. "What do you mean?"

"There was a slow acting poison soaked into the bandages. As if someone wanted her to survive the accident inside the building, and then die slowly wrapped up like that. And that's not the only weird thing. They also used a very particular type of poison."

Martinus looked at Dr Manners, who uttered the only word to pass his lips since Spalding had arrived.

"Formaldehyde."

Martinus leaned over Spalding and placed both his hands flat on the table. It creaked as he did so.

"So that's what we have, Mr Spalding. And why, before you do us the courtesy of identifying the crushed and mutilated body of Margaret Upchurch, I have to ask you if you can think of any reason why someone would want to crush a young woman to the point where she was nearly dead, and then wrap her up in bandages soaked with embalming fluid?"

4

"Is it much further?"

Michael Brennan mopped his forehead as he followed the girl down the dirt track, doing his best to keep his eyes off parts of her anatomy that a man of his age could probably go to prison for staring at, much less touching these days. Of course it would help if she wasn't wearing the kind of school uniform he could have sworn went out of fashion in the nineteen fifties, complete with straw boater, tightly buttoned blue blazer, and skirt the shortness of which he was sure he had described as 'one of the reasons our country is in the state is now' in an article of his on declining moral standards in one of the more popular tabloids.

Of course, that had been a long time ago, and he had been the author of a lot more outraged newsprint since that article about the morally bankrupt state of many of Britain's teenaged girls. That was the one that had got him in the door, though. That, and the supremely angry column he had provided about the threat to the children of both today and tomorrow as a result of the kinds of films they were allowed to watch. "If we are not careful," he remembered writing with some degree of pride, "we are creating within our midst a whole generation of Dr Valentines, who would not hesitate to recreate some of the shocking things they have seen on screen just for kicks". It had helped that he had been the one to cover the

Dr Valentine affair for the paper as well, making the most of his contacts in the Bristol police force to give him the inside facts, as well as plenty of gossip and conjecture that he had been able to weave into a seamless whole to give him his first major set of headlines.

That had been some time ago now, of course, and while the paper had been happy for him to ride on the back of the story's success for a while, he had known it wouldn't last forever. His regular column, "Brennan's Britain", had been the answer. Ostensibly a look at contemporary culture, he had been encouraged to use his weekly 1500 word allocation to express horror at the kinds of things he knew the paper's very specific kind of middle class, middle-aged readers would be similarly outraged by. Once he had exhausted such old standbys as linking movie violence and crime, immigration with unemployment, and video games with short attention spans, he found himself having to try harder to come up with things that would keep his column popular, and himself gainfully employed.

He hadn't had to look far to find the answer. In fact he hadn't had to look any further than the trunk he kept in his own attic, the one with three padlocks on it, all of which required different combinations to get them open. He had always been worried that it might get discovered one day and so, embracing the philosophy that the best defence is a good offence, Michael Brennan had become a crusader against pornography. The pleasant, and thoroughly unexpected, side effect of this had been discovering that having a serious moral objection to such material also happened to be the best way of acquiring it.

Some of his more enthusiastically horrified readers had directed him to the very best outlets, establishments and websites that purveyed the sickening material he was determined to expose for the nation's safety. Soon he found himself having to buy another trunk with the extra money the paper was now paying him, and that one was nearly full now as well. In fact, if he acquired any more 'specialist research material' he was going to have to think seriously about moving house.

And this girl he was currently following might just lead him to the story that would bag him the funds to buy one.

He could remember the letter she had sent him two weeks ago almost word for word. After all, he would use it to kick off the article he was intending to write, an article that would portray her as one of the poor helpless victims that he, crusading journalist Michael Brennan, had saved by exposing the immoral filth that was taking place and, worse, being filmed, at one of Britain's more out-of-the-way public schools.

Of course what she had put in her letters could also turn out to be nonsense, which is why he had agreed to meet her at the very place where she claimed the events were taking place. Well, not right at the school. His car was parked in a lay-by on an isolated country road a mile or so back, and he had walked the rest of the way, meeting her at the main entrance to the school by a pair of heavy iron gates painted green.

They had also been locked.

"It's the holidays," she had explained. "Don't you have kids of your own?"

Brennan had shaken his head, suddenly embarrassed that she thought him old enough to be her father. "But if that's the case why are you dressed like that?" he had asked.

A coquettish smile. "Because I've said I'll be in one of the films," she had whispered conspiratorially. "Term's only just ended, and my parents aren't expecting me back for another week, so I thought it would be the perfect time for us to work on this story together."

Brennan had groaned internally at her words. So that was it. She wanted her name on the piece too. Well, she was about to get her first hard lesson in the world of journalism, he thought, if all this came to anything.

The way in to the school grounds was through a much smaller gate further along. It led onto a dirt track that she had explained was only used by the school gardener. "When he's sober enough to drive that little cart of his," she had giggled.

Now they had been walking for nearly a quarter of an hour, and there was still no sign of anything remotely resembling a school.

"Nearly there," said the girl, skipping ahead as if daring him to chase after her, which he duly did, if only not to lose sight of where they were supposed to be going. They rounded a corner, and there was the school.

Brennan's first impression was to be distinctly underwhelmed. "It looks more like an old manor house," he said.

The girl shook her head. "It's nowhere near as old as it looks, or as old as its owners would like people to think. It's like a reproduction. My daddy calls it 'Stockbroker Tudor', whatever that means."

Brennan wasn't sure, but he made a point of remembering the phrase for his writeup.

"It's very quiet," he said, looking at the empty car park and the litter blowing around the deserted cricket pitches.

"Of course it is," said the girl. "I told you – term finished last week. Now come on."

The school's main doors were unlocked, and she led him into a high-ceilinged hallway with a pine floor so polished Brennan almost slipped. The wood panelling of the walls came up to waist height and had been painted a pale green. The white of the plaster above was all but obscured by numerous pin boards with green velvet backgrounds, documenting sporting fixtures and arrangements for end-of-term prize giving. Brennan nodded. If the locked gates and empty grounds had given him any doubts about this place being a real school they were gone now – only a madman would go to this level of detail to give an aura of authenticity.

"Well you've convinced me this is a school," he said, trying hard not to leer at the girl. She had unbuttoned her blazer now she was inside in the warm, and her white blouse was under a pleasurable degree of tension. "Now what?"

"Now you stay here, and wait for my signal," she said, skipping off down the corridor. Her regulation school shoes clattered on the wood as she rounded a corner, the sound of her footsteps vanishing as soon as she did. Brennan assumed the floor must be carpeted round there, and settled down to wait.

He wondered what her signal might be. Would she

wait until they started filming? Or perhaps until she and whoever might be with her were, well, doing something his readers might consider morally outrageous? He licked his lips and hoped so, grateful for the digital camera that was nestling in his jacket pocket. He had carried one with him for the past two years, and it had got him a lot of 'worthwhile research material' in its time, so now he never travelled without it.

After fifteen minutes, he wondered if she was going to make a signal at all.

After twenty, he decided to find out what was going on for himself.

He was surprised to discover that the corridor she had turned into had the same kind of wooden floor tiles as where he had been standing, making him wonder why the sound of her footsteps had vanished so abruptly. Perhaps she had skipped quickly into one of the classrooms here, he thought. He made his way down the passageway, his own footsteps echoing noisily in the empty space, until he came to the first door. Set into its own little alcove on the left, the black letters on the anaemic green paint read: Mr K A Johnson – Mathematics.

Brennan listened at the door and, when he heard nothing, tried the brass meringue-shaped knob.

The door opened noiselessly to reveal the kind of classroom Brennan thought had gone out of style years ago. Twenty open-lid desks of the same polished pine as the floor tiles were arranged in five columns of four, all facing a large wooden table and chair that stood atop a wooden dais. Behind the chair, and to the right of it, an easel blackboard the colour of slate was propped on its wooden tripod, and held in place by three supporting pegs.

There was nothing written on the blackboard, no books on the master's desk, and not a soul in the room.

Except Brennan, of course.

He gave a cough and its echo cracked back at him. At least the girl was telling the truth about it being school holidays, he thought, although he wondered what kind of pupils kept their desks so spotlessly clean, the lids unblemished by even the slightest suggestion of biro-etched graffiti or an ink-splattered fountain pen mishap.

The classroom of Mr J N Partleton – English, was a little further down the corridor on the right. It was arranged in the same way as Mr Johnson's and it, too, was empty.

You'd think they'd at least have some textbooks scattered around, Brennan thought, before realising the pupils probably had to buy their own and bring them along to lessons.

The next room on the left belonged to Mr M V Bradborough, who taught Geography. Brennan expected to see at least a globe or some maps on the walls, but the room was the same empty place of learning as the others.

He was about to give the final room in the corridor, the last door on the right, a miss, when there was a sound from behind it.

Brennan read the name on the door. Mr M Carmichael – Classics. Good God, did they still teach Latin and Greek these days? Brennan put his ear to the door. Yes, there was definitely something going on in there. It was faint, but as he concentrated he thought he could make out words.

No, not words.

Chanting.

Boys' voices, chanting Latin.

Increasingly furious at the thought that his time was being wasted, Brennan yanked open the door to confront the Latin summer school or whatever the hell it was.

The classroom was empty.

That was impossible! He had heard them!

Brennan strode inside and looked around. The room was like all the others – no books, no teacher, no pupils.

Nothing.

The voices had stopped now as well. In fact, Brennan realised, they had stopped as soon as he had come through the door.

"Ah! I see we have a new pupil in the class!"

Brennan whirled to see a figure standing in the doorway, a figure clad in a worn dark suit. A pocket watch had been tucked into the fraying pocket of the man's waistcoat. The mortarboard had seen better days as well, and the black teacher's gown had smears of chalk dust here and there from times when the blackboard rubber had probably been hidden by an especially mischievous pupil, or misplaced in a moment of absent-mindedness.

This new arrival peered at Brennan through a pair of tiny rimless spectacles. Vision through the circular lenses must have been almost entirely obscured by the myriad tiny splintered cracks in the glass. Nevertheless Mr Carmichael, if it was he, seemed to have no trouble seeing Brennan.

"Well answer me, boy," he said, taking a step forward and closing the door behind him. "I don't know where you were before, but here, if a master asks you a question, you answer. Promptly, politely, and respectfully."

Brennan was so shocked he found himself momentarily lost for words.

"Who the hell are you?" he eventually managed to stammer.

"Oh my," said Mr Carmichael. "That won't do. That won't do at all."

In the corner by the door was what looked like an umbrella stand, but instead, it housed a collection of what looked like very thin walking sticks. Carmichael took a step to his left, and as he drew one out, Brennan realised they weren't walking sticks at all.

They were canes.

"I can see we're going to have to teach the new boy a lesson," said Carmichael to no-one that Brennan could see. He gave the cane a couple of experimental swishes through the air, once to the right and once to the left, as if he was preparing for a fencing duel rather than the delivery of corporal punishment. Then he pointed at the table with it.

"I suggest you make yourself ready, young man."

Brennan was about to splutter an objection when Carmichael continued. "However, I see no reason why the misbehaviour of one especially bad apple should ruin this morning's lesson. Boys, continue with what we were doing while I deal with this miscreant. Second declension – begin."

Carmichael pressed a switch near the door. Suddenly the air around Brennan was filled with boys' voices, almost as if the classroom had become home to a Latin lesson for ghosts.

"Dominus, Domine, Dominum," the boys chanted as Carmichael advanced, the cane held high. Now he was closer, Brennan could see the tiny razor-sharp steel points that had been fitted along the length of rattan.

If he was hit with that it would open him up like a pig being gutted.

"Domini, Domino, Domino," the voices chanted as Brennan held up his hands.

"Now look," he said. "I'm sorry I'm trespassing, but I was led here under false pretences. I'm a journalist and—"

The cane descended, tearing into both of Brennan's outstretched palms. He screamed and took two steps back.

"Domini, Domini, Dominos," said the boys.

"For God's sake!" he screamed as Carmichael pursued him, the man raising his cane to deliver another blow. "I haven't done anything wrong!"

"Oh I wouldn't say that," said Carmichael. With a flick of the wrist he ripped open Brennan's right cheek, then the left, finishing off by making a deep gouge across the man's forehead.

"Dominorum, Dominis, Dominis," came the voices over the speakers as Brennan fell to his knees, blood streaming down his face. The chanting stopped as the man who had been beating him removed his spectacles.

"In fact, I'd say you've been a bad boy," he said,

bringing his face close to Brennan's own beaten features. "A very, very bad boy indeed."

Through bloodstained vision, Brennan looked into the face of the man who, for no reason, had decided to torment him.

And then he realised that the man actually had a very good reason indeed.

"Valentine!" he croaked, his voice quaking with fear. He spat blood onto the otherwise spotless floor. "Oh my God."

"Not quite," said Edward Valentine. "But certainly someone sent to show you the error of your ways." He raised the cane for yet another attack, and then paused as he looked into the middle distance.

"That's very good, boys," he said. "Now – the third declension."

Silence.

"Oh of course," said Valentine with a smile to the weeping mess that Brennan had become. "I have to change the tape. Excuse me."

As his tormentor went over to the doorway, Brennan realised this might be his only chance to escape. He pushed himself to his feet, bent his head down and, ignoring the dripping blood pooling on the floor, cannoned his body towards the door.

Valentine pushed another button.

As Brennan found himself in the corridor, more boys' voices surrounded him, coming from the speakers that had been set into the ceiling at regular intervals.

"Rex, rex, regem," the voices said as Brennan staggered towards the exit. He turned and through a bloody mist saw a caped figure close behind him.

"Regis, regi, rege," the boys chanted. Brennan ran back the way he had come and quickly found himself in the open air.

"Reges, reges, reges," came the voices from all around him, from the speakers set into the trees, into the walls of the building, from everywhere he looked.

"No escape for naughty boys," said Valentine from behind him. "And you, Mr Brennan, are a very naughty boy indeed."

From behind one of the trees that skirted the tennis courts appeared the girl who had first enticed him here. She waved to him.

"Come on!" she called, her tone urgent. "This way!"

"Regum, regibus, regibus," said the boys on the tape, concluding their latest task.

Brennan had no time to think and so he ran towards her, under the horizontal tree branch that arched ten feet over her head, and straight into the hangman's noose she looped over his head and tightened around his neck.

"What are you doing?" he said in choked tones as the girl backed away, leaving Brennan tethered by the rope that had been strung over the branch above him.

"She's doing what she was asked, Mr Brennan," said Valentine, coming up to the hapless journalist and raising the cane once more. "Now, can you remember the Latin for 'to love or to like'?"

Brennan started to cry, the mixture of blood and tears obscuring his vision entirely for a moment as he desperately tried to avoid another flogging.

"Amo!" he said eventually in between the sobs. "Amo! It's amo!"

Valentine tutted. "I would have hoped that a man of your age and presumed education would have at least been able to present the verb in the classically accepted manner." He raised the cane as the man before him struggled. "Allow me to refresh your memory. The Latin verb for to like or to love is Amo – I love," he whipped the back of Brennan's neck. "Amare – to love," another slash across the face, "Amavi – I have loved," a hard blow across the back of the knees that caused Brennan to collapse, "and finally, Amatus, which is?"

Brennan didn't know, or he was bleeding too much to be able to answer. Valentine took hold of the end of the rope that had been coiled around the hook screwed into the back of the tree trunk. He unwound it, and began to pull.

The journalist was yanked to his feet, then to tiptoe, and then into the air.

"The supine stem!" Valentine said as he pulled the rope still further. Brennan, coughing, choking, his eyes watering, pulled at the constriction around his neck as he rose higher and higher.

Once he was satisfied, Valentine wound the rope around the hook once more before making his way round so that dying journalist could see him.

"I hope your education here this afternoon will allow you to at least understand me, Mr Brennan, when I say Non Te Amo. Non Te Amo one little bit."

Dr Valentine and his companion watched Brennan's death throes together. Once he was satisfied that the journalist was dead, Valentine turned to the young lady beside him.

"I think that concludes our lesson for today," he said. She smiled back at him as he added, "And now, I think, for tea on the lawn."

They walked away from the hanging body of Michael Brennan, the man's torn face a mask of blood, his eyes glazed in death, hung out to dry like so many of those whom his column had shamefully and needlessly destroyed over the years.

But would no longer.

5

This time the phone call came at a far more convenient time, and performed the useful function of getting John Spalding out of a preview screening of something low budget and intensely violent. At first he thought the surround sound had been cranked up a little too high before he realised the vibration in his pocket was the police trying to get hold of him again. Grateful though he was to be excused the cavalcade of blood-drenched atrocities being depicted on screen, he wasn't at all happy when it was explained what was required of him.

"You want me to go *where?*" he said.

"Bristol, sir." It was Martinus again. "Since we last spoke to you there's been another death, in another part of the country, and your name has cropped up as knowing him as well. Plus it would seem something happened a week or so ago that might involve you too. The investigation's become national, and it's been decided to base operations in Bristol. I've been asked to go along to supply information regarding the death of Margaret Upchurch, and they're requesting that you come along too."

Spalding shook his head in disbelief. "What are you talking about? Who else is dead?"

There was a pause on the other end of the line while Martinus presumably consulted his notes. "Earlier this morning a Mr Michael Brennan was found hanging from a tree in the grounds of a former public school in Buckinghamshire," he said. "And just over a week ago, near the A470 coming out of Cardiff, a Mr David Bradshaw was found dead by the roadside."

Spalding could tell from the way Martinus broke off that there was obviously more. "He wasn't just found dead by the roadside, was he, Inspector?"

Again there was that pregnant pause that Spalding was starting to get used to. "No sir, he wasn't. Mr David Bradshaw was found impaled on a five foot high brass crucifix stolen from St David's Cathedral. So I hope you understand why I've sent someone round to where you were watching your film, sir."

Spalding looked up to see a uniformed police officer getting out of a squad car. "Yes I do, Inspector," was all he could say as he allowed himself to be led to the vehicle.

~

The Bristol police station meeting room Spalding was shown into was considerably bigger that the last room he had been questioned in. Windows at the far end looked out over a city that just then was bathed in late afternoon sunshine.

There were two other people in the room.

Spalding recognised Derek Martinus, and the young serious-looking woman with the short blonde hair turned out to be DI Susannah Graves from Cardiff. Apparently a DI Wentworth was coming over from Buckinghamshire as well, but he hadn't arrived yet. After the introductions, Spalding decided to be the one to break the ensuing awkward silence.

"So, do either of you know why I'm here?" he asked.

"Well," said Martinus, "you knew Margaret Upchurch."

"And," added Graves, "you knew Mr Bradshaw. Your number was in his phone. We didn't realise you might be connected to what was going on until your number also turned up on Michael Brennan's phone as well."

Spalding suppressed a nervous cough as he poured water from the jug on the table into an empty plastic cup. "Do you think I did it?" he said.

"In an ordinary case you'd be the prime suspect," said Martinus, clasping his hands on the table. "But this isn't ordinary."

Spalding frowned. "Then who do you think is responsible?"

"I'll tell you who's responsible," said a voice. "He was last seen heading over the Bristol Channel in a hot air balloon shaped like a giant raven."

DCI Jeffrey Longdon, late of the Avon and Somerset Constabulary, but recently very much reinstated and promoted, eyed the three of them from the doorway.

"And who saw him doing that?" said Spalding with a barely concealed chuckle of disbelief.

"I did, sunshine," said Longdon, stepping into the room, "and I very much hoped I would never hear his bloody name ever again." He waved an empty mug in their general direction. "Nice little job down in Cornwall, that was all I wanted. Nice bit of peace and quiet while I waited for my pension to come through. Maybe a bit of sheep rustling to sort out, the occasional bit of petty larceny or vandalism perhaps, but definitely not outrageously contrived deaths that no-one in their right mind would believe possible if they hadn't seen them with their own eyes. Which, of course, I have."

"Dr Valentine," Spalding breathed.

"Too right Dr Valentine, son, too bloody right." Longdon took one look at the water cooler and yelled out of the door. "For Christ's sake can't we get some coffee in here? I didn't come back to drink something from a bloody mountain spring. If I wanted that I'd have got a job in bloody Tibet."

Graves turned to Spalding. "You've heard of him, then?"

Spalding nodded. "Rather more than that I'm afraid." He looked at Longdon. "Can I use my smartphone in here?"

"Well I hope you can, son," Longdon looked as if he had just been asked something in ancient Greek, "because I certainly wouldn't know how to."

Spalding tapped the screen until the relevant site came up. Once he had found what he wanted he held the phone up to Longdon. "It's a book," he said.

Longdon peered at the picture on the screen.

"'The Nine Deaths of Dr Valentine'," he read, before giving Spalding an incredulous stare. "Are you telling me you wrote a book about that lunatic?"

"Not me, Inspector," said Spalding, passing the phone around so the others could also see the picture. "We. Once all the fuss had died down I contacted the journalists who covered the Dr Valentine story for the national dailies. I thought a book about his crimes might sell well, and that their input would be invaluable. Unfortunately, because we could never agree how best to do it, it ended up being just a rehash of the original articles they wrote."

Longdon didn't seem impressed. "And what were these articles like?" he asked.

Spalding looked confused. "Like, Inspector?"

Longdon nodded. "Yes, like. I mean were they sensitive, well-researched, accurate?"

"Well I wouldn't quite say—"

"Or might they just have been given the usual tabloid treatment?" Longdon continued. "Might they just have been a little bit embellished? Sexed up? Made more appealing to the readers? In a word, Mr Spalding, might they have been what we in the force would refer to as Total Bollocks?"

"That's two words, Inspector," Spalding said, only to instantly regret it as Longdon gave him a look that could blast rivets through steel.

"Don't try my patience, sonny. I know what you do for a living, and no matter what you've seen on the cinema screen, it's nothing compared to what he did to all those doctors. Nothing." Longdon took a breath. The silence in the room was palpable. "What the hell were you lot all thinking?"

"The story was so popular it seemed the obvious thing to do," Spalding replied. "And I have to say the book did very well."

"Yes," said Longdon. "And I have to say that now it appears he's planning to do you lot 'very well', doesn't it? Did it never occur to you that we never caught him? Did it never even for a moment enter your heads that he might come back?"

"He was a wanted man, Inspector." Spalding was doing his best not to shout now. "What possible reason could he have had for wanting to come back here?"

"I think you and your friends have given him a perfect reason," said Longdon. He went over to the window and gazed out over the sun-blushed buildings. "A brilliant, rich, unstoppable psychopath, and you and your friends have gone and waved the biggest red flag anyone could ever conceive of right in his face. Well done. Well bloody done. It's because of you I'm not down in St Ives now checking that Mrs Humphries' Scone and Jam Shop hasn't decided to engage in a little bit of illegal Sunday trading, before popping over to the local for a pint."

"Where do we go from here, sir?" DI Graves looked at Longdon expectantly.

"The first thing we need to do," Longdon replied as he turned to face them once more, "is find out what he's basing the murders on this time."

"Isn't that a bit of an assumption, sir?" That was Martinus. "He might not be basing them on anything."

Longdon snorted. "A bloke run through with a massive crucifix? A girl wrapped in bandages soaked with embalming fluid?" No-one dared say a word. "The only I thing I am sure of so far is that it's not Vincent Price films this time. I had to watch nearly every bloody one of them two years ago and none of them have deaths like those in them."

"No," said Spalding with quiet confidence. "They don't."

All eyes turned to him.

"You say that as if you might know where they are

from," said Longdon, his tone no longer quite so admonishing.

"I might," said Spalding. "You see, I don't think he's gone too far from his original inspiration."

"Well, out with it, lad," said Longdon, dragging up a chair. "Even if it's ridiculous I'm more than willing to give it a serious listen at this point."

Spalding took a deep breath. "In the film *Dracula Has Risen from the Grave*, Christopher Lee, as Dracula, is finally killed at the end of the film by being dropped from a great height onto a huge metal crucifix."

"So it's films starring Christopher Lee this time," said Longdon. "At least that's a start." Spalding tried to interrupt but it was no good. "Can you put together a list for me of this bloke's most memorable film appearances, especially including ones where he—"

"It's not films starring Christopher Lee." Spalding eventually managed to shout Longdon down. It wasn't a pretty sight. "At least, not specifically him."

Longdon's eyes narrowed. "What do you mean?"

Spalding waited until he was sure the DCI was going to keep quiet before continuing. "In the film *Blood from the Mummy's Tomb* the character of Margaret, played by Valerie Leon, is crushed beneath a falling building and the final shot is of her wrapped in bandages pleading for help to the camera."

"And Christopher Lee's not in that one?" Graves asked.

"No, he's not." Spalding replied.

"Damn!" Longdon thumped the table. "So there's not going to be a pattern this time. It'll just be any old daft film he can think of."

"No Inspector, not just 'any old daft film'." Spalding was getting tired of having to fight for the stage, but it was still most likely the quickest way he would be able to get out of here. "In the film *Fear in the Night* Ralph Bates is hanged from the branch of a tree in the grounds of a deserted public school, just like Michael Brennan."

"Is Christopher Lee in that?"

"No, Inspector, he's not."

"Or this Valerie girl you mentioned?"

"Inspector Longdon," Spalding said, getting to his feet, "do you want to know the link between these three films, or don't you?"

Longdon's eyes widened at that. "So there is a link?"

"Yes!" Now it was Spalding's turn to thump the table in frustration. "Good God, man, I'm trying to tell you! All three movies were made by Hammer Films, arguably the most famous British picture company ever!"

"I thought that was Ealing," said Derek Martinus.

"Shut up, DI Martinus." Longdon turned back to Spalding. "You've got a good point there, son, I'll give you that. What better way to bump off a load of British journalists you hate than by using a British institution like that."

"Are Hammer Films a British institution?" asked DI Graves from the back.

"Even I've heard of them," said Longdon. "Therefore they must be." Then it was back to Spalding. "Can you give me a list of their key films?"

Spalding sat down again, leaned back in his chair and rolled his eyes. "I could give it a go," he said. "But it would go on for several pages."

"Doesn't matter," said Longdon with a shake of his head. "If there's one thing I learned from my previous encounter with our Dr Valentine, it's that he's nothing if not obsessive. Get me that list, and somewhere on it will be what he's planning next. In the meantime," he said to Spalding," I also need a list of everyone who contributed to that book of yours."

"It shouldn't be too difficult to remember," Spalding replied, taking out a pen to scribble on the notepad Longdon had just handed him. "After all, there aren't too many of them left."

He ignored the inspector's expression as he did his best to remember everyone who had contributed to the book, and was still alive. By the time Spalding had finished he was sure he had all of them, except perhaps one.

Spalding stared at the list of names in front of him and willed himself to remember the one that was missing. It was a woman, wasn't it? A woman who had written for the *Daily Express*, or possibly *The Sun*, he couldn't remember which. Spalding drummed his fingers on the table while the others waited. Longdon had sent out for a copy of the book but Spalding knew it would be quicker if he could just remember.

Her name was on the tip of his tongue.

For Christ's sake, he thought. What *was* it?

6

"Fran?"

Francesca Warren stopped stirring her coffee, an action she had been performing for the better part of the last five minutes, and looked over to see who had shouted to her from the door of the coffee shop.

Oh God, she thought, it was Yvonne Carstairs, the very last person she needed to see right now.

Fran had been 'friends' with Yvonne for the past six months or so. She always thought of the term in inverted commas because, as far as she was concerned, people in the media didn't have real friends so much as people they could use to get the next gig, and that was certainly how the two of them treated each other. Fran didn't mind that – it was just the sort of thing one did if one wished to get on. What she did mind was the woman herself. Yvonne was chirpier, prettier, but worst of all, younger – something Fran had never been able to forgive her for. Even though Yvonne had yet to achieve the kind of success Fran had enjoyed with the Dr Valentine thing, she was sure it would come. Meanwhile, Fran was spending far too many hours in coffee shops wondering if her five greatest column inches of fame were already behind her.

"I thought it was you." Yvonne had already glided across the room, effortlessly avoiding the messy three year old in the buggy (she had dealt it and the child's mother the kind of understanding look that had her interviewees opening up in spades, and how Fran hated her for it), and with a swish of her white knee length Louis Vuitton skirt the girl was sitting beside her. Whether Fran wanted her there or not.

"Hello Yvonne," Fran said, forcing a smile and putting down the spoon she might do something silly with if the other girl said the wrong thing. "How's the world of fashion?"

"Oh, much the same." Yvonne accompanied the words with the sigh of mock boredom that all her kind seemed to acquire once they had been let loose on unsuspecting Paris couturiers. "How about you?"

Fran tried to imitate Yvonne, but instead of evoking a sense of chic ennui, her sigh just came out sounding vaguely depressed. "Fine, fine," she said, in a way that meant it was anything but.

"Oh you poor love." Yvonne folded her hands in her lap and leaned forward. "Tell me all about it."

Of course, Fran couldn't really do that. Any chink in the journalist's armour, especially the female journalist, would just get widened and ripped into by her female colleagues. So she put away thoughts of her latest relationship breakup, and the consequent loss of the possible headlining story she had been using him to get to, and elected to remain non-committal.

"Just the usual, darling," she said, drawling on the last word with all the false sincerity of many years of practice. "Men. And editors. And anything else you'd care to suggest."

"Oh no!" Fran knew that Yvonne wasn't really the

slightest bit concerned, but she was capable of putting on an exemplary job of pretence. "Editors can be a bitch sometimes, can't they?"

Fran nodded, grateful the conversation had been skilfully diverted into something they could both have a nice, manageable non-specific moan about. "They can," she replied. "And the women are even worse!"

They both giggled at that. Fran sipped coffee. Yvonne looked at her watch.

"Are you in a hurry?" Fran asked, hoping that the other girl was.

"Kind of," Yvonne replied. "In fact, it's absolutely serendipitous me finding you here. You couldn't do me the most *enormous* favour, could you?"

Fran's ears pricked up at that. Any favour could always be exploited. "That depends what it is," she said, smiling sweetly. "But you know I'll always do my best to help."

Yvonne leaned further forward and lowered her voice to a conspiratorial whisper. "Well," she said. "You know that lovely young model I've been exhausting most nights?"

Fran didn't, but she nodded enthusiastically anyway. "Of course!" she lied, determined to get more information in case she could use it later. "What did you say his name was again?"

Was it Fran's imagination, or did the other girl's cheeks blush a little pinker at that? "It's not a *he*, my love. That's why I've had to keep it absolutely one hundred percent quiet. You *know* how people wouldn't understand."

Fran nodded, doing her best to rein in her excitement. People certainly wouldn't understand, not in the industry and certainly not the readership of middle England. In fact they'd not understand to the point of at least wanting to read about it all on page three, or even page one if it was a slow news day. Fran reached over and gave Yvonne's wrist a squeeze that was tight with empty reassurance.

"What can I do?" she said.

"Well." Yvonne licked her lips. Was this difficult for her? How delicious! "We've been having a bit of trouble, and so I've arranged for us to meet up this afternoon. The problem is, that bloody editor of mine has set up an interview that I'm supposed to be doing at the same time." Yvonne looked at the now infinitely superior-feeling Fran with wide eyes. "You couldn't possibly do the interview for me, could you?"

Fran let a few deliciously painful seconds pass as she pretended to think about it. She stroked her chin, gazed off into the middle distance, and generally milked the moment for all it was worth before answering.

"I've quite a bit of work lined up this afternoon myself," she lied. "But, yes, of course I'll do it. What are friends for?"

"Oh, thank you!" The girl seemed genuinely grateful and, for a moment, Fran felt almost guilty for revelling in her misery. Almost. "It's a new company." Yvonne was already searching in her bag. "The magazine wants me to interview their managing director, get the lowdown on their products, philosophy, all that sort of thing." It took a bit of struggling but eventually Yvonne produced a slightly creased business card.

Fran peered at the elegant font.

"'Ayesha Industries'," she read. "'Come And Bathe In Our Eternal Flame'."

"That's their new cosmetics line," Yvonne explained. "They're launching it next month."

Fran tucked the card away. "Well it's nothing if not dramatic," she said.

Yvonne nodded. "That's what I thought. They could be the next big thing. To be honest I'm probably shooting my career in the head not taking it myself, but I really can't. Are you still happy to do it?"

Oh yes, Fran was happy all right. Fran was bloody ecstatic.

"Only if you're absolutely sure," she said, crossing her fingers.

"Oh I am," said Yvonne, already getting to her feet. "Thank you so much. You'll never know how much this means to me."

Perhaps not, thought Fran. *But I just might do my best to find out.* "Don't worry, darling," she said. "Fran will take care of everything."

There was no answer to that and so, after brushing lips against both cheeks the two women parted. When Yvonne had gone, Fran allowed herself a little chuckle as she looked at the card once more. A cosmetics interview, she thought, blessing her good luck. What could possibly go wrong?

~

The offices and distribution warehouse of Ayesha Industries were located in an industrial park on the south side of Nottingham. A tiny map showing the establishment's exact location was printed on the back of their business card. Fran also liked the little optical trick the company had thought to include on the front. Next to the company name and slogan was a picture of the face of a beautiful girl. That wasn't so surprising, but if you held the card up to the light and angled it just so the picture changed to that of a haggard old lady.

Cute, Fran had thought, and it was also a decent little bit of manipulation. Show the customer what she thought she looked like now, and what she would look like after Ayesha Cosmetics had finished with her. At least that was what she presumed it was intended to convey, but it hadn't been terribly well made – the 'before' and 'after' pictures seemed to be the wrong way around.

She parked her two-seater BMW in the empty car park, got out and looked around. The place seemed deserted for a Wednesday afternoon. Then she remembered the numerous 'To Let' signs she had seen on the way in. That didn't bode well. If Ayesha Cosmetics could only afford to set up in a place where industrial property prices were at a minimum, she wondered if they might have cut corners with 'Eternal Flame' as well.

She pushed the buzzer to the left of the glass panelled door labelled 'Office', noting as she did so that at least the sign looked as if it had been professionally put together. The red-lettered gothic font on a black background felt a little severe for a company that was trying to present itself as the future of beauty, but that was just something else she could write about.

Fran didn't have to wait long for an answer. She did, however, have to pause for a moment to take in what the individual who opened the door was wearing. She thought pink could look all right on a man if it was just a shirt, but an entire suit and tie to match was going over the top a bit.

No, she thought, stifling a giggle. A *lot*.

"Miss Carstairs?" the man's overly bouffanted Liberace hairstyle gleamed silver in the afternoon sun, but the swathes of lacquer in which the locks seemed to have been coated prevented the slight breeze from disturbing its almost mathematical perfection.

Fran shook her head. "Yvonne couldn't come," she said, extending a hand and giving him her most winning smile. "I'm Francesca Warren."

His grip was oddly synthetic. Probably the result of too much all-over body Botox, she guessed. When he smiled the corners of his face looked as if they might fold in on themselves. Definitely Botox, she thought.

"How lovely to meet you, Miss Warren," he replied. "I'm sorry your colleague couldn't come, but I'm delighted that she managed to find someone even more beautiful to come in her stead. I am Dr Chantler Day, managing director and indeed founder of Ayesha Cosmetics. And my, do I have some intoxicating things to show *you* this afternoon."

I'll believe that when I see it, Fran thought as she followed him inside. Still, she had to give him full marks for being a quirky character, and they were always so much easier to write about.

Dr Day led her down the length of a narrow brightly-lit corridor. At the far end stood a pale olive coloured door, next to which was a numeric keypad. He paused and turned to her.

"Do you wish to see what lies behind the green door, Miss Warren?"

Fran shrugged. "Of course," she said. "That's what I'm here for."

Dr Day's eyes tried to crease for a second, in spite of whatever treatments he had applied to the skin around them, before he typed in a number on the pad. There was a whoosh of air as the door opened.

"Air tight," he explained. "But don't worry, the room is fully air conditioned in a very special way that I'll explain in a minute."

Fran suddenly had visions of being pushed into this air tight room by this strange man and she held back.

"There's nothing to be afraid of here!" Dr Day chuckled. "But if it makes you feel any better, I'll go in first."

The room inside was surprisingly large and echoingly bare. White walls and a white ceiling added to the atmosphere of sterility, and the air from the vent in the ceiling had a strange, ozone-like smell to it.

"Please take a seat." Day motioned to the chair positioned in front of the remarkably elaborate makeup counter that was the room's only other item of furniture.

"Where are you going to sit?" Fran asked, putting her bag down and positioning herself before the makeup mirror. Christ, she looked a bit rough today.

Day stood behind her and put his hands on her shoulders. "I shall not be sitting," he said. "I shall be showing you the magic of Eternal Flame."

Fran craned her neck to look at him, but Day gently but firmly turned her head so she could only see his reflection as he towered over her. "You're not going to give me a makeover, are you?" she said, looking at her own image again and rather hoping he was.

"Not just a makeover," said Day. "I am going to turn you into a different woman. Believe me, by the time you walk out of here you will feel as you never have before."

"Well, not to cast aspersions on you or your products," Fran said, wrinkling her nose, "but that's going to a hell of thing to try and pull off."

"Nevertheless," Day said, his hands still on her shoulders, "I very much feel that today I shall achieve it. Now, the first thing I need for you to do is to take a deep breath." In case she wasn't sure of his instruction, he demonstrated it for her.

Fran did as she was told, and again that was that slight sting in her nostrils. "Why?" she asked.

"Do you know one of the main threats to beauty?" Day asked, his face grave. "One of the worst things to harm beautiful skin, the perfection of youth?"

Fran shrugged. She couldn't imagine he was going to come up with anything revolutionary, but she let him have his moment.

Dr Day raised his arms and looked up at the ceiling. "Why, the very air itself!" His gaze snapped back down to regard her. "Did you know that air is mainly made of nitrogen? Nitrogen filled with bacteria and dust particles, toxins and poisons, all of them quite, quite terrible for your pores?" Fran knew what air was made of but she kept quiet. "That is why we insist that Eternal

Flame cosmetics be applied in a pure oxygen environment. What you are breathing in at the moment is not common air, Miss Warren, but one hundred percent pure and unsullied oxygen! It's used in hospitals all the time to treat patients with breathing problems. All I am doing is using it on the beautiful to make them even more so!"

Okay, Fran thought, so he's a little bit potty. In fact he might be quite a lot potty. Did she trust him to put stuff on her face?

She needed the article.

"Okay," she said, cautiously. "But surely if this makeup has to be applied in this sort of atmosphere, you're shooting yourself in the foot with the home cosmetics market?"

"Ayesha Products will *not* be for home use," Day explained. "They will be salon only. It will increase their exclusivity, and therefore their popularity."

Just another fad then. But that was fine. Fads made good copy. In fact the more over the top, the better. Fran gave him a regal wave.

"In that case, carry on, maestro," she said with a wry grin.

Day clapped his hands. They made a curiously dull sound. "Excellent! Now, first we need to apply the foundation. If you would be kind enough to look up and close your eyes."

He reached over her shoulder and took a small unlabelled aerosol canister from the table. He shook it twice and then, holding it at arm's length, proceeded to spray a liberal quantity of it in the air above Fran's upturned face. She coughed, and then grimaced as the particles began to settle on her skin.

"I wasn't expecting perfume," she said.

Dr Day shook his head. "I didn't say it was, Miss Warren. It's an entirely new concept in foundation makeup. The substance I have applied to your face and neck and now…" he added another couple of squirts "…to your hands, is a fast acting foundation and moisturiser combined. Do you feel anything?"

Fran opened her eyes. "Now that you mention it," she said, "my skin does feel kind of tingly."

The beauty specialist clapped his hands. "Excellent! In that case, we're ready to move onto the next stage. If you will allow me." He placed his hands on Fran's shoulders and swung the swivel chair round so she was facing him. "All you need to do now is let me work my magic, and then you'll have the most amazing story to write about."

Fran remained unconvinced as the man began to – rather inexpertly – apply a blusher of an unflattering shade to her cheeks, followed by some glittery lilac eyeshadow that she thought had gone out of style thirty years ago. Still, the eighties were supposed to be coming back, and she supposed she should wait for the overall effect.

"Oh my," said Dr Day as he applied what felt like swathes of the stuff, "you really are looking hot, young lady." He uncapped a lipstick of an especially violent purple hue. "Yes," he said, pausing, his voice lowering in tone. "Very hot indeed. Tell me, Miss Warren, have you ever been hauled over the coals?"

Fran frowned. "What?"

"Oh nothing, nothing," came the reply, almost as if the mask she imagined was now firmly back in place had never actually slipped. "I was just thinking." He began to apply the waxy substance to her mouth. "The kind of job you do, you must have given some people a rough ride in the past. In your articles I mean."

"It's all part of the job," said Fran. "To tell the truth, to give the public what they want."

"That's not always the same thing though, is it?" The voice had dropped in tone again. "The public don't always want the truth, do they? They want to be entertained, to be told a story, a story with a happy ending that can let them sleep in their beds at night, safe in the knowledge that at least it's not they who have been raked through the mud and filth of what passes for journalism nowadays."

"What are you on about?" Fran tried to stand, but her limbs felt unnaturally heavy.

"You're not drugged, in case you're wondering." The man's entire demeanour was different now, and the man himself seemed to have changed into someone much more serious. "It's something rather more effective than that."

Fran suddenly felt very scared. "What do you mean?" she said in a very small voice.

"Just a taste of your own medicine, Miss Warren." The man was peeling off the fine latex coverings that sheathed his hands. Now he was picking away the paper thin substance that he had used to coat his face. "You see, that's my specialty. Medicine, that is. Or rather, it was. Yours on the other hand is being paid money to tell lies about people who have had quite enough turmoil in their lives already."

Now he was lifting off that absurd hairpiece to reveal a visage that made Fran want to cry and go running to her mother. She was so terrified she could scarcely utter his name, but she managed it somehow, the word coming out as little more than a whisper.

"Valentine."

"Dr Valentine or, to be even more accurate, Mr Valentine, if you would be so kind. Although your sort rarely are, are they? Kind, I mean." There was barely-concealed malice in his voice now. "Which is partly why I've had to go to all this trouble and expense to teach you a lesson, to make you an example to your kind that you cannot just write what you like, and think you can get away with it."

Her heart filled with dread, Fran forced herself round to see what she looked like in the mirror.

And breathed a sigh of relief.

She looked ridiculous, certainly, as if someone with little or no experience had tried to make her up, but she wasn't scarred, she wasn't bleeding, and she wasn't teetering on the brink of a painful death.

She was, however, very angry.

She spun back round to face him. "I don't know if you think this is funny," she snapped, "but you've wasted an afternoon of my time with this little charade of yours, and so let me assure you that I certainly will be writing about it. And about you. Again."

Valentine merely shook his head and tutted. "You don't watch many horror films, do you, Miss Warren? I'm presuming this because, if you did, you'd know what happens to the victim who calls the villain of the piece all sorts of unpleasant names. Let me assure *you* that it never ends well."

Fran already had a tissue out and was rubbing at her makeup. Which wasn't shifting.

"It won't come off," said Valentine. "Not until you leave this room, anyway."

Fran stood up. "Then that's what I'm going to do," she said. "Right now."

Valentine stepped to one side and gestured to the door. "By all means," he said, "although I should probably warn you before you do."

"Why?" Fran sneered. "Have you got an axe waiting to drop on me on the other side? Or a pit waiting to open up?"

"Nothing so lacking in finesse for one so beautiful," he said, with a smile that had no humour in it. "You may remember I mentioned this room is being supplied with pure oxygen?" Fran nodded. "That's because the substance I have applied to your face reacts with the nitrogen in air, turning it into a highly corrosive acid. You cannot leave this room, Miss Warren. Ever."

Fran snorted. "That's ridiculous," she said. "You must have got some of the stuff on you when you were spraying me!"

"Indeed I did," Valentine replied. "Hence the need for the protective coverings you have just seen me remove. It takes a couple of minutes for the spray to combine with your skin, and then it's fixed there. Permanently." He took two steps towards the door. "And so now I hope you can understand why it is I who am going to leave this room and not you. The door is airtight and I've arranged for the oxygen to last for another half an hour or so. After that you get to decide whether you breathe your last in here or..."

"Why were you going to do this to Yvonne?" Fran cried, trying to decide if this madman was telling the truth. "She never wrote anything about you."

"She never wrote anything about anyone," said Valentine as the door opened and the familiar face of Fran's 'friend' appeared on the other side. "In fact she never wrote anything at all. You see," he said as he and the young woman exchanged smiles, "Yvonne is a very good friend of mine. Although I know her under a different name."

"Yvonne!" Fran screamed, on her feet but uncertain if it was safe to proceed any further. "Help me!"

"Oh no, darling," said the woman Fran had thought she knew well enough to trust. "You've only yourself to blame for this. I would say 'see you later' but we both know that's not going to happen."

The door swung shut with an air-tight hiss, leaving Fran to ponder her fate. Her only company was the noise from the air vent, and she knew that would be stopping soon enough.

She looked at herself in the mirror, and rubbed an experimental finger across her face. Her skin felt strange, but not exceptionally so. The stuff was all over her hands as well, like a fine coating of lacquer. Was it really capable of dissolving flesh? And there was so little of it, just the faintest trace, really. She couldn't accept that it was capable of doing what Valentine had said.

He just meant for her to suffocate, didn't he?

Fran got to her feet again, angry now that she should have been conned by such a cheap trick. She strode to the door. *It had better be locked, Valentine,* she thought, *because if it isn't I'm coming after you.*

The door opened with a sucking sound.

Fran hesitated, then took a single step into the corridor.

Another.

And another.

She looked at her hands.

Nothing.

Fran took several deep breaths and laughed out loud. That bastard! How dare he scare her like that!

She strode back the way she had come, determined to catch Valentine and that bitch Yvonne to give them both a piece of her mind before she got back to her keyboard to annihilate both of them on paper.

The door at the end of the corridor opened easily and Fran stepped into the open air of the car park.

At first she felt almost nothing, just a slight tingling as if her extremities had been numbed. Then there was not just pain, but searing, burning agony eating into her skin and burrowing into the deeper tissues beneath. Fran raised her right hand to see the flesh had already dissolved from the fingertips, revealing nubs of white bone that were already beginning to be eaten away before her eyes. She turned to run back the way she had come, but the door was now closed and locked, the company logo replaced by a sheet of paper on which were typed six words:

PURE OXYGEN IN THE CORRIDOR TOO!

They were the last thing she ever saw. As Fran clawed at the melting flesh of her face with fingertips of bleached crumbling bone she wondered if there would be anything left of her for the police to recover.

There was, but not very much.

7

The ceiling was ribbed and vaulted, and perfectly suited the drawing room of the elegantly appointed country house for which it had been constructed. The beautiful cornice work, always in shadow these days, rose twenty feet above the oak floor tiles, which were themselves over a hundred years old.

The room was almost in darkness, the bright sunshine of the day outside kept away by the heavy red velvet curtains that had been drawn across the double bay windows. The only illumination afforded this chamber was a single bare bulb burning above the pipe organ that took up the entire wall opposite.

The organ had two manuals. Its owner had initially wished for three, but to include a choir manual as well as the swell and the great would have meant extra expense that he had preferred to spend on other things. Right now he was playing Bach's *Prelude in E Minor* with an arrangement of stops so gentle it was best appreciated in otherwise absolute silence.

The man to the left who was currently bound to a wooden chair was preventing that.

The owner seemed not to mind, but it was difficult to tell because of the mask he wore. It was a rough, papier mâché affair that concealed his left eye and left a gap for his nostrils but not his mouth. Every now and then his right eye darted to his helpless victim, the eyelid creasing with annoyance. He should have anaesthetised this one as well as gagged him.

The music came to an end, and almost immediately the door opened. It was a heavy piece that dated back to the seventeenth century and had been imported from France. Despite its age, the excellent condition of it hinges and heavy floor runner had meant that some considerable time had been spent on making it creak appropriately.

A beautiful girl stood in the doorway. The same beautiful girl who, over the past couple of weeks, had posed as a socialite, a taxi driver, a schoolgirl, and finally and most recently as fashion writer Yvonne Carstairs, friend of the now late Francesca Warren.

The figure at the organ turned and acknowledged her presence. She in turn glanced at their latest prisoner, the poor man mistakenly taking her for a potential saviour. The pleading in his eyes was wasted on her.

"You've decided, then?" she said, as the phantom altered the combination of organ stops.

She was rewarded with a shake of the head as Valentine peeled off the mask. His suit was about fifty years out of date but was no less immaculate for it.

"I'm afraid not," he replied, before playing a few bars of something infinitely more threatening and definitely more flamboyant. He stopped and gave the man in the chair a worryingly insane look.

"Tony and I have been having a little chat, haven't we Tony?"

The man mumbled something in reply. The girl removed the gag and the words "My name's not Tony" tumbled from his tear-stained lips.

"Of course it isn't," said the girl. "That's not the point, silly. That's not the point at all." She looked back at the man sitting on the organ stool. "You couldn't decide, then?"

Valentine picked up the tattered mask. "Between *Phantom of the Opera* and *Paranoiac*? No, I'm afraid I couldn't. But as we're both aware, the time for procrastination is at an end. The police are not exactly closing in, but I would imagine they are at least trying to get themselves organised now. I'd be very disappointed if they weren't."

"Really?" said the girl.

Valentine nodded. "We've left them enough clues," he said. "That last one was the most obvious of all. Plus we made sure we left plenty of the 'Ayesha Cosmetics' business cards lying close to what little was left of poor Miss Warren. Anyone with access to a search engine should be able to work out her death was inspired by the film *She*." He gazed off into the distance. "You know," he said, "I wouldn't be at all surprised if the police are watching poor Ursula Andress dissolve in front of Peter Cushing and that other chap right now." He chuckled. "I wonder if they've dragged Inspector Longdon back from wherever he probably thought he'd been sent to live out his days. It would be rather delicious if he happened to be in charge of things again."

"Who are you?" the sobbing man in the chair asked the girl. "Why would you want to help him?"

Valentine answered for her. "I'm afraid even I don't know her real name," he said. "Either because she cannot remember it, or because she would prefer not to say. Whichever the reason may be I have always respected it, and have no intention of prying further. Suffice to say I call her Christina, because of the circumstances under which we met."

"He rescued me, you see," said Christina. "I had jumped from a very great height into a very deep body of water with the full intention of killing myself." She gave Valentine an apologetic look. "For reasons I have no intention of elaborating upon. Not just for now, anyway. It was only when I surfaced for the third time that I realised that it was not my time to die yet. And that was when I saw the raven."

The man looked confused. Bloody and tearstained as well, but mostly confused. "Raven?" he asked.

Valentine nodded. "A little affectation of mine," he said. "My escape route from the forces of the law, as well as a little flamboyant flourish to signify that my revenge was at an end. Something you and your friends have regrettably caused me to realise is not the case. Not the case at all."

"He picked me up in his balloon." For the first time since she had entered the room Christina smiled. It was utterly bewitching. "A strange man in a huge raven-shaped balloon saved my life. How could I not help him after that?"

"But that's a great story," the man spluttered. "You could sell that alone and get twenty thousand for it. I could arrange it for you, if you like."

"Be quiet, Tony," said Valentine.

"Yes, shut up, Tony," Christina added, pulling the gag back up for good measure. "Was it a good idea bringing him here?" she asked Valentine.

The doctor shrugged. "No-one saw him, and we go out so often. I rather liked the idea of entertaining at home for a change."

"True." The girl was making her way across the room now. "Well, if we're staying in, would you care for some champagne?"

Valentine nodded but held up a hand. "Afterwards, though," he said. "Nothing takes the chill out of good champagne more than excessive screaming."

Christina smiled again. "So you'd better hurry up and choose," she said. "Are you going to be Herbert Lom or Oliver Reed?"

Valentine pondered for moment, and then a brainwave struck. His eyes were gleaming when he next looked at her.

"Neither," he said, producing the syringe he had been intending to use anyway when his patient got a bit too noisy. "I'm going to be Eric Porter. Get the car while I make a couple of telephone calls."

~

"Before you go up, I just need to warn you that you can't take photographs in here."

The man in the cloak and pointed beard sighed at the words, and gestured with his silver-headed cane to the semi-conscious man propped up by the pretty nurse.

"I am not here to take pictures, young man," he said. "I am here in a final and desperate attempt to cure this poor young man of his inner demons!"

The elderly ticket vendor of the Whispering Gallery at St. Paul's Cathedral scratched his chin. "Oh yes," he said, adjusting the name badge that stated his name was Ronald. "We did receive a phone call about you earlier from someone high up in the Royal College of Psychiatrists. Will you be able to manage, Dr Pritchard, or would you like me to locate some assistance?"

The man calling himself Dr Pritchard shook his head. "Thank you," he said, "but we should be fine. Nurse Laura and I will ensure that he gets up there safely."

"Come on Mr Hannah," the girl said firmly, propelling the man in the direction of the stone spiral staircase. "You know this is for your own good."

"He doesn't look very well," said Ronald as Mr Hannah groaned and tried to resist the ministrations of his two carers.

"Of course he isn't well!" said Pritchard as his patient was helped onto the first step. "That's why we've brought him here, why he's had to be sedated, and why we really cannot be kept chatting when we have important work to do."

"Oh of course," said the little old man, staying with them rather than shuffling back to his ticket booth. "You're sure you don't need any help?"

"No."

Mr Hannah groaned and reached out an arm to the ticket vendor.

"I could call an ambulance if you like," the man added.

Pritchard and Nurse Laura had managed to get the man onto the third step now.

"Thank you," said the doctor, putting away the syringe he had just used to administer something to the poor man, "but that won't be necessary. At least not right now. If my patient does anything silly I can assure you that you will be the first to know."

Mr Hannah, suddenly more cooperative now he had received his injection, allowed himself to be manhandled the rest of the way as Ronald the ticket vendor, mumbling to himself all the while, made his way back to attend to a group of Spanish tourists who had just entered the building.

He had just finished the long and laborious process of selling individual tickets to all thirty of them, when there was a muffled thump from behind him.

He didn't need to turn round to know that something quite catastrophic had happened, something that caused most of the tourist group to run screaming from the building. But he did anyway, giving the broken body of poor suicidal Mr Hannah a cursory glance before turning back and calmly announcing to the few visitors remaining that the cathedral would need to be closed for the rest of the afternoon.

As he put the 'Closed' sign on his desk, Ronald realised he was going to need to ring for an ambulance after all.

8

"Are you telling me you didn't suspect anything?"

Longdon had taken the next available train to London while DI Martinus, DI Graves, and DI Colin Wentworth, who had finally turned up from Buckinghamshire, had been despatched elsewhere. John Spalding had insisted he accompany Longdon, partly because he thought being present at the crime scene might help spark some suggestion as to where Valentine might strike next, but mainly because he no longer felt safe on his own.

"I've told you twice." Ronald Turner-Wyatt was unhappy at having been kept behind at St Paul's so late, and he had already explained to the police officers that his cat Mungo was going to be even more unhappy about the delay in getting his dinner. "He was a doctor."

Longdon sighed. "And how did you know he was a doctor?" he asked.

"Well for a start," the little man replied, "he said he was one."

"Oh that's marvellous." Longdon's spell in Cornwall hadn't helped his diplomacy skills. "And if I told you I was the Queen of Sheba, would you believe that?"

Ronald shook his head. "You haven't got a crown," he said, before adding with a sniff, "besides – you're not a lady."

"He's got a point, Inspector." Spalding was gazing up

at the gallery and marvelling at the distance from the balcony to the floor.

"That's enough from you," Longdon snapped. Behind the three of them the lifeless broken remains of Valentine's latest victim was being lifted onto a stretcher. Even ten feet away it was possible to hear the man's broken bones crunching as the fractured pieces jarred against one another. Longdon tried to cover up the noise with the sound of his own voice. "Why else did you think he was a doctor?"

"He had a patient with him," Ronald said. He looked over Longdon's shoulder as the flattened, vaguely man-shaped outline beneath the red blanket was wheeled away. "Poor man. Poor, poor man."

"Didn't he ask you for help?" Longdon was getting nowhere but he persisted anyway. "Didn't he try to tell you he was in danger?"

Ronald shook his head. "He wasn't very well at all. Dr Pritchard said he wasn't. Said he was troubled with all sorts and that they were going to help him clear his head."

"Well they did that all right, didn't they?" Longdon rolled his eyes. "They cleared his head clean off."

"He had permission from the Royal College of Psychiatrists." Ronald was indignant now and was showing signs of having had quite enough. "I don't know what else you want me to tell you, Inspector. He seemed a perfectly charming gentleman. A little eccentric, perhaps, what with that top hat and cane, but charming nevertheless. I can't believe they meant that poor man harm. I mean my goodness, even the nurse who was with him was lovely, and the essence of politeness."

Longdon's eyes blazed at that nugget of information and it was all he could do not to grab the little old man by the lapels. "What nurse?" he said, his voice barely a whisper.

"The one who was with him. Lovely girl. Really pretty. And just as well-spoken as he was. Lovely couple they were. Shame you don't get to see more well-dressed people like that around these days."

Longdon did his best to remain calm as he put an arm around Ronald and pointed to a young man standing close to where the body had recently lain. He was making notes on a sketch pad. "Mr Turner-Wyatt, you've been of the utmost help to us," said the Inspector, "and I cannot begin to tell you how grateful we all are for you giving us some of your valuable time."

"Mungo won't be happy," Ronald said again.

Longdon ignored him. "All I need you to do before you leave is have a word with Steve over there. I want you to give him as accurate a description of this girl as you can. He'll draw it for you as you go along and I want you to stop him and get him to change it if what he draws isn't exactly like the nurse you saw here this afternoon. Do you understand?"

"I really have to be going."

"I understand that, Mr Turner-Wyatt, I really do. But you see, it's vitally important that we find her as her life could be in danger."

Ronald seemed to wake up at that. "Oh dear," he said. "Oh dear, oh dear. Well in that case I suppose Mungo will have to wait a little longer."

He went over to give Steve his description while Longdon tapped Spalding on the shoulder.

"Which film was this one from, then?" he asked.

"*Hands of the Ripper*, Inspector," Spalding replied. "A 1971 film famous for its climax in St Paul's Cathedral. It's actually a girl who falls to her death but otherwise I'm quite surprised at how faithful Valentine managed to make his reconstruction."

Longdon failed to be impressed. "Let's stick with Valentine himself, shall we?" he said. "I don't suppose any of you journos did any detailed research on him? You didn't by any chance find out about any wives? Lovers? Sisters? Anyone else who might be the girl he had with him?"

Spalding gave him a wry grin. "It probably won't surprise you to learn that 'we journos' had a good old look into Dr Valentine's history. And no – he had one wife, now deceased, no sisters, and no illicit affairs."

"At least none who would own up to it," Longdon pointed out.

"We offered a very tidy sum to anyone who could come forward with any dirt on the doctor," said Spalding, "especially of the lurid and debauched kind, and we came up with nothing. Until he decided to go on his rampage of death he seems to have led a pretty spotless life. Cared for his patients, loyal to his staff. The bugger was probably kind to animals as well."

"He probably still is," Longdon was rubbing his chin in thought. "And he probably still believes that some human life should be preserved – just not the kind that crosses him. Which means we could be looking for a very grateful patient, or even someone who sympathised with his story and somehow managed to find him out."

"That's a bit far-fetched, don't you think, Inspector?" Spalding shook his head. "Are you suggesting someone might have sympathised with him enough to want to commit murder? To actually take a human life?"

"I'm not sure everyone in this country would go so far as to describe your kind of journalist as human, Mr Spalding." Longdon raised an eyebrow. "And I'd suggest you don't forget that."

Spalding gave the Inspector a cold look. "Meaning what, exactly?"

"Meaning that I have been dragged back here to investigate a series of murders where even I can sympathise with the murderer," said Longdon. "Don't forget I read those newspaper articles too, and I and my staff didn't exactly come out of the whole thing unscathed. You people don't care what you write as long as it sells papers, and yet the minute your own health is threatened and your own lives are endangered, you come to us expecting to be protected by the very hands you've bitten time and time again. I can understand our Dr Valentine's motives only too well, Mr Spalding, and while I am not the most sensitive of men I certainly have a little bit of sympathy for him, something that is somewhat lacking when it comes to you and your colleagues."

Spalding, stunned at Longdon's outburst, said nothing. Now that the Inspector had stopped speaking, the gaunt silence that surrounded them seemed claustrophobic, despite the vast space in which they were standing.

"I see, Inspector," he said eventually. "I'm sorry you feel that way. I hope it isn't going to affect the investigation."

Longdon shook his head. "Just because I don't like you doesn't mean I'm going to let you get killed, Spalding, and I'm sure you realise that. Don't get me wrong – I've every intention of capturing our Dr Valentine. He got away from me once and you people made me a laughing stock. I've no intention of that happening again."

Longdon turned to see that Ronald was making for the door.

"All finished are we?" Longdon called after him. The little man quickened his pace in case he was about to be called back, but Longdon was already on his way over to Steve the artist.

"Very nice," he said as he inspected Steve's sketch. "I'm not surprised our Mr Turner-Wyatt could remember her. She shouldn't be too difficult to find." Spalding was peering over his shoulder. "I don't suppose you recognise her, do you?"

Spalding shook his head and coughed to clear his throat. "I've never seen her before," he replied. "More's the pity."

"We'll get this picture circulated," said Longdon. "See if anyone knows anything about her."

"Do you think that's wise?" said Spalding. "Surely it will simply alert Valentine to the fact that now we know what his accomplice looks like."

"I don't bloody care what Valentine knows," Longdon snapped. "The bugger's always two steps ahead of us anyway. This is the first lead we've had and while it's probably going to turn out to be part of some master plan of his, I'm going to milk it for all it's worth."

"Well you'd better hurry up, Inspector," said

Spalding, no longer veiling the cynicism in his voice now that Longdon had revealed what he thought of him. "After all, there are only two of us left. If the entire might of the British police force can't prevent us from being killed you deserve everything that any of my currently uninvolved colleagues end up writing about you."

"Oh we'll stop him," said Longdon. "Don't you worry about that. Right now there are three DIs on their way down to where Martin Peyton, formerly of the *Daily Mail*, is currently on holiday."

"And where might that be, Inspector?" Spalding asked. "Wales? Bournemouth?"

Longdon shook his head and said the name of a place that gave both of them a feeling of dread inevitability.

"Cornwall."

9

Penzance was a wonderful place for a holiday, Martin Peyton thought as he stretched in the midday sunshine. He should have done this ages ago. The deck chair in which he was currently sitting creaked against his weight as he put his half-empty can of lager down on the folding table beside him. The minute they had arrived at the caravan site the kids had insisted they go swimming, and so his wife Caroline had volunteered to do child supervision as long as he promised to have the caravan opened up by the time they got back. It hadn't taken long, and now Martin was enjoying a quiet beer before the inevitably noisy return of five year old Oliver and seven year old Melanie, with no doubt a damp and weary Caroline trailing behind them.

What he did not expect was for a police car to pull up and three plainclothes detectives to get out.

"Can I help you, officers?" he asked, getting to his feet and suddenly feeling rather foolish in his gaily coloured Hawaiian shirt, shorts and flip-flops.

The one who looked like a wrestler flashed an ID badge at him. "DI Derek Martinus, sir. Can you confirm that you are Mr Martin Peyton?" Martin nodded. "Of 27 Palmentry Row, Birmingham?"

"If I have to admit I live there then, yes," Martin replied with a grin. The officers did not seem amused.

Now the severe-looking woman spoke. "DI Susannah

Graves," she said, with a flourish of her badge. "Can you also confirm that you are the author of the articles 'Sick Surgeon Killed His Own Kind', 'Demented Doctor Dealt Death to Nine' and—" there was a pause before this one, "—The Medical Madman and the Incompetent Inspector: How Malpractice Cost Taxpayers Thousands'?"

Peyton nodded slowly. "I am," he said. "Might I ask why any of that is important?"

The third man identified himself as DI Colin Wentworth. He had a thin face that Martin imagined probably rarely smiled, and today was no exception. "We have reason to believe your life is in danger, sir."

"What?" The journalist did his best to look properly incensed. "Who on earth would want to kill me?"

Graves raised her eyebrows. "Those newspaper headlines haven't given you a clue, then?"

"No they haven't, Miss Graves," Martin tried to look behind them to see if there was any sign of Caroline and the kids coming back. "And if you don't mind I'd appreciate you leaving before my family returns. I don't want them upset by you being here."

"With all due respect, sir," said Martinus, shifting awkwardly from foot to foot, "I think they'd find it more distressing if they came back to find you'd been skewered through the chest."

"Or crushed," added Graves.

"Or hung by the neck from a convenient tree, like the one just over there." Wentworth helpfully pointed to a big old oak towering over wooden slats that demarcated the camp's toilets.

Martin sank into his chair. "What the hell are you lot on about?"

"It's Dr Valentine, sir," said Martinus. "Over the past few days we believe he's killed a number of your colleagues, and there's a good chance you could be next."

"Ah." Martin Peyton went quiet as he stared hard at the ground. Eventually he looked up at them again. "And I suppose you've been sent down here for my protection, have you?"

"Something like that, sir," said Wentworth. "Of course, the best thing for you to do would be to come with us so we could keep you in protective custody until this is all over."

"But you know I'm going to refuse," Martin replied. "Don't you?"

"I can tell from your face, sir," said Wentworth, "even if you haven't actually said it yet."

Martin rung his hands, checked again to make sure there was no sign of his family, and then gave the officers a pleading look.

"This is my last chance with Caroline and the kids," he said. "She's threatened to leave me a couple of times now, and to take them with her. She doesn't like what I do any more than you do. In fact I've been thinking of chucking it all in and getting a nice quiet job down here working on the local paper. You know, covering church fêtes and local sporting events. And I just might do that. But if she sees you people here she'll leave me for certain."

"We can't leave you alone, sir," said Graves. "We're under orders."

"And what do your orders say, exactly?"

"That we are to keep you under observation at all times," said Martinus, "and intervene if your life appears to be in any kind of danger."

"So you could keep an eye on me from a distance, then?"

None of them looked happy about that.

"But you could?" Martin looked desperate. "You could follow me anywhere you need to, watch me all the time, but keep yourselves out of the way enough that my family won't know you're there?"

"We're not exactly trained for covert operations, Mr Peyton," said Wentworth. "We're just simple coppers who want to prevent you from being strung up."

"Or stabbed," said Graves.

"Or crushed," added Martinus.

"Or dissolved in acid," said Wentworth for good measure. "You do see our problem, don't you?"

Martin nodded. He was starting to sweat now. "I do, I do, but please. You don't know how important it is that the kids don't think there's anything wrong. And Caroline too." Martin looked around nervously. "Especially Caroline."

The detectives conferred. It wasn't long before there was the sound of children's laughter from behind them. Martin jumped and Wentworth gave him a sour look.

"You have to promise us you won't do anything to endanger yourself," he said.

Martin nodded. "Of course."

"And that you won't go wandering off on your own," said Graves.

"I promise," Martin agreed.

"And whatever you do," said Martinus, "do not allow yourself to be drawn away by any kind of weird invitation, no matter how attractive a prospect it might be."

"I'm with my family," Martin said, too loudly and with a laugh so insincere it could only have been intended for the sun-tanned attractive woman behind them who was doing her best to herd her children towards the caravan.

"Darling?" Caroline's pretty face was already creased into a frown. "Who are these people?"

Martin did his best to look nonchalant, but despite years of working on a national daily he couldn't quite dispel his aura of shiftiness, especially not in front of his wife.

"They're policemen," he said, before quickly adding a "sorry" in the direction of DI Graves.

"Oh God, I warned you," Caroline said. "Any more funny business with bloody oil sheiks, or exclusive interviews with people on the run, and I told you what would happen." She called to the two children who had scampered into the caravan to change out of their moist clothes.

"It's not what you think!" Martin said, his eyes darting from her to the three detectives in the hope of some corroboration.

"Isn't it?" Caroline's eyes narrowed as she waited for one of them to say something.

"Your husband isn't in any trouble, Mrs Peyton," said Martinus eventually. "Quite the opposite, in fact. Hopefully he's helping us to prevent a murder."

Caroline gave her husband an accusing look. "Just as

long as it's not his own," she said. "You won't believe how many scummy low life types he's rubbed mucky shoulders with in the past, in the hope of some bloody headline the world would probably be better off without anyway."

"I'm afraid we can't say any more," DI Graves interjected, saving everyone from digging themselves into ever-deepening holes. "But if you see us around, don't worry. It's all just a precautionary measure."

The three of them got back into the car. As they drove away Caroline turned to Martin, her eyes blazing. "Precautionary against what, might I ask?"

Martin shrugged and held out his hands. "I can't tell you," he said. "If I did I'd be in trouble."

"You're in trouble already," said Caroline. "And if you don't tell me you're going to be spending the rest of the fortnight here on your own."

"Mummy!"

"Daddy!"

The first voice was Oliver's, the second Melanie's. The couple turned to see their children standing in the doorway of the caravan. The little girl was holding a crumpled piece of paper.

"What's that you've got there, Mel?" Martin asked, desperate for any form of distraction.

The girl came forward and shyly held the paper up with one hand, while hooking the index finger of the other firmly inside her mouth.

"The scary lady gave it to us," said Oliver from behind her.

"She wasn't scary," said Caroline, in way that was

probably intended to sound reassuring, but in her current state of anger it just sounded as if she was telling them off. Melanie cringed away from Mummy's outstretched hand as she gave the paper to Daddy.

Martin did a better job of smiling than Caroline had managed as he read the garish red print out loud.

"Dr Terror's Haunted Cornish Funfair," he said, at the same time taking in the array of gruesome characters that surrounded the words.

"Can we go can we go can we go can we can we can we can we?!!" Oliver came tearing out of the caravan with a battle cry and rammed straight into his father.

Martin hugged his boy and gave both his children his best funny face. It made them both giggle. "You don't want to go to a Haunted Funfair do you?" he said.

"Yes!" the two children chorused.

"But won't it be too scary for you?"

"No!"

Martin crouched down and gave them both a serious stare. "Not even if I make you go in the Haunted House... by yourselves!"

There was a pause as the children considered this. Then Melanie took Oliver's hand and said "I'll look after him."

"Yes, Melanie will look after me!" Oliver's trust in his slightly older sister's ability to protect him from danger caused both parents to gaze at him adoringly for a moment.

"Hey guys, it'll all be fine," Martin said with a glance to his wife. "Nobody's going to go on anything without one of us with you."

"Thank you Daddy!" Melanie ran forward to give Martin a big kiss.

"We're going we're going we're going we're going!" Oliver was already charging around demonstrating how he was going to fight zombies, as Martin Peyton realised he had somehow been duped into taking his children to the fair.

~

The field in which Dr Terror had decided to erect his Haunted Cornish Funfair was just beyond the outskirts of the town, but that didn't seem to have harmed its business at all. In fact, on this midsummer Saturday afternoon, the place was packed. Martin found a narrow parking space in the next field along, squeezing the family's four wheel drive between a camper van and a black Audi. Martin couldn't help taking a closer look at the tiny toy voodoo doll with the needles through its heart hanging from the Audi's rear view mirror, before the relentless cries of his children urged him to follow both them and his wife in the direction of the glittering summer noise.

"Don't think I've forgotten what we were discussing," Caroline hissed as Martin dug in his pocket for his wallet. The bored-looking girl in the ticket booth ignored the bouncing children and barely registered Martin as he slid two notes across. They were all rewarded with barely-legible stamps of black ink on their hands and a sheet of tickets for the rides.

"Look at this!" said Martin as they tramped across grass that looked ready to die. "A free ride on each attraction!"

"Me me me me me me me!" With all the egotistical zeal of a five year old, Oliver had already assumed that the tickets were intended for him.

Melanie jumped up and down, trying to read the sheet as Martin walked. "Where's mine?" she whined.

"You forgot to get two sheets," Caroline spat.

"I wasn't given two sheets, was I?" Martin snapped in return. "Besides, I think I can afford rides for everyone."

"That's not the point, is it?" said his wife, determined not to let it go. "Whichever child gets the free ticket will think they're special in your eyes, and the other one's sense of self-worth could be ruined!"

"Then I'll alternate who gets the tickets," Martin sighed, wishing she'd never read that child psychology book. He looked at the tickets and wondered which they should try first. The 'Zombies in the Haunted Tin Mine' sounded as if it might be a bit too scary, and something claiming to be 'Dr Blood's Coffin' would probably be a bit too much for them as well. They might find the waxworks museum boring, and these local things were never up to much, so they could give the 'Crucible of Terror' a miss. Judging by the absence of a queue outside the tent's rather scarred-looking entrance, everyone else had decided to do the same thing.

"Now you seem like a man willing to take a challenge!"

The man who had suddenly appeared in front of them seemed far too well dressed for a carnival showman. He didn't sound like one either, Martin thought.

"I'm not so sure about that," Martin said, stepping to one side.

The man mirrored his movement. "Oh I think you are,

my dear sir. Allow me to introduce myself. My name is Dr Franklyn." He noticed Caroline's frown. "Not a medical doctor, my good lady, oh goodness me, no. My doctorate is in the twin disciplines of entertainment and excitement, and," he turned back to Martin now, "I do not believe for one second that you are the kind of man who would shirk a test of bravery before his entire family!"

Martin looked at his scowling wife, and then down at his two children, who were regarding their father with all the trust and adoration he didn't deserve. He remembered the words of the police officers, but this wasn't something out of the ordinary, at least not in the context of a fairground. What possible harm could come to him here?

"All right," he said, flashing Caroline a determined look. "Lead me to it."

"Why, my dear sir," said Franklyn with a gesture of his cane, "we are practically upon it."

The Peyton family looked up at the banner over the fairground ride ahead of them. "Dare You Ride 'The Reptile'?" screamed ivory-coloured letters. The first and last of each word had been embellished with blood-dripping fangs. Rather than lend the phrase a sense of spooky fun, Martin thought it all looked rather sinister. He looked down at his sheet of tickets. The free ride on The Reptile was in the bottom left hand corner.

"We only have the one ticket," he said with a shrug.

Franklyn tapped the height restriction sign. "I'm afraid the little ones aren't quite grown up enough to enjoy this one yet," he said, "and I imagine you'll be wanting your wife to look after them if you're going to take a spin?"

Martin shook his head. "In that case it's probably best if I don't bother with it at all," he said.

"Oh go on, Daddy," said Oliver. "I want to see the fangs. Rahhhhhhhh!!!!"

"What kind of a ride is it?" Melanie asked.

"Merely a waltzer of the old fashioned variety," said Franklyn, indicating the green-painted merry-go-round, "but with a few little surprises thrown in."

Martin took a closer look at the ride. The whole thing had been painted an unappetising green. Each carriage had room for one, or possibly two at a squeeze. But that wasn't the thing that bothered him.

It was the fact that each carriage was in the shape of a snake's head.

The seat was red, the scarlet plastic presumably intended to emulate the interior of the snake's gaping mouth. The moulded plastic canopy boasted a pair of glaring yellow eyes set into green-black scales. Two huge fangs descended from the canopy to touch the floor, matched only by the pair that curved upwards from the cigarette-burned linoleum to meet the roof. They were obviously the safety bars, but they looked more likely to do harm than protect.

"I suppose it'll be all right," said Martin, trying to keep the uncertainty out of his voice.

"Of course, my dear sir," Franklyn assured him.

"Why isn't there anyone else on it?" Caroline asked.

"It's only just been re-opened," was the reply. "In fact my assistant is just this moment about the ticket booth."

They all turned to see a pretty girl in a slinky emerald dress making her way into the tiny cabin at the front.

"My daughter, you know, and late again," said Franklyn with a slight trace of irritation. "She can be a great burden to me."

"Well I don't fancy going on it by myself," said Martin.

"Oh you won't, my dear chap, you won't! As you can see, there is already a queue beginning to build." They all looked behind them to see that indeed there was. "But as you've been good enough to lend me your time and attention, you get the opportunity to ride in the best seat." Franklyn indicated the chair closest to the entry gate. "Now what do you say? You won't get another chance like this all day. It's always one of our most popular rides."

"Go ON, Daddy!" Oliver was insistent. "I want to see you in the shark's mouth!"

"It's a snake, darling," Caroline patted Oliver's head. "Go on, then," she said to her husband. "We haven't seen anything suitable for the children to ride on yet, so you may as well entertain them by going on this."

With no alternative but to go along with everyone else's wishes, Martin gave a resigned nod. Dr Franklyn lifted up the snake's upper jaw to allow him to sit within the red raw lining of its mouth. Once Martin was comfortable, the fangs were brought down, and locked into place.

"Comfortable?" Franklyn asked. Martin gave him a weak smile in reply. "Good! Now we just have to wait for some more of the cars to fill, and then you'll be on your way."

Martin's family were herded back behind the safety railing as Martin watched others taking their place inside the cars. They were mostly teenagers, although there were a couple of people older than him, so he didn't feel quite as self-conscious as he might have done otherwise.

He looked around the inside of the carriage. The green paint was peeling, revealing what was probably zinc plate beneath.

Except no, it wasn't.

Martin craned his head forward and picked at a tongue of crumbling green enamel to his left. It came to pieces in his fingers. What was revealed looked odd, and certainly not what he would expect the bare bones of a fairground carriage to look like.

It almost looked like...words.

The carriage began to move off as Martin fumbled for his mobile phone. He thumbed a random button to cause the screen to light up, and then held it close to the place he had stripped the paint from.

There *were* words.

Tiny words.

Newsprint.

Martin felt a spasm of concern as the chamber rattled and rocked a little from side to side. He hoped they hadn't done a swift repair job on it by plugging any holes with newspaper.

The carriage rounded a corner as Martin reached out and picked more paint away. This time he revealed enough that he could read whole sentences.

His sentences.

The carriage jerked again as Martin found himself

reading his own article. The last one he had written for that paper. The last headline that policewoman had quoted at him with something approaching disdain in her voice.

The carriage began to turn round.

Martin, not strapped in, reached out with both hands to either side of the carriage to brace himself.

The paint there crumbled and came away, too, revealing more newsprint, more news stories.

All his news stories.

All about the same thing.

The same man.

The carriage was starting to spin, now, faster and faster. Despite his flailing efforts to keep himself steady, Martin found himself being flung from side to side.

The first time he saw blood he thought he must have scratched his hand on a rough piece of metal.

As the carriage slowed he saw the spike that had emerged from the wall on the left. It was only a couple of inches long, but the point was sharp and diamond shaped, designed to create a wound that wouldn't heal well. But that wasn't the worst of it. The skin where the metal had penetrated was swiftly swelling and turning black, the infection or poison or whatever it was spreading over his palm.

Almost as if he had been bitten by a venomous snake.

Martin barely had time to inspect the wound further before the chamber began to spin once more. Martin pushed himself away from the penetrating metal, only to feel something pierce his back from the other side of the carriage. He pulled himself away to see another spike had appeared there as well. Burning agony shot up his spine.

Now more spikes were beginning to appear, from both sides, the back and from the roof as well. The seat on which Martin was sitting was slippery with blood. It was impossible to tell how much because the material was the same colour as what was flowing out of him. His skin was swelling everywhere, now, the flesh turning black and mottled. He felt foam begin to bubble between his lips.

As the carriage began to spin faster and faster and Martin gave up all hope of keeping himself away from the spikes that were still appearing, all he could think of was how horrified his family would be when the jaws of what had become his tomb were finally prised apart.

10

The atmosphere in the incident room in Bristol was decidedly chilly.

Martinus, Graves and Wentworth had arrived back from Cornwall in the early hours of the morning. To say Longdon had been unhappy with what they had to report would have been an understatement. Now they sat with nothing to say while Longdon leaned back on his chair and stared at the map of the British Isles next to the door. A red drawing pin indicated the site of each murder, and a piece of red wool led from each pin to a mini reproduction of the poster for the corresponding Hammer film.

There were now six of them.

"That wall looks more like an advert for a horror film festival than a murder investigation," Longdon growled. He took a gulp of coffee so strong that even he found himself coughing at the bitterness of it. He looked at his three colleagues. "How the hell could the three of you have let Peyton out of your sight?"

"We didn't, sir," said Martinus under his breath.

"What?!" Longdon bellowed, causing the bigger man to physically recoil.

"What he means, sir," said Graves, "is that we were there all the time. In fact we were practically standing behind his family while the ride was going. We couldn't possibly have known that—"

"Of course you could!" Longdon tipped forward on his chair and put the coffee cup on the table. He got up, thrust his hands into his pockets, and began to pace before them. "This is Valentine, remember? A man who seems to be able to do anything, from catapulting someone off a cliff to rigging up an entire fairground to suit his demented purpose." He placed his palms flat on the table and glared at them. "Did none of you recognise him?"

They all shook their heads.

"He didn't look anything like the pictures we were given," said Graves. "But he was very well spoken."

"And what about the girl?" Longdon pointed to the sketch Steve the artist had made at St Paul's. A portrait-sized reproduction was now stuck on the wall next to the Hammer posters.

"Yes sir," said Wentworth. "That was definitely her. But with respect, sir, that picture didn't get transmitted to us until after Mr Peyton's demise, so there's no way we could have identified her."

"I know, I know," Longdon waved his hand in a dismissive gesture. "It just means we've only one more chance to stop him."

"And you better had, Inspector," said Spalding from next to the water cooler. "Because for your information I've already written a nice little exposé about this investigation so far. And if anything happens to me, my lawyers have instructions to deliver it to the highest bidder."

Graves gave Spalding a weary glance. "Why should you be bothered about how much money it sells for if you're dead?" she said.

"Because," said the journalist, "the more it sells for, the more the newspaper concerned will make sure that the story isn't just plastered all over the front page for several incisive, thought-provoking issues, it'll make sure the thing is shouted from the rooftops so everyone knows how incompetent you all are."

"I'll provoke your thoughts in a minute, Mr Spalding," said Longdon. "And I can assure you it won't be with a newspaper."

"Shouldn't you be hard at work trying to apprehend Valentine rather than sitting here thinking up new ways of insulting me?" said Spalding, looking round the room. "In fact, shouldn't all of you?" Before he could say anything else, the reporter grimaced and got carefully to his feet. "If you'll excuse me," he said, clutching his stomach, "I think all these events are beginning to get to me." He began to walk awkwardly towards the door. "By the time I come back I hope you'll have thought of something else to do other than just sit here trading insults and apologies."

Once the door had closed Martinus spoke up.

"Do we have to keep him with us all the time, sir?" he asked. "He's starting to get on my nerves."

The others nodded as Longdon shook his head. "We have to have him under maximum police protection," he said. "You've all seen how skilful Valentine is at murdering people under our very noses. In fact for all we know he could be hiding in the cubicle outside preparing to abduct Spalding as we speak."

The room went very quiet at that. The silence was only broken by the distant sound of a toilet being flushed.

"What *are* we going to do, sir?" said Graves. 'We're still without any useful leads at all. There have been no identifications of that girl, and we've made no progress working out where Valentine might be based."

Longdon regarded the map. "You're right there," he said. "I was hoping the murders might have been centred around one particular area of the country, but they're scattered all over the place."

"What about where he used to live?" said Wentworth.

"You mean the former residence of 'Dr Richard Patterson', the name he hid behind the first time around?" replied Longdon. "That was one of the first things I had checked out. It was bought for a song at an auction held a couple of months after it was clear Valentine wasn't coming back, and if he was it would be to a nice cosy prison cell rather than his mansion in North Somerset."

"Who bought it, sir?" asked Graves.

Longdon looked around him, and then lifted a bulging file off the floor. "I made a note of it in here somewhere," he said, flicking through papers before selecting a tissue-thin yellow sheet. "It would seem the property was sold to an elderly widow by the name of Mrs E Brandt."

"And that's not a Hammer film character, is it?" Graves was already typing the name into a search engine on her tablet.

"I don't think Valentine would do anything quite so obvious," said Longdon. "It's been checked but it wouldn't hurt for you to take another look."

Graves was already shaking her head. "There are too

many entries for Brandt on IMDB," she said. "It could take ages to go through them all."

"Spalding might know," Martinus piped up.

"He might at that." Longdon looked over to the door. "Where the hell is he anyway?"

"Perhaps we should go and check?" Wentworth was already on his feet.

With Longdon in the lead, the four of them made their way down the corridor outside as quietly as possible. They halted when they came to a white door on the left. A black outline indicated it was the gents' toilet.

The door was closed.

Longdon knocked twice, rapid and loud, before speaking even more loudly. "Are you all right in there, Mr Spalding?"

There was no reply.

Longdon tried the door handle. It was locked. He took a step back and aimed his shoulder at the plywood.

"Shouldn't you try once more?" asked Martinus as the door splintered inward.

"Mr Spalding, are you in here?" Longdon bellowed to the empty toilet cubicle before them. He stepped inside and looked around.

"Maybe he went to get something to eat," said Wentworth.

"I don't think so." Longdon was reaching above him to take down a gold-bordered invitation card that had been wedged above the inside of the lintel. "It would appear our Dr Valentine has left us a message this time."

The four of them stared at the seven words that had been written on the card in Prussian blue ink:

At home this evening.

Guests are welcome.

The four police officers arrived at Valentine's Somerset mansion just after sunset. The Victorian country house was in darkness as they got out of the car.

"Are you sure this is where Valentine meant, sir?" Martinus was searching the mullioned windows for a trace of light, but none was forthcoming.

"Of course I am," said Longdon, making sure his special issue firearm was loaded. He had insisted the others be armed as well, and they all looked equally uncomfortable about the possible need for them to wield guns.

"I really don't think he's going to attack us, sir," Graves argued. "And anything he has in store for Spalding is bound to take the form of some complex creation that guns will be useless against."

"They might just convince him to stop whatever he's doing, though," Longdon replied with a snarl. "We're going in with guns, and that's an end to it."

Wentworth turned up the collar of his jacket against the cold breeze that had sprung up. "How can you be so certain this is where he's holding Spalding, sir?" he asked.

"A couple of reasons." Longdon tried the cast iron handle of the front door. It swung open with a creak. "First, if he wanted us to be his guests for the evening then the venue couldn't be that far from Bristol. Second, this is the most likely place for him to want to meet, especially as it probably appeals to his sense of humour to have a final face-off in the place where I met him before. But finally, and the one that really clinches it, the name 'Mrs E Brandt' is in a Hammer Horror film after all. She's a minor character in something called *Frankenstein Must Be Destroyed*, a film that also happens to feature an isolated country house."

"What happens in the film?" asked Wentworth with yet another shiver.

"Oh, apparently Frankenstein saws some chap's head open to try and swap his brain with someone else, but it all goes a bit wrong." Longdon shone his torch into the hallway. "Still," he said, looking behind him at Wentworth, "the house burns to the ground at the end, so if that happens tonight at least it'll warm you up a bit. Right now, though, I'd appreciate it if you would kindly cover my back."

Wentworth followed Longdon into the building, while Martinus and Graves were given instructions to go round the back of the house and find another way in "Just in case we end up strung up by the staircase," Longdon said, with little trace of amusement in his tone. "If you hear us screaming, you come running. Understand?"

Graves and Martinus nodded, drew their weapons, and went off to circumvent the house from the right.

"What's it like being back here, sir?" Wentworth whispered as Longdon flicked a nearby light switch.

"Bloody electricity must have been disconnected," said Longdon as he swiped at the switch once more. The house stayed dark. "Bloody disconcerting is what it is, son," he said, answering Wentworth's question. "Bloody disconcerting." He shone his torch up the broad staircase on the left. "Valentine kept his mummified daughter upstairs," he said. "My colleague Jenny Newham found her body propped in front of a television set showing old Vincent Price films over and over."

Wentworth nodded. "I remember reading about it," he said, looking around the entry hall. "Was the place as bare as this when you were here?"

Longdon shook his head as they inspected the oak-panelled walls. "There were all sorts of trophies and paintings," he said. "But it looks as if they all got sold off in the auction." He indicated a door to his right. "If I remember correctly," he said, "in here was what he liked to call the drawing room."

This door creaked as well, and utter blackness lay beyond it. Unsurprisingly, the light switch for the lounge also failed to work.

"You'd think he'd have made things a bit more welcoming," said Longdon, as he shone his torch ahead of him.

"Perhaps we've got it wrong," whispered Wentworth from behind him. "Perhaps he didn't mean this place after all."

"Rubbish!" Longdon was still certain. "Besides, if I'm wrong, where's Mrs so-called Brandt? Why hasn't she furnished this place rather than leaving it like a tomb after the grave-robbers have been in?"

"You're starting to sound like those old films, sir," said Wentworth with a nervous chuckle.

"I certainly feel as if I'm living in one of them sometimes," Longdon replied.

Then all the lights came on.

The two men shielded their eyes against the harsh glare as, from the speakers that had been positioned all around the room, well-spoken tones that were familiar to Longdon began to address them.

"Good evening, gentlemen," said Valentine. "And in particular, may I say how pleasant it is to see you again, Inspector Longdon. I must confess I rather hoped we had not seen the last of each other. How strange to be talking to you once again within the walls of my old home."

Longdon took his hand from his face as the lights dimmed a little to reveal their source – four floodlights set up on gantries positioned to the left and right of the far side of the room.

"Is that better?" Valentine said. "I must apologise. It was not my intention to dazzle you to such an extent. At least, not with mere stage lights."

"As opposed to your searing intellectual genius?" Longdon shouted into the void above them created by the glare. "I'm not sure what you're hoping to prove, Valentine, but my advice is for you to give up now. The house is surrounded."

There was a chuckle at that. "I hope you'll forgive me, Inspector," he said, "but I believe I've heard that line somewhere before. And it didn't do you or your sergeant much good last time, did it? Now forget about barking whatever you believe will pass for your next pithy witticism and please pay attention to what, or rather who, is in front of you."

Longdon followed Wentworth's horrified gaze to the man sitting in between the spotlights at the far end of the room. For a moment he almost didn't recognise that it was Spalding. This was partly because "sitting" wasn't an entirely accurate way of describing how the man had been secured there. His wrists and ankles had been attached to the stout metal supports by thick clasps. Another broad band of shining steel ran around his waist to keep him upright. But the most intricate method of restraint had been reserved for Spalding's head and neck. A stout leather brace around his throat prevented him from lowering or raising his chin. The cushioned rubber ends of rigid steel supports had been placed tight up against each cheek, so any movement of the head from side to side was an impossibility.

But the thing Longdon was most concerned about was the drill that had been placed perpendicular to the apex of Spalding's shaved skull. There was a gap of about three inches between the pointed tip of the heavy drill bit, and Spalding's recently scraped scalp, which still bore tiny traces of fresh blood where the razor had nicked the skin.

"I'm looking, Valentine," said Longdon. "What am I supposed to do now?"

"Oh nothing, Inspector," said the voice. "By which I mean if you do anything at all, even move, in fact *especially* move, it will spell the downfall for poor old Mr Spalding."

"What do you mean?" Longdon was about to take a step back when Wentworth stopped him and pointed at the floor.

Which was now laced with a spiderweb of fine metal strands that glinted in the glare of the spotlights. But only if you looked at them at just the right angle.

"Any movement of the fibres will start the drill," said Valentine. "And the more fibres that are broken, the faster the drill will spin."

"What bloody Hammer film is that in, then?" said Longdon, now shouting at the ceiling again.

"It's not," said Valentine. "But the man before you awaiting some rather blunt Victorian-style brain surgery is certainly from one. I'm sure I don't have to help you with it, Inspector. It's exactly what you're thinking."

"What?" Longdon looked confused and almost took a step forward before his colleague stopped him again.

"*Frankenstein Must Be Destroyed.*" The muffled words from between Spalding's compressed lips were just sufficiently intelligible, even to the ears of the gruesome scene's offstage creator, who responded with another low chuckle.

"Indeed!" Valentine said. "But I very much suspect it is I whom Inspector Longdon would like to see destroyed at this very moment."

"You'd be bloody right about that," Longdon growled. He lifted a foot, one of the wires went twang, and the drill started turning.

"Oh dear, Inspector," said Valentine. "I do believe you've put Mr Spalding one step closer to a nasty death. A very nasty death indeed."

"This isn't a very Hammer way to end it all, Valentine," said Longdon. "I'd have thought you'd want to finish this little series of murders with more than a few pieces of clanking metal."

"Oh, this is not the end, Inspector," came the reply. "Not for you, and certainly not for me. But I wanted to see you tonight to tell you that by now you should hopefully have worked out where our final showdown should be. If not, then I'll ask you to think once again about Mr Peyton's death. If that doesn't help, then go back to your source material. For now, however, I agree with you. This scene isn't quite typical of the Hammer horrors I have been taking such pains to try and reproduce. I'm sure you know what's missing, as well."

There was the sound of an electrical circuit being completed, and the curtains to the left of the window burst into flame.

"Enjoy trying to save yourselves, Inspector," Valentine was laughing now. "To say nothing of our journalist friend. And if you do make it out of here alive, have fun working out where to come looking for me."

As Spalding struggled against the steel restraints the flames spread along the floor and made contact with the cables running up to the left bank of floodlights. There was a hiss as the plastic insulation melted, and then a loud bang from the left lighting gantry. Tiny fragments of burning glass and metal peppered Spalding, making his struggles all the more frantic.

"You can't, sir!" screamed Wentworth as Longdon made to lunge forward. Another metal thread broke and the drill began to descend towards Spalding's skull.

"Well, what are we supposed to do?" Longdon shouted in return. "Just stand here and watch him die?"

There was no response from above them. Valentine was already making good his escape.

"That's obviously what we are bloody well are supposed to do," Longdon added, shielding his brow from the heat with his left arm while he stared at the intricate criss-cross pattern of metal, now glowing orange from the reflected flames. His concentration was interrupted by a crash from ahead of him.

The window panes to the right had exploded inward, and the faces of Graves and Martinus were now poking through.

"Don't come in here!" Longdon shouted. "You'll kill him!"

But it was already too late. The flames, drawn towards the fresh air, ignited the right hand lighting gantry. As Spalding continued to pull helplessly at his bonds, the lights exploded and the metal framework fell forwards, straight into the mesh of tripwires.

The moment he saw where the gantry was headed, Longdon lunged forward. But by the time he got there, the drill was firmly lodged in Spalding's skull. Spalding, meanwhile, had ceased to care.

12

"He said I would know where it would all end."

Longdon stared at the map. The faces of seven dead journalists stared back, their photographs pinned next to the posters for the movies that had inspired their deaths.

"It has ended, hasn't it?" Martinus was being even more tentative than usual, even though Longdon seemed to have lost his fire since Spalding's death the night before. "I mean, there's no-one else for Valentine to kill."

Longdon ran a weary hand over his face. "I know that," he said, "in the same way I know that if our good doctor hinted that he isn't finished, then he isn't finished."

DI Graves handed him a fresh cup of coffee. "Sir." She was having a hard time finding words this evening as well. "Have you considered that if you do manage to work out where he wants to you go that it might be..."

"...a trap?" Longdon regarded her with bleary eyes. "It's all I have been thinking about, DI Graves, believe you me."

The door creaked open and Wentworth pushed his way in, holding a cardboard box out in front of him. He dropped it onto a nearby table.

"Those are all the Hammer films I could get hold of on DVD," he said with a sigh. "I had no idea there were so many of them."

"Christ, neither did I." Longdon looked at the

widescreen television that had been set up in the far corner. From his expression, watching anything on it was the last thing he wanted to do.

"Okay," he said eventually, getting to his feet. "We'll do it in shifts. Eight hours each, and in pairs in case one of us misses anything." He rummaged in the box and pulled out a disc. "I feel a bit like I'm running the lucky dip at the local fair," he said. His colleagues stayed quiet. "Yes you're quite right," he added. "That wasn't funny at all." He looked at the garish picture of a woman with snake's eyes and fangs poised to leap off the cover. "He said to think about the death of Martin Peyton, so who fancies watching *The Reptile* with me?"

Martinus jerked a thumb towards the map. "Is there any point, sir? He's already used that for a murder."

Longdon put a hand on his shoulder. "All the more reason for watching it and paying close attention then, DI Martinus," he said, "and thank you for volunteering. Valentine said we'd know where it would end so maybe the clue is in one of the films he's already used as inspiration. We should be able to get through at least five of them before Graves and Wentworth take over."

Longdon urged the other two out the door, with instructions that they were to "read a book, get pissed, take sleeping tablets, whatever" as long as they got some sleep.

"I'll expect you back here at 7am sharp," he said. "And if DI Martinus and I have nodded off, you'll have the pleasure of our company as we watch what we've missed again."

Once Graves and Wentworth had gone, Longdon

scraped two chairs into place. "Come on then, detective!" he said when he saw Martinus hesitate. "I'm afraid we haven't got a sofa we can cuddle up on, so it's going to have to be the Avon & Somerset Constabulary's finest moulded plastic for our viewing pleasure. At least it'll keep you awake."

Martinus gave a shrug and took the chair on the left as Longdon loaded *The Reptile* into the machine and pressed 'play'. Just over ninety minutes later, the crashing music that heralded the titles of *Dracula Has Risen from the Grave* served to wake them up. *Blood from the Mummy's Tomb*, however, had them both nodding off in front of the flickering screen. As the end credits rolled on Valerie Leon's bandaged form reaching out for help, Longdon got up and switched the lights on.

"What's the time?" he asked.

Martinus looked at his watch. "3.45am, sir." He yawned. "Which one do you want to watch next?"

"Bloody none of them." Longdon shook his head in exasperation and looked at the notes he had been taking. "None of the films we've watched have had anything in common, except that the villain dies in the end."

Martinus still had his eyes half closed against the brightness of the fluorescent lighting. "Could that be what Valentine means, sir? That he's going to perform some kind of flamboyant act of suicide?"

Longdon shook his head. "That's not his style," he replied. He punched the carton of DVDs. "I'm convinced it's got something to do with these buggers."

Martinus rubbed his eyes but still couldn't open them more than a crack. "Perhaps we're barking up the wrong tree?" he said. "Maybe we need to watch some that Valentine hasn't tried to recreate yet?"

Longdon nodded. "You might be right," he said. He picked a film at random and held it up. "How about *Slave Girls*?" he said with a tired smile.

Martinus returned his grin. "Could be just the ticket for this time of the morning, sir," he said.

Longdon was already studying the synopsis. "Apparently this one's set in the jungle," he said. "So unless Dr Valentine plans on carting us all off to the back of beyond, I think we can safely give it a miss." He tossed it into the corner. A minute later *The Viking Queen* followed it, as did *The Pirates of Blood River*. "We're not going to Hong Kong either," said Longdon, as he put *The Legend of the Seven Golden Vampires* with the others.

Next was *Plague of the Zombies* which, no matter how hard he tried to find a reason for it, Longdon couldn't reject. Into the DVD player it went and *Crash Bang Boom* went the opening title music.

"At least they do their best to wake you up at the start of these things," said Martinus as he did his best to sit a little more upright.

"Probably to get all those 1960s kids to sit down, shut up and watch," said Longdon, taking his seat.

They were about fifteen minutes in when Martinus tapped Longdon on the shoulder.

"We've seen all this before," he said.

Longdon rubbed his eyes. "No we haven't," the inspector replied. "I made sure to put the ones we've seen on a separate pile."

Martinus shook his head. "I don't mean that, sir. I

mean we've seen this village before. In that first film we watched." Now there was a scene of the place where the villain lived. "And that house." Martinus was pointing now. "That house was in the other one as well."

"Good work, detective," said Longdon, getting out a notepad. "Maybe we are onto something after all."

The old tin mine was burning and the credits were rolling as Longdon levered himself off his seat and over to an adjacent computer terminal. With weary fingers he typed in a search for the locations of the two films.

"All shot on the same sets, apparently," he said as he peered at the screen. "And the house is somewhere called Oakley Court." He typed that in too. "It's certainly been used in a few films over the years. And it was at the end of *The Reptile*. Could that be what Valentine meant?"

There was a snoring from the other side of the room. Longdon looked at the clock. That was probably enough for one night, anyway. On a hunch he typed in 'Oakley Court events', added the month, and hit return. There were the usual wine tastings and musical tributes, and no doubt on the weekends there would be a few weddings as well. In fact something called the 'Wedded Bliss' organisation was having a conference there in five days' time. Longdon scrolled down to the relevant section and read it more closely. According to the information posted, the head of the agency, a 'Very Reverend Dr Bliss' would be revealing to select members of the press how he had founded the organisation and allowed for so many to meet with "that for which they were always intended".

"That's far too bloody fishy," said Longdon to himself.

He typed in "Dr Bliss" and was rewarded with a picture of the actor Peter Cushing in clerical garb.

"'From the film *Captain Clegg*'," Longdon read. "Otherwise known as *Night Creatures* and made in 1961 by..." Longdon was off his chair and shaking Martinus awake in a second.

"Up you get," he said, his eyes burning with the intensity of a zealot. "We've got a lot of work to do when the others get here."

"What?" Martinus almost fell off his chair as he struggled to wake. "Have you found something?"

Longdon nodded. "Too bloody right I have, and I have to say I'm more than a little fed up with being one step behind all the time." He pointed at the box of DVDs. "We're going to beat Valentine at his own game."

13

"They're ready."

Christina turned away from peeking through the crack in the heavy curtains. Beyond them lay the room in which the more than thirty guests had been assembled.

Valentine checked his reflection and picked up his black cloak.

"If you're debating whether or not to wear it," she said, "you should. They're going to want to take photographs."

Valentine nodded and shrugged it on over his black suit. "It's only appropriate, really," he said. "And I would hate to disappoint my public."

He seemed ready to go. Just as he was about to step through into the other room Christina stopped him.

"Are you sure this is what you want to do?" she said.

Valentine nodded. "If my story must be told, I would rather it was I who did the telling," he said. "Otherwise the same thing will just happen all over again, and we both have better things to do with our lives than spend them killing journalists." He took her hand in his own. "Is everything prepared?"

Christina nodded.

He looked her in the eye. "You don't have to do this with me, you know. I'm grateful to you for having come this far. I would understand if you wished to leave at this point and continue with your own life."

Christina returned his look. "This has become my life," she said, "and whether or not what we have done is for the good, I know that if I had not met you my life would have been nowhere near as worth living. I thank you for that."

Valentine smiled. "I imagine I'm never going to learn exactly why I found you in the state you were in all those months ago," he said.

"Maybe some time," the girl replied. "But not now. Now it's time to stop all this sentimental nonsense." A mischievous gleam appeared in her eye. "You have an audience awaiting you, doctor, an audience keen to hear from the lips of Dr Valentine himself his quite remarkable story."

"Indeed." Valentine smiled. "And provided our Inspector Longdon has done his homework, this should provide a most satisfying climax to it all." He reached for the curtain, and drew it aside with a flourish.

The room had been arranged so that Valentine would enter from the back. As he strode down the central aisle the assembled individuals quietened, and by the time he had reached the lectern at the front the room was silent. He gripped either side of the polished wood, took a deep breath, and began to address them.

"Ladies and gentlemen," he said. "May I first of all thank each and every one of you for coming here today. I'm sure you will agree with me that Oakley Court Hotel is one of the most pleasant venues one could wish for in which to hold what is essentially a press conference."

There were murmurs of agreement at this.

"Sad to say," Valentine continued, "I believe the

owners are thinking of selling it, and that would be a great shame. However, today they have done me the gracious gesture of allowing me to hire the entire main building. Just to ensure that we are not disturbed." He gestured to his right. Through the French windows the nearby river glittered through the net curtains. "So let us enjoy the peaceful atmosphere of this place while we can," he said. "The grounds are beautiful, and the Thames has never looked so inviting. In fact I may take a little trip on it later on myself."

There were a few chuckles at that as the atmosphere in the room began to relax.

"But now to business." Valentine looked out over the room, checking the time on the heavy clock hanging on the back wall as he did so. "I have no doubt that the police will be here soon, and I want you members of the press to hear my story before they arrive. You are journalists I have specially selected and whom I trust to report the account I am about to give you accurately and faithfully. I am sure you will not let me down."

There was a flurry of opening of notebooks and switching on of recording devices. Then the room went quiet again.

"I suppose the best place to start would be in Bristol, two years ago," said Valentine. "I had just managed to drag the body of Andrew Wells, Consultant in Accident and Emergency, to the Clifton Suspension Bridge. I had debated whether or not to dress him in the gorilla suit when I got there, but eventually decided it would be better if I encouraged him to put it on himself before I knocked him out."

Valentine was about to continue when a voice stopped him.

"That's enough, Dr Valentine."

DCI Jeffrey Longdon appeared from between the curtains at the back. He pointed a revolver at the man who had just stopped speaking. "If you'd be kind enough to come quietly with me, sir. We don't want a scene, now do we?"

Instead of looking upset Valentine gave the policeman a broad grin. "Why Inspector! How lovely to see you! Even if it is a little before time. Did your mother never tell you that punctuality is the politeness of princes?"

Longdon was unfazed. "No sir, she was too busy showing me how to put the boot in the groin of the kids who were trying to bully me at school."

Valentine raised his eyebrows. "Really?"

"No," came the reply. "Now, are you going to come quietly or not?"

The doctor raised his arms. "But I can't possibly leave now, Inspector," he said. "Not with all the press here. They're waiting to hear my story, you see."

"Your story?"

Valentine nodded.

"You mean the one about how you've just killed seven of them in the style of the deaths in Hammer horror films?"

"I was certainly going to touch on it, Inspector," said Valentine. "Along with how I was sorely misrepresented by those particular individuals."

"Sorely misrepresented in how you killed all those

doctors before you went and killed all those journalists, you mean?" Longdon was edging forward.

"Well, if you must put it so crudely, Inspector, yes."

Longdon was halfway down the aisle now. "And might it not have occurred to you, Dr Edward Valentine, that any journalist invited to a press conference like this might decide to do something other than accept their invitation? That they might instead run a country mile in the opposite direction, possibly informing the police of their intentions as they did so?"

"That thought had crossed my mind, Inspector." Valentine was moving back from the lectern now.

Longdon kept his gun trained on him. "Tell me," Longdon said, "how much research did you do before you started killing all those reporters?"

"What do you mean, research?" Valentine was against the back wall now, and there was nowhere for him to go.

"I mean," said Longdon as he approached the lectern, "how many Hammer films did you watch?"

Valentine chuckled. "Since you asked, Inspector, most of them. I rather hope that you have since done the same."

Longdon nodded. "Oh I have, sir, I have. Even stuff like *Straight On Till Morning*."

Valentine wrinkled his nose. "A pretentious thriller written by someone with art house aspirations, but lacking the talent to achieve them."

"I wouldn't know, sir," Longdon replied. "I fell asleep during that one. I stayed awake during the others, though. The old black and white psycho thrillers for example. There were some classics amongst that lot."

Valentine smiled. "Ah, yes," he said. "*Scream of Fear, Paranoiac*..."

"...and *Nightmare*." Longdon narrowed his eyes. "Do you remember the plot of *Nightmare*, sir?"

"One of many in which people try to drive a young lady mad," said Valentine. "Not especially memorable."

"Perhaps not, sir," said Longdon. "Although the way in which they tried to drive her mad did fascinate me. It's actually someone with a mask on, isn't it? A very realistic-looking mask."

Longdon raised his left hand, and as one the collected members of the press removed their remarkably life-like masks to reveal thirty members of the Metropolitan police force's finest.

Longdon gave Valentine a steely look.

"You are surrounded, sir," he said. "I suggest you give yourself up. I do hope, however, that you appreciate our little gesture to your own modus operandi."

Valentine was smiling now as he edged to the corner of the room. "Indeed I do, Inspector," he said, "just as I hope you will appreciate this."

Valentine unhooked the stout rope he had arrived at. Immediately a heavy net fell from the ceiling, trapping the police officers.

"From *Curse of the Mummy's Tomb*, Inspector," Valentine said as he ran for the exit.

Longdon swore and gave chase.

Valentine crashed through the lounge, leaping over chairs and avoiding tables. Police officers had been stationed at the main entrance and so Valentine swerved to the left and ran up the main staircase, taking the steps two at a time, his cloak billowing out behind him.

Longdon was in hot pursuit. He stopped the officers as they made to follow.

"He can't go anywhere," he shouted back to them as he ran up the stairs. "Just make sure all the exits are covered, and instruct back up teams two, three and four to do exactly what I told them."

Longdon caught up with Valentine on the first floor landing. It ran the length of the building. Longdon was at the near end, Valentine at the far.

"Very impressive, Inspector," said Valentine, panting a little. "You know, I was rather hoping for something like this. A more suitable ending to our little tale than you carting me off in the back of a police car."

"Oh I intend to do that too, sir," said Longdon, glancing behind him at the floor-length curtains that had been drawn across the first floor windows. "But first of all I intend to do this."

With that Longdon charged towards the curtains, and pulled them down.

Blinding white light filled the landing from the bank of floodlights that had been erected behind the glass.

Valentine shielded his eyes and took a step back, almost tripping over his cloak as he did so. Just as Longdon was almost upon him Valentine grabbed a heavy candelabra and heaved it in Longdon's direction. The policeman ducked just in time, and when he looked up again Valentine was taking the next flight of stairs.

Longdon arrived on the second floor just in time to see Valentine disappear through a door marked 'Staff Only'.

It led to a poorly lit flight of concrete steps, again leading upward. Longdon clattered after Valentine as the doctor opened a service door at the top that led onto the roof.

Despite the sunshine there was a distinct chill to the air as Longdon pursued Valentine past chimneys and over ventilation ducts. Finally, there was nowhere to run.

"Come on, Valentine," said a breathless Longdon as his quarry edged toward the end of the building. "You've had your fun. It's time for this particular story to end."

"What?" Valentine looked disappointed. "Don't you have anything else, lurking out there in the grounds, Inspector? A horde of bats at your command to destroy me? A strategically placed windmill whose shadow will somehow overcome me? Aren't you even going to just try and bonk me on the head with a rock?" He looked over the edge of the building to the lawns below and frowned. The grounds were covered with mist.

"Fog canisters," said Longdon. "I thought you'd appreciate that. Of course it means even if you did make your way down you wouldn't have a hope of finding your way out of here. All my men down there are wearing gas masks. Gets in the throat, you see. Makes you cough and then probably makes you cry, too – as good as any tear gas."

Valentine nodded. As he moved slightly to the left he raised his hands and applauded. "Excellent, Inspector. I have to say I'm actually touched that you went to all this trouble."

"You've killed sixteen people, Valentine. Let me assure you that it's worth all the trouble and expense."

Valentine looked over again.

"Only if you catch me, Inspector," he said, with a grin. "It looks like it's almost as windy down there as up here. It shouldn't be too long before all your tear gas is blown away."

"There's still nowhere for you to go, Valentine." Longdon took a step forward and wielded his revolver. "I suggest you give up now. I won't hesitate to use this if I have to."

Valentine look horrified. "You wouldn't shoot a man in cold blood, would you, Inspector?"

Longdon aimed the pistol at Valentine's left leg. "You are a highly dangerous criminal, sir. All I would be doing is incapacitating you in order to make an arrest."

Valentine seemed to give that some consideration. "I suppose you have a point there, Inspector," he said. "In which case all there remains for me to say is that I really have had the most tremendous time here, and that I must thank you for all the effort you have gone to. But now it's time for me to bid you farewell."

Dr Edward Valentine raised his right hand, smiled, waved, and took a step backwards.

Straight off the building.

"Oh, shit." Longdon peered over the edge to see, through the thinning fog, the crumpled body of Valentine on the grass below.

A female police officer was already running towards him.

"Keep your distance!" Longdon shouted down. "And don't let him out of your sight!" He took out his radio to speak to Martinus. "Get an ambulance here pronto," he said, "and make sure it really is one."

"What do you mean, sir?" said the voice on the other end.

"I mean," said Longdon as he made his way back across the roof, "make sure they've got ID and that the driver is who they say they are. I don't care how many pieces Valentine might be in at the moment, he's not getting away from us this time."

By the time Longdon had made it to the front of the hotel he could already hear sirens.

"That's a bit bloody early," he said to himself, as he rounded the building to where Valentine had fallen.

The body was gone.

Wentworth, Graves and Martinus were still staring in disbelief at the spot. Martinus was on his radio to the police cars that were already in the process of cordoning off the area.

"Don't tell me," said Longdon as he approached, "you didn't check the ambulance ID."

"The ambulance hasn't got here yet," said Wentworth. "And by the time we did he'd gone."

Longdon looked at the soft Valentine-shaped depression in the grass. "What about the officer who was first on the scene?" he asked.

Graves gave him a querulous look. "We were the first on the scene, sir," she said.

Longdon shook his head. "No, no, no," he said. "There was another officer, a girl, who came running across as soon as Valentine fell. About medium height, dark hair, wearing a uniform."

Wentworth looked at his colleagues, who both gave him the same embarrassed look. "We haven't got any uniformed officers on this one, sir. They're all plainclothes."

Behind Longdon, on the Thames, a cortege of a funeral barge and two accompanying black boats was slowly making its way past the building. Meanwhile he was kicking at the ground in frustration.

"I cannot bloody believe he's got away again," he said, looking for something, or someone, to punch.

"Sir, that ground doesn't look right."

Longdon looked down to the patch of ground at which Martinus was pointing. The patch where Valentine had fallen. The patch he had just kicked.

The patch that had broken away a little, revealing the cushioned surface beneath.

Longdon crouched down and tore at the corner of the artificial grass. Then he prodded a finger into what was under it. "Sponge," he said, getting to his feet. "Bloody sponge." He looked at the others. "He knew. Valentine knew. All the time I thought we had the upper hand, that we'd managed to surprise him, and that bastard knew what we were doing every step of the way. Well, I hope his bloody bruises don't heal for a month."

"There's something else there as well, sir." Graves crouched down and pushed the green plastic cover out of the way. In the far corner was something white. She plucked it out and handed it to Longdon.

"Probably a farewell note," said Longdon as he began to unfold it. "Have you made sure all the road blocks are in place?"

Martinus nodded as Longdon read what was on the note. "All being sorted now sir," he replied. "Don't worry – he won't get far."

The funeral barge was beginning to disappear around a bend in the river as Longdon's face turned purple.

"What's the matter, sir?" asked Wentworth.

"What does it say?" asked Graves.

Longdon showed them what was written on the paper.

Don't Look Now, Inspector

As the four of them turned to face the river, the air was suddenly filled with music. Fireworks erupted from the front of the cortege as a dark figure emerged from the funeral barge, stood on the deck, and waved at them.

"Shall I send the men after him, sir?" said Martinus.

"No," said Longdon resignedly, "he's probably got a private jet waiting round the corner to fly him somewhere far, far away."

"Maybe it's not him, sir," said Graves, "and if it is, at least he won't be coming back."

That did little to lighten her DCI's mood. He raised a hand and pointed in the direction of the now vanished cortege.

"That's Valentine, all right," he said. "And he always comes back."

Longdon later put it down to his imagination, but right then he was sure that behind all the noise and the music and the showmanship, he could also detect the faintest sound of laughter.

The End

The Hammer Films
of Dr Valentine

If you have just finished *The Hammer of Dr Valentine* (and what are you doing here if you haven't? Go back and read the book now. You'll enjoy both it, and this bit, more if you do) I'm sure you'll appreciate that, amongst other things, it's a love letter to Hammer Films, a company that produced so many memorable and entertaining pictures that helped to make my childhood a lot more special than it would have been otherwise.

At the end of the special edition of *The Nine Deaths of Dr Valentine*, there was an appendix that provided my thoughts on the films referenced in the text, along with the usual collection of autobiographical reminiscences that I like to include at the end of my books. What follows, therefore, is not intended as a critical analysis of some of my favourite Hammer films. Rather, it is merely meant to provide an insight into the creative process that resulted in the book you now hold in your hands. As well as that, I hope it provides you with a window onto the life of a ten year old boy who, having discovered the treasure trove of fantasy that was British horror cinema, has remained spellbound and entertained by it ever since. It's impossible for me to describe just how important the films of Hammer were to me when I was growing up (and the films of Amicus, Tigon, Titan, Glendale and all the other companies that existed at the time, even if it was only to produce one or two movies before vanishing) but

I hope the following notes give you, the reader, some idea.

Dracula Has Risen from the Grave (1968)

This must have been one of the first Hammer films I ever saw – in ATV's 'Christopher Lee - Prince of Menace' Friday night film season back in the late 1970s. It's the third of the Draculas to star Christopher Lee, and features all kinds of things guaranteed to please thrill-hungry late 1960s audiences. Apart from the climactic impaling that inspires Dr Valentine in this story, my favourite moment has to be the apparently heretical scene where Dracula, having been staked, proceeds to wrench the bloody piece of wood from his chest because the atheist hero doesn't know how to pray. In hindsight it's a bit ridiculous, but to my wide-eyed ten year old self it was a stunning and unexpected highlight of the picture. In fact I'd go so far as to call it Hammer's Italian moment – it doesn't really make any sense at all, but it must have had audiences wide-eyed in disbelief and shock in cinemas in 1968. Out of all the Dracula films Hammer made, this was the most successful. Some think it was because of its female stars (I'm sure Hammer boss James Carreras did, and it was even retitled 'Dracula et les Femmes' in France). I like to think it was because of the film's many over the top moments. The first victim is found trussed up in a bell inside a church, with that lovely effect of blood running down the rope. No-one seems to question that Dracula hadn't actually been brought back to life yet. When he is, it's because of blood unconvincingly trickling all the way from priest Ewan Hooper's gashed head into Dracula's mouth as he lies beneath some extremely thin ice on a mountain slope. A moment later and Dracula's up and about, reflected (Shock! Horror! Heresy!) in the icy mountain stream, and busy bending the fairly hopeless (and very dubbed) Ewan to his will. After this Dracula decides that, rather than vampirise the local female populace (who would all no doubt resemble 1960s busty British starlets on the make) he would rather get his revenge on the Monsignor (Rupert Davies) who has locked him out of his castle. If I was Dracula I'd have got Ewan to shift that cross and then gone looking for Jacqueline Pearce or Barbara Shelley (again), but instead we end up meeting beery Barry Andrews who's in love with blonde busty Veronica Carlson. Before you can say "Dracula's not actually in this very much, is he?" Mr Lee is hissing, acting menacing, and saying very little. But never mind, there's a fun chase across rooftops, via horse and carriage, and finally that climactic battle that results in Dracula getting flung off a cliff and onto the handily pre-positioned crucifix. Mr Lee thrashes around very effectively, thank you very much, before dissolving in a puddle of goo. Roll credits to James Bernard's theme, in a major key for a change.

I must admit I've seen *Dracula Has Risen from the Grave* many times and writing this makes me want to watch it again. It doesn't make a lot of sense and it doesn't even feature Dracula that much, but it's Hammer Films at the company's pinnacle of success. Thrilling, gory, sexy, colourful, crazy, over the top, beautifully designed, gorgeously photographed and bombastically scored. Heaving bosoms, hissing Dracula and hysterically over the top at points, if you stopped people in the street when I was growing up and mentioned Hammer to them, this is what it meant.

Blood from the Mummy's Tomb (1971)

While Hammer managed to do a number of interesting things with Dracula and Frankenstein, it wasn't until their fourth mummy picture that they managed to do something truly original with this particular classic movie monster. Shot in red brick environs in the middle of an early 1970s winter, can you think of any other successful mummy picture that has a contemporary setting? Good old Hammer. Only at the height of their powers could they take a minor Bram Stoker novel, fill it with slashed throats, a crawling severed hand (what exactly was the point of that, by the way?) and a sexy leading lady, and just by accident produce an original and satisfying spin on the mummy theme that still works over forty years on.

Valerie Leon is Margaret, daughter to Andrew Keir's Professor Fuchs, an Egyptologist of distinctly dodgy inclination, who seems to have half a rebuilt tomb in the basement of his ordinary-looking suburban house, a whole load of Egyptian artefacts, and a number of colleagues who want nothing more to do with him after some escapade abroad many years ago, which culminated in their breaking into the tomb of Queen

Tera (Leon again). Tera, by all accounts, was a pretty naughty piece of work (well, she was definitely pretty, and sadly we don't get to find out how naughty she was capable of being). What's far more worrying is that the professor seems to have some poorly researched and badly thought out plan that involves the life of his daughter and the supplanting of her existence by said evil queen on the occasion of her next birthday.

Even more dodgy but better organised Corbeck (James Villiers) is keen to see Tera rise again for his own ends, and he aims to assist the queen in reclaiming the artifacts needed to complete the ceremony. George Coulouris is locked up in one of the best Hammer loony bins and, in a superbly edited and shot bit of mayhem, ends up dead and his snake statue gone. Hugh Burden has a heart attack and has his jackal skull stolen, and fortune teller Rosalie Crutchley gets her cat pinched while her companion (labelled 'Saturnine Man' in the credits) looks on. It's all for nothing of course as the surviving cast members succumb to another what-shall-we-do-to-end-it-oh-let's-have-the-roof-fall-in Hammer climax, with either Margaret or Tera ending up being mummified for real in a closing shot that's possibly the best one in a film that's really rather good all the way through.

With a title that means nothing other than that James Carreras had learned to copy Tony Tenser's approach to titling films by reaching into a box of cards labelled with 'horror' words until the right combination came up, a director who died before filming finished, a star who left once filming had started, and a script by a writer who was both banned from the set and notorious for screenplays that were a bit difficult to make any sense of sometimes, it's a wonder that *Blood From the Mummy's Tomb* is any good at all. What's more surprising than that is that it's actually well worth watching, and is easily the best (along with the 1959 *The Mummy*) of the films Hammer made that had a connection to ancient Egypt. It's rare that the fourth movie in any horror film cycle has anything to commend it, and following in the wake of *Curse of the Mummy's Tomb* and *The Mummy's Shroud* one could be forgiven for expecting Hammer's Mummy IV to be a right load of derivative old rubbish. Instead it's original, well directed, and being shot in what looks like the depths of winter only serves to heighten the creepy atmosphere that pervades the movie right up to that classic final shot. That image scared me silly, by the way, when I watched this on its 'First Showing on British Television' (the Radio Times always told you if a movie was a premiere in those days) as the second half of a BBC2 double bill. Which if course is why it's here as the second of Dr Valentine's Hammer-inspired deaths.

The acting is fine throughout, with the usual collection of British character actors and eccentrics (Aubrey Morris take a bow you lovable weirdo, you) and Valerie Leon, having been used as decorative set dressing in a number of Carry Ons, getting the role that she was born to play. Hammer didn't always get their casting right but she is uncannily perfect for the roles of both Tera and Margaret. Fine stuff all round, *Blood from the Mummy's Tomb* is a Hammer film that's definitely worth preserving. A personal favourite.

Fear in the Night (1971)

I well remember watching this for the first time. I had just got out of hospital having suffered a particularly nasty case of appendicitis. The extent of the peritonitis I had suffered as a consequence of the organ's rupture was entirely my own fault. At the tender age of eleven I refused to be taken to hospital, and even pretended I was recovering from the appalling abdominal pain from which I had been suffering, solely so I could stay up to watch Peter Cushing star in *Corruption* (1967). Seeing as the film was never shown on television again, and didn't surface on DVD uncut until this year, I have to stay I still feel justified in having watched Sir John Rowan hack a prostitute's head off while I clutched at my own abdomen and wished that the awful pain in my right iliac fossa would go away.

But enough of my medical history. The next week I was back at home and sitting in the armchair, some heavy silk sutures holding my right sided gridiron incision together, as I settled down to watch the next in ATV's Peter Cushing season. *Fear in the Night* was the last gasp of the Hammer psycho thriller. I don't really count the pretty dire *Straight On Till Morning*, as that's a different kettle of fish altogether, one that I like to call dull, pretentious, and failed. *Fear in the Night* is the hoary old plot of trying to drive some poor young girl mad and get her to think events are not at all as they seem. Pretty Judy Geeson marries Ralph Bates and goes to live with him at an isolated public school run by Michael Carmichael and his prosthetic arm (Cushing in tiny spectacles) and his wife Molly and her twelve bore shotgun (Joan Collins, doing her usual black widow routine even though her husband is still alive – for the moment anyway). The school is entirely bereft of pupils but the empty classrooms have tape recordings installed so mad Mr Carmichael can relive the glory days when he was still allowed near children.

The Hammer of Dr Valentine was originally going to open with someone being chased down empty school corridors while children's voices screamed at them through loudspeakers. I liked the idea so much I thought it deserved more space than I was intending the opening chapter to have. So it got pushed further into the book and also allowed me to have a lot of fun trying to remember all those noun declensions and verb conjugations from my own school classics lessons.

She (1965)

I didn't want every death in the book to be from a Hammer Dracula, Frankenstein or Mummy picture. Similarly I didn't want to include too many obscure films that people might not know about. Having someone chased by stop-motion dinosaurs and girls in fur bikinis was an appealing prospect, but the book wasn't going to be called *The Hammer Acid Trip of Dr Valentine*, so I reigned in any ambitions for some more bizarre Hammer homages. Besides, at this point I was still contemplating a *Slave Girls* chapter, where someone was going to get skewered on a giant white rhino horn while a room full of

Martine Beswick and Edina Ronay lookalikes swayed and gyrated while wearing very little. Sometimes people ask me why I write and I hope that's helped provide an answer.

Anyway, having dispensed with a room full of Edinas, I thought epic Hammer would do very nicely. Plus, the climactic scene of *She*, where Ursula Andress turns into an old hag and then falls to bits before a horrified John Richardson's eyes, was one of my first memories of being terrified to the point of running out of my parents' lounge. I think it must have been a Saturday afternoon BBC2 screening, and I must have been about five. Lots of horror writers have fears about peculiar things. One of mine is old ladies, for reasons I won't go into too much here, but I'm sure *She* didn't help things.

So I had to have a lady dissolve, because for me that's the whole essence of the film. The rest was working out how to do it. I also hope that this chapter, with Dr Valentine as a cosmetics expert, will hopefully have those familiar with the first volume thinking nostalgically of Vincent Price's turn as 'Butch' in my favourite film of all time, *Theatre of Blood*. Hammer buffs will already have worked out where 'Dr Chantler Day' is from, and a quick check of the film's credits will explain it to anyone else who wants to know.

Paranoiac! (1965)

This one's only mentioned in passing (along with 1963's *Phantom of the Opera*). I wanted a reference to it because it's my very favourite of the black and white Hammer psycho-thrillers that tended to play as B-features to their more colourful A pictures. A lot of people prefer Susan Strasberg in *Scream of Fear* (1961) but I'll take mad old Oliver Reed chatting to his rotting brother as he plays the organ anytime. Another one from BBC2 double bill days, I now own this on a sparkling Blu-ray and wonder, like I do with so many films, how on earth I watched this one in pan and scan. Freddie Francis' direction is often creative and never dull, there's a nice creepy score from Elizabeth Lutyens (daughter of Sir Edwin), and Janette Scott makes for a pretty put-upon heroine. I've got Dr Valentine playing Bach's *Prelude in E Minor* because that's one of the first pieces I learned when I started playing the church organ. Sadly, I don't have one in my house. I don't have a terrified Daily Mail reporter tied to a chair, either, I promise. Would I lie to you?

Hands of the Ripper (1971)

Now, here we have another favourite of mine. *Hands of the Ripper* is a fascinating, gorgeous, and superbly made mixture of tragic love story and (for its time, certainly) gory slasher picture. I first watched it during one Christmas in the early 1980s (the BBC were good to us back then), came upstairs and related the entire plot to my ten year old younger brother, who was still awake at well past one in the morning, and since then I've revisited it regularly. It's another Hammer that I could wax lyrical about for ages because I love pretty much everything about it. Eric Porter is splendid as the movie's 'mad scientist' where in this case the science is psychology rather than surgery or any 'physical' discipline. Angharad Rees is tiny, delicate, and yet somehow believable as both the helpless Anna and the spirit of Jack the Ripper. In fact it's impossible to believe that any other actress could have done a better job. Christopher Gunning's music plays up to the film's emotional core and this could quite possibly be director Peter Sasdy's best film. All this and Dora Bryan getting skewered with a poker when we're barely past the credits – what more could you want?

The Reptile (1966)

Another one I had to include and, after *Fear in the Night*, the second 'creative death' I came up with for the book. What better Hammer film to suit a fairground ride? Originally it was to be a roller-coaster but I felt the practicalities of being able to construct such a thing were beyond the bounds of even Dr Valentine's capabilities. (Although one of my favourite moments in the non-Hammer *Dr Phibes Rises Again* is when someone says they wouldn't be surprised if Phibes had created the storm they are currently experiencing. Quite where he gets a giant fan from in the desert is one of those marvellous movie moments that is simply Not To Be Questioned.)

Back to *The Reptile*. This is a Hammer it took me a long while to catch up with (the Studio Canal Blu-ray is a treat, by the way) but the still of Jacqueline Pearce in her Roy Ashton snake mask had been a familiar feature of horror film books ever since I started reading them. I remember being delighted when, at age ten, we had a school trip to Newport to view an art exhibition about masks. It was there as part of the display. I gave a short summary to the rest of the class about what I knew of the film, much to my form teacher's surprise.

The Reptile is a fairly minor Hammer film, but I think there's a lot to commend it. Miss Pearce is splendidly sensuous in her slinky green dress, and the bit where she has a little bit of dialogue while in her snake form is actually oddly sexy – shades of what movies like Robert Siodmak's The Cobra Woman (1944) promised on the posters but never delivered. The colour photography is lush and Don Banks delivers music that's subtler and more varied than James Bernard's work for the company.

Dr Terror's Haunted Cornish Funfair also features references to a number of other Cornish horror films, including Hammer's own *Plague of the Zombies* (1966), Sidney J Furie's *Dr Blood's Coffin* (1961) and Tom Parkinson and Ted Hooker's 1971 Mike Raven-starrer *Crucible of Terror*, where Me Me Lay gets coated in bronze.

On a note that's probably not at all interesting to anyone, this chapter also features a cameo appearance by my car. It's given me years of faithful service and so I thought it deserved a mention. I wonder if this is a first. There's also a cameo by my wife's voodoo doll. If that's not a first I'd like to read the book that did that one before me.

Frankenstein Must Be Destroyed (1969)

Here's another favourite of mine, and one I first saw under unusual conditions. Back in the old days (i.e. the late 1970s) HTV Cymru was the Welsh regional broadcaster on behalf of Independent Television, or ITV, which is now vastly more homogenised and dull in its programming than it was back then. Or at least that's how it feels. Anyway, it was not unusual for HTV Cymru to broadcast popular movies dubbed into Welsh. Seeing as neither I nor my family spoke the language, this often led to some confused but nevertheless amusing evenings. I well remember watching George Stevens' classic western *Shane* (1953) with my dad as we tried to work out what Alan Ladd was actually talking about, speaking as he was in Welsh with a strong Blaenavon accent.

I kept my fingers crossed that a Tuesday night showing of Hammer's *Frankenstein Must Be Destroyed* was not going to suffer the same indignity, but sadly it was not to be. The hand-drawn title card 'Rhaid Distro Frankenstein' should have warned me, of course (I think that's what it said) but bear in mind that the first few scenes of the film feature no dialogue at all. By the time we got to Thorley Walters interrogating Harold Goodwin, both of them sounding as if they came from the far side of Merthyr Tydfil, I was so involved with the film that it was difficult to tear myself away. And hearing Peter Cushing speak in Welsh was, I am sure you will appreciate, a quite singular experience.

It was only many years later that I got to see

Frankenstein Must Be Destroyed in English, but even now I can remember my ten year old self staring at that Welsh version, wishing desperately that I could understand what on earth was going on. Who knows? Perhaps that's why I developed such an affection for the more surreal and dubbed Euro-Horrors of the 1970s later in life.

I haven't talked about the film at all, and I apologise for that, but I'm sure you'll understand that's something I've wanted to get off my chest for many, many years. *Frankenstein Must Be Destroyed* is a cracking piece of Hammer horror. Peter Cushing's Baron Frankenstein had, by this time, become ruthless, amoral, and a complete and utter bastard. Of all of his performances as Frankenstein, this is my favourite, and I can watch him endlessly in it. Never mind soppy Simon Ward and busty Veronica Carlson, bastard Peter Cushing is the reason I love this film, whether he's sawing open a skull to get at the facts the poor chap's brain holds, or being deliciously pretend-sympathetic to Maxine Audley when she comes to unexpectedly visit. Everyone complains about the rape scene (put in at James Carreras' insistence) and it doesn't need to be there, but it does make us think Frankenstein's even more of a bastard than we do already.

Originally I planned to have the climax from *Frankenstein Must Be Destroyed* be mirrored as the climax of *The Hammer of Dr Valentine*, but when I came to write it I realised the story couldn't end there. And so we come to...

All the Others

I wanted to try and include references to as many Hammer films as possible. When the epiphany struck that the climax had to take place at Oakley Court, I thought it was about time the police sat down with a crate of DVDs and worked their way through some old favourites. *Slave Girls* (1968) finally gets a mention. (If you haven't seen it, by the way, it's really not that great. My great friend and fellow movie enthusiast Guy Adams called it "invariably the last movie in your Ultimate Hammer Collection to draw attention. It rattles at the bottom like a semi-crushed Orange Cream in the Christmas Chocolate Tin." I rather like Orange Cream, but I don't think I need to watch Slave Girls again in a hurry.) *The Viking Queen* (1967) is another one that probably won't get screened again soon, along with *The Pirates of Blood River* (1962). Hammer managed a nice line in kids' adventure pictures for the Saturday morning crowd (so Mum and Dad could go shopping or recover from hangovers from the night before) but I must confess I find them mainly curios now.

Legend of the Seven Golden Vampires (1974), however, is a picture I love. Made just after the blink-and-you'll-miss-it early 1970s craze for martial arts movies reached its peak, it's a crazy mélange of East meets West, with Dracula in pantomime greasepaint, rotting vampires where you can tell the make-up is a mask even from quite a long way away, loads of chop-socky action, Julie Ege's chest wobbling about a bit in a vest, Peter Cushing holding it all together, and one of James Bernard's best scores. The whole sequence near the beginning where the dead rise from their graves to create a weird zombie army is an all-time classic bit of Hammer.

Captain Clegg, or *Night Creatures* (1961) is another Saturday morning pic that I must confess a sneaking liking for, probably because it has Cushing, Oliver Reed, Patrick Allen and Yvonne Romain, all of whom add colour to the swashbuckling adventure. Oh, and dear old Milton Reid, tied to a post after having his ears cut off in an opening scene that misleads us into thinking this is going to be a gorier pirate adventure than it actually is.

Sorry *Straight On Till Morning* (1972), but I never really liked you, so you get it in the neck from both Dr Valentine and DCI Longdon at the end here. *Nightmare* (1964) is the Hammer psycho-thriller where I finally wondered how audiences of the time could believe it was possible to produce an accurate, realistic, life-like mask of someone that could fit perfectly over someone else's face and, in some cases, alter their body shape and language so they looked exactly like the person they were impersonating. So here's my little homage to that particular bit of 1960s implausibility.

And then we have a net drop from the ceiling, just like in *Curse of the Mummy's Tomb* (1964) – I said I wanted to pack in as many references as possible. For the record, I consider this to be Hammer's worst mummy picture. I much prefer *The Mummy's Shroud* (1967) which exhibits a cruelty and creativity to its murders (and especially in the way they're filmed) that elevates it a bit above Michael Carreras' pedestrian effort. Dickie Owen's mummy appearing at the top of a flight of fog-shrouded stone steps is almost worth the price of admission, though.

For the climax, I pondered for all of a microsecond if it might be too clichéd to pay homage to *Dracula* (1958), and then I remembered what kind of a book this was meant to be and wondered how on earth I could have considered leaving it out. Hammer's version of Stoker's novel is one of my favourite remakes of all time. It's a great film for so many reasons – performance, photography and music being just a few, but the reasons I think it's one of the greatest are twofold. First, until it came out (*The Curse of Frankenstein* being a bit of a warm-up act) horror as a film genre was all but dead, considered to be black and white kiddie matinee monster fare but certainly not something worthy of adult attention. Then along came *Dracula*, with its vivid, marvellous colour, its blood and gore and pretty girls with heaving bosoms. The film single-handedly changed the face of the horror film forever – and in so many good ways. It also showed that sometimes British really was best, and gave us a chance to shine in the international market at something we could be really good at – quality, atmospheric well-made horror. Stop people in the street today and they can still tell you what Hammer Horror is because it really was that momentous a sea change. Second, *Dracula* really is the way to approach a remake – it doesn't slavishly copy the original, or the book on which it's based – instead it swirled its satin-lined cape, bared its fangs and did its own outrageous thing in the context of the social and cultural climate of the time. It was one of the first horror films I ever saw and I still consider myself very lucky to have encountered the good stuff so early on. So here's that splendid climax once more, this time à la Dr Valentine, complete with curtain-pulling-down scene.

And we're still not finished! Once he's been chased across the rooftops of Oakley Court (someone has to put that in a film sometime) Valentine references, in order, the climaxes of Don Sharp's *Kiss of the Vampire* (1963), Terence Fisher's *Brides of Dracula* (1960) and *To the Devil a Daughter* (1976) – Hammer's last horror film until things started up again recently, and possibly the worst climax to a Hammer horror ever.

Finally, Valentine's escape. I'll confess that right up until the last page I wasn't sure if he was going to get away this time or not, but the idea of a funeral cortege on the Thames was too good not to use, even it if felt more Phibes than Hammer. It's neither, of course. The message Valentine leaves Longdon reveals what film is being referenced here, and it's nothing to do with Hammer at all.

Because in the next book, Dr Valentine will be...

...oh, I'll leave that for next time, shall I?

Yes indeed ladies and gentlemen, provided that *The Hammer of Dr Valentine* is favourably received, I can assure you that the good (bad?) doctor will be back, larger than life as ever, and with a whole new collection of creative murder methods for those he deems deserving of them in the third volume. All will be revealed in due course.

Until then, take care of yourselves, be nice to each other, and I (and Dr Valentine) will see you all again soon.

John Llewellyn Probert
Floating Down The Thames Amidst Fireworks
February 2014

Acknowledgements

This time, my thanks have to go first of all to everyone who bought *The Nine Deaths of Dr Valentine*. You're the reason this second book has seen print, everyone, so if you enjoyed this one too give yourselves a big pat on the back for being so supportive of this little indulgence of mine. I had at least as much fun writing it as I did the first, so thank you very much indeed.

Simon Marshall-Jones of Spectral Press will always deserve my eternal gratitude for giving me the opportunity to write the first one, and this sequel.

This book would not exist if Hammer Films had not existed. Indeed, I probably wouldn't be the person I am now if Hammer Films had not gone down the route of producing elegant, gory, sexy, well-acted gothics from the late 1950s. I'm not going to thank specific individuals, partly because the films Hammer made always felt like a group effort to me, but mainly because I would hate to miss anyone important out.

The story you have just read would not exist without Hammer Films. The book you are holding would not exist without the efforts of my publishers. I, on the other hand, would not exist without Mrs Kathleen Probert (aka the horror writer Thana Niveau). And so this last thank you is for her. Once again, she has had to sit and listen to me reading out the entire text of *The Hammer of Dr Valentine*. Her support and companionship is, and always had been, priceless. Thank you, my love, I know you enjoy all this stuff just as much as I do, and that in itself has a value beyond measure.

The Last
Temptation
of Dr Valentine

This one is for all those who have followed the adventures of Dr Valentine so far.

(Because you're the reason he's back, you know)

1

Marcie Conran was pissed off.

This was not an unusual occurrence. It didn't take much to piss off Marcie, and right now her intolerance level was at an all-time high. It had been turned all the way up to eleven by her bristling bulldog bastard of an ex-husband, the fact he and his synthetic bitch of a new girlfriend had custody of their two kids, and that all of them were still in sunny California while she was over here in this miserable place.

She tried to light a cigarette but a chill gust of wind blew out her last match. Then it began to rain.

She shivered and hugged herself, her stilettos beating out a tattoo on the railway station platform as she tried in vain to warm up. Fucking weather. Fucking weather in this fucking town in the middle of fucking nowhere in this piece of shit fucking country.

Her latest internal rant (and there had been many this day, oh yes indeed) was interrupted by her mobile phone vibrating in her jacket pocket. Two sharp shivery bursts.

Text message.

Have you left yet?

It was Ryan. Again. Ryan who had got to spend the day in a city approaching civilisation talking to film distributors while she had been stuck in this piece of shit dive.

No. Train delayed. Couple of hours.

It would take at least that to get to London, she figured.

The phone buzzed again.

Have to fly out tomorrow then. No way we'll make the last one tonight.

Shit.

Book first one in the morning, then. Don't want to stay here a minute longer than I have to.

No worries. Hotel is nice.

It fucking well ought to be, seeing as the studio was paying. 'Good. Get champagne and other expensive shit. I need cheering up.'

Ryan sent her a winking face. After that her phone stayed quiet.

Marcie looked up and down the platform. Where the fuck was the train? The digital readout above her head said it should be here now. Perhaps they had cancelled it. Perhaps they did that in this country when there were only a couple of people who wanted to escape from what they called the West Country on a Wednesday evening.

The wind picked up. She was about to go back up the stairs and complain to the guy at the ticket gate when she realised the breeze was because of the approaching Inter City 125.

About fucking time, she thought, picking up her black bag. She teetered a little, having momentarily forgotten just how heavy it was. *Bloody screenplay. Bloody documents that had to be signed by the mayor and the council and the historic buildings people and Christ knew how many others just so we can do a little bit of filming in their shitty town.* Well she'd managed it – everything signed and sealed. When the cast and crew arrived in earnest there wouldn't be a single bit of red tape in their way. Neither a single protesting local nor pissed off architecture enthusiast would be able to do a thing about them being there. All above board, all legal. She'd even got them all to sign a duplicate set of the forms she'd mailed to the studio an hour ago, just in case something happened to her bag between here and LA.

She waited for the train to slow and began to make her way to the first class carriages, lugging the case behind her. *Why the hell couldn't they have done everything electronically?* Some of the council members had been older than God, but surely even God had heard of pdfs by now?

The compartment door was locked.

Marcie pulled at the handle and then emitted a groan deliberately loud enough to be heard by everyone in the vicinity. Not that there was anybody. The other passengers must have slipped into the cheaper carriages further down.

Perhaps she had her reservation wrong? The ticket was buried somewhere in the bag and she couldn't be doing with ferreting it out. She moved even further towards the growling locomotive and tried the next door.

Locked.

Jesus H fucking Christ! What was wrong with British fucking Rail or – she stepped back to read the red letters on white – Great Western Fucking Trains? Did they not want anyone travelling in first class? She'd heard of the funny attitudes of these Brits. Perhaps you had to do a weird handshake or know some kind of password to get on.

She looked up and down the platform for a rail official.

Nobody.

"Hello?" Which school did you need to have gone to in order to get on a fucking train in this town? "Hello?"

She moved down to the end of the platform. One door left to try. If this was locked she was going to get in with the fucking driver. Let's see how he'd like to have her ranting in his ear for the next two hours!

She was already composing a letter of complaint to 'Not So Great Western Trains' as she pushed down the handle of the very end carriage.

The door swung open.

At last! She climbed inside, hefting the case behind her. Marcie could not for the life of her remember the number of her seat reservation, but as the length of the carriage met her gaze she realised it didn't matter. The entire compartment was empty.

I'm not surprised, she thought. *If it's this hard to catch a train in this country everyone probably goes by bus.*

She dragged her case halfway down the compartment and chose two sets of seats facing each other, separated by a table. She took out her laptop, dumped her bag on the seats opposite, and then sat facing what she hoped would be the direction of travel. By the time the train moved off Marcie was too engrossed in sending an email to studio vice-president Jerry Fabricius to realise she had chosen correctly.

Hi Jerry

Fixed up the locations. Took the whole damned day. Know it cost to send us over here but if Ryan's done his part it should be worth it. On train to London now, flying back to LA in the morning. I'll have the release forms with me but I've mailed you a duplicate just in case. Has Chuck finished the rewrite on the 5th draft yet? Or the 25th? I can never keep track of these fucking writers – they never seem to do what they're told until you've dragged them through a year's worth of meetings on a pay-check. Anyway, let me know if I need to do anything else before I leave. I know I'll be back in this place before I know it, but I wanted to ask just in case.

And before I go, I'm going to ask you one more thing: at this moment I'm on an empty train travelling past what looks like a pig farm. It's raining and it's cold and they say it's Spring. In a moment someone is going to serve me the milky sheep shit they call coffee here. You want me to come back here for six weeks of location shooting. So I ask you:

What have I done to royally piss you off??

Love and hugs,

Marcie.

She read it over once, decided she was happy with it – not too fawning but not too abrasive, either – and pressed 'send'. Then she shut the laptop off and relaxed back into her seat.

The pig farm was behind her now, and she found herself looking out over green fields and hedgerows, made all the more lush by the rays of setting sunlight now prodding their way through the cloud cover. It was still raining, though.

Can't this country even make up its mind what weather to have?

She sighed and looked around. No sign of the drinks trolley. She'd give it another ten minutes and then go on the hunt.

She tried reading the complimentary newspaper that was lying on the table but it was no use. Once she was on a new project it was all she could think about, and this was a good one. It seemed like every other movie these days began with the caption 'Based on True Events', whether or not there *was* any truth to it. Her latest project actually was. Well, it was based on a book that had documented the events, but that was just as good – better in fact. A series of horrific and at the same time almost absurdly creative murders of doctors, many of them in the same area of the United Kingdom. The book had been a bestseller both in the UK and overseas, with it being especially popular in the US. Even so, they wouldn't be calling the movie *The Nine Deaths of Dr Valentine*. That was far too long. She had no idea what title the movie would end up with, but that would be decided soon. Chuck was under strict instructions to come up with it by the time she got back. She had emphasised it had to be one word, two at the most. Market research had shown that was what appealed most to the demographic they would be aiming at. Something like 'Devilish', she thought, or perhaps 'Diabolical'. Nice, non-specific horror titles that would show up easily on the spine of a Blu-ray or on a streaming movie channel menu. Chuck would doubtless throw in a 'The' but that could be got rid of easily enough.

She was aware that there had been some trouble after the book's publication, and that the maniac responsible for the killings had gone after the book's authors, killing them in even more outrageous ways than his original victims. Needless to say, that had merely fuelled the public's thirst for the case, and book sales had doubled with every new death. It had made sorting out the rights a bit of a problem, but with Jerry's team of lawyers behind him there hadn't been too much of a struggle in the end.

And the best bit of all?

The killer was still on the loose.

Marcie allowed herself a smug smile. They were still making films about Jack the Ripper, weren't they? And most importantly, still making *money* from films about Jack the Ripper. Well, with any luck Dr Edward Valentine would remain free and the box office would continue to roll in. Maybe they could even do a sequel.

Nobody knew where the lunatic was now. If he had any sense he'd be on some island off the coast of South America, keeping his head down. Marcie wondered if he'd ever end up seeing their movie. If so it would probably be years from now, on some battered old television behind a local bar while he sucked the dregs from filthy whiskey glasses.

"Would you like a drink?"

Marcie jumped. It wasn't like her to be so distracted,

but she was tired. That had to be the reason she hadn't heard the train steward. And therefore there was only one answer to his question.

"Coffee. Black."

The middle-aged man in the smart green uniform with red piping around the collar and cuffs seemed to be waiting for her to say something else.

"Don't you have coffee?"

"We do, madam," came the well-spoken reply. "It's just that in this country it's customary to add 'please' when requesting an item from someone such as myself."

Oh was it? "Tell me..." she squinted at the little silver badge pinned to his left breast pocket "...Edward, is it customary for you to be such a pain in the ass? Are you immune to your company's customer complaints department?" She leaned into the aisle, her gaze never leaving his. "Would you like to keep your job?"

"Of course madam." That was better. He seemed a little more appropriately servile now. And he seemed to have poured her coffee without her noticing it. "Sugar?"

"No."

He paused for a moment before handing it over. If he expected her to say "Thank you" he had another thing coming. The moment passed, by which time the man was already making his way down the aisle to the next carriage along.

Marcie sipped the steaming coffee. Why did they always make it too damn hot? She added the risk of being scalded to her letter of complaint. She had nothing better to do for the rest of the trip and it would do her good to forget about Dr Valentine for a bit. Yes, she thought, returning her attention to her laptop, a good old rant about the service she had just had to endure would be just the thing. She should even be able to get it emailed off before she reached London.

But the words wouldn't come. Or rather, the first two or three sentences came easily but then, for some reason, her mind froze.

I must be more tired than I thought. Marcie sipped, and then gulped at the swiftly cooling coffee before looking at the screen once more.

There was something wrong with it. The display was blurring.

No, not the display. Marcie looked down at the keyboard. That was blurring too. So was the countryside beyond the window – rushing past in a swiftly darkening haze. She had been told the sun didn't set especially quickly here this time of year. It was only when the interior of the carriage began to darken that she understood it wasn't the outside world that was the problem at all. The last thing Marcie saw was the Dr Valentine script poking out of her briefcase. The last thing she did was collapse on top of it. And the last thing she felt was that script being levered out from beneath her now-paralysed form.

But it wasn't entirely over for Marcie Conran.

Not yet.

~

When the train pulled into platform five at Paddington Station, those to whom such a thing might be important merely assumed that the lights in Coach L had failed.

However, anyone who looked closer would be able to see that it wasn't just dark inside the carriage.

It was impossible to see anything.

Almost as if the windows had been painted black on the inside.

When conductor Errol Steadman realised the doors to the coach could not be opened (including the connecting doors between carriages) he called his next in command. Station Supervisor Sarah Bannister confirmed that none of the carriages were supposed to be locked, and suggested Errol use his pass key to get one of the doors open.

This Errol duly did.

Five seconds later he called the police.

They could deal with what was in there, he thought as he bit back the urge to vomit. He worked in a railway station, not an abattoir.

He used that quote a total of fifteen times in the next couple of days to the variety of newspaper, radio and television journalists who were keen to interview him. The police asked him all sorts of questions as well, none of which he was able to answer terribly successfully. After all, how was he supposed to know what Marcie's now-empty briefcase had once contained?

2

Organ music filled the room.

'Room' did not really do it justice. It was more of a chamber, an auditorium, as befitting the country house it was a part of. The rippling glissandos of Bach's *Fantasia in A Minor* echoed off the ribbed ceiling and vibrated the diamond teardrops of the elaborate chandelier, whilst the sustained pedal line caused the glass to rattle in the lead frames of the vast bay windows, covered now by heavy velvet curtains to shut out the daylight and dull the sound from the loosening glass.

The house was vast, a palatial construct on a par with a Chatsworth or a Longleat. Indeed, in common with that latter country estate, this too possessed an animal park that was opened to the public on days when there were enough of them around to make it worthwhile, allowing a few more pounds to fill the coffers and contribute to the building's considerable upkeep.

The man playing the organ did not own the house, but he was currently pretending to, having assumed the mantle and persona of the elderly Marquis who was at that moment enjoying a holiday on the French Riviera. Such holidays had been known to last for months and, on one occasion, for over a year. Arrangements had recently been made to ensure he would be kept away for as long as was needed.

His usurper had work to do, and the staff had been accepting of the Marquis' 'long-lost cousin' having arrived to take control of the running of things, especially when it turned out that the new arrival was rather better at the job than His Lordship had been.

At the opposite end of the room to the organ, close to the door and away from glass-fronted cabinets displaying oxidising silver sporting trophies, stood a straight-backed wooden chair. The small figure propped upon it might initially have been mistaken for the life-sized doll of a little girl; fraying blonde pigtails tied with pale blue ribbon, polished but slightly scuffed shoes on feet that weren't quite able to reach the floor. While she was no doll, it was true to say that it was now five years since those feet had moved, since that hair had been pulled away from the attentions of a brush with a grizzly 'I don't want to!' No, it was a long time since she had complained about anything, but the attentions of a remarkably talented Viennese taxidermist had rendered her almost lifelike for as long as his preservative techniques would last. The man had promised a lifetime guarantee, and in return his client, the little girl's father, had promised the man would be held to that.

The music segued into the piece's corresponding fugue as a remarkably beautiful woman entered the room, closing the heavy door behind her. She ignored the child in the chair, and instead crouched to pick up the manuscript that had been tossed near its feet. A glance at the title revealed why the man at the organ had been playing so loudly. She knew he didn't like to be disturbed when he was thinking, but the music had woken her before dawn, and now it was late in the afternoon. Even for someone of his single-mindedness she worried that it was too long a time to be spent wrapped up in such thoughts, and while he would probably resent being disturbed, she cared sufficiently for him that she was going to do it anyway.

After all, he had saved her life.

Her right hand toyed with strands of hair as she approached. She had it in a black bob today. The vast number of wigs he had obtained for her meant she could adopt virtually any hairstyle she desired, but today her hair was her own. He had insisted on little except that she kept it cut short, the easier to conceal if necessary.

He did not hear her approach. He would not have heard an elephant approach, so loud was the music and so lost was he in his plans and deliberations, how he would obtain the necessary equipment, make the necessary arrangements. She knew he must be planning something even more extraordinary than what they had previously been through together, and what he himself had been through alone before that, otherwise they would not be here, in this fabulous house filled with all manner of things that could be put to so many creative uses. For all she knew he had already installed a torture chamber in the cellars she had yet to explore.

The keyboard playing paused. A rest of two bars to allow the pedal line to catch up in the fugue.

Then the pedal line stopped, too.

"You're behind me, aren't you. Christina?"

She nodded, almost forgetting to speak. "I was wondering how best to disturb you, but the music has helped with that. Are you all right?"

Edward Valentine swung himself round on the organ stool and regarded her, his steely grey eyes ablaze with whatever was going on in his head. "Have you read it?"

She glanced behind her. "You mean this bundle of papers you left lying next to Victoria's chair? No. Should I?"

"With all haste." He was nodding, the corners of his mouth creased into a smile that was anything but benign. "It is to form the basis of our next project. Hopefully our final one." He slid himself off the stool and took the manuscript from her. "You read the title, at least?"

"*The Diabolical Deaths of Dr Valentine*." Now it was Christina's turn to offer a wry smile. "Don't tell me we're moving into the world of film production?"

"No." Valentine riffled through the script. "But someone is. A group of individuals from Hollywood, California, no less. They will be coming over here soon to take advantage of the current economic climate, and to make use of a number of locations in Bristol that will apparently make their misguided piece of celluloid more 'authentic'."

"They don't use film these days," Christina said, although she knew there was no point in correcting him. "It's all shot on digital."

He thrust the manuscript at her. "Do you know what it's about?"

She smiled again as she wrinkled her nose. "My guess would be that it's all about you?"

"They have 'adapted' that book. That wretched book written by those wretched reporters I saw fit to punish for their sensationalist actions. And what is even worse, they have had the effrontery to change virtually everything about it."

"That's not uncommon. It's called making it more appealing to a wider audience so they can make more money. They do it to books all the time."

"Perhaps they do." Valentine threw the increasingly ragged-looking sheaf of papers to the ground. "But not to me. Not to my story. It has been perverted enough already by those journalists. It would seem there are those working in other media who also need to be taught a lesson."

Christina picked the manuscript up and dusted it off. She probably ought to read it if it was going to occupy their lives for the next few months. "So when do we start?"

"We already have, my dear girl." Valentine got back on the stool and played four notes in a minor key – E, E flat, E, A flat. "I have left a little message for the police at Paddington station that should hopefully indicate to them that I have returned."

3

Detective Sergeant Jenny Newham stifled a yawn and tried to get herself comfortable. It was impossible. The church hall that had been co-opted as the incident room was draughty, and the plastic chairs had presumably been designed to discourage sitting for more than five minutes. The drizzle of rain down the frosted glass windows just added to the overall feeling of gloom.

Plus, she had a raging hangover.

It was her own fault, of course, but even though she had been working in London for over two years she still felt the need to prove herself on nights out with the rest of the team. Proving yourself often included how many shots you could down at two in the morning after a serious night of drinking, dancing and dodging the fumbling attempts of blokes whose idea of romantic gestures seemed to involve their outstretched fingers being unceremoniously thrust into places she was determined they would not go.

Jenny was tired and uncomfortable, and at that moment her brain felt as if it was two sizes too big for her skull.

She was also very excited.

During her time in the big smoke she had been involved in all kinds of serious crime investigations, everything from rape to kidnapping to bank raids.

But very few murders.

And no murders at all like this one was rumoured to be.

DS Andy Slater had told her all about it while they sipped Frangelico mojitos (Andy's knowledge of cocktails was superb, his taste in music less so) at some awful 1980s retro bar last night. Over the high pitched screeching of the Communards begging not to be left this way, Andy had shouted that tomorrow's briefing was about something special, something weird, something no-one had ever seen before. His words had given her the kind of tingle she hadn't experienced since she had worked on the case of all those doctors being murdered in Bristol. Jenny had assumed London would be packed with cases like that of Dr Valentine – complex murder investigations that would challenge her abilities and satisfy her intellectually. But all the good stuff always seemed to end up being dealt with by other departments and other officers.

Now, at last, it sounded as if something was coming her way that she would be able to get her teeth into.

Andy made it in just as the briefing was about to start, sliding into the seat she had kept free next to her in the front row. If anything he looked worse than she did. She flashed him a smile of sympathy as he sat down and took out his notebook. Jenny glanced behind her. Quite a few of the assembled officers had been to the bash last night - someone's birthday? Jenny couldn't remember – but no-one looked as rough as her and her gay best friend. She felt perversely proud as DCI Helena Martin took to the stage, the lights were dimmed, and the powerpoint projector switched on.

"At approximately eight thirty pm yesterday, the 1729 Intercity service from Swansea arrived at London Paddington. When it did so it was immediately noticed that the windows to coach L had been blacked out." DCI Martin's words were accompanied by an image of the exterior of the carriage in question. "When conductor Errol Steadman opened the access door to the left using his key, what he found prompted him to call the police."

Andy put his hand up. "Are you saying that the doors to that carriage were locked?"

DCI Martin nodded. "Somehow the automatic device that causes the carriage doors to unlock once the train has come to a halt had been over-ridden. The connecting doors to the adjacent carriages had also been incapacitated and the glass in them blacked out. Mr Steadman sensibly locked the door behind him and contacted his superior, maintaining a calm composure that I am sure you will all agree is highly admirable bearing in mind that this was what he had just seen."

The next picture flashed up on the screen and suddenly Jenny wished she hadn't had so much to drink last night. She fought to keep the bile down as she took in the image. Andy's self-control wasn't quite as impressive and suddenly the chair next to her was empty. The groans from around the room suggested they weren't alone in finding the scene disturbing.

The interior was like no railway carriage she had ever seen.

First, the seats had been removed. How this had been achieved she had no idea. They hadn't just been unscrewed and pushed aside, or hacked through in parts to clear an area. Everything was gone, leaving the carriage an empty, blacked-out space.

With an operating table in the middle of it.

Of course, it was what was *on* that operating table that had stimulated the chorus of gagging. The 'patient' looked to be female, her wrists and ankles bound to the gleaming chrome by heavy buckled brown leather straps. She was still dressed, and much of her outfit was soaked in blood.

Someone had taken off the top of her head.

Or rather, her skull. Because her intact brain was present for all to see, exposed and illuminated by the flood lamps that had been set up to shine upon the glistening cerebral tissue.

"The victim died from loss of blood," the DCI continued. "It is assumed that the top of her skull was removed either while she was awake, or in a state of light anaesthesia. Toxicology screens are still awaited, but we are presuming that as she was strapped down her killer planned for her to be awake for at least part of what has been carried out here. The victim sustained no other injuries, and as far as we can tell there were no witnesses."

Jenny coughed and then had to force back down the vomit that was threatening to pop from her throat into her mouth. Her actions caught the DCI's eye.

Oh well, she thought, *you wanted adventure, may as well show willing now you got her attention.*

"So are you saying, ma'am, that someone blacked out the windows of that carriage, cleared it of all its seating, moved an operating table in there, secured someone to that operating table, performed a surgical procedure delicate enough that the skull was removed and the brain was left untouched, then locked everything up for someone to discover when the train eventually arrived in London?"

The DCI nodded. "That's an excellent summary, Newham. Glad to hear you're with us as you certainly don't look it. Were you actually going to ask a question?"

Jenny narrowed bleary eyes. Actually, something was nagging at her. Oh, it was worth a shot. "Did the killer leave any kind of message?"

DCI Martin gave a brisk nod. "Actually, they did. We're getting the psychological profilers onto it now. I'm guessing they'll say it's the work of a psychopath with a superiority complex who feels the need to demonstrate his greater intellect to the world at large. Either that or it's some bizarre revenge killing. Obviously once we know more about the victim we'll have a better idea of who might have harboured a grudge against her."

Jenny hardly heard that last bit. She was too busy staring at the third picture her DCI had put up, the one of the ceiling of the carriage, where six words had been written, each letter daubed in blood. Right at that moment she couldn't explain why, but Jenny felt as if she should know what they meant. Perhaps it was because of her experiences in Bristol, or possibly she was still a little drunk from last night, but somehow she suddenly felt at an advantage compared to everyone else in the room. She hadn't written down anything else during the entire briefing, but she copied out the phrase onto her notepad, carefully and laboriously, punctuation included.

Like chalk, erased from a blackboard.

4

"...and I thought I had already told you to change that fucking title!"

If the pale, crushed-looking young man seated at the other end of the long table sank any further into his chair he would end up on the floor, which was exactly where Elliot Edwards thought he deserved to be right at this moment.

"I'm sorry Mr Edwards I'll..."

"...leave now and do what I told you to do in the first place?"

Grateful for the excuse to get out of there, screenwriter Charles Herman – unaffectionately known as 'Chuck the Fuck' because of his lack of success with women, and even more poorly regarded as 'Chuck the Fucking Loser' by Elliot – slid out of his chair and left the room. Elliot tended to add that suffix to almost everyone he knew – Jerry Fabricius was a fucking loser for thinking they could make some stupid horror book into a decent picture – and film it in the UK of all places for Christ's sake! The casting director was a fucking loser for not having yet secured them a star for the lead role. "We're still waiting on Nic Cage," she had said, before folding her arms and retreating behind all those fucking beads and bangles she wore like some walking fucking hippy store. Christ, every time she moved it sounded like a door was being opened into one of those places that stank of incense and false reassurance. They made money, though. Maybe he should get out of this business and into something like that.

But not yet. First he had to produce *The Diabolical Deaths of Dr CrazyFace* or whatever fucking useless title Chuck the Fuck was going to come up with next. Elliot knew he should fire him but Chuck was cheap. And yes, all writers were cheap (or at least the ones employed by American Enterprise Pictures were) but Chuck was especially cheap, because Elliot still had the pictures and wasn't going to give Chuck the memory stick until he'd got at least another couple of free screenplays out of him

He looked round the room. Losers, all of them. To his left sat Raymond St Pearce, directing his first feature under his real name, as opposed to all the adult 'work' he'd been churning out in the San Fernando valley for the last couple of years. Ray had convinced Jerry that he had the skills to make his first legit feature. Plus he was willing to work for guild minimum, which always tended to swing things at AEP. But not as much as Ray swung at those filthy parties he held, or so Elliot had heard. Next to him was casting director hippy woman whose name he really couldn't be bothered to remember.

After that came Ryan Patrick, location manager, just back from that godforsaken country where they would be shooting this project, thanks to a sudden crash in the value of the pound against the dollar.

"We're shooting in England," Jerry had told him from

behind a fog of blue cigar smoke in the one remaining bar in Hollywood where you could still give yourself lung cancer if you wanted to. "Their currency's all gone to shit – it'll be so cheap to shoot there it'll make even one of *our* pictures look classy."

Which of course was why Elliot was really still on board. Call it some misplaced sense of personal pride in a business that was always trying its hardest to punch any sense of self-worth out of you, but Elliot wanted to make one decent picture, just one, so that all his years spent in this business could count for something. One movie that was actually okay. No blockbuster, but maybe something that would get written about favourably in those horror movie magazines his son read. He hardly ever saw Max these days because his actress ex-wife (or was it the one who had been the model?) had moved to the east coast, but maybe if he made something that his son ended up reading about he could finally earn the boy's respect.

Ryan Patrick was a fucking loser because when Marcie Conran had failed to turn up at the airport, Ryan had left without her. He also had no idea where she was or what she was doing now. Nobody did. Marcie wasn't answering her phone, which was a very un-Marcie thing to do. Elliot hoped she hadn't decided to dump the project – or worse, found a new job over there working on some floppy-haired Hugh Grant picture that would benefit from her ruthless skills as line producer. Elliot had always felt great pride at how she had taken on board everything he had taught her (including the swearing). He repeatedly told Jerry he wasn't paying her enough, and that she'd leave for the majors the minute she had the chance.

"Let her," Jerry had said in between tumorous coughs. "We can always find someone else."

It sounded as if Marcie had, which put Elliot in the shit. There would be no time to find someone else in the window of opportunity they had to shoot in the locations they'd secured permission for. Which meant he would have to go. To the UK. Himself.

Fuck.

Ray, hippy girl, Ryan to his left. Straight ahead was a recently vacated screenwriter's chair, possibly wet with Chuck's loss of self-control. Elliot had only ever known one writer to piss themselves in a meeting, but since then he had insisted on all the chairs being upholstered in wipe-clean vinyl.

To his immediate right was director of photography Mac Armitage. Mac had worked on the last five AEP productions, mainly because he was quick, cheap and unhireable by any other studio because of various vices he so far seemed to have been able to keep under control during his time with them, thank god. Production designer Lisa Wallcroft was as tightly buttoned as her set designs weren't. Elliot suspected that her minimalist, highly restrained appearance concealed a heart of rampant undisciplined mania, and as long as she kept it to her work that was fine. Next to her was an empty seat reserved for Mike Parello, AEP's resident composer, who was rumoured to have connections to the Mob. Mike never came to the pre-production meetings but Jerry insisted a seat be kept for him out of 'respect'. Next to that was the empty chair that Marcie should have been sitting in.

Where the hell was she?

His phone buzzed.

"Nobody leave! I'm not finished with you yet." Elliot frowned as he listened to what the voice on the other end was saying. Then he frowned some more, then he felt his face going a shade of purple so dark that the other people in the room began to slide their seats towards the exit in case he needed CPR. The caller rang off, and Elliot took two deep breaths. Once he'd dismissed the meeting he'd have to get his electric sphygmomanometer out and check his blood pressure.

"It seems that Marcie has gotten herself killed." He waited for the news to sink in. Then, when it became clear that the shocked expression on everyone's faces wasn't going to fade as quickly as his he added, "Which means I'll be going to England with you."

As he registered their responses, Elliot Edwards noted with a sense of grim satisfaction that if there was any news that could possibly be worse for them than a colleague's death, it was obviously that.

5

"You wanted to see me, Newham?"

Away from the noise and organised chaos of the rest of the station, DCI Martin's office should have been an oasis of calm. Instead, the atmosphere within the room was more akin to stifling suspense, not helped by Jenny's senior officer appearing none too pleased to see her.

"Yes." Jenny put her briefcase down on the one available chair and remained standing. "It's about the case."

DCI Martin leaned back in her seat and tapped an expensive-looking ballpoint against teeth Jenny was certain was capable of tearing the heads off kittens, or whatever else it was the woman did to relax. "Go on."

Jenny took out a disc in a slim blue case and handed it over.

Martin raised an eyebrow. "A DVD?"

"Blu-ray." Jenny gave a nervous smile. "It was all they had left in the shop."

Martin picked it up, glanced at the title, then flipped the case over. "This says 'Region A', Newham. Not for play in the UK."

Jenny nodded. "Yes, but..."

"The UK is 'Region B'. We know this because..."

"Because you've told me before."

"Because..."

"Because before you came to work here you put in five long years as part of customs and excise." Jenny was trying hard not to bob nervously from one foot to another, but it was difficult.

"And so while it's very kind of you to want me to watch 'One of the most enjoyable horror films of the '70s', according to…" the DCI seemed to be summoning all the disdain she could muster "…*Mondo Esoterica* magazine, I really do have more pressing things to do at the moment."

"I think it's connected to the murder."

If anything, that seemed to make things worse. Martin threw down the pen, clasped her hands in front of her on the desk, and gave her a cool look. "Jenny, I appreciate you're trying to help, but…"

"If you'll just let me show you the relevant scene."

"… the fact remains…"

"It's about half an hour in. I can find it easily."

"…that you have come in here every other month for the last year with some lunatic attempt to connect a contemporary crime to any one of a number of ridiculous films made over forty years ago!" Martin lowered her voice. "You're a good DS, Jenny, but you're not going to get any further if you keep coming to me with these ludicrous ideas." She tossed the disc back to her. "I know that case in Bristol made a major impression on you, but if you think you're ever going to encounter another one like it you're mistaken. I am also well aware that we encourage members of our team to develop blue-sky thinking, but your head is currently operating in outer space. What are you doing now?"

Undeterred, Jenny had taken a laptop from her bag, inserted the disc and was now punching buttons. She found the bit she was looking for just as Martin was getting to her feet. "Just watch this, ma'am. It's just a few seconds. Please."

DCI Martin squinted at the scene, which depicted an elderly man explaining to a shorter, slightly younger woman the findings of an autopsy. Between them was a body, the top of the skull removed and the brain exposed. The room in which the scene was taking place was swaying from side to side, almost as if the autopsy was being conducted on...

Martin looked at the blu-ray case again, at the title of the film, while Jenny backtracked the scene so that Peter Cushing could say that line once more, those same words they had found on the ceiling of the carriage.

"*Horror Express*." Martin's throat sounded dry. "I saw that headline this morning. I never knew there was a film called it." She sat back down. "Do you think he's back?"

Jenny shrugged. "Maybe. Or it could be a copycat killer."

The DCI looked dejected. "They never caught him, did they?"

"No."

"How many people did he kill again?

"Seventeen, that we know of. Nine doctors and eight journalists – the ones who wrote the book about him killing the nine doctors."

Martin sighed. "Well, once we have more on the victim than just her name and why she was over from the US, we'll have a better idea if we are dealing with your old friend."

Jenny took a document from her case. "With respect, ma'am, the intel has come through. They were bringing it straight to you but I intercepted it on my way in here."

Martin blinked. "Well get on with it, then. What was Marcie Conran doing on a train from Bristol?"

"She had been getting permission, ma'am."

"Permission? To do what?"

"For the film production company she was representing to shoot a movie on certain locations here."

Jenny noted with the tiniest amount of satisfaction that the blood was draining from DCI Helena Martin's face.

"What movie?"

"A film version of *The Nine Deaths of Dr Valentine*."

"Oh, shit."

"And apparently she had the screenplay with her."

"We didn't find any screenplay."

"No. Which means someone else may well have it."

"Oh, shit."

"Along with the location list."

"Bollocks."

"And the shooting schedule."

"You know what this means, don't you?"

Jenny wasn't sure. "You'd best tell me anyway."

Martin stroked her chin and looked away for a moment. "We're going to have to get *him* involved."

"I understand he's left the force, ma'am. Considered his failure to apprehend the perpetrator of seventeen murders as a failing on his part. Lives somewhere in Cornwall now."

"I don't care where he lives. Former Inspector

Longdon is the only one who has any chance of second guessing how this man's mind works. I'll contact the studio Marcie Conran worked for and try to convince them not to come over, not that it will do any good. These film types seem to regard this sort of thing as good publicity, in which case I'm going to have to assign officers to watch them all while they're over here. Staff I do not have."

Jenny jumped at the opportunity. "I'd be happy to hang around a film shoot, ma'am."

The DCI gave her a cool look. "Oh no, I've got another job lined up for you."

"Yes ma'am?

"You're off to Cornwall."

6

Ryan Patrick hated flying.

In actual fact, he hated most forms of public transport, but flying was the worst. The most claustrophobic (even in business class), the worst kind of other passengers (especially in business class) and a journey that no matter how long it was always felt much, much longer. Ryan hated train travel, and hadn't taken a bus trip since his heady days as a teenager in the 1990s, but it was flying he hated most.

Which had been his excuse, before leaving LA, for hiring the most expensive motorbike the rental company had to offer to get him around the UK. All on the studio's budget, of course. His luggage could follow on later. Eight hours of cheap champagne, fat business types complaining all around him, and the still-audible sticky screams of children in economy (they really needed to come up with something better than a curtain to divide those who were willing to pay from the unwashed masses), meant that once he was through passport control and customs, what Ryan really needed was to feel the wind in his hair.

The man from the hire company apologised profusely that they didn't have the Ducati Supersport Ryan had requested, but explained that the Triumph Explorer 1200 XCA should meet all his needs.

"Our website calls it 'the ultimate go anywhere, do anything transcontinental motorcycle'." He passed some forms across for Ryan to sign. "And our customers agree."

Ryan wasn't so sure. "I've got a Ducati back at home," he said. "It's been my favourite machine for the last couple years. Are you sure you don't have one?"

The man looked apologetic. "I'm afraid the last one has just gone out, sir. May I venture to ask, are you American?" Ryan nodded. "Here for long?"

"Couple months tops. Making a movie."

"Oh, the film business. We get quite a few of you coming through here. Well, may I say that the Triumph should look after you nicely on our roads. They were originally a British company, after all."

Ryan sighed and scribbled his name, eager to get out onto the open road. "Not any more then?"

"No sir." The forms were taken back and checked. All seemed to be in order. "They are owned by BMW now."

"Seems like everything in this country has been bought up by somebody else." Ryan picked up the keys. "It won't be long before you don't have anything left." He had intended it as a joke, but from the man's expression it obviously didn't go down well. He looked Ryan up and down.

"Do you require some leathers, sir?"

Oh hell, yes he did. His would be trapped in his luggage, which apparently wasn't going to arrive until tomorrow.

"We can offer you full outfitting at a very reasonable price."

More likely it would be very unreasonable, but there was little Ryan could do. Besides, the studio would be picking up the tab. He signed yet more forms.

"If you would care to follow me, sir."

The changing room was cramped, but was nowhere near as disappointing as the outfit Ryan was handed.

"Don't you have anything else?"

More apologetic looks. If there was one thing the British did better than anybody else, it was look embarrassed. "I'm not sure how to say this, sir, but it would appear we are very low on hire apparel at the moment. Very low indeed."

Ryan regarded the scuffed black leather jacket. "You mean..."

"Yes, sir. This is the only set we have left at present. However, I think you will find it fits nicely." Who was this guy? A motorcycle hire clerk or a menswear consultant? "The alternative would be, of course, for you to reclaim your luggage and obtain your own leathers, but I cannot guarantee that the bike would not have been rented by somebody else when you returned."

"Or I could go to another company."

"Of course you could, sir. Unfortunately, however, we do offer a no cash return policy. I could provide you with some vouchers should you wish to visit the UK at some other time?"

More flying, more coming to this crappy country that couldn't even get him the bike he wanted? No thanks. Once this shoot was over, Ryan had no intention of ever coming back. Besides, there was no way the studio was going to authorise another bike for him, especially as he hadn't technically been cleared for even one at the moment. And Elliot had emphasised he wanted Ryan in Bristol for their pre-shoot meeting this afternoon. No, there was no way he could do anything but agree.

The rental clerk nodded. "Very good, sir. I shall leave you to get changed."

After all that, Ryan was surprised to discover that the guy was right – the trousers fitted very well indeed, almost as if they had been made for him. And in retrospect, the leather jacket had a touch of worn class about it. What had been written on the back of it? No matter how much Ryan squinted, or what angle he held it at under the light, he couldn't quite make out the letters. Nevertheless, when he made his way out of the fitting room he felt quite the 1950s heartthrob. His sense of self-cool lasted for all of thirty seconds, right up to the point where he was handed the helmet.

"Again, sir, I have to apologise."

"Let me guess." Ryan hefted it and flipped the visor up and down. "It's the only one you have?"

"I'm afraid so, sir."

Ryan shook his head. "Why the hell would you even stock a helmet that looks like this?"

"I have no idea, sir. I am afraid I only work here."

"It looks like a skull."

"I know, sir."

"Someone has actually painted eye sockets on the visor."

"Again I can only apologise, sir. However, I think you will find that vision through it is quite adequate."

Ryan couldn't believe he was actually trying the thing on, but he was becoming increasingly desperate to get out of there.

The rental clerk was right. Despite the decoration, the vision through the visor was actually fine.

"Won't I get stopped by the police?"

"I think you'll find them quite accepting of certain eccentricities in this country, sir. As long as you're wearing it, you should be safe from their attention."

"Well, as long as it gets me to Bristol."

The man said nothing. Ryan tucked the helmet under his arm. Feeling every bit the rebel biker of pulp novels he would never read but did have on his shelves back in LA, Ryan followed the rental clerk's directions to where his ride was waiting. He supposed he shouldn't have been surprised when the bike turned out to be rather older, and considerably less shiny, than the one he had been shown in the brochure.

It turned over nicely, though, which was what mattered.

Ryan sat there for a moment, revving the engine. Oh yes, it turned over very nicely indeed. And with that, all his concerns about the hire company and what they had given him to wear fell away. He was going to have the best time riding this baby around those English country lanes, but first he had to get to Bristol.

The machine handled well on the roads out of Heathrow and soon he was on the M4. Time to see what it could really do.

He spent the next seventy miles in the fast lane, only slowing down when he saw the bright markings of police vehicles. Then it was back up to faster than was legal, the sense of speed exhilarating, the feeling of control absolute.

It was at the Swindon exit that everything went horribly wrong.

At first Ryan thought his rear tyre must have burst. The bike veered sharply to the left, narrowly avoiding a black Audi that blew its horn at him. Through no fault of his own Ryan continued his trajectory and soon found himself in the slow lane. To his relief the bike righted itself but continued to slow down.

Ryan tried to speed up.

The accelerator refused to respond.

Now the indicator was blinking of its own accord.

What the hell was going on?

Helpless, Ryan held on tight as his motorcycle left the motorway, indicated left again at the exit roundabout, and began to make its way along a main road he identified through his skull-painted visor as the A3102. He tried the accelerator again.

Nothing.

He tried the brake.

No response.

Ryan considered throwing himself from the bike, but it was going too fast. All he could do was hang on as he was driven through the English countryside, through tiny villages where he tried to wave for help and those present on the streets waved an angry fist back at him for going too fast.

Then he was out in the country again, on straight, open roads. The bike, still beyond his control, began to speed up. And now something else very strange was happening.

He could hear music.

It had to be coming from inside the helmet. Either that or he was hallucinating. The words were faint but Ryan could just make them out. What was the singer going on about? How the world never knew the name of whoever was the subject of the song, how he had ridden his motorcycle 'just like a bomb' and how you were being encouraged to join him, 'riding free'.

Riding free...

Oh, shit.

He had to get off this thing.

He was in the countryside. Those grass verges would be soft, wouldn't they? Even at the speed he was going, if he jumped he stood a chance of, at worst, getting away with a few broken bones. That would likely be better than being driven straight off a bridge into the river or into (or even through) a brick wall. Yes, that was what he had to do.

Jump.

Up ahead the road curved to the left. The bike would have to slow down to take it. That was where he would make his bid for freedom.

Ryan braced himself as he felt the bike decelerating. As it veered into the turn, he raised his hands.

He tried to raise his hands.

His hands suddenly felt glued to the handles.

He couldn't raise his body either, or take his feet from the footrests.

Despite the buffeting wind, Ryan Patrick felt a new

chill as he realised he was trapped on the machine. He scarcely registered that he was now passing through yet another village, or that the bike was showing no signs of slowing down as another corner presented itself.

With a juddering thwack the bike mounted the grass verge and crashed through the flimsy wire fence. Now Ryan was being bumped up and down as the bike careered over grassland. What was that up ahead? Were they rocks? Why were they so regularly arranged?

Standing stones. That's what they were. A circle of them.

Ryan hung on for dear life as the bike veered in and out of the stone circle, as it turned and zig-zagged, as the wheels churned the grass, as he was driven straight at a huge, leaning stone only for the bike to turn aside at the last minute. The song had stopped now, but Ryan could hear something else.

Police sirens.

Thank God. They must have been alerted by his speeding through all those other villages. They'd know what to do. They'd be able to stop things before this fucking machine killed him.

Wouldn't they?

The bike's wheels spun once more, sending up a spray of soil as the vehicle performed one more circuit of the stone circle and then headed back to the road, to the main street through the village and back the way he had come. In the far distance, Ryan could see blue lights flashing as the authorities neared the town. Straight ahead of him a truck had been parked on the road, one of those big cement-mixing things.

Ryan waited for the handlebars to tilt so he would avoid it.

The handlebars didn't shift.

And he began to speed up.

Tears filled Ryan's eyes as he realised that whoever was controlling the bike had no intention of his avoiding the obstruction in his path. He only had seconds to take in the green painted truck, the picture of an enormous amphibian glaring at him from the back of it, and the words 'Green Frog Constructions' beneath, before the bike came to a crashing halt, one which executed the cement delivery system in a way any Hollywood executive would have described as 'spectacular'.

~

Two hours later, in a conference room in Bristol, exceedingly pissed off movie producer Elliot Edwards surveyed the assembled 'talent' that had been brought together for their pre-shoot briefing. It was essentially a rerun of the previous Hollywood meeting, but with one significant absence.

Where the fuck was their location manager?

His cellphone wasn't picking up. Well, it was, but the voicemail message was less Ryan's voice and more a series of grumbling croaks, as if someone had recorded it by holding a frog close to the microphone and squeezing it. What kind of guy recorded a stupid-ass message like that?

The others in the room shifted uncomfortably in their chairs as Elliot tried Ryan's number for the final time. If he didn't answer he was out of a job, and they'd have to get somebody local to fill his position. Wouldn't that be fun?

Elliot was punching the 'hang up' button when the receptionist from downstairs knocked on the glass door. He beckoned her in. The girl looked nervous, but then they all did.

"I hope you've got good news for me."

She seemed to have difficulty in getting the words out. "I'm not sure what this is, actually, but the message is for you if you're Mr Edwards."

Elliot nodded. "Go ahead."

"The message is that Mr Patrick is waiting downstairs for you."

Elliot raised his eyebrows. "That's it?"

"Yes."

"And why, pray, did Mr Patrick not come up here and tell me that himself? In fact, why did Mr Patrick not just come up here and present himself to the meeting that he is now late for by..." he looked at his watch "...one hour and fifteen fucking minutes?"

The girl cringed. Her next words were uttered in a voice that sounded more suited to a mouse than a human being. "I think you probably need to come downstairs."

"What?"

Elliot stood and gave his team a glare. "You all stay here."

They didn't listen, of course. Instead they followed him to the concourse of the modern office block where, taking up an inordinate amount of space on the clean tiled floor was what looked like a truly terrible sculpture of a man on a motorcycle.

"What the fuck is this meant to be?"

Elliot reached out to take the piece of paper that had been taped to the motorcyclist's right hand.

"'Really sorry to be late for the meeting but I got stoned'. That's not even funny."

But the rest of the group wasn't listening to Elliot anymore. They were staring at where, when Elliot had pulled free the message, some of the grey, rocky substance had crumbled free, revealing the leather-gloved hand of the man who had been encased within it.

7

It was raining, which meant the teashops were busy.

Jenny Newham had to wait for two elderly ladies to finish their tea and cake in The Copper's Kettle before a space finally became available. She was still brushing crumbs from the table when a waitress approached, notepad in hand.

"You're not supposed to do that."

Jenny looked up at the girl, who couldn't have been more than twenty. "I'm sorry?"

The waitress offered her a chirpy grin. "It should be me saying that really, shouldn't it? You know – 'Sorry, but it's so busy in here today'. The owner doesn't like customers brushing food onto the floor. Something about it encouraging mice."

Jenny returned the girl's smile. "That's ok. In actual fact, the reason I'm here is that I'd like to see the owner. Is he around?"

The waitress nodded but it didn't look promising. "You're not from the police, are you?"

Jenny hadn't been expecting that. "I might be."

The girl leaned over and lowered her voice. "It's just that he always says if the police come looking for him we're to say he's not here. I've gone and got that wrong already, haven't I?"

"Don't worry." Jenny laid a reassuring hand on the

girl's arm. "You could say an old friend is here to see him. It would more or less be the truth."

"All right." The girl brightened, but still looked unsure. "He's not in any trouble, is he? I mean, we've all been wondering why it's the one thing he goes on about so much. He's not some major wanted criminal or something?"

Jenny restrained herself from issuing a nervous laugh. "Oh no, nothing like that. He's very much on the side of the good guys."

"And you really are a friend of his?"

"I like to think so."

The girl pointed at the menu. "Well, if you're not sure if he'll see you, it would probably help if I told him you've ordered something."

Jenny picked up the laminated card. "I'll do better than that," she said. "I'll buy him something as well. Are you licensed?"

The girl looked over at the clock hanging behind the counter.

"Just gone eleven so yes we are." The pencil was poised over the notepad. "What can I get you?"

"I'll have a cup of blueberry rooibos tea and one of your granola slices."

"And for him?"

"You'd better get him a double brandy."

The girl raised her eyebrows at that and then she was gone, leaving Jenny to contemplate the condensation-fogged windows as she wondered once more exactly what she was going to say. She had gone over various options on the drive down, everything from 'Long time no see' to 'We need you...desperately', but none of them sounded right. The last time she had seen him had been years ago, just after the two of them had watched a huge raven-shaped balloon float away over the Bristol Channel as Dr Edward Valentine, serial killer extraordinaire, had made good his escape. Would her then-senior colleague have changed? Would the second encounter with the maniac have left him a burned-out shell of a man, incapable of doing little other than skulking behind the scenes of a tea shop in a tiny village in Cornwall? Would coming down here be a mistake that would leave her depressed, disenchanted and with little else to report back to DCI Martin other than that they were on their own?

"Newham! What the bloody hell are you doing here?"

The entire patronage of The Copper's Kettle fell silent.

Fourteen pairs of elderly female eyes swivelled towards the source of the bellow from the back of the teashop, and so did Jenny's.

Jeffrey Longdon hadn't changed much. His greying hair was a little thinner, and he had lost a bit of weight (or perhaps it was because he wasn't in that trench coat he had insisted on wearing in all seasons) but the passage of time hadn't treated him too badly at all. He didn't smile, but for a man who had never used those muscles of expression in the entire time she had known him, that would probably have been asking too much anyway. As he squeezed between customers to make his way to her table, his clientele resumed their chatting and the rain began to hammer even harder against the windows.

"Is that for me?" He was looking at the brandy.

"I thought you might appreciate it."

Longdon pulled out his chair, scraping the floor as he did so.

"Bloody linoleum." He regarded the gouge mark he had just made on the floor. "I knew I should have gone for the more expensive stuff." He sat down and the chair creaked. He rocked back and forth on it, and was rewarded with more sounds suggestive of imminent cracking. "Whatever happened to good old English craftsmanship, eh? The bloke down the road said his family had been in the furniture business since the Victorian era. Sounds as if the skills have decided to skip a generation, doesn't it?"

Jenny tried to get a word in but Longdon held up his left hand. "I'll save you the trouble, shall I? It may seem impossible for you people in London to believe but we do get the newspapers down here. Occasionally I even read them, and I especially read them when my regulars keep going on about the main story." He turned and waved at a table of six old ladies in the far corner who were currently demolishing a mountain of scones. They offered him a collective giggle as they waved back, their fingers thick with strawberry jam.

"Do they know what you used to do?"

"Have you ever tried to keep any kind of secret from a bunch of old ladies in an out of the way village where very little happens?" Longdon rolled his eyes, but she could detect a hint of an affectionate smile. "You would think this is the kind of place where you can escape your past, but I swear those old dears keep better records than MI5."

"You don't seem too bothered by it."

Longdon shrugged. "I can't allow myself to be. Besides, it's made me into something of a local secret celebrity. That lot sitting over there eat enough cakes and scones to let me pay the utility bills on this place, so God bless 'em, I say. Running a place like this is certainly easier than inner city police work, which I have absolutely no intention of returning to before you even ask."

"Not even if I tell you we think he's back?"

"Especially if you tell me that. Look, Newham, I had two chances to catch this bloke and both times it all went horribly wrong. Seventeen people died and nothing I did helped stop any of it."

"In case you're forgetting, I'm still here because of you."

"I know, and that gives me some consolation, but even that was a stroke of luck, a chance bit of information gleaned in a pub. Standard police procedure gave us nothing."

"Because this wasn't – this isn't – a standard case. Nobody knows this lunatic like you do. That's why we need you back."

Longdon's hand strayed to the brandy glass. "No you don't."

Jenny had no intention of letting this go. "Yes we do."

The drink barely touched the sides. "Are we going to do the entire pantomime routine, Newham? If so you're going to have to buy me a lot more drinks if you think I'm going to sit here and listen to you."

"We think he's going after a film crew this time."

"I don't care."

"From Hollywood."

"Now I care even less."

"They're coming to Bristol."

"I feel sorry for Bristol."

"Two of them are already dead."

"Then they're stupid if they don't bugger off back to where they came from aren't they?" Longdon's eyes narrowed. "Hang on – you said two?"

"Yes."

"The newspapers have only mentioned one. Isn't that right, ladies?" Scone-stuffed mouthings of agreement came from the far corner. "So what's the second?"

Jenny paused for effect. "Only if you agree to come back on the case."

"No. Absolutely not."

"In that case, the photos stay in the briefcase I have under the table here." She could see from Longdon's expression that she nearly had him. "In fact, seeing as I've finished my tea, I may as well be going. It must be challenging work running this place, and I applaud you for it."

Jenny made to get up. It was her make or break moment. Either she was walking out of here with Longdon or without, and now would be the decider.

Longdon folded his arms and stayed silent.

Shit.

She was at the door. In fact, she had opened it and was listening to the little bell tinkling, tolling out the sound of her failure, when his voice boomed from behind her.

"All right."

It wasn't enough. She had to push this.

"All right what?"

The shop went silent once more, such drama having not been experienced in the village of Lanston Bassett for many a year.

"All right I'll look at the pictures."

"And?"

A pause, followed eventually by "And offer what help I can."

Jenny closed the teashop door. This time the tinkling of the bell was impossible to hear over the sound of so many old ladies applauding.

8

"This is ridiculous! It's just damned nonsense!"

Recently (and hurriedly) reinstated Inspector Jeffrey Longdon leaned heavily on the table and glared at Elliot Edwards. It had little effect on the fuming producer, but that just made Longdon glare all the more.

"No, Mr Edwards." Longdon spoke in the calm, clear, purposeful tones of someone with a lifetime's experience of telling people things they didn't want to hear. "It is neither ridiculous nor nonsense. You and your little group—" he indicated the remaining members of Edwards' crew, huddled on uncomfortable chairs and bearing expressions that ranged from miserable to near-catatonic "—have attracted the attentions of one of the most notorious serial killers of all time." He picked up the copy of the screenplay one of them had brought along. "What were you thinking?"

"That he had left the country after killing those journalists and escaped to some godforsaken third world country to lie low." Edwards took out a cigar and was about to light it when Jenny coughed and pointed at the No Smoking sign.

"Lie low?" Longdon snorted. "A man who took over an entire village so he could drown someone in acid? Who constructed a catapult capable of firing a body into a Welsh gorge and impaling it on a massive crucifix just because it would look a bit like the ending of a Dracula film? A bloke who dressed up as a clown for two years to entertain kids at the bloody zoo just so one day he could dump a bucketload of deadly poisonous scorpions onto the head of someone who had pissed him off? This is not the kind of criminal who likes to skulk in the shadows at the best of times." He threw the screenplay at Chuck the screenwriter, who dropped it. He was still scrabbling to pick it up as Longdon took a deep breath. "For two years there's been peace, and you had to bring him back."

"Now you sound like someone in one of your Hammer pictures, Inspector." Edwards couldn't smoke his cigar, but he was doing his damnedest to chew on it. "The thing I would like to know is, if he's killed so many people and, as you say, has done it so flamboyantly, why the hell haven't you guys caught him yet?"

"That's what I was wondering." Lisa the art director, clad in an immaculately pressed grey suit, crossed her legs and gave Longdon a cool look.

The Inspector risked a glance at Jenny. "He's very good at getting away. Look, I'm not saying we haven't made a few mistakes, but we're not dealing with a normal human being."

"You mean you believe he has supernatural help?" Casting director Caitlin Dufresne pushed strands of her lengthy, corkscrew-styled auburn hair out of her eyes. The amount of jewellery she had on around her wrists and neck meant she rattled as she did so.

"No, Miss Dufresne, I do not. What I mean is that he possesses a brilliant intellect, a vast fortune, and, perhaps the greatest indicator of how raving mad he is, a detailed working knowledge of all the horror films made between the mid-1950s and the 1970s. As you presumably all know if you've read your own script."

"Okay, so we know that" Raymond St Pearce piped up, "and we know that the first time round it was Vincent Price films, and the second it was Hammer horrors. What is his theme this time?"

Silence descended on the room. Longdon resisted the urge to rap his fingers on the table. "We're not sure," he said, eventually. "DS Newham has identified, correctly in my opinion, that your line producer, Marcie Conran, was killed in the style of a scene from the 1972 Spanish-British coproduction *Horror Express*, starring Christopher Lee and Peter Cushing. Oh, and Telly Savalas, in case that's important."

"And Ryan?" DP Mac Armitage was leaning forward in his chair now, eager to hear Longdon's answer. "Is there a film where a guy on a motorbike gets smothered in concrete?"

Longdon continued to feel and look uneasy. "We believe that, in view of the 'witty' message that accompanied Mr Patrick's body, the clothes he was dressed in and the nature of his death, that in this case the death was intended to represent a scene from the film *Psychomania*."

"*Psychomania*?" That was Elliot again. "What the fuck is *Psychomania*?"

Longdon fell silent at this point, so Jenny chimed in.

"Another film from 1972. British. A motorcycle gang gets turned to stone after becoming immortal due to the breaking of a pact with a frog god."

"What the fuck did you just say?"

"You'll watch your language in front of my junior staff, Mr Edwards. DS Newham has just provided a more succinct summary of that particular film than I ever could."

"And the link between the two films?" Lisa wanted to know.

Longdon spread his hands. "It's difficult to say. They were both made in part by Benmar productions – a short-lived film company, but I'd be surprised if that's what he's taking as his theme. Our worry is..." Silence descended as the six Americans in the room awaited his reply, "...that this time he's using British horror films in general as his inspiration. And if he is, there are an awful lot of horrible ways in which he might be thinking of doing you in."

"So what do you suggest we do?" Raymond had taken out his cigarettes now and was nervously toying with the packet.

"I would have thought that was obvious." Longdon allowed his gaze to rest on each of them in turn before speaking again. "Go home."

"Out of the question," Elliot barked. "We've already spent too much on this project to back out now. Plus, we don't know if we'll ever be able to get permission to shoot in the authentic locations ever again."

"Is it really worth risking your lives for?"

The group looked uneasy before Elliot spoke up on their behalf yet again.

"I say it is. Can you imagine the publicity we're going to get out of this? The cast and crew of American

Enterprise Pictures risking their very lives to bring this tale of murder and horror to theaters!"

"And what are you going to say about Marcie and Ryan?" Caitlin asked.

"Did you not see *The Exorcist*? Or any of those other movies where there were deaths on the set? Did it keep people away? Hell no! It just made audiences want to see them all the more!"

"I believe Miss Dufresne was talking more about the appropriateness of using your friends' deaths for publicity, Mr Edwards," said Jenny.

"Friends?" Elliot spat the word out. "They weren't friends, and if anyone in this room claims anything more than the most superficial acquaintance with either of them it's a goddamned lie. We all need the money, we all stand to make a hell of a lot of it, and we are all staying."

"Is that the decision of all of you?" Longdon eyed the group once more.

The group's collective gaze drifted down to the floor.

"He's given us all new contracts," Chuck eventually whispered.

"Profit points," said Mac.

"We're all going to be rich," said Lisa.

"According to Mr Edwards," Caitlin added, sounding none too sure.

"We just need to get the picture in the can," said Raymond, "and then we'll be out of your hair."

"You're out of your minds is what you are," said Longdon. "And I can't stop you going about your daily business, but I want you all to consider yourselves duly warned."

"Yes, yes." Elliot got to his feet. "If you don't have anything else to add, Inspector, we have a picture to shoot. Our principal players should have arrived at Bristol airport an hour ago, so if you'll excuse us, we intend to get to work."

"An hour ago? That's working them a bit bloody hard isn't it?" They were filing out of the room as Longdon was struck by another thought. "Hang on...you haven't got somebody playing *me*, have you?"

9

It had been a hell of a day.

Caitlin Dufresne threw her room key onto the scuffed table and sat on the edge of the narrow bed. It creaked ominously as she did so. Outside it was still light, just not enough to keep shooting, otherwise Elliot would still have them at that suspension bridge now. She had ceased wondering why he wanted her to come on location with them. He obviously hated her. Not, she thought with a tired smile, that their producer was in the habit of showing any degree of affection to anyone. He had told her it was cheaper to keep her around to look after the cast than employ anyone extra who might be more suited to the task.

The cast! She had been with Elliot when they had met 'the cast' at the airport. The first disaster had been the absence of Nicolas Cage, their (at the moment still nominal) star. A couple of telephone calls had revealed that apparently he still wasn't happy about the pay and whoever Elliot had spoken to (she still wasn't sure if it had been Mr Cage's agent or not) was going to get back to them after Elliot had grudgingly agreed to increase his offer by an amount so paltry even Caitlin would have been insulted. She strongly suspected that neither she nor anyone else on the shoot would ever get to meet the man Elliot wanted for the lead role.

But they would get to meet his stand-in.

Elliot had explained that, as a backup, he had arranged for someone who looked very similar to Nicolas Cage to be flown over, so that they could at least proceed with long shots, back-of-head shots, and profile views (provided the scene was very dark). Thus it was that she found herself shaking hands with Franklin Robbins, professional Nicolas Cage impersonator. Admittedly he looked quite a bit like the man, but as soon as he opened his mouth the much higher pitched Texas twang confirmed that he most certainly was not.

And that was it for their 'international cast'. As they drove back from the airport Elliot had explained that he had scrapped many of her casting decisions and had instead employed the services of both local and London talent agencies to provide more individuals who resembled the actors she had chosen for the roles.

"I need you to tell them exactly how to behave. You know, how to be like the American actors we would have flown over if we'd had the money." Elliot had threatened to fill the car with cigar smoke, forcing Caitlin to roll down the window.

"But I'm not a dialogue coach, Mr Edwards. In fact I'm not any kind of instructor. I don't really know how I can help."

"You cast the original actors, didn't you?"

"Yes."

"And I'm guessing you met them all?"

"I did."

"Well then!" As if that was all the proof he needed, Elliot folded his arms, cigar jammed between his teeth.

"If they don't behave the way your original choices did you can step in and correct them. Raymond's going to be far too busy making sure Mac is pointing the camera in the right direction."

So that was what he had meant by needing her to 'look after the cast'. Dear God. They had driven straight to the suspension bridge where the (Bristol-based) technicians were busy setting up under Mac Armitage's guidance. Raymond was studying the script with Chuck, and when their car pulled up, all eyes were briefly on Franklin as he got out, before everyone went back to work. The noticeable uplift in the general mood swiftly returned to normal as the news spread that it wasn't actually Nicolas Cage at all.

They had only been allowed a few hours to get the shots they needed, and so as soon as Elliot emerged from the car in a fog of smoke like Dracula rising from his grave, the producer was already clapping his hands loudly and bellowing, wanting to know when they were goddamned well going to get started.

Caitlin had stood on the sidelines and watched as they had filmed Franklin (from the back and the side and never too close) pull a body out of the trunk of a car, drag it to the side of the bridge, and tie a rope around its ankles. In the script he was then supposed to set the body on fire and throw it over, but Bristol City Council had expressly forbidden the use of any naked flame at one of their historic landmarks.

"Never mind," Elliot had said. "We've got a cheap CGI guy back in LA. He'll put the flames on afterwards."

And that was pretty much it for the first day of shooting. As there would be no actors in the scenes,

Caitlin had been released, while the rest of the crew had gone off to get the long-shots. Now here she was, in the tiny bedsit that was all the company was willing to pay for her to stay in. She would probably go out in a bit and find somewhere cheap to eat. She might even have a couple of drinks to go with the meal. She had no wish to contact the rest of the crew. No doubt a group of them would be going out somewhere, but she knew that, even if it didn't start off that way, the conversation would soon turn to Marcie and Ryan, and as the evening drew on and the empty shot glasses piled up, at some point somebody would ask who everyone thought might be next because, after all, they hadn't caught the killer, had they? In fact, he could be watching them right now.

He could be watching *her* right now.

She jumped at that, and even found herself going over to the window to check, drawing back the flimsy gauze curtains and peering into the empty street beyond.

No-one.

No black-cloaked maniac waiting with a scalpel, no ordinary-looking man with what might be a Bowie knife concealed beneath his coat, no 'workman' with a variety of power tools at his disposal. Nothing.

God, she felt lonely.

But what was the alternative? A night of drinking and inevitably talking about death. She couldn't handle that. Not now.

Caitlin reached into her bag, and took out the business card she'd been handed by that friendly-looking girl wearing all the charm bracelets, the one she'd bumped into as she'd entered her hotel.

There were all sorts of leaflets and brochures in the lobby. Most of them were for tourist attractions, and a couple were for local churches of various denominations.

The gold-embossed pink card in her hand, however, was for nothing like that. Instead, it was for something Caitlin had been placing more and more reliance on recently, especially after her latest relationship breakup (ironically, or tragically, because of her dependence on the very same thing). But it had always played a major part in her life, helping her make decisions, choose career paths and even decide on lovers. Now, a stranger in a foreign land with no friends and with an aching desire to be back home, she needed that help more than ever, and it had been with almost aching relief that she had spotted the little box of business cards positioned near the staircase.

Madame Dorothy
Medium
Guide to the spirit world
Tarot Readings a Speciality

A tarot reading was what Caitlin needed more than anything right now, something to impose order and make sense of the confusion she was feeling. But would Madame Dorothy be willing to see a customer this late? The sun had not yet fully set but it was still well past business hours.

Only one way to find out.

The phone rang three times before it was picked up. An elderly female voice answered.

"Yes?"

"Is that Madame Dorothy?"

A pause. Caitlin crossed her fingers that Madame Dorothy was not away, or perhaps even occupied with another client.

"It is."

Caitlin sighed with relief. "I don't suppose you're still doing readings, are you?"

"I have been doing readings for many years, my dear and, the spirit world willing, I shall be doing them for many more."

"I'm sorry, what I meant was, are you still doing readings this evening?"

Another pause. Caitlin crossed her fingers so tightly they hurt.

"Well it is getting rather late, my dear, and we old ladies have to get our beauty sleep. We're not quite as agile as we once were, you see."

"I understand that." Oh God, what could she say to convince her? Best to be honest. "It's just that I've come over from the United States and things aren't going too well. I'm in need of spiritual guidance and you will appreciate that without my usual advisor I'm feeling a little lost."

"Lost in what way, dear?"

"Spiritually, mentally, psychologically..." Every way she could think of, really. "Two people I worked with and knew well have died, and to be honest I just don't know how to cope with any of it."

"Two deaths, you say?"

"Yes."

"Friends of yours?"

Not at all but it would probably help if she lied. "Yes."

"Close friends?"

"Young friends. Friends nobody expected to be killed by a maniac."

There was a sharp intake of breath on the other end of the line. "A maniac, you say?"

"That's what the police think. I'm not even sure if I should be telling you this, but then I don't think they're completely sure the killer is who they suspect." She was rambling. "Oh I don't know, I'm just so confused."

"Indeed you are," said Madame Dorothy. "Or at least, that is most definitely the impression your psychic vibrations are giving me."

Caitlin found herself choking back a sob. "Really?"

"Oh yes. What you need is more certainty in your life at this moment. I believe I can give you that. Oh yes indeed, my dear, that shouldn't be a problem at all."

"Oh thank you," said Caitlin, and meant it. "*Thank you.*"

"You can thank me afterwards dear, if you're still feeling up to it. Now, I am afraid I do not make house calls, so you will have to come out to my farm. It's a bit off the beaten track but local taxi drivers know it. Do you have a pencil?" Caitlin didn't, but she had a notepad on her phone. She typed in the address to give to the cab driver. "I shall expect payment before we begin, by the way."

"Sure. No problem." Even though she knew she had money she checked her purse anyway, just to make sure the sheaf of ten pound notes was still there.

"That's good. Now, don't you go worrying your little head about getting here too late. Some people are better in the daytime but my daughter and I find it so much more fun being night people. I shall await your arrival."

There was a click and Caitlin was left sitting in silence. But not for long. There was a card for a cab company in her room and the next thing she did was dial the number. She only understood about half the words the gruff Bristolian voice on the other end of the line said to her, but she eventually gleaned that the earliest they could send someone to get her was in half an hour.

It would have to do.

She agreed, rang off, and settled down to wait.

Five minutes later there was a knock on her door.

"Taxi here for you!" The voice of the guest house's landlady was already fading as the woman retreated downstairs. Caitlin frowned, got to her feet, and peered once more through the window. Sure enough, a car was waiting outside the building. But it couldn't be for her, could it?

Maybe there had been a cancellation.

Maybe things were looking up for her for once.

Caitlin grabbed her bag and her shawl and made her way down to the entrance, where a girl dressed in jeans and an afghan coat was waiting. She didn't stop chewing as she talked.

"You Miss Dufresne?"

Caitlin preferred to be called Ms, but she was worried if she corrected the petulant-looking girl she might lose her ride, so she just nodded.

"Taxi for Yates' farm?

"Yes."

"Let's go then."

The phone number on the side of the taxi was different from the one Caitlin had dialled and, though she didn't want to delay things, she couldn't help but mention it.

"Oh that? All the taxi companies share the bookings round 'ere. I was the closest so they sent me. It's not a problem is it?"

Caitlin was sliding into the back seat as the girl started the engine. "No it's fine. Sorry I asked."

"Don't you worry. You just sit there and relax and we'll 'ave you there in no time at all."

She couldn't relax, though. As the car drove her back over the now-empty suspension bridge – the cameras, gantries and other moviemaking equipment having been cleared away – and took her down tree-lined roads, Caitlin suddenly realised she had no idea how far away Madame Dorothy's farm was, or even if she was being taken in the right direction.

And there was a maniac on the loose.

And she hadn't told anyone where she was going.

"Whatcha doin'?"

Caitlin dropped her phone at the girl's barked question. She knew she was nervous, but she hadn't realised just how much until that moment. She tried to smile as the driver eyed her in the rear view mirror.

"Just phoning a friend."

"Oh. Right. You might have trouble getting a signal out here, mind."

It took a few tries and some wriggling around on the

back seat, but eventually she got a signal. Nobody was answering, of course. Every single undoubtedly drink-addled one of them had set their phones to go straight to voicemail. The signal cut out just after she left the address Madame Dorothy had given her on Raymond's phone. After that the bar indicator remained stubbornly at zero.

Caitlin breathed a sigh of relief. At least somebody knew where she was going, now. Not that she was going to get into any trouble. Dr Valentine was a man, wasn't he? Not a kindly-sounding old lady who lived with her daughter out in the middle of nowhere.

Relax, Caitlin.

Even so, it was getting darker and the roads were getting narrower. There wasn't even the benefit of moonlight to better see the narrow lanes the cab was now taking her down. The vehicle took a sharp right turn, and then there was the sound of gravel beneath the tyres as the car began to jerk over the bumps and potholes of a dirt track.

Dear God where was she being taken?

"Are you sure this is right?"

The driver said nothing, just kept her eyes fixed on the stretch of track ahead that was illuminated by the car's headlights.

"Excuse me?" Caitlin tried the door.

Locked.

"Excuse me – are you sure we're going to the right place?"

Now there was a light ahead, a pinprick of glowing yellow in the otherwise all-pervading blackness. It grew as the car neared it, and Caitlin realised it was a lantern, hanging outside the door of the farm the car was now pulling up outside.

"That'll be a tenner," said the girl, after she had pulled up the handbrake and switched on the light.

Caitlin gathered her bag and shawl. Apart from the light by the door, the building was in darkness.

"Would you mind waiting?"

"It'll cost you."

"That's okay. Keep the meter running until I come back."

The girl rolled her eyes as if the concept of a meter was something that belonged in another world. "Yeah, sure."

Caitlin half expected the driver to open the door for her, but when the girl showed no signs of budging, she flipped the handle herself and found to her relief that it opened.

The night had turned chilly and she wrapped her shawl around her shoulders as she made her way across the muddy forecourt to the door. There was no bell, and the heavy, rusted knocker creaked as she lifted it to hammer it against the wood.

Once.

Twice.

Wait.

Caitlin glanced back nervously at the cab. The driver ignored her, engrossed in something glowing in her lap. Probably texting that she'd brought the weirdo to the weird place and she'd be a while yet because the damned woman wanted her to wait.

Wait.

Should she try again? There was no evidence of any lights coming on. Thank God she'd asked the girl to stay, otherwise she'd be in real trouble, stranded out here.

She knocked again.

And again.

Silence

Okay, that was enough. For all she knew this was the wrong place, anyway. If she took the cab back now she'd be in bed by eleven and no harm done.

She was just turning to go back to the car when she heard the door open.

"Are you the young lady for the reading?"

Caitlin took a moment to reply. Madame Dorothy (for it had to be she) looked like everything Caitlin could have hoped for in a rustic English fortune teller. Gypsy skirts, hand knitted top covering a blouse that looked beige in the weak light, headscarf wrapped tightly but with a few wisps of silver hair poking out from beneath it. And that face! Old, and wise, and full of confidence, no doubt from her many years communing with the spirit world. It was most likely that confidence that leant Madame Dorothy's visage just the slightest hint of masculinity.

"Yes." Madame Dorothy waited. Caitlin didn't know what else to say. "Well, not exactly young, but I am definitely here for a reading. If, that is, you are Madame Dorothy?"

The old lady flung the door wide so Caitlin could see the fire burning in the grate at the back of the house, raised her arms, and bellowed a most unexpected invitation.

"Hail to thee, Queen of Pentacles!"

It was such a shock that instead of moving forward as she was probably meant to, Caitlin took a step back.

"Oh goodness me, did I startle you?" And the fortune teller was back to kindly old Madame Dorothy. "I'm terribly sorry my dear, sometimes I do get a little carried away. Follow me, if you would be so kind."

The corridor to the back room was almost as dark as the night outside, and Caitlin narrowed her eyes as she inspected the floor for the inevitable cats lurking in wait to trip her up. She made it to the parlour unbrushed, where both the roaring fire and an oil lamp on the circular table leant her surroundings a cosy orange glow.

"That's something I'd never see in LA."

"I'm sorry, dear?"

"A fire." Caitlin pointed at the flickering flames. "It would be far too hot."

"Oh, these English summer nights can get rather chilly, and we mustn't have you getting uncomfortable, must we?"

As if to prove the point, Dorothy took the poker and gave the coals a thorough going over, before leaving the tip of the implement wedged deep in the glowing embers.

"I find if I do that it stops it the silly thing from sparking when I have to use it again. Do take off your shawl, dear, you can't possibly be cold in here."

Caitlin wasn't, in fact it was a relief to be free of it. She sat on one of the two wooden chairs while Dorothy closed the door they had entered through, drew the curtains closed, and turned the light from the lamp down so it was barely a glow. Then Dorothy sat so that she was facing

Caitlin, laid her hands on the crimson damask tablecloth and turned them so the palms faced upwards.

"Your hands, please."

"I thought we were going to do a—"

"Your hands. Please."

Caitlin noticed Dorothy had big hands, but she still didn't expect their grip to be quite so powerful. She gasped as Dorothy tightened her hold.

"Very interesting. I see you have been through some traumas in the past."

"You mean those scars on my wrists?" Caitlin gave a nervous giggle. "Those aren't what you're probably thinking. In fact they're—"

"—surgical. Yes, I know. Carpal tunnel releases."

"Yes. How did you know?"

"I am Madame Dorothy, I know all. Now, please be quiet while I examine your future."

From Madame Dorothy's expression Caitlin's future seemed to start off well but quickly became either confusing or frankly worrying.

"You are a stranger to this land?"

"Yes." But she could probably tell that just from the accent.

"You have not been here very long."

"No." That was true, but it could still be a guess.

"And you're not going to be here for much longer."

"Aren't I?" That was a relief. Truth be told, Caitlin couldn't wait to get away from this country and back to the warmth of LA, where the people were just as weird as the ones here but it was her kind of weird – the kind she could deal with, put up with, and sometimes even embrace.

"I don't think so. Your lifeline suggests that things are about to undergo a sudden change."

"For the better?"

Madame Dorothy gave her a thin smile. "We shall have to consult the cards to learn more about that." She released Caitlin and held out her hand.

"Oh yes, sorry." Caitlin rummaged in her bag and brought out four ten pound notes, which she handed over. "Will that be enough? I'll probably need the rest to pay the cab driver when I get back."

"That will do nicely my dear. After all, it's not as if we're going to be here for very long, is it?"

Caitlin didn't know what to say to that, and so she just shrugged as Madame Dorothy produced a Ryder Tarot deck and began to look through the cards.

"Aren't you supposed to shuffle them first?" Caitlin's enquiry was met with a brief glare that quickly resolved itself into an expression of benevolence.

"I have to find you first, dear. Aha! There you are."

The Queen of Pentacles was drawn from the pack and placed in the centre of the table. Then the pack was shuffled – deliberately and with Dorothy's eye on Caitlin the entire time she did it. Then nine more cards were dealt in rapid succession, face down this time and forming the traditional Celtic Cross pattern.

"This forms the base of your question, this crowns you, this is behind you, this ahead of you, this where you find yourself, this the views of other, then we have your hopes and fears and finally..." Madame Dorothy laid down the final card "...this will be the outcome."

"But I haven't asked a question."

"You want to know what's going to happen to you, don't you?" Madame Dorothy's voice was almost a whisper. "What the immediate future holds?"

"Yes, I suppose so."

"I suppose so." Was that a sneer on the fortune teller's face? In fact, was she imitating Caitlin's Californian accent? "Well why don't we take a look then?"

Madame Dorothy ignored all the preceding cards and went straight for the final one. Caitlin braced herself as it was turned over. Then she relaxed.

"Happy with that one, are you?"

Caitlin shrugged again. "I'm just relieved... really pleased, actually, that it's not Death."

"Deary me." Dorothy tutted. "Now why would a young lady like you be expecting that card to be your final outcome?"

Caitlin gave a giggle of relief. "I don't know, and I don't really know why I was so worried about it appearing anyway, because it's actually a very good card, isn't it?"

Madame Dorothy's expression grew grim.

"No."

The word sent a chill down Caitlin's spine. To shake it off she returned her attention to the upturned card.

"It's not the Tower either, is it? Thank goodness."

"No it is not. Thank, as you say, goodness."

Caitlin wrinkled her nose. "It *is* a bit grim though."

"So many of the cards are, my dear."

"But even so. A dead body with ten swords sticking out of it?" Caitlin gave Madame Dorothy a nervous smile. "I hope you're going to tell me it means something good is going to happen to me."

"*Something* is going to happen to you, that much is certain." Madame Dorothy got to her feet and moved over to the fireplace. "You'll have to excuse me a moment my dear, it really has got a little chilly in here."

Had it? Caitlin hadn't noticed.

"You said you were glad it was not the Death card, a card that represents change, an old life ending and a new one beginning." Dorothy picked up the poker and raked through the fire's smouldering embers once more.

"Yes."

"And yet you find yourself relieved at a card that signifies not a change, but an ending, for that is what the ten of swords is." The old lady held the poker aloft like a schoolmistress addressing her class and using her cane to emphasise a point. The tip of the poker was a brilliant orange. It made Caitlin sweat just to look at it. Was it her imagination or could she feel the heat from it?

Dorothy took a step forward. "The ten of swords represents a dark time in life, when one sees something as it really, truly is, and realises that there really is nowhere...further...to go."

The old lady was coming forward now, the glowing poker still held out in front of her. Only she wasn't old at all, not now that she had pulled off the headscarf and the silver-haired wig beneath. In fact, she wasn't even a woman.

Oh God.

Him.

Caitlin pushed her chair back, got to her feet, and tried to back away, immediately stumbling over the chair in which she had just been sitting.

"Get away!"

The figure holding the poker merely shook his head as he moved slowly but purposefully forward.

Caitlin pushed the chair aside, turned, and ran back down the corridor that led to the outside door. If she screamed loudly enough perhaps the cab driver would hear her!

The cab driver was standing in the entrance.

"Oh God please! You have to help me! There's this man and he's been killing us – the people I work with – and now he wants to kill me! Please, please we have to get out of here!" Caitlin added a 'Now!' when the cab driver didn't move. In fact, the girl didn't seem to be listening to her at all.

She was looking over Caitlin's shoulder.

"Everything all right, mum?"

"Oh yes," said the man in his Madame Dorothy voice. "It certainly is, now that we're all a family again. Caitlin, have you met my daughter?"

Caitlin didn't know which way to turn, between the man wielding the poker and the girl who had now raised the meat cleaver she was holding in her right hand. "They said I was well again," said 'Dorothy' as the searing heat became almost unbearable. "They said I was well."

In the end, Caitlin didn't know whether it was the poker or the cleaver that hit her first, and even if the cards could have foretold which, it wouldn't have really mattered.

10

CLIFTON SUSPENSION BRIDGE, BRISTOL
EARLY THE NEXT MORNING

Very early, in fact.

Mac Armitage stamped his feet to keep out the chill as he adjusted his camera. "Why in God's name did Elliot want us back here at four in the goddamned morning?"

Raymond St Pearce shook his weary, hangover-ridden head. "His text to my cellphone said the shots we got yesterday weren't authentic enough."

"Pah! Authentic my goddamned ass!" Mac zoomed in and out on their 'star', clad in a black cloak. "Does he know how much more difficult it is to get night shots? I thought that was why Chuck was told to write as many scenes in broad daylight as possible."

"That's what I did." Charles Herman sipped steaming coffee from a polystyrene cup. "Maybe Mr Edwards has had a sudden change of heart and wants to be more faithful to the book."

That resulted in a cackle of laughter from Mac. "Sorry boy, but that idea that Mr Edwards has anything other than pure soulless greed pumping blood around that money grabbing shell of his has just made my morning."

"Let's just get on with the shot, shall we?" Raymond sounded irritable. "Some of us would like to spend the rest of it back in bed."

"With that little piece of tail you picked up last night,

Ray?" Mac's eye was obscured by the viewfinder but his raised eyebrow wasn't.

"None of your fucking business, Mac. Just start rolling, will you?"

"In case you've forgotten, Mr Director, you have to shout 'Action' or the rest of these good ladies and gentlemen who have also been dragged from their beauty sleep won't know to shut the fuck up."

Raymond gave Mac one last scowl before calling for quiet. His voice seemed swallowed up by the darkness enveloping the vastness of the Avon gorge beneath them.

Silence.

"Action!"

The cowled and cloaked figure of Franklin Robbins moved to the boot of the car, just as he had done the day before. He flipped it open, reached in, and dragged out a heavy object sheathed in sacking.

The object moved.

No, the object *struggled*.

"No-one told me Elliot had hired a stuntman," Chuck whispered.

"No." Raymond was concentrating on the scene. "I suppose Caitlin might have. Where the hell is she, anyway?" Chuck shrugged. "You must admit it's adding a lot to the scene."

Indeed it was. Unlike yesterday, 'Dr Valentine' seemed to be having genuine difficulty in dragging the bound, writhing body over to the edge of the bridge. He paused for a moment to get his breath.

"That's overdoing it a bit isn't it?" Chuck took another gulp of coffee.

"No, this is great," Raymond murmured. "It's real. That's what people want nowadays. I bet Dr Valentine himself had the same trouble when he performed the actual murder."

Mac was still rolling as 'Dr Valentine' reached between folds in the blanket and pulled out a rope.

"Brilliant," said Raymond. "We can cut in a close-up of him wrapping it around the guy's neck but this is still so much better than yesterday. Did you have a word with him?"

"No." Charles looked around. "Maybe Caitlin did. Still no sign of her, though."

Now 'Dr Valentine' was heaving the struggling body up onto the wall that ran the length of the bridge, pausing only to tie the free end of the rope to one of the bridge's metal support cables.

"He's forgotten the gasoline," Chuck was doing his best to keep his voice to a whisper, but it was obvious some of the crew members could hear and they were giving both him and Raymond disdainful glances.

"Didn't you read Elliot's memo?" Raymond hissed back. "Or Marcie's? The Bristol police said if we set anything on fire here they'd make sure we were put away for longer than Tom Cruise's career. We've had to just settle for hanging. Don't worry, we'll shoot the burning when we get back to LA and edit it in."

Meanwhile, after a degree of pushing and shoving, the stunt person bound tightly in the blankets had finally slid from the bridge and was now hanging, suspended in mid-air.

"Cut! Excellent!" Raymond was clapping his hands.

"Let's get some close-ups of the hanging body from the bridge and then we'll haul him up. Franklin, we won't need you for this."

The actor playing Dr Valentine nodded and slipped away.

"Frankie's being a bit quiet this morning." Mac stepped back as two grips moved in to position the camera equipment closer to the side of the bridge.

"Did you see the two girls he left the club with?" Raymond whistled. "I'd be struggling to drag *myself* onto that bridge this morning, never mind whoever that stunt person is. He's probably gone for a lie down, and I don't blame him."

They waited while the crew set up a shot looking straight down onto the body through the gaps in the bridge's metal framework. Mac made sure everything was in frame, then nodded to Raymond.

"OK everybody, let's have quite again! And...action!"

Silence descended as the camera rolled, framing perfectly the body of Dr Valentine's latest struggling victim.

Except the victim wasn't struggling. In fact it had stopped moving altogether.

Raymond rolled his eyes. "Could we have some squirming down below there, please? Perhaps a few jerks? Come on, you've got a rope around your neck and you're about to be burned alive, show a little terror, could you?"

Nothing.

"Maybe he was at the party last night too?" Chuck was peering over at the motionless form.

"If he's passed out I'll fucking kill him, but only after we've shot the entire thing again." Raymond called over to the crew. "Has anybody got something we can poke him with?"

Chuck grimaced. "I don't think Health and Safety will be very happy with you doing that, Raymond."

"Health and Safety aren't fucking well here are they?"

Raymond's snarl was cut off by a woman's scream behind them. "Oh my God he's not moving! For Christ's sake pull him up!"

Before Raymond had a chance to protest the motionless body was being hauled up and back over onto the bridge by crew members. They proceeded to unwrap the blankets.

There was another scream.

"Fucking hell, what is it now?"

Raymond pushed the crew aside to see what they were staring at.

They were not staring at a stuntman.

They were staring at Franklin Robbins, the Nicolas Cage lookalike.

"But...but that's Dr Valentine!" Raymond spluttered.

"I know," was all Chuck could say.

"He just pushed that body off the bridge!"

"I know.'

"How the hell could he be in two places at once?"

There was a pause then while an ambulance and the police were called.

"Maybe he wasn't playing Dr Valentine just now?"

Raymond turned on Chuck then. "Then who the fuck was, eh? Who. The Fuck. Would tie up Franklin like in the book, chuck him off the bridge, and let us all watch while he died."

"Probably the same guy who got us all here at four am to film it."

Raymond's eyes narrowed. "Elliot Edwards?"

Chuck was still shaking his head as they settled down and waited for the police to arrive.

CLIFTON SUSPENSION BRIDGE AGAIN,
BUT A SHORT WHILE LATER

"This is all a bit too bloody familiar."

Jeffrey Longdon peered into the Avon Gorge before moving his attention to the horizon. The sun was just beginning to come up.

"That was happening last time we were here, wasn't it?"

"I think your memory's better than mine." A crackling voice on Jenny's radio asked what they wanted to do with all the crew members they were detaining.

"Let 'em go. No, wait. Keep behind anyone who isn't local and is still alive. That means the director, that bloke with the camera and anyone else. Is that Robbins bloke dead?" The paramedic nodded before getting into the back of the ambulance. "I don't know why I even bothered to ask."

"Valentine could still be nearby, sir."

"Oh he could be, Newham. For all we know he might be driving that ambulance out of here right now. Or he could be one of our own men. Or he could even be you."

"I think that's a bit far-fetched sir."

"You're right, of course. You get an apology for that, Newham. Sorry."

"That's quite all right, sir."

"Now, where are those Hollywood types?"

Longdon's inquiry was swiftly answered as the three men were brought over to him. None of them looked happy.

"Is this all of them?"

"I've phoned Elliot," said Raymond. "He's on the way and he's bringing Lisa, our art director. I can't get hold of Caitlin."

"That's not surprising. Gentlemen, I am sorry to have to inform you that the body of Caitlin Dufresne was discovered in a barn by the side of the M5 just a short while ago. She had been covered with straw, but the perpetrator had reckoned without the farmer's cows."

"Did she have a power drill injury to the head?" Jenny asked.

"Poker to the abdomen and meat cleaver to the face, but very good thinking nevertheless, Newham."

"What the fuck are you two talking about?"

Raymond's words caused the corner of Longdon's left eye to crease slightly. "Now, now, sonny. I've already warned you about language in front of my DS. She was describing one of the murders in the 1974 Pete Walker film *Frightmare*, and even though we've yet to get the full post mortem report, I have very strong suspicions that it provided the inspiration for Dr Valentine's latest murder."

"Don't you mean second latest, Inspector?" Even in the wan light of the lazy Bristol sunrise, Chuck had gone a lighter shade of green.

"Yeah." Mac lit a cigarette and blew the smoke in the direction of the retreating ambulance. "What film is Franklin's killing from, then?"

"My guess would be that he couldn't pass up the opportunity to bump someone off under your noses in a scene from his actual life story. Was the whole thing by any chance more accurately enacted than in your script?" The three men nodded. "Well there you are, then."

"What the fucking Goddamned Christ is going on here?"

Elliot Edwards had arrived with a bewildered-looking Lisa Wallcroft in tow.

Longdon's face was grave. "I'm afraid Dr Valentine has killed the actor who was playing Dr Valentine."

"He wasn't an actor, he was just a stand-in."

Longdon sighed. "In that case the stand-in for the actor playing Dr Valentine has just been killed – by the real Dr Valentine."

"Who was playing the movie Dr Valentine, at the time." Chuck added.

"What?"

"The real Dr Valentine, playing the movie Dr Valentine, has just killed your stand-in for the actor playing Dr Valentine who wasn't playing Dr Valentine in the scene but was playing one of Dr Valentine's victims and ended up as an actual victim of the real Dr Valentine." Jenny took a deep breath.

Elliot frowned. "I still don't get it."

Raymond had a go. "Franklin is dead."

"Shit." Elliot took out a cigar. "Any idea who did it?"

"Yes," said Longdon, and left it at that. "We've also found the body of your casting director."

Elliot looked around. "Where?"

"Some distance from here." Longdon thought it best not to elaborate. "She's dead as well."

The producer clenched his cigar so tightly between his teeth he almost bit the end off. "Just what kind of half-assed operation are you people running here?"

"You know precisely what kind of a criminal we are dealing with, sir." Jenny was trying to keep her voice calm. "You're the one making a film about him, after all."

"Yeah!" Elliot's face was turning red to compliment Chuck's green. "Making a movie! Something we should be able to do in your goddamned country safely and without any risk of getting ourselves killed!" His index finger was poised to poke Jenny in the shoulder. "Now I wanna know what the hell you are gonna do about it!"

"I'll tell you what we are going to do...sir." Longdon's bellow shut everyone up and probably woke any residents who had managed to sleep through the events so far. "We are shutting down your little production."

"What!"

"It is simply too risky for you to continue. I would suggest that all four of you pack your bags and go home. It might be your only chance of surviving the next week."

"Christ!" Elliot was reaching boiling point. He took a step forward so that he was right in Longdon's face. "I'd heard you Brits hated foreigners, but I never thought I'd actually experience such blatant xenophobia!"

"I never thought I would meet a film producer who knew that word." Longdon didn't move an inch.

"You are fucking rude, Inspector."

Longdon raised an eyebrow. "Am I?"

"Come on Elliot." They were the first words Lisa had spoken. "You're just getting yourself worked up." She laid a hand on his arm and tried to pull him back. The man backed away, but it was obviously a struggle.

"You won't stop us, you know! And neither will he! If you won't let us shoot here we'll find somewhere else! I've still got my director, my director of photography, *and* my production designer, and I am going to—"

"And your writer..." came a choked voice from the back that was presumably Chuck's.

"Oh yeah, and him too. Anyways, I swear to you now that I am going to get this damned film finished if it kills me."

"That's up to you, sir," said Longdon. "As long as you realise that Dr Valentine will most likely kill you long before your attempt to finish the film has a chance to."

"Fuck you!" was all Elliot seemed to have left to say. It certainly was all that he did say, repeatedly, as he was led back to the waiting car, the remainder of his production team shuffling in tow.

Longdon and Jenny waited until the fucks had receded into background noise before saying anything else.

"He's not going to stop, is he?"

"Do you mean Elliot Edwards, Newham? Or Dr Edward Valentine?"

"Both, sir, but I thought I'd leave it like that so it could mean either."

"Well I think you're right on both counts, Newham. We've got a crazed producer intent on risking his and his team's lives to finish his project, and a crazed killer intent on stopping them in the style of old British horror movies from the 1970s, but apart from that we have no idea how or where or when he might strike next."

"So what do we do next, sir?"

The sun was up, now. Longdon pointed to a cafe on the corner.

"Breakfast."

12

A Car Heading Into the English Countryside

So that was it, then.

Chuck Herman tried to relax as he gazed out at the countryside passing by. Another job finished. Or rather, stopped by the police before anyone else could be murdered. And would Elliot be paying him? He didn't think so. He was going to starve to death before Elliot gave him back those pictures of him with that girl, the one whose father had sworn he would kill Chuck if he went near his daughter. It wouldn't have made any difference how many times he explained that it was she who had gone near him. Such things, rare as they were, never seemed to work out in his favour.

He gave a deep sigh. He needed money, he needed a future, but most of all right now he needed to escape the clutches of Elliot Edwards, producer and blackmailer extraordinaire. All he needed was the first to achieve the second and the third.

Which was why he was being driven into the depths of Wessex.

He unfolded the printout of the email he had responded to earlier, and read it through one more time.

Dear Mr Herman
I apologise for approaching you without going through your agent...

Chuck smirked. Elliot acted as his 'agent', and for all he knew the man had been suppressing gigs like this for the last couple of years.

> ...but I learned you were in the country working on a new picture for AEP and I could not pass up the opportunity to enquire as to whether or not, after your current project is finished, you might be conducive to working on one of my projects?
>
> I already know what you are thinking. Why, when there are so many screenwriters in England, would I want to employ somebody from the US? Well, aside from your considerable skill and experience, I need someone who can turn out a script from a distinctly American point of view. Also, I would be very grateful if you could perhaps do a little script doctoring on projects that are not quite ready for the camera?
>
> If you are interested in any or all of these I would be delighted to meet up with you for an interview. Our studios are located within Dunsmoor House, the kind of stately home many of your countrymen believe we all live in. I can provide transport, and, if nothing else, it will give me the chance to show you some of the old props we have hanging around here, just to give you an idea of the kind of thing we want.
>
> I very much look forward to hearing from you.
> Yours sincerely,
> Max Milton

Chuck folded the paper back up and put it in his pocket.

The email had arrived before all the trouble had started, and he had replied saying yes, he would very much like to consider working for a new company. When the car had arrived at his hotel this morning to pick him up he had quite forgotten his appointment. The driver was very good, though, and waited while Chuck made a couple of telephone calls to make sure the car company was genuine (which it was). He had considered contacting the police, just to let them know where he was going, but they were having a difficult enough time of it controlling Elliot, and the one thing Chuck didn't want was for his producer to learn he was going for a job with another company. In the end he had put the phone down, reasoning that he had kept the driver waiting long enough and chances like this didn't come along every day. Or ever, in fact.

Now he was here, with dark clouds glowering overhead making it feel more like night than ten in the morning, being driven along a busy main road through the heart of England.

Even with the weather so threatening, Chuck had never felt so free.

He was just beginning to relax when the car turned off. They passed between two tall wrought-iron gates and proceeded along a narrow gravel drive that wound its way through a forest of beech. There was a rumble of thunder overhead and Chuck had to repeatedly tell himself he couldn't see things moving between the trees. He made his living by his imagination, but there were times when it was more his enemy than his friend.

Raindrops began to spatter the windscreen.

This all feels like the start of a movie in itself.

Stop thinking like that, Chuck told himself, because in a minute you're going to reach your destination and it's going to be a great big old country house, the kind that's haunted, or inhabited by a couple of old ladies who keep their lunatic brother in the cellar when he isn't out killing the locals at night, or used as a women's prison, the kind where no-one ever gets out, and you are going to go in there and be interviewed and you are not going to appear at all nervous, okay?

Okay?

Chuck allowed himself a nervous giggle. At least he'd have plenty of ideas to pitch if he was asked.

There was light up ahead – dim and grey and suggestive that the driveway was coming to an end. The car emerged from the forest and there it was in all its glory – Dunsmoor House.

It looked exactly how Chuck had imagined it. In fact as he got out of the car he half expected a girl to emerge screaming from its entrance, begging him to take her far away from here, and not to believe the women in uniform who were following who would claim she was sick, that this was a private clinic, and that she needed to be taken away for more treatment.

Really stop that now.

Chuck approached the broad double doors, took hold of the heavy iron ring held in the mouth of what looked like the blackened head of a lion, and knocked.

As he waited there, in the cold and the rain, he half expected the car to drive away, leaving him alone in the middle of nowhere and awaiting the attentions of the servants who lived and lurked in this forbidding place.

But the car stayed where it was, the rain was already improving, and now the door had opened. Of its own accord, somehow. Chuck peered inside.

"What are you doing?"

The girl at the reception desk was attractive, dark haired, and the way she had the tip of her pen placed between her lips made Chuck's legs feel decidedly wobbly. He also felt an immense sensation of relief.

"Chuck Herman," he held out his hand. "I'm here for an appointment with..."

"...Mr Milton, yes I know." The girl picked up the phone and announced Chuck's arrival. She nodded at whatever was said on the other end and put the receiver down. "I'm afraid he's a little busy at the moment, but he will see you if you're willing to wait."

Chuck nodded, perhaps a little too vigorously. "No problem." He looked around the broad entrance hall. There was nowhere to sit.

The girl pointed to a doorway on the right. Her fingernails were scarlet. "Mr Milton suggested you might like to take a look at the props museum while you're waiting? Something about it hopefully providing inspiration for what he would like to discuss with you."

"Sure." Chuck pulled on his glasses and squinted at the sign over the doorway. "Dr Diabolo's Temptations Limited," he read aloud. "A circus picture?"

"Kind of." She gave him a big smile. "It certainly had a few acts that killed them in the provinces, Mr Milton always says. You've heard of it?"

"Yeah." Or had he? He couldn't be sure, but it was always best to play along. "Of course."

The girl's smile broadened. "Great. Then you'll be prepared for the kind of things you're going to see in there."

"Sure." Chuck was already making for the doorway. "But it'll do me good to refresh my memory."

"Of course." She waved him farewell with a crimson-tipped claw. "See you later."

"Er...yeah. See you too."

"If you say so."

Chuck was still pondering what the girl might have meant when a door he hadn't previously noticed swung shut behind him with all the finality of the closing of a vault. It made a loud clang, too, one that made him jump so much that he almost missed the first exhibit.

Because that's what it was. He had expected the studio's prop room to be a dusty cupboard filled with rotting plasterboard glories of productions past, but this was nothing like that.

It was almost as if he was in a museum.

"Dr Diabolo's Temptations Limited Museum!" he said aloud to nobody in particular, just to break the cloying silence.

The corridor he was in was narrow and dully lit. To his left were a series of booths, each displaying their own atmospherically-lit tableau. It seemed to be an awful lot of trouble to go to just to display a few items from old movies but hey, maybe these were classic pictures in this country, revered by fans who wanted this stuff preserved. And it made sense that any film company that intended to last would explore all kinds of platforms for making money.

"You're starting to sound like Elliot," he chided himself. "Just shut up and see the show."

The first booth depicted a hairy creature on its hind legs attacking a cowering man on an unrealistic-looking glen. For some reason a blue flag with a white cross on it hung in the background.

Chuck peered at the explanatory card stuck to the railing that was presumably there to prevent people from straying into, and damaging, the exhibits.

"'Werewolf'." Well that was obvious, wasn't it? But perhaps not to Brits who had never seen that picture with... who was it... Benicio del Toro? From a few years back?

The next exhibit was more disturbing. A man was being dragged from his desk (and the microscope balanced upon it) by what could only be described as rampant foliage.

"'Creeping Vine'," Chuck read. "Obviously."

The third had a guy holding a trumpet while his head disappeared inside the giant, wide-open mouth of something out of a nightmare but was actually, according to the card, the voodoo god Dambala. Next to that a man wearing spectacles fought off a dismembered hand that was trying to strangle him, while the fifth booth along showed a sombre young man staking a sexy lady while a hatchet-faced man looked on from the background, a vulpine grin on his face.

"'Vampire'," Chuck sniffed. "Well, if you say so."

He had come to a right turn. He hoped it was going to lead to an exit. Instead it took him to the next set of displays.

An overweight tabby cat was eating the remains of a human head in a prison cell. A girl had skin scratched from her face to reveal metal beneath. Chuck didn't see the point of the grand piano until he saw the blonde girl pinned beneath it surrounded by splinters of broken glass.

"And Edgar Allan Poe!" Now Chuck was facing a portrait of the famous author. "I wonder if they spelled his name right." He had never bothered to learn it.

A strangler, the severed head of Salome on a plate, a half-melted wax doll next to a screaming man and finally an old cloak, the label 'Property of Shepperton Studios' prominently displayed for some reason, formed the next stage of what was becoming a decidedly peculiar tour.

Chuck was starting to feel disorientated. Here was another right hand turn. Surely he had gone round in a circle by now? The Santa Claus carrying a bloodstained axe suggested not, neither did the decaying corpse of a man screaming into a mirror, the horribly realistic-looking heart sitting on a blood-smeared Valentine's day poem, the coffin filled with squirming body parts (animatronic of course, but they looked so real), nor the blind men hard at work on something Chuck couldn't quite make out.

Another right turn, and a dead end.

And the final tableau.

It was a mixture of things that made no sense to Chuck at all. On the left was a collection of paper-wrapped parcels, presided over by what looked like a dressmaker's dummy. Next to that was a mannikin of a pretty girl, her face jammed up against another mirror, but instead of screaming, her face was contorted into a macabre, deeply unsettling expression of amusement. Then, on the far right, was a table on which were posed a number of small dolls.

One of the dolls was moving.

As it edged its way to the end of the table, Chuck peered at the doll's head. Was it his imagination, or had its face been modelled after his, glasses and all?

He stood, entranced by the little automaton as it half-slid, half-scuttled its way across the scratched wooden surface. He held his breath as it took one step too far – and plunged to the stone floor beneath.

The tiny clay head, its features fashioned so carefully to resemble the screenwriter, was dashed to pieces as the doll struck the ground. So accurate a reproduction was it that Chuck could feel his heart hammering in his chest as it toppled and fell, and when the little face crumbled he drew an anxious breath.

But there was little time to mourn the death of Chuck's homunculus. There was movement at the opposite end of the tableau, now. Those curious brown paper parcels were starting to move, to shuffle towards him. As they began to emerge into the light, Chuck took a step back.

The first one looked like an arm, a human arm wrapped up and tied with string. It was using its fingers in a pincer-like movement to pull itself along.

Both engrossed and repelled by what had to be a piece of clockwork machinery, Chuck stood spellbound as a second arm appeared, followed by a leg. This limb was on its side and employed the knee joint to help it move.

All three limbs were coming closer.

To him.

Chuck moved to the right.

So did the limbs.

He moved to the left.

So did the limbs, all the while getting closer. Soon they would be past the barrier and within touching distance. Chuck felt that would be a very bad idea. He was about to return the way he had come when there was a dull thud, followed by the sound of crackling paper.

And a brown paper-wrapped head rolled out from the shadows, past the limbs, and came to rest at Chuck's feet. It was the paper moving in and out where the mouth should be that made him take a further step back.

He wasn't ready to run yet, though, not even when the dressmaker's dummy straightened itself and turned its chipped, lacquered waxen head, staring at him with its unblinking boiled-egg eyes.

He ran when the dummy began to walk towards him. Stiff-limbed and awkward of gait, he could hear its clumping, measured footsteps as it pursued him, past the coffin and the Santa, past the cloak, the doll, Salome and the strangler, past Poe, the piano, the robot and the brain-eating cat, past the—.

The exhibition came to an end. Or rather, Chuck found himself facing an abrupt narrowing of the passageway. So narrow was it that he was going to have to turn sideways to negotiate it. He looked at it, momentarily confused. There had been more exhibits, hadn't there? Where was the werewolf and the weed wrapped around the guy?

Stomping footsteps echoed behind him, creaking sounds from limbs unused to movement, swiftly drawing nearer.

There was no time to try and remember what may or may not have been here. Perhaps he'd taken a wrong turn.

In a place where there was only one way you could go?

Never mind that. Chuck turned sideways and squeezed himself between the rough plywood boards.

He had just managed to get his entire body inside when the first razor blade sliced his flesh.

Chuck screamed, a mixture of shock, surprise, and pent up fear. What the hell was something sharp doing in here?

Make that two somethings.

More than two somethings.

Jesus Christ, he was being cut everywhere!

Stomp-creak, stomp-creak.

He couldn't go back, he just couldn't, not into the waiting, rigid arms of whatever the hell it was exactly that was chasing him.

But could he go on?

He had to. Chuck kept his eyes shut tight and clenched his teeth every time he felt a new incision in his clothes and in his skin as he moved forward.

It was like being in hell.

And, like hell, it felt to Chuck as if it was never going to end. By the time he pushed himself from the other end of the narrow walkway he was a sobbing, staggering, bleeding mess barely able to keep himself upright.

Chuck wiped blood from his vision and looked ahead. Was he out? Was he back at the entrance to the exhibit?

If he was it wasn't obvious. All he could see, ahead of him in the middle distance, was what looked like something propped on an easel. It was illuminated by a spotlight somewhere high above.

Chuck dragged himself forward, no longer worried about the mannikin-thing. There was no way it could get through that razor-lined passageway. He concentrated on what he could see ahead of him. Was it a painting?

A few more steps confirmed that it was. A portrait, in fact.

Please don't let it be a portrait of me.

But it was, and a startlingly accurate one, seeing as it portrayed Chuck not as he was when he entered this dreadful place, but as he was now, blood-smeared and with his clothing in tatters.

But what was it doing here?

He leaned forward to inspect it further, and as he did so he unwittingly tripped a filament-thin wire. The wire led to a can of paint thinner perched precariously above the picture, and his movement upended it.

Turpentine poured across the painting, causing Chuck's already bloody image to melt, his features to slide, the portrait to become so hideously distorted that it only barely resembled its subject.

But only for a moment.

The movement of the can had set a second mechanism in motion, one which pushed the painting from the easel. It fell to the floor with crash and revealed the spray gun that had been positioned behind it. This all happened so quickly that Chuck had no time to recoil before the acid the spray gun had been loaded with hit him full in the face.

Chuck screamed and clawed at his eyes, his face, at the tissue that was already coming off in his hands as he fell backwards, writhing in agony on the floor.

By the time he was dead he very much resembled his portrait again.

13

"He's what?" Longdon didn't look happy.

"Disappeared, sir." Jenny handed him a printout of the film crew's latest whereabouts. "We've got tabs on Elliot Edwards, Lisa Wallcroft, Raymond St Pearce and Mac Armitage, but Charles Herman seems to have vanished off the face of the earth."

"Or under it."

"Sorry, sir?"

"Nothing, Newham, it's just that we know if one of Dr Valentine's intended victims disappears it's usually a sign to start contacting the relatives. God knows what state we'll find him in." Longdon looked down at the paper in his hand. "Edwards and Wallcroft seem to have toddled off to the same country hotel together."

"Yes, sir."

"Anything going on between them, do you think?"

"They're Hollywood types, sir. It would be odd if there wasn't anything going on, wouldn't it?"

"You've been watching too many American soap operas, Newham."

"I can't say I've had the time, sir, not with all these British horror films to watch. Over and over and over again."

"I know." Longdon rolled his eyes. "It does get a bit wearing, doesn't it? Sometimes I think there's only one person in the world who knows more about these films than we do." He put the paper down and gazed out of the window at the Bristol skyline. "And I would give my eye teeth to know what he's up to right now." He looked back to Newham. "They're all under police protection? The four of them?"

Jenny nodded. "There's a PC with them all the time, except for toilet breaks and anything else that's a bit too personal."

"I'm not sure if that's a good idea – a lot can happen in a bathroom."

"Our coppers have been instructed to knock every couple of minutes and to report in if any of the intended victims don't reply."

"And for the other 'personal' stuff?"

"Same drill, sir," Jenny grinned. "Unless of course it's possible to hear what's going on anyway."

"May the Gods save us from the comings and goings of show-business types." Longdon got to his feet. "It would help if we knew their weaknesses, their obsessions, even their hobbies. If we'd known Ryan Patrick was into motorbikes we could have kept him away from them, and it was a given that Miss DuFresne would be into all that Tarot-reading stuff." Longdon's eyes lit up. "Have any of them got criminal records?"

"No, sir. I already checked. I also tried going through US newspaper archives, but the broadsheets had nothing and the scandal sheets were just filled with rubbish."

"Probably a damned sight more creative than the work of this lot we're trying to protect I'll bet." Longdon rapped his knuckles on the desk. "You know, if this was one of their wretched films this would be the point where someone comes in who's able to tell us who the next victim is going to be, and how they're likely to be done in."

They paused.

They looked towards the door.

They waited.

"It's not going to happen, is it sir?"

"I'm so desperate it was worth a try, Newham." Longdon sat back down. "It's no good. We're going to have to rely on our own boys in blue, and hope to God none of them turn out to be Valentine in disguise."

"Or his assistant, sir."

"What?"

"His assistant. That girl you said was helping him last time."

"Oh I haven't forgotten her, Newham, but Valentine's already dressed her up as a copper – that's how he got away last time, and if there's one thing I've learned from this entire, lengthy case, it's that he doesn't like to repeat himself." Longdon tapped his pen on the desk as he thought. "It's a good point, though. You'd best get the message out that none of our suspected targets should spend any undue amount of time with either a man *or* a woman they aren't one hundred per cent sure of."

~

"I bet I know what you like."

The girl was blonde and very pretty, with that rustic accent common to the area that reminded Mac Armitage of farms, and girls on farms, and movies about girls on farms, ones that you couldn't even buy in this country without going into some sleazy store where your chances of getting out uninjured looked slim. Of course he had his laptop, but the WiFi in his hotel was terrible and the last thing you wanted was for a streaming video to start buffering at a crucial point.

That was what had brought him into town, that goddamned cop bodyguard in tow. He had explained he wanted to go to a store that sold DVDs. After an unsuccessful trip to two different malls, he had resorted to making his requirements obvious, and Constable Alan Mathers had explained, a little red-faced, that 'one needs to go to a specialist shop for such items, sir, and to be honest, the very particular type of things you're after aren't strictly legal in this country, so shall we just pretend this conversation never happened?'

Yes, Mac was very happy to pretend the conversation had never happened. If only he could do the same for this country, this trip and this goddamned fucking movie. He knew he couldn't say no to Elliot – for all kinds of reasons, the least of them being the money – but perhaps this was the one time when he should have just run away, or gone into hiding. Now he was here in this shitty country with its shitty porn laws being watched by the police night and day – not because of anything he'd done (thank God) but because there was a chance he might never make it back to God's own blessed US of A if this Dr Valentine managed to kill him first.

So now he was in a coffee shop in what the cop had told him was 'one of the nicest parts of Bristol'. The fact that the guy had then proceeded to point out to him the roof of the building where Dr Valentine had skewered one of his victims onto the horn of a golden unicorn a few years ago meant he no longer felt like sipping his coffee or eating the pastry the man had bought for him, not once the policeman had realised that Dr Valentine's previous methods of dispatch were probably not a suitable subject of conversation with someone who was now on the hit list himself.

But then he had spotted the girl.

He couldn't be sure if she had followed him in, or if she had been one of the customers in the queue in front of him. Either way, now she was sitting opposite, sucking on the straw of some creamy strawberry milkshake thing. Every time he caught her eye she smiled.

"You'll have to excuse me a minute, sir." PC Mathers was making for the restroom, having drunk only half of his gargantuan Americano. Mac didn't know what to do, but evidently the girl did. She got up from the crushed brown leather sofa where she had been sitting and came over to him, her opening line putting ideas into his head that he was sure she didn't intend. When he didn't respond, she repeated it.

"I said, I bet I know what you like."

"I heard you the first time. And you think so, do you?"

The girl's eyes widened, just like they might do when she was being—

"Oh! An American! I love American men! Say something! Please!"

Mac gave her a broad smile and puffed out his chest, feeling the material of his red plaid shirt tightening. "Well, what exactly is it you'd like me to say?"

"Anything! I mean, that was great but just...would you mind if we chatted? Just for a little bit? If you're not too busy?"

Mac patted the seat beside him. "Never too busy to talk to a pretty lady, ma'am." He took off his denim jacket, which was old and tatty and he knew didn't show him to his best advantage. He held his stomach in and crossed his fingers that PC Mathers got stuck in the john, or discovered some crime in progress that would keep him occupied for the next half hour.

"Great! Thanks!" The girl took out a questionnaire. Mac's face dropped. "I'm here today on behalf of SmileyChild, a charity that helps kids with incurable cancers enjoy the life they have left." She filled something in at the top. "And I bet you're just the kind of lovely guy who likes to help kids."

For a moment Mac didn't realise she'd stopped talking. Now he was too busy hoping PC Mathers would hurry up.

"I beg your pardon?"

"SmileyChild." The girl tapped the clipboard. "Would you be interested in making a donation? All I need are your direct debit details. It's only three pounds a month, cheaper even than that coffee you're drinking."

Mac already had his hands up. "I'm sorry to have to tell you, but as you may have guessed, I don't actually live in the UK."

The girl's cheeks reddened extremely becomingly. Mac wondered if other parts of her were capable of turning the same shade of gently flustered pink. "Oh, I really should have guessed. Sorry."

Mac smiled. "No problem."

"So are you here visiting relatives? Are they here?" The girl had picked up her pen again and was surveying the coffee shop. "Do you think they would like to contribute?"

"I'm not here with anyone." And Mac was back to hoping PC Mathers stayed put. "I'm in the UK because of work."

He assumed that would be the end of the conversation, but it wasn't. Instead, the girl made herself more comfortable by tucking her right foot beneath her (flexible as well, Mac noted, better and better) and leaned forward.

"What kind of work?"

If there was ever an opportunity to make the most of being employed by AEP to shoot their cheap pieces of crap, this was it. Mac took a sip from his coffee to make her wait a little, then he fixed her with his best important stare and said,

"I'm in the movies."

That was all, he thought. Short and sweet. Let it sink in. He watched as it did, signified by a delicate fluttering of her eyelashes and a quick lick of the lips. He bet her heart rate had gone up a little bit, too. His certainly had.

"Oh wow!" She spoke so loudly several heads turned. She went even redder and almost whispered. "Are you an actor, then?"

Mac shook his head. "I'm what they call a DP." She looked confused at that. "A director of photography. I'm in charge of how we light the scene, what kind of lens we use in the camera, that sort of thing."

"A photographer!" The words came out with the same

girlishly provocative enthusiasm, but with the volume dialled down to avoid eavesdroppers. "From Hollywood?"

Mac tipped an imaginary cap. "Yes ma'am."

The girl shuffled closer and held out a hand to shake. He couldn't help but notice her fingernails were painted bright red. "Milly Powell. Pleased to meet you."

Her skin was soft and warm and worryingly intoxicating. "Likewise," Mac replied.

"So, are you shooting a movie over here?" He nodded. "Oh my God, that must be exciting!"

"It is." And Mac bet she had no idea how exciting it had been for the last few days. He looked over to the far corner and the sign marked 'Toilets'. There was still no sign of PC Mathers. Good. "We've spent most of our time up at the suspension bridge, but we should hopefully be shooting in other areas of Bristol, too."

"Great. Could I come and watch?"

"That's probably not a good idea." What could he say? "Film shoots can be quite dangerous if you're not trained. I'd hate for you to trip over a cable or get electrocuted on something."

"Oh." Milly seemed despondent for a moment. Then she perked up again. "What kind of a film is it?"

"Horror." Should he have said something else? No – girls loved horror movies, didn't they? It certainly looked as if Milly did.

"Wow. That's great. Have you always shot horror films?"

"No." He wasn't sure how far he should go with this. "Thrillers, comedies, race car pictures, and...other stuff."

The last one made her eyes light up. "What kind of... other stuff?"

He leaned in, close enough to smell her peach skin cream. "Now I just couldn't go telling a nice girl like you about things like that. Besides," he said, conspiratorially, "I wouldn't want to offend the other fine people in this coffee shop."

"Of course not." Milly was whispering now, and she seemed deadly serious. "Are you any good at still photography?"

"Did plenty of that in my time working for the stroke mags," Mac said, and then clamped his fingers to his mouth as if he'd just committed the most terrible faux pas. It had the effect he desired. After her flutter of laughter Milly got serious again.

"Would you be able to take some pictures of me?"

That surprised him, so much so that he disguised it with a bout of coughing, which he relieved by taking a deep swig of coffee. "I'm not quite sure what you mean, little lady."

"I mean, I don't want to be hanging around coffee shops for the rest of my life trying to get people to donate money to charities even I've never heard of. I want to go places, meet people, be someone. Modelling opens doors." She tossed her head back, ran a hand through her hair, and gave him a coy smile. "Don't you think I could do it?"

"Maybe, but there are a million kids out there just like you, so don't ever think that a few skin pics are going to miraculously open doors for you. Even if they do it's likely they'll be the wrong kind."

Milly pouted. "For your information I was planning on you taking some pictures of me wearing clothes."

When Mac's face obviously fell a bit she added. "Most of the time, anyway. Oh please, if you could I'd be really, really grateful."

"Well..." it was tempting, but "...it could be difficult to fix up. I've no idea when they'll need me over the next couple of days." It probably wouldn't be at all. In fact please let it not be at all.

"You're free now, aren't you?" He was. "And I'll bet you're free for the rest of the afternoon?" That, too.

"But what about your charity work?"

Milly was already getting to her feet. She held out an encouraging hand. "I'll have to ask people to give me extra tomorrow, won't I?"

When Mac touched those soft fingers for the second time he realised there was no way he was going to say no to this girl who, for all he knew, might want some pictures taken wearing all manner of creative stuff, and if she didn't have any, maybe they could pop into one of those places where he was going to buy the DVDs and dress her up in some. Only if she was willing, of course.

He managed one final swift glance over to the toilets as he was led from the coffee shop. No sign of PC Mathers. He hoped nothing had happened to the policeman, and promised himself he would apologise profusely when he saw the man again.

If he ever did.

~

Mac had been expecting something of a walk, but it turned out Milly lived just around the corner. This was just as well, as he was quite winded by the time they had climbed the stairs to her top floor flat. Mac did his best not to show it but he could feel the giveaway reddening of his features. He hoped she didn't notice.

As if on cue, Milly said "Don't worry, we're here!" and produced a set of keys.

Mac was gasping for breath as he all but stumbled into the bare, stark studio apartment. If he wanted to keep chasing girls like Milly he was going to have to go back to the gym once he was home. He grasped the stem of a flood lamp, took a few deep breaths and looked around. There was no furniture, and no carpet to cover the bare boards, which were scratched and splashed with drops of white paint. No curtains hung at the windows overlooking the street outside, and it was with some disconcertment that Max realised he could see the horn of one of those gleaming gold unicorns PC Mathers had told him about.

"Do you live here?"

"Oh no." Milly took off her jacket and draped it over a weary-looking three-legged stool. "Daddy rents this for me. The plan was for me to have somewhere to paint, but I got so bored with all that art stuff. It just wasn't working for me, so I convinced a friend to lend me a couple of cameras and here we are."

Mac was already looking at the wealth of photographic equipment strewn across the table to his right. His breath regained and the unicorn forgotten, his eyes widened at some of the high tech stuff Milly's friend had presumably 'loaned' her.

"This stuff's great!" He picked up the nearest camera. "Do you know what this is?"

Milly shrugged and undid the top two buttons on her shirt. "I'm guessing the answer isn't a camera?"

Mac chuckled as he switched the device on. "It's a top of the line Hasselblad. Your friend must be rolling in it if he's happy to let you just play around with one of these."

Milly assumed a mock-serious demeanour. "I'm only supposed to let qualified people use it," she said. "But from what you've told me, I guess that means you."

"It sure does." Mac adjusted the focus and looked through the viewfinder. "We should be able to get a few nice shots with this baby."

"Great. Are you okay to have me up against that wall?"

Was she doing that deliberately? She had to be. Mac followed her pointing finger to a spot opposite the door. Against the white-painted brickwork had been erected a black sheet, the bottom edge of which spilled across the floorboards, covering them nicely.

"Should be fine." Milly moved over to strike a pose and Mac dragged a couple of the lamps into position. When he looked through the viewfinder again Milly was leaning forward provocatively.

"Are you happy like that?" his voice came out as a croak.

"The question is, are you happy with me like this?"

All Mac could do was nod as he fired off a few shots. He asked her to move slightly to her left, to tilt her head back, to lean inward a little more, all the while clicking the shutter button and caring less and less about the pictures and more and more about how long he should leave it before he suggested she get out of some of those clothes.

He was about to when he heard a noise behind him.

At first he assumed the faint whirring was the air conditioning coming on, but as it got louder he realised it was a sound he hadn't heard for a very long time. In fact, so nostalgic was it that for a moment he felt himself transported back too many years to count. Back to a time when movie cameras actually contained moving film that had to be loaded and threaded, and then unloaded and developed and screened using a good old fashioned projector.

Was someone really behind him with a 16mm Paillard Bolex?

Someone was.

Someone wearing a pale brown duffle coat with the hood thrown back, and the top open to reveal the tightly buttoned white shirt and tartan necktie beneath. The blonde hair was combed in a style that might just have been in fashion fifty years ago. Mac couldn't see the man's face because, whoever this person was, he was intent on filming him with the Bolex.

"Hey! Who are you?"

Milly giggled. "That's my friend Mark. You were so busy taking my picture you didn't hear him come in. This is all his equipment. He loves cameras and film and movies. That's why he's filming you now."

"Well, you can tell him to stop." Mac backed towards Milly. Mark the cameraman took a disconcerting step closer. "I'm a behind the scenes man. I have no interest in being in a film."

"We know that, Mr Armitage," Mark said. Did Mac detect a slight German accent? "But we are very interested in you being in our film, a film that we are sure is going to turn out much better than the one with which you are currently engaged."

"We've even got special equipment for it." Milly stepped out from behind Mac and took up a position to Mark's left. She was holding something.

A camera tripod.

"Ah! The very thing! Thank you my dear."

Mark placed the Bolex on the tripod and arranged it so that one of the tripod's legs was directly in front of Mac. Then he began to lift that leg into the air.

"What are you doing?" Mac tried to back away further, but now he could feel the black sheet behind him.

"Teaching a lesson to someone who should know better."

The leg was level with Mac's throat now. He tried to step to one side but Milly shoved him back, unsheathing the spike concealed at the leg's tip as she did so.

Far too late, Mac realised what was happening. As he turned to claw at the sheet and it fell away to reveal the original British poster for the film he was now part of a reconstruction of, and as the spike entered his neck and emerged from his throat to pin him to that poster, as he coughed blood over it with his dying breaths, Mac couldn't help but acknowledge that at least they had killed him in the style of a true classic.

14

"*Peeping Tom*, sir."

"I beg your pardon?" Longdon looked up from holding the door open so the forensic team could carry Mac Armitage's body away.

"The movie, sir." Jenny pointed at the poster. "Infamous nearly sixty years ago for destroying the career of Michael Powell, its director."

"And responsible just a little while ago for destroying both the career and life of a hack American cameraman. Yes, Newham, I am capable of reading the poster that our latest victim has been found stapled to, thank you very much." Longdon gave the latest of many deep sighs. "Who called it?"

"The flat beneath this one. Heard some banging and crashing but it was the scream that alerted them that something might be wrong."

"Oh something's wrong, all right." Longdon looked out of the window. The shining golden horn of a previous Dr Valentine murder weapon made him turn back to face the room. "Something's very wrong. The press are calling for our blood, DCI Martin won't replace us because nobody else wants to take this case on, and to top it all I understand bloody *Panorama* did an hour-long television special on it last night."

Jenny winced at the mention of it. "They did, sir."

"And they had reconstructions?"

"That's correct."

"Including actors playing us?"

"Trust me, sir, you don't want to go there."

"Inspector Longdon?"

Newham and Longdon turned at the sound of the words, spoken in an American accent.

"How the hell did you get up here?" Longdon did his best to refrain from snarling. He failed.

Raymond St Pearce, movie director and potential victim of Dr Valentine, looked as if he had shrunk in stature since they had last seen him. "I told your men outside that I'm the next victim and they let me up."

Jenny got in before Longdon could. "And what makes you think that, sir?"

St Pearce dug into his pocket for his wallet, from which he gingerly removed a strip of tissue-thin paper. "I have no idea how it got there, but with everything that's been going on I figured it had to be a clue."

Longdon stared down at the strip, and at the words printed on it. "'Seven days are allowed', and some funny symbols printed about it."

"Runes, I think you'll find, sir." Jenny was peering over his shoulder.

"Yes."

"As in *Night of the Demon* from 1957."

"Yes, thank you Newham. I think we're both familiar enough with that particular classic of British horror cinema to know what this means."

"Well?" St Pearce was searching their faces. "What does it mean?"

Jenny looked uneasy and said nothing. Meanwhile Longdon was scratching his head.

"You're not planning on going anywhere near a railway station are you, sir?"

"No. Why?"

"Oh, just don't." Jenny took the strip from Longdon. "In fact, stay away from railways in general. We'll assign you a bodyguard to make sure you don't happen to stray too close to one."

"Does someone get killed by a train in that one, then?"

Longdon joined Jenny in looking uncomfortable.

"Well?"

"You'll have to forgive us for finding it difficult to explain, sir, but I suspect that, like me, DS Newham is wondering quite how even Valentine could pull this one off."

Raymond St Pearce looked at the blood-splattered poster of *Peeping Tom*, then back to the two police officers. "For God's sake, just tell me."

"A demon, sir." Longdon looked away as he said it.

"A what?"

"In the film, a giant demon is conjured up out of nothing and kills someone on a railway track." Jenny thought she should help. From St Pearce's expression it didn't seem to.

"And on a deserted country road at the beginning of the film," Longdon added.

"Oh yes," Jenny added. "Mustn't forget that. And then of course there's that giant invisible thing that pursues Dana Andrews through the trees at Karswell's house."

"You're quite right, Newham." Longdon was nodding

as St Pearce stared at them both in horrified disbelief. "That had slipped my mind for a moment."

"You're both insane!"

"On the contrary, sir." Longdon's voice was grave. "It's Valentine who is insane. He's also perfectly capable of hijacking a train and creating a remote control motorcycle, and that's only this time around, so we're not discounting the possibility that he has a hundred foot-tall demon model concealed somewhere waiting to crush the living daylights out of you."

What little colour Raymond St Pearce possessed had drained from his face.

"But don't worry." Jenny did her best to sound reassuring. "If it's something that enormous then hopefully we'll see it coming."

"Also, sir," Longdon added, "don't forget that we have a whole seven days to work out what he might be up to this time." He pointed to the runes that Jenny was still holding. "When did you find these?"

Raymond's face fell even further. "Six days ago."

"Ah."

"I didn't think it was anything important. Then, when all of this started happening, I forgot all about them. I only remembered this morning, and when I went to the police station they told me you'd been called out. They eventually told me where you were after I showed them...that." Raymond now regarded the runes fearfully. "So are you saying that tomorrow I'm gonna be killed?"

"No sir." Longdon brought himself up to his full height. "I'm saying that tomorrow may well be the day that we finally catch Dr Valentine."

"You mean...?" Jenny tucked away the strip of runes.

Longdon nodded. "Exactly, DS Newham. You and I are not going to take our eyes off our Mr St Pearce here for the next twenty four hours."

15

More than a day.

Jenny Newham looked at her watch once more, just to check. There was no doubt about it. Over twenty four hours had passed since Raymond St Pearce had shown them the runes, inscribed on the strip of paper that was still tucked into her pocket. Did that mean he was safe? He certainly looked it, sat in one of the library's armchairs, his feet up, nodding off after his attempts to read the latest online issue of *Variety* on his tablet had dulled him into a stupor. Before that he had been viewing decidedly more adult material, until Jenny warned him that the library staff would revoke his WiFi privileges if he was caught. Now he was snoring gently. Above him the overhead clock's display read nineteen hundred hours.

Jenny wondered how long she needed to keep Raymond here. She and Longdon had decided to take six-hour shifts keeping an eye on the director, and hers was due to end in another sixty minutes.

The library had just closed.

It had seemed the most sensible place to bring him. There had been some debate (in which Mr St Pearce had taken an active role) as to where might be safest. For obvious reasons it couldn't be anywhere near a country road, a railway line, or an isolated mansion. St Pearce himself was not keen on spending a day in the police cells, and his hotel had been deemed insecure. The library was nearby and when St Pearce himself mentioned it as somewhere quiet that he could sit so they could keep an eye on him, neither Longdon nor Jenny could think of any better alternative.

And now it looked as if their efforts had been successful. Jenny wandered the bookcase aisles, stretching her legs while Raymond snored. Should she ring Longdon? She knew he slept only rarely, and no doubt even now he was checking round all the likely places where Dr Valentine might strike.

As if on cue, her phone began to chirrup.

Raymond snorted and turned a little, but failed to wake up.

"Hello?"

"Vincent Price was the best Dracula." The signal wasn't great but it sounded like Longdon's voice.

"...and my favourite Christopher Lee film is *Theatre of Blood*," she replied. Their decision on the best coded responses to identify each other had been based on the most likely things Dr Valentine would never say. "Raymond, the director of *Virgin Witch*, the best film of all time, is safe and sound."

"Actually, you can drop all that, Newham. I think we've got him."

For a moment Jenny couldn't answer. Instead she just stared, slack-jawed, at her phone screen.

"Are you still there, Newham?" said the tinny voice of her superior.

"Um...yes...sir." Jenny coughed to clear her throat. "Are you sure?"

"Not yet, but our surveillance team have spotted what looks like a forty foot tall inflatable demon outside Pearce's hotel. Chances are Valentine must think St Pearce is inside. We're cordoning off the area now. Get up here as soon as you can. And bring St Pearce with you."

"Is that such a good idea, sir? Bringing Valentine's intended victim right to him?"

"I understand what you're saying, Newham, but if he's not with us then we can't protect him, can we? And you're needed here – we're short staffed enough as it is."

"All right sir, I'll see you soon."

Jenny pocketed the phone and approached the sleeping form of Raymond St Pearce. Gently rocking him by the shoulder did little, and so, rather than waste any more time, she clapped her hands loudly next to his left ear.

"Hey!" The director didn't look pleased at the rude awakening.

"It's time to go."

"What do you mean?"

"They think they've got Valentine and they want me over there. And you're coming with me."

That didn't seem to sit well. "Oh no I'm not. If he's somewhere else then I'm staying here."

"Well I'm afraid that's not possible. I'm under orders to keep you in my sight at all times."

St Pearce folded his arms. "Then you're just going to have to stay here with me, aren't you?"

"I am not going to argue with you, Mr St Pearce." Jenny gave him a hard stare. "You are coming with me. Right now."

"I. Am. Not."

Jenny had her phone out to ring Longdon back when there was a crash from outside the main doors.

Raymond was on his feet in an instant. "What was that?"

"Probably nothing." Jenny glanced at the exit. "So are you coming with me?"

"No way!" Raymond pointed at the exit. "Make sure there's nobody out there!"

He had a point. "All right. You stay here until I get back." Instead of doing as he was told, Raymond was edging away from her into the depths of the library. "Do NOT get lost in there – do you understand?"

Raymond poked his head out from behind a bookcase and nodded. "Just go and find out who it is! You're supposed to be protecting me!"

That was true, and it looked as if it was the only way she might get him out of here. "All right. But stay hidden, and don't move until I come back."

"Don't worry." Raymond was retreating into the stacks. "I'm not going anywhere."

As she made her way to the exit, Jenny hoped he was right. She knew she shouldn't be worrying, especially as Longdon himself had rung in to say they had Valentine surrounded.

Thought they had Valentine surrounded.

But hadn't actually seen him.

Had actually only seen a giant inflatable demon.

And not the greatest criminal mastermind the country had ever known.

Jenny thumbed redial on her phone.

No signal.

She backed into the library, hoping the bars at the top of her display would leap back into activity.

Nothing.

"What are you doing?"

"Stay down!" she hissed. "Something's not right."

Jenny climbed onto a chair and did a quick survey of the room. Nothing suspicious.

There was another loud bang from outside, a sound like a heavy piece of metal being dropped. Was somebody trying to get in?

"I'm going back to check out the exit doors," she shouted. "If you see or hear anything suspicious, just shout and I'll come running."

Raymond's muffled reply sounded as if he understood.

The doors were still locked. Jenny took out the key the chief librarian had entrusted her with and slid it into the lock. The door opened noiselessly and she stepped out into the arched entrance of the old Victorian building.

A brisk wind was blowing, and from where she was standing, Jenny could just make out the council building, with its twin golden unicorns perched at either end of the lengthy, curving roof. She well remembered the time they had discovered the body of one of Valentine's first victims skewered on the horn of the one that was the furthest away.

Something appeared to be hanging from it right now.

In fact, the more she looked at it, the more she convinced herself that it could be a person.

Had Valentine skipped a victim? Had the whole thing with Raymond St Pearce been an elaborate distraction while Valentine went after somebody else? Had those words 'Seven Days Are Allowed' been referring to one of St Pearce's colleagues and not the director at all?

Should she investigate? Not without locking the library doors again first. Jenny made sure nobody could get in before making her way across the cobbled street. A crowd had already gathered around the far side of the building

"Police." She was already holding up her badge to the onlookers. "What's happening here?"

"Dunno," said a young man with a beard and an interesting line in rainbow-coloured woollen headgear. "Perhaps the circus is coming to town."

Jenny looked up. What she had first thought was a human body she now realised was a rapidly deflating simulacrum of one.

One that had been dressed strangely.

Like so many around her, Jenny held up her phone, but in her case it was to make use of her camera's zoom setting.

It was a clown.

Jenny peered at the picture. Perhaps it had nothing to do with Dr Valentine at all. There was no clown in *Night of the Demon*, was there?

Was there?

She tried to think. Wasn't there a bit where Dana Andrews went to visit the black magician Karswell at his country house? And he ended up interrupting a children's party? Hosted by Karswell himself dressed up as a...

But what was the significance of the ex-clown hanging up there?

Because it was after Karswell had taken off his clown makeup that he summoned that creature that chased Andrews through the woods.

Something invisible.

Meaning not visible at all.

Meaning not the thing that Longdon and his team currently had surrounded.

Jenny had her phone to her ear as she ran back to the library. But there was something wrong. Longdon's phone wasn't ringing. She checked the screen. Instead of the normal display, now all it showed was nonsense - a multitude of stick-like symbols. She dug out the strip of paper.

The symbols were the same, repeated over and over and over.

When she got back to the library the doors were still locked.

And now the key the 'chief librarian' had given to her no longer fitted.

~

Even though he had assumed he would feel safe inside the library, as soon as DS Newham left, Raymond St Pearce felt anything but.

He had heard her lock the doors behind her. All the lights were on. There was no chance anyone else could be in here because they would have had to get past Jenny to do so.

And yet...

As he sat in the cosy armchair that up until just five minutes ago had been possibly the most soporific-inducing piece of furniture he had ever had the delight to nod off in, he suddenly felt that he was not alone. He had not heard any strange sounds, he had not seen any strange movements out of the corner of his eye, but something in the library had changed since his bodyguard had left.

His suspicions were confirmed when all the lights went off.

Raymond was on his feet in an instant.

"Hello?" The word came out just before the realisation that he would be revealing his whereabouts to any intruder.

Time to move, then.

For a moment Raymond considered hiding in the corner, the back of the armchair pulled across to help keep him concealed. But if he was found there would be no escape, and right now all he wanted to do was run.

Perhaps he could get out through the fire exit? The building had to have one, although as he looked around for one of the mandatory well-lit signs he couldn't spot it. Whoever was in here with him had presumably cut the power to the emergency lights as well.

Whoever was in here...

He was kidding himself. As if there was any doubt as to who it might be. And in that case, perhaps talking wasn't such a bad idea.

"Dr Valentine?" He began moving between the stacks, all the while aiming to get to the main exit doors. Perhaps there was a fire extinguisher there he could use to smash the glass. "Dr Valentine, I'm sorry. I didn't know that making this movie would upset you. If I did I would never have had anything to do with it."

The doors were in sight now, but they still seemed an awfully long way away. Raymond paused and listened, hoping for a sound in the darkness that would give away any pursuer.

Nothing.

Perhaps there was no-one. Perhaps there was a legitimate reason for the lights going out.

And the emergency exit lights?

Okay, maybe not, then.

"Dr Valentine." He tried a different tack. "If there's anything I can do, that any of us who are left can do, to make amends, all you have to do is say."

Silence.

Keep moving.

"I just want you to know I'm sorry." What else could he say? "Surely I don't deserve to die? Not for something I didn't realise was wrong?"

The doors didn't seem to be any closer. In fact, if anything they seemed to be moving away.

And...swaying from side to side.

Or was that just him? Raymond rubbed his eyes, blinked and looked about him.

Which was when a gust of wind hit him with the force of a typhoon.

So strong was the force of the gale that Raymond was

blown back the way he had come, past the stacks, past the chair, back further until he ended up pinned against the bookcases at the back of the library. He struggled to escape, but the blast was so strong and so broad he found it impossible to move. Whatever was being used to create such a windstorm had to be enormous, but whether that was responsible for the roaring sound, or whether it was just the wind itself, it was impossible to tell. Raymond brought his hands up to his face, covered his eyes, and then tried peering through the cracks in his fingers.

He could see it now. Right in front of the doors. A massive rotary fan that must have been dropped from the ceiling so softly and so suddenly that he hadn't had time to register it before the wind started up. And now he was trapped.

But what exactly was Valentine intending to do? Blow him to death?

The first book hit him on the left temple.

At first he thought it was an extra severe blast of wind. It was only when the next hardback hit him in the face and he felt the bridge of his nose crack through his protecting fingers that he realised what was happening.

Now more volumes were hurtling towards him, thumping into his chest, bruising his legs. Was it just the force of the gale that was thrusting them forward? Raymond tried his best to see if there were human figures next to the fan, but just as he did so, the library erupted into a snowstorm of paper. Loose pages, torn bindings, ripped covers, all came hurtling towards him, along with intact volumes so bulky that the only way to get them to fly so fast must have been to fire them out of a cannon.

The first serious break was his left wrist, still flat against his ribs as he sought to protect his face. Like his nose, he felt rather than heard it. He screamed and coughed blood at the same time, and paper found its way into his mouth. He spat it out as an encyclopaedia cracked his right knee. He would have fallen then, but the force of the fan kept him upright as book after book smashed into him and a tumult of feathery paper threatened to clog his nose and mouth.

His left hand fell to his side, the pain from his shattered wrist finally too much. The fingers of his right offered little protection for his face. Through the cracks between his fingers, through the storm of flying paper and gusting wind in this building where he thought he would be safe, the last thing Raymond St Pearce saw was a metal-bound volume the size of a family bible come flying straight at his head.

~

By the time they got the library entrance open, Jenny had been joined by two uniformed police officers, one of whose radios she used to get Longdon down to where they were. The application of a crowbar and a lot of brute force finally got the doors to yield. Getting the power back on proved to be more difficult.

Longdon took a torch from one of the uniformed officers and then sent the man off in search of the fusebox.

"Mr St Pearce?" The library offered nothing but darkness and silence. Longdon switched on the torch. "Bloody hell, what a mess."

Jenny stepped inside and bumped straight into the object that had been blocking the entrance.

Longdon shone the torch in her direction. "What have you found, Newham?"

"It appears to be a fan, sir. A very big one."

"So we've found the cause of all this mess, then. The question is, why? How does any of this tie in with *Night of the Demon?*"

Jenny shrugged. "Maybe we got the film wrong?"

Longdon shook his head. "No, Valentine doesn't mean to trick us," he spat, "he just wants to demonstrate how creative he is." He shone the torch ahead of them.

Where the Demon was waiting.

The library ceiling was high, as befitted an old Victorian building. Even so, the horns of the twenty foot monster that had been constructed at the back of the room almost scraped against it. As Jenny and Longdon approached, they saw the entire construct had been fashioned from paper – books, magazines, loose leaves, all piled up to create a shape that, at a distance and in the semi-darkness, resembled the gargantuan creature that appeared at both the beginning and the end of the 1957 British classic.

But that was not all.

The grisly centrepiece of this bizarre tableau, a shocking glare of red amongst the black and white, was a human body, pinned and splayed so that its head rested just beneath the demon's head, the arms extended into the demon arms, and the mangled legs thrust downwards towards the demon's own.

"Jesus Christ." For a moment even Longdon was

speechless. "He's turned Pearce into the bloody monster from the film."

It turned out that the monster was not just bloody, but also extremely unstable. As they approached the stacks of books began to topple, and the body of Raymond St Pearce fell forward with a crash.

Jenny was feeling the pulse in the man's neck.

"I'm guessing he's no longer of this world?" Longdon was shining his torch so Jenny could see.

"Correct, sir."

Longdon pointed at St Pearce's mouth. "What's that?"

Jenny winced as she tugged at the sheaf of paper protruding from between the dead man's lips. "Just more paper, sir."

Longdon's eyes narrowed. "Is it?" He held out a hand. "I'm not so sure."

Jenny passed it over and Longdon shone the torch onto it.

"Thought so," he said. "It's not like our Dr Valentine to pass up the opportunity to ram his point home, to make absolutely sure we haven't missed it."

Longdon threw the document on the floor. From the glare of the streetlights outside, Jenny could just make out the title and author of the short story that had been used to finally choke Raymond St Pearce to death.

"Casting the Runes", by M R James.

16

"And that's the story *Night of the Demon* is based on?"

The interviewer's name was Carola Peterson. She was obviously clued up on the Valentine case, her questions were incisive, and she had a stern attractiveness to her that would likely cause men of a certain disposition to fall in obeisance at her feet.

Jeffrey Longdon was not one of those men.

He was, however, extremely uncomfortable, both with his attempts to answer Ms Peterson's questions and with having to be there in the first place. But he had orders from on high that, after all his failed attempts to catch the killer, a national appeal, onscreen and at peak viewing time, was what was now needed. At this point the general feeling from his superiors seemed to be that anything was worth a try. He wished this hadn't been so soon after that bloody *Panorama* reconstruction the other night, though – the one they had insisted on playing clips from on this very programme.

"That's correct." He shifted in his seat and it made an unfortunate noise. Someone in the audience coughed. Why the hell did they even have to have an audience? Why couldn't it have been just the two of them? This was almost as bad as a press conference. "We believe the killer was demonstrating his sense of irony by placing the story where he did."

Peterson crossed her legs. "Just that?" She pursed her lips. "Just his sense of irony? Nothing to do with his sense of superiority over the might of the British police force?"

"Well, I suppose..."

"A police force that has now failed to save the lives of more than twenty people?"

"Yes, I imagine that..."

"A police force that appears to have been wasting taxpayers' money with inadequate manpower, an inability to conduct appropriate research and, with respect, staff lacking the appropriate skill set?"

Whatever you do, don't lose your temper, he had been ordered. Oh well, it wasn't as if he'd been forced back into the job. In fact, now more than ever he would be happy if he never did any policing ever again. He leaned forwards.

"Listen, Mrs Peterson."

"It's Ms."

"Whatever. How much do you know about British horror films?"

"Quite a bit, now." Her expression didn't change, but Longdon could tell he was getting to her. Good.

"And why do you know?"

"Because..."

"Because it's your job to know everything about a set of murders that have already happened, isn't it? To be the one who can grandly, and very publicly, shut the stable door well after the horse has bolted, preferably with as loud a bang as possible to draw the maximum amount of attention to yourself."

"I hardly think…"

It was no good. Longdon was off. "Do you know how many British horror films there are? Do you know how many Valentine still has to choose from? Do you know that whatever we do, whatever we try, despite every single approved and unapproved method of police work, he keeps managing to slip through our fingers? Do you know what that feels like? Does it surprise you that no-one else wants to take on this job that even I have done my best to get away from? Twice? The so-called finest minds in the country haven't got a clue. They were the ones who suggested – no, ordered – that I come on here, and if you want my honest opinion I don't think for one minute that it's going to do a bloody bit of good." Now he fixed Ms Peterson with a steely glare. "So I ask you, *Ms* Peterson, what would *you* do next?"

It'll be all over the papers tomorrow, Longdon thought. Policeman loses his rag on national television. Then I can get back to tea and cakes in Cornwall. I doubt Valentine will come after me. Those Cornish-filmed movies are pretty awful. *Doctor Blood's Coffin* and that one with Mike Raven covering naked girls in bronze.

"Rather than me, why don't we put it to our studio audience?" The interviewer had recovered quickly, but it didn't surprise him that she was now diverting attention from herself to the others in the room. A flurry of hands went up. Suddenly the whole thing felt much worse than a press conference.

An elderly woman wearing a crucifix so huge and heavy-looking Longdon was surprised she was capable of standing up wanted to know why the government wasn't talking steps to ban all horror films to stop this kind of thing from happening again. A red-faced man waved a copy of the Daily Mail as he asked what nationality Dr Valentine was and if he had links to Islam. When a middle-aged woman wearing what looked like a red woollen tea cosy on her head claimed Vincent Price was her spirit guide and that he had told her where the next murder would take place, Longdon had to fight the urge to cover his face with his hands.

An angry-looking woman with grey hair and an electric purple blouse wanted to know why so many Americans had been allowed to come to England to work anyway, and perhaps Dr Valentine was doing this as a warning to other foreigners who might want to come over here and take British jobs. Most frightening of all, when she finished speaking there were grumbles of assent from elsewhere in the audience.

The Q&A went on for half an hour and was very much Q and very little A. Carola Peterson nodded and frequently glanced at Longdon, who repeatedly responded with an expression he hoped signified 'How am I supposed to answer that?' The 'discussion' was just getting to onto how UK citizens should be allowed to have guns to defend themselves, just like in America, when Carola was signalled that it was time to stop. Longdon never thought he would be grateful for live TV, but right now anything that would get him out of there was welcome.

The feeling of utter exhaustion suddenly upon him, Longdon watched as the studio emptied quickly. When he turned to ask Carola which way he should go he discovered she had already left. Within what felt like moments Longdon found himself alone in a darkened studio.

He got to his feet, surprised at how shaky his legs were. Well, he wasn't used to this sort of thing, was he? He'd done his fair share of press conferences in his time, sat behind a desk and with other members of the force close by. This, however, had been something else entirely. A sideshow. A lunatic circus of horrors where the true frights had been less the murders recounted in all their grisly detail and more the attitude of the audience assembled in a no doubt calculated manner to provide the maximum degree of controversy the papers could report the next day.

"They all feed off each other," Longdon murmured to himself as he searched for the exit.

"They do, don't they?"

Longdon froze. He knew that voice. He may have only confronted the man twice in the last five years, but there was a time when they had worked together, albeit with the other using an assumed name.

"Valentine?"

"Dr Valentine, if you don't mind. I didn't spend all those years working for all those degrees and doctorates just for anyone – even an esteemed member of the police force such as yourself – to refer to me simply by my surname. I tired of that quickly enough when I was a schoolboy, so you can imagine how it might affect me now."

While Valentine talked, Longdon's eyes were busy searching the studio. Was it his imagination or had the lights been dimmed further? And where was the voice coming from? Up at the back row of the stadium seating? In the sound booth beyond that? Or somewhere to the side? He had to get him to speak again.

"You saw the show, then?"

"Oh my dear chap, once I heard about it I wouldn't have missed it for the world. I was in the audience the entire time. I wouldn't have expected you to spot me, though. I've become very good at this disguise thing since I began my little crusade."

Now the voice was coming from everywhere. Which meant Valentine had to be in the sound booth. Longdon stepped off the stage, careful not to stumble in the now near-darkness.

"I wouldn't come any closer if I were you, Inspector. Television studios can be terribly dangerous places. I'm sure you've seen Norman J Warren's *Terror*?"

Longdon stayed put. "I doubt even you have the powers of an eighteenth century witch."

"True. Neither am I a doctor of metaphysics, otherwise I would be happy to foretell your future using my Tarot cards." The voice was behind him now. Valentine was messing with the speakers. It was possible he wasn't in the studio at all. But Longdon had the feeling he was. "That reminds me. Have you found Charles T Herman, former screenwriter for American Enterprise Pictures, yet?"

Damn. Longdon had hoped the man had escaped the country, but obviously not. "No."

"Ah, well, don't worry, you will. I was going to punish him in the style of an Amicus anthology film but there are so many good ones that I ended up using several of them to give him a true 'portmanteau death', as it were."

"I'm sure you found it very amusing."

"Oh I did, Inspector, but not nearly as amusing as the little charade I planned for you."

So this was it. Cut down not by a drunken mob in a deserted warehouse, or shot dead in some grimy reconstruction of an early 1970s crime film. This was it. Killed in the dark in a crappy television studio where he had just spent possibly the most embarrassing hour of his life.

Longdon gritted his teeth. "Well, as Ian Hendry says in *Theatre of Blood*, get it over with, then."

Was that chuckling? "My dear Inspector. It has already happened. Please don't think for one moment I would want to kill you. I'm having far too much fun with you still alive. You and that intrepid detective sergeant of yours. No, I'm referring to the little entertainment I staged and which you have been a part of for the last hour or so."

Now that was unexpected. "You mean... that was all faked?"

"That depends on what you mean by the term. Those were real people, and weren't they terrifying? You were filmed by real cameras, and the programme was indeed broadcast in the time slot the BBC planned. The programme they intended to show didn't go ahead, of course, because you didn't turn up for it. The real Carola Peterson was most disappointed. I think they planned a repeat of *Doctor Who* to fill in the time. Not that anyone saw that, of course, because I arranged for our little production to be broadcast in its stead."

Longdon was having trouble processing it all. "You're saying that the girl who interviewed me was..."

"...a friend of mine, yes. She has been of invaluable help to me over the years. In fact I believe you have met her before, but like me she is very good at altering her appearance."

Longdon knew it would be useless, and quite possibly dangerous, to proceed any further, so he went and sat back down on the stage.

"Nothing more to say, Inspector?"

"I was just wondering why you bothered with all this."

"Because it amused me, because I needed a little more time for all the pieces of my next creative endeavour to fall into place and finally and most importantly, because it pleased me immensely to rise to the challenge I set myself."

"You're not stopping then?"

"There are two more tableaux to construct. You know that as well as I. Two more and then, hopefully, we can put this little matter to bed. Which is where you should probably be going, Inspector. After all, you've had a hard day, and there's a fair bit of travelling in store for you over the next week."

"What do you mean by that?"

Longdon's question was met by silence. A moment later the lights came back on, including the one marking the exit. As Longdon dragged his terribly weary self towards it, he wished it was the case he was leaving and not just the building.

17

"Well that was embarrassing." Lisa Wallcroft thumbed the 'Off' button on the remote, placed it next to her on the red velvet divan, and turned to look at her producer. From behind her, Elliot Edwards finished his fifth whiskey and soda of the evening and placed the empty glass on the nightstand. He regarded her from the huge double bed where he was currently reclined, and on which she had persistently refused to join him during the course of the evening.

Thinking about it now, she shouldn't have accepted his invitation to watch Longdon's television interrogation. She should have stayed in her own room and started making the plans to leave the country that she had kept promising to herself she would but somehow still hadn't got around to arranging. Contrary to the belief of the police team back in Bristol, she and Elliot were not an item (much as Edwards would have preferred it otherwise) and on arriving at the hotel she had insisted they check into separate rooms. As a result, the two police bodyguards they had been assigned had found themselves standing outside not just different doors, but on different floors. Elliot thought it was because the hotel was full, and Lisa had no intention of enlightening him that the considerable distance between their respective bedchambers had been at her specific request. Of course it hadn't stopped him from asking her to come and see him for 'production meetings' and technically she was still on his payroll, so she could hardly say no.

She wished he would just drop the whole idea, though. It, too, was getting embarrassing.

"It was embarrassing, wasn't it?" Now Elliot was tapping on an iPad. "And it was so good we have to put it in the movie, show just how incompetent that police inspector really is and always has been."

Lisa stopped her jaw from dropping. "But he's the one who's trying to prevent us from being killed!"

"And not doing a very good job of it!" Elliot leaned over and picked up a sheaf of broadsheet newspapers from where he had tossed them on the floor. "Mac Armitage pinned to a wall? Raymond St Pearce beaten and choked to death with books? Probably the first time he had been beaten and choked with anything not intended to get him off as well."

"Elliot, that's not funny."

"And it wasn't intended to be. Chuck the Fuck missing? I never thought he'd be the one to get through this but if he's back in Hollywood now I might just keep him under contract while he writes the story of how he got out of this damned country. But of course he probably hasn't left. Why, I bet right now he's trapped somewhere being eaten alive by people dressed up as vampires or some shit."

Lisa was shaking her head. "Well if he is, you know what that means, right?"

Elliot was back to tapping but stopped to raise an

eyebrow and give her a hard stare. "That we're the only ones left? Of course I know that. It's why I'm getting this outline done so when we get back to LA I can put a new writer on it."

"Your optimism touches me almost as much as every other part of you disgusts me."

That made him give her his full attention. "You watch your mouth, missy, if you want to keep this job."

"Elliot, all I want to do right now is stay alive." That was it. That was enough. Lisa got to her feet. "I'm leaving in the morning. I'm going to get a taxi to the nearest airport and a flight to the US if they fly there, or pretty much anywhere else if they don't. You're welcome to come with me. Otherwise I dare say I'll be reading about you in the papers at some point during the next few days."

"You'll be reading about me in a year or so, about how much money I made off of this story and how much I'll still be making from the sequels." Elliot was back to tapping. "I can't believe you're being so short-sighted about this."

"Better short-sighted than short-lived." Lisa couldn't think of a better exit line, so she opened the door and left. For all she knew Elliot was writing it down right now. Well, he could have it for all she cared. She nodded at the on-duty officers, one of whom remained outside Elliot's door while the other, a PC Travers, accompanied her back to her room.

"I'll be right here if you need me in the night, Miss," he said, taking up a position beside her own door as she went to open it.

"Don't you want to get yourself a chair or something?"

"No, Miss." Travers gave her a brief smile. "Wouldn't want to risk getting too comfortable, now would I?"

"I guess not. Goodnight, officer."

"Night, Miss, and don't forget to lock your door once you're inside."

As if she wouldn't. Once the door was closed she didn't just turn the key and flip the deadbolt across, she dragged the largest, heaviest chair in her suite over and jammed it beneath the door handle, just as she had done the previous night. Then she checked the sash windows to make sure they were locked, and placed the various ornaments with which the hotel had seen fit to decorate her room in precarious positions on the window sills so that the slightest tremor would send them toppling to smash on the floor.

It was only when she had done all of this that she noticed the doll.

Her room was the same size and general design as Elliot's, with the same large double bed facing the same widescreen television and with the same kind of divan in between the two.

The doll was sitting on the divan as if preparing to watch the television. Or perhaps it had just finished and turned the set off before Lisa came in?

Why the hell are you having thoughts like that?

"So who put you here, I wonder?" She spoke the words aloud just so she wouldn't feel so alone. She was well aware help was on hand outside, just a few feet away, but she didn't need to bother him with this.

Then she noticed the doll was dressed just the same as she was.

It looked a bit like her, too.

The doll was the size of a five year old child, and was surprisingly heavy when she picked it up. It was only when she turned it over that she realised exactly what it was.

"Well aren't you a doozy?" She pulled at the toggle lever hidden in the dummy's back and the mouth opened and closed. Another control caused the head to swivel on the neck joint with the creak of freshly sanded wood that hadn't yet been given room to breathe. Lisa's index finger found a switch that made the eyes open and close.

Unable to resist, she sat on the divan and positioned the dummy on her lap.

"Well hello, Lisa."

It felt too weird with the dummy not replying, so Lisa clenched her teeth and tried out a few words.

"Hello Lisa."

"So what am I supposed to do with you?"

"I don't know. Maybe tell the policeman outside you found me."

"I suppose I should, shouldn't I?"

"Mind you, I do seem to be pretty harmless."

"You do."

"And if I was some kind of trap you'd probably be dead by now. I could have had poisoned spikes on the controls, or perhaps there's a bomb in me. Can you hear any ticking?"

Lisa couldn't resist holding the doll's rigid belly up to her ear. "Now you mention it, no I can't. Doesn't mean you're safe, though."

"Then take me outside to that nice policeman."

She should, shouldn't she? In fact what was she doing messing around with it?

"Good point," she said. "You're coming with me."

She tucked the dummy under her arm and went to open the door.

Which was locked.

Of course it is. Who's the real dummy – you locked it yourself, didn't you?

Lisa removed the chair, turned the key, threw back the deadbolt, and turned the handle.

The door still refused to budge.

She tugged at the handle. Then she pushed. Then she thumped the unyielding oak of the door.

Still nothing.

"I don't think it's gonna open."

Lisa hadn't said anything. The words had come from under her arm. The voice was nothing like the one she had been attempting. This one was higher pitched, grating, the kind of annoying voice a ventriloquist's dummy in an old movie might have.

Shit.

"What did you say?" Lisa held the dummy before her. It regarded her with lifeless eyes. She resisted the urge to shake it, then remembered it was a piece of wood and shook it anyway before repeating her question.

"Hey, careful lady! I cost a lot of money to make, y'know! If you're going to play rough the least you could do is put me down!"

"Please open the door." She spoke the words slowly and carefully, trying her best to quell her mounting panic.

"You must be goin' nuts or somethin'. I mean, look at me. Do you really think I can open a door? I ain't even got arms that move!"

Lisa threw the doll on the bed, which earned a *"Hey!"* as she recommenced hammering on the door.

"That's not gonna work," came the voice from the bed. *"You should have known better than to stay in the same room two days runnin'."*

"What?"

The thing emitted a horrible giggle. *"Soundproof door, soundproof door, whatever did I fit you for?"*

"Say that again."

"Come into my parlour said the spider to the fly. Wooden spider, wooden spider, tryin' hard to get inside her."

"Shut up." Lisa ran to the window.

"The question you need to be askin' is, is it just your mind I want to get inside?" This was accompanied by another horrible laugh.

As Lisa hammered on the glass she stayed focused on the doll, still prostrate and crumpled on the bed where she had flung it. She kept expecting it to sprout blades from its fingers, to spring to its feet and come trundling towards her in the awkward, jerky fashion of something she'd seen in some Italian art film once.

The glass sounded dull, and her fists bounced off the surface as if it was made from—

"Reinforced plastic. Can't think of anythin' to rhyme with that, so you'll just have to take my word for it. While you're givin' up tryin'. The perspex is smoked, so no-one's gonna see what happens in here. At least, not until I'm ready for 'em to see."

Lisa turned back to the thing on the bed. "Why are you doing this?"

"You know why."

"But I never did anything to you."

"That is true, and it's why I left you until close to the end, to give you plenty of time to leave. But you didn't, and so now you're goin' to be part of the big lesson I'm going to teach your Mr Edwards and all his friends back in Hollywoodland."

"Elliot doesn't have friends."

"He has you. But not for much longer. Besides, that wasn't what I meant and you know it."

Lisa ran a hand through her hair and glared at the dummy. "So what are you going to do? Have you sealed the room? Am I going to suffocate with a suffocatingly unfunny dummy? Is there really a film where that happens? If so I'm glad I'll never get to watch it because it sounds like a pile of shit."

"You're not going to suffocate. But I do need you to go to sleep now. Don't worry, when they find you, you'll be a brand new woman."

Now Lisa could hear a hissing sound. She looked around but could see nothing.

"It's only in movies that the gas is green."

Lisa didn't know what to do and so she panicked. She picked up the nearest chair and threw it at the window. It bounced off. She ran back to the door and started hammering on it once more. Each blow she struck was a little weaker, a little less forceful, and by the time she was sliding to the floor her blows were lighter than a feather.

~

It was only late the next morning when anyone suggested that there might be something amiss.

Neither Lisa nor Elliot were early risers, and their

police bodyguards had already grown used to never having to escort them down for breakfast. By lunchtime, however, Elliot was finally up and about and wanting to know where Lisa was. He arrived outside her room with his bodyguard in tow.

"Is she in there?"

Constable Travers nodded and yawned. "Has to be. I've been here all night and I haven't seen her since she went to bed. I'll be glad to get there myself once my relief turns up."

Elliot banged on the door and called her name.

Nothing.

"She's always awake before I am. Can you get that door open?"

Travers frowned. "But she may be... indisposed, sir."

"She may be dead for all we know." He thumped the door again. "Have you got a key?"

Travers was already on his radio, seeking permission from Longdon. His barked affirmative could be heard by all three of them. The police officer rummaged in the pocket of his uniform for the key and then slid it into the lock.

The deadbolt was still on.

"Are you all right, miss?"

There was no answer to Travers' question.

"Lisa! It's Elliot!" The producer turned to the two men, his shoulder against the door. "Come on, then! Help me break the lock off."

It took several heavy shoves before the teak into which the deadbolt screws had been set split with a squeal and the three men fell into the room.

To behold a scene of horror.

Because it was a scene. The papers would describe it as a 'macabre tableau', 'sickening statuary' and 'more horrific than anything from Madame Tussaud's'. One US paper used the headline 'Vaudeville Violence', while one of the more downmarket UK tabloids had a rare day of wit combined with nostalgia for a long-ceased BBC TV show of Victorian variety acts and ran the headline 'The Bad Old Days'. Only one broadsheet made reference to the classic 'dummy' story in the 1945 Ealing anthology film *Dead of Night*, while none mentioned the 1964 Richard Gordon production *Devil Doll*. Which of these two likely candidates Valentine was actually paying 'tribute' to did become the subject of several articles, but that was much later.

The opposite side of the room had been converted into a tiny theatre, complete with raised platform, proscenium arch and plaster Doric columns flanking the wings.

On the stage sat the 'act'.

It was not difficult to make out what it was. In fact it was all too easy, all too horrible.

To begin with, there was the ventriloquist's dummy, which bore a frightening resemblance to the ventriloquist, right down to the clothes it wore and the wide-open horrified stare it bore.

But that was nothing compared to the ventriloquist herself.

Lisa Wallcroft's skin had been coated with a glossy substance to give it the appearance of recently varnished wood. What looked like black, tarry paint had been applied to her scalp, moulding her hair into a style from the 1940s. Tiny sutures held her eyelids open. Worst of all, two large incisions had been made, one at each corner of her mouth. These cuts had been extended into the bone of her jaw and down into her throat. The detached piece now flapped forward, giving the whole thing the appearance of a dummy's mouthpiece.

It was only when they approached that she made a noise.

Then they saw her mouthpiece was moving.

The two policemen and the hard-bitten film producer stared in horror as both the dummy that was Lisa and the doll on her lap began to talk, in unison.

"You've... come... this... far..." The voice was a tinny monotone, high-pitched and all the more disconcerting for having been given an electronic timbre. "Only... a... little... further... to... go... now... Inspector."

"Inspector?" The colour had drained from Elliot's face, while Travers had his radio held up to the grotesque 'speaker'.

"A... nice... location... for... our... finale... I... think."

There was a pause, then, one which went on for so long they could hear Longdon's voice on the other end. "What's it saying?"

"Nothing yet sir, we're still waiting for it... her... to say any—"

"Summerisle."

"WHAT did it say?" Longdon bellowed down the line.

"Sir, I think it said—"

"Summerisle," the Lisa-doll said again. And then again. And again. In fact her 'mouth' kept emitting the word until they were able to get her body to the local mortuary and find a pathologist capable of making it stop.

"Summerisle... Summerisle... Summersle... Summerisle... Summerisle..."

18

"Who the hell is Summerisle?" The discovery of Lisa's body had done nothing to quieten Elliot Edwards' abrasiveness. If anything, he was now even more unbearable.

"It's not a who," Longdon replied. "It's a where."

"Except it isn't." Jenny Newham was studying a map of the north coast of Scotland and its associated islands. "Not really."

"Well no wonder my entire cast and crew didn't have a chance with guys like you in charge." Elliot slurped coffee. Noisily. "I don't understand a word of what you're saying."

"Last night, Edward Valentine sent us a message." Longdon spoke as he would to a five year old, which to be honest wasn't very different from how he addressed most adults. "Summerisle is the location of one of the most famous British horror films ever made, if not one of the most famous films ever made full stop."

Longdon and Jenny allowed the pregnant pause which followed to play out.

"And that film is?" Elliot's face was turning red with exasperation.

"Forgive me sir," Longdon raised his eyebrows. "I had forgotten your occupation, which presumably doesn't afford you any working knowledge of the history of the medium I understand your countrymen refer to as moving pictures."

"Are you trying to be funny?"

"I wouldn't say I was the one in the room who was trying, sir, in any sense of the word."

"That's enough now from both of you." Jenny held the map up to Elliot. "The Summer Isles are an archipelago in the Highlands of Scotland."

"I saw *Highlander* once," said Elliot. "Okay TV show. I don't think anyone died in it, though."

Jenny shook her head at Longdon, who stayed quiet. "The film Dr Valentine is referencing is *The Wicker Man*—"

"Oh yeah." Elliot's eyes lit up. "With Nicolas Cage!"

"Jesus Christ." Longdon turned his back on both of them, Jenny could see him biting his bottom lip as he did so.

"That was a remake. The original is a British film from 1973 in which a policeman is lured to a remote Scottish island called Summerisle, where he is sacrificed to pagan gods by being burned alive in a thirty foot high effigy of a man made of wicker."

"Good summary, Newham," said Longdon's back.

"Thank you sir. Now, the question is, was Valentine referring to one of the islands in this archipelago, or was he, in fact, referring to where the film was actually shot?" Her finger moved down the map, but only a bit. "Which was mainly here – Newton Stewart in Dumfries and Galloway."

Elliot snorted. "So have you by any chance been in contact with your buddies up there?"

"We have contacted the relevant constabularies, yes

450 | John Llewellyn Probert

sir." Longdon had been unable to stay out of the conversation for long.

"And have any of them reported the construction of a..." Elliot looked at Jenny as he raised his fingers to enact quotation marks "'...thirty foot high effigy of a man made of wicker'?"

"No sir, they haven't. But that doesn't mean Valentine hasn't got one hidden away somewhere."

"Even if he has, I'd be more worried about you guys than me." Elliot slurped more coffee. From his expression it was presumably cold.

"And why do you say that, sir?"

Elliot gestured to Jenny with his cup. "You said it yourself. He burns a policeman. Not a film producer." Then he pointed at Longdon, just to emphasise his point. "A policeman." He put the cup down. "And therefore, officers, if you will excuse me, I have a flight to catch back to LA, where I have a lot of work waiting for me. The footage we've already shot isn't going to edit and score itself, and I want to make sure they get it right."

Elliot made for the door but Longdon blocked him. "Exactly how much of this project of yours has already been filmed?"

The producer shrugged. "Quite a lot of it, actually. We were only over here to get location shots."

"In that case, sir, I must ask you to reconsider."

Elliot blinked at Longdon. "What? Why?"

"If Valentine knows you've already made some of the movie, and don't doubt for a second that he does, there's no way he's going to let you leave this country alive. You should have told us this sooner."

"And if I had, would Lisa and the others still be here?" Elliot pushed Longdon aside. "That's hardly likely is it, Inspector? So if you don't mind, I'll continue to make my own life my responsibility, and right now the best thing I can think of is to put as many miles between me and this godforsaken country as I possibly can."

The door was barely shut as Jenny said,

"He's not going to get back to the US, is he, sir?"

Longdon was already shaking his head. "Not a chance. Did you put the tracker on him?"

She nodded. "While you had him distracted by turning your back on him. It's in his jacket pocket. We just have to hope he doesn't take it off."

"If he's going to try and leave the country I think we can rest assured he'll be taking everything with him," Longdon replied. "Let's go and have a chat with the signals boys."

"And girls, sir."

"And girls, Newham. I stand corrected."

19

Elliot Edwards stumbled out of the taxicab and resisted the urge to vomit. Who the hell would build an airport you could only reach via winding roads you couldn't even fit a pickup truck down? He paid the driver and provided a generous tip. This wasn't something Elliot was in the habit of doing, but his relief that the guy hadn't tried to kill him, or at the very least drive him somewhere other than his requested destination, had expressed itself in an act of atypical generosity.

He picked up his suitcase and made his way to the first class lounge, where the girl on the phone had assured him he would be met by a representative of the airline who would check him in. He hated flying at the best of times, and when it was on the company account he always made sure it *was* the best of times. Business class if first wasn't available, personal service all the way, and God help them if they didn't make his trip so comfortable it was as if the plane had never taken off.

"Mr Edwards?"

The smile came to Elliot's lips completely involuntarily. Being met just inside the sliding doors – now this was service! He handed over his case and passport to the girl in the pale grey uniform (the little hat was a nice touch) and followed as she led him down a corridor to a room where it appeared he was to be the sole occupant.

"If you'll wait here I'll just get you checked in." She gave him the brightest smile he had seen in ages, although it dulled a little when he prevented her from closing the door.

"I've had a weird couple of days," he said by way of explanation. "Right now I've got a thing about confined spaces, so the door stays open, if you don't mind."

"Of course not, sir, as long as you understand we won't be able to do that on the flight."

She was just trying to be charming, that was all. Elliot dismissed the image of him being bundled out of an exit door at 37,000 feet and instead gave her a brisk nod, before turning his attention to the well-stocked self-service bar.

He should have done this the minute the trouble started, Elliot thought as he poured himself a generous measure of scotch. For a split second he felt a pang of remorse that if he had, at least six people might still be alive. Then he slugged back the drink and comforted himself with the thought that at least he was still here, and likely to remain so.

After his second drink he wondered where everyone else was.

After his third he started to worry.

"Hello?"

The corridor outside was empty. Where was everyone?

"Hello?"

Now he could hear footsteps. He hoped it was the same girl. If there was one thing you needed if you were planning on complaining, it was continuity.

"Is everything all right, sir?"

"I was just wondering..." he peered at her name badge "...Sylvia, where everyone else was and..." he added for good measure "...when we might be boarding?"

Again that smile. Elliot wasn't sure he liked it quite so much this time around. "You are our only first class customer this morning, sir. And as to when we are boarding, you are welcome to take your seat whenever you like."

Elliot knocked back his fourth scotch. Had he poured that himself? His memory was a little hazy. "Great. Do you have my passport?"

"Right here, sir." She handed it over. "We've cleared passport control for you, all you need do now is follow me."

And so Elliot did, down more corridors, across a deserted concourse area, and outside, where a plane much smaller than he had been expecting was waiting for him.

"I'm flying to LA in that?" He tried to stop his words sounding slurred. "Surely that plane can't fit more than six people."

"It's a personal jet, sir." Sylvia was doing her best to stop her hair from blowing into her eyes. "I believe you asked for the very best the airline had to offer?"

That was true. "Yes, but I didn't expect..."

"Perhaps we could talk about this further inside, sir? It is rather chilly out here."

It was. The wind whipped around the two of them as they ascended the fold-down steps. Once they were inside Sylvia closed the door. "We'll be taking off very soon so if you'd like to get yourself strapped in?"

The single passenger seat looked very comfortable and as Elliot fastened the clasp around his middle he could feel himself drifting off. Lack of sleep, relief, booze, all no doubt had their part to play in his sudden torpor. "I'm just going to chill if that's okay."

"Of course it is, sir." That same smile. "You just relax and leave the driving to us."

~

When Elliot awoke, he could hear music.

It wasn't the usual rubbish, either, the popular crap that usually got piped through on flights. This was...strange. Old. The instrument sounded like someone blowing through a squashed harmonica, and what was the girl singer going on about? Having a hundred sheep? That couldn't be right, could it?

He rubbed his eyes and looked about him. Either this was the quietest flight he'd ever been on or—.

"We've landed, sir." There was Sylvia and there was that damned fake smile again.

Elliot looked at his watch.

"That's impossible. We've only been in the air for a couple of hours."

"Sorry if I didn't explain it properly, sir. This was just the first stage of the journey to our hub. If you'll follow me I'll show you to your final destination."

Elliot was building up to showing her his 'both barrels' complaining mode, but the door was open and Sylvia was already on her way down the steps. He released some of his frustration by muttering loudly as he staggered to his feet to go after her.

Outside didn't look like an airline hub. Not one little bit.

~

"They've landed." Lieutenant Charlotte Blackmore of Bristol's Ministry of Defence Signals Division indicated the flashing dot on the computer screen.

Jenny Newham peered at it. "Doesn't look as if Elliot was going abroad after all."

"Oh he was going all right." Longdon was already noting down the location. "But I very much suspect our Dr Valentine chose the destination." He turned to Blackmore. "Presumably it's highly irregular for a flight to leave Bristol Airport and end up in some random site within the UK? I mean one that has no official landing pad?"

The lieutenant shrugged. "I'm just in charge of signals, sir, but we do sometimes pick up private helicopters on their way to country residences, that sort of thing."

"A country residence..." Longdon looked at the computer map once more. "Can you narrow down where they've landed?"

Blackmore looked at Jenny, who gave the lieutenant a 'humour him' look. "Yes, sir. If you've ever used Google Earth you'll know that these days it's possible to pinpoint locations extremely precisely."

"Then where are they?"

Blackmore zoomed in on the image. "It looks like a field."

Jenny was shaking her head. "Typical. *A Field in England*."

Longdon frowned. "Explain, Newham."

"It's another British horror film, sir, but much more recent than that others. Part of my research when I was reading around the subject, as it were. What they refer to as a folk horror picture."

Meanwhile, Blackmore was pointing at the screen. "It's a field next to an enormous country house."

"That's more like it." Longdon sniffed.

"And it looks like they've been setting up for some kind of country fair, which I guess isn't surprising, really." Blackmore's eyes widened as she caught sight of something in the grounds close to the house. "I wonder what that's for?"

Longdon and Jenny knew exactly what it was for. Even with the image slightly blurred it was obvious that, in the grounds of a Wiltshire country house, someone had constructed a thirty-foot tall man. From wicker.

"We were right all along," Longdon muttered.

"With Valentine's considerable help, sir."

"Never mind that."

Jenny frowned at Longdon missing her point. "I'm just wondering if, because he's never given us any clues before, he might have something else up his sleeve?"

"Then we'd better have something up our sleeves too, hadn't we, Newham?" He turned back to the screen. "He's escaped before but this time we've got him. Oh yes, Dr Edward bloody Valentine, your days of engineering utterly ridiculous deaths for people are coming to an end. Come on, Newham, we'd better get over there."

"Excuse me?" Lieutenant Blackmore appeared to be packing up. "But I'm guessing you don't need me for anything else?"

"No." Jenny gave her a grateful smile. "But thanks for staying."

"No problem," Blackmore replied. "To be honest, you guys were lucky to get hold of anyone. My boyfriend's already going to be unhappy I've delayed the start of our long weekend away."

"Bit of annual leave?" Longdon whistled. "Wish I could have that right now. Mind you, once this is over I intend to go on permanent leave. Nothing but tea and cakes and the gossip of old ladies for me."

But Blackmore was shaking her head. "Just the long weekend. You know, Bank Holiday and all that. What with summer a-coming in, hopefully the weather will be nice."

Longdon blinked.

Jenny laid a hand on the woman's shoulder. "What did you just say?"

"Oh, you know, it's the May Bank Holiday weekend. I know the weather's usually rubbish but we thought we'd go away anyway."

"We're sorry to be so picky," said Longdon. "But what both my colleague and I are wondering is, what made you use that specific phrase?"

"Oh, you mean 'Summer a-coming in?'" Blackmore gave an embarrassed laugh. "Sorry. We've all been making fun of it round here since the flyers arrived this morning." She got to her feet.

"What flyers?" Jenny asked.

"Oh they're all round here. I assumed they must be all round Bristol. This can't be the only place they were sent. Mine's probably still in the bin."

"Would you mind getting it for us?" Longdon asked.

"Please," Jenny added, to take the edge off what had sounded like an order.

"Look, I need to get going. I'm probably already in trouble with my boyfriend."

Longdon looked as if he was about to say "You'll be in more trouble with us if you're not careful," but Jenny's hand on his arm prevented him.

"Please," she said. "I know it sounds strange, but that flyer may actually have a bearing on this case."

"Oh, all right." Charlotte Blackmore put down her bag and reached under the desk. Despite being small, the black plastic bin was home to a remarkable amount of rubbish that seemed to consist mostly of crisp packets and chocolate wrappers. Eventually, after rummaging through what looked like the off-casts of a gargantuan party pack of Mars Bars, the lieutenant pulled out a crumpled colourful piece of paper.

"There!" She handed it over. "None of that other stuff's mine, by the way. We had a leaving do for one of the temps and I seem to be the only one who wants to keep this place tidy."

Longdon and Jenny were no longer listening. Instead they were staring at the flyer, or rather the words on it. After they had taken in the image of a large wicker effigy positioned next to a palatial country house.

A Weekend of Folk Wonders!

Come and Marvel at Our Heritage and History With...
Live Performances!
A Beautiful House and Gardens!
Bring the Whole Family!

Summer Is A-Comin' in at Summerisle House Come and Celebrate it with us!

Admission FREE - Only on May 1st!

"That's tomorrow," said Jenny. "Do you think Valentine will wait that long?"

"To bump off Elliot in some pretend-but-actually-real ceremony in front of hundreds of members of the general public? With the added novelty of humiliating the police before once again making good his escape?" Longdon stuffed the flyer into his pocket. "What do you think?"

"I think he's rather overdoing the 'pointing us in the right direction' thing."

"Because he obviously wants us to be there." Longdon didn't sound tired now. Instead, his voice was filled with a steely resolve. "Does that surprise you? It's his final big performance before he intends to disappear from the public eye yet again. But even that's not enough. He has to demonstrate, publicly, that even with all this information, even with all this forewarning, and with all the manpower we can put together, he can still outwit the police force. Well, not this time. This will definitely be Dr Valentine's last bow, but not the way he thinks."

20

"There are an awful lot of people here." Despite the warmth of the day, and the crowds, and the general gaiety, DS Jenny Newham shivered.

Longdon nodded as he swung his gaze from the country house to the left ('Guided Tours every half an hour!) to the fairground that had been erected in the grounds to the right. "I doubt even our Dr Valentine realised the distance people will travel for a bit of a free knees-up."

"Do they even say knees-up anymore, sir?"

"They do where I'm from, Sergeant. Now, come on. The chances are Valentine's got Elliot locked up somewhere in the house, so I suggest we go on one of their guided tours and then split up once we're inside and try and find him."

"What if they bring him out and burn him—"

"Try to burn him."

"What if they bring him out and try to burn him while we're in there?"

Longdon pointed at the sun. "He'll wait until that's close to setting. He's not going to go to all this trouble and then get a dramatic detail like that wrong. We've got a good few hours to find him yet."

They joined the queue for the tour of 'Summerisle House'.

"Has it occurred to you, sir—"

"Most everything has occurred to me Newham, but go ahead anyway." Longdon was obviously in an interrupting mood, but Jenny couldn't blame him for being on edge.

"Has it occurred to you that everything here – every single person, every piece of equipment, even this house – might all have been put on for our benefit?"

"I don't doubt it for a second, Newham." Longdon took her arm as the queue shuffled forward. "Even so we need to remember that most likely nearly everyone here is an innocent member of the general public who has no idea they are here under false pretences."

The elderly man in front of them dressed in the traditional British spring garb of grey raincoat, tweed trilby hat and umbrella turned at Longdon's slightly too-loud expostulation.

"You what?"

"Nothing."

"No." The man wasn't going to let it lie. "What do you mean about 'false pretences'?" He leaned forward and whispered. "They're not going to charge us once we're inside, are they? I've hardly brought any cash and Elsie's already given me an earful about being too tight to buy ice creams."

"Albert! What are you bothering these nice people about?"

"Nothing, dear." Now Albert was winking at Longdon with all the verve of a desperate man.

"It's all right, madam." Longdon gave Elsie what passed for a smile. "We were just commenting on how kind it is of the owners of Summerisle to let us look round it for free."

"I bet." Elsie shot a scowl at Jenny. "Men. They're all the same, aren't they? Always grabbing the chance to save a bit of beer money."

Jenny didn't know what to say so she just shrugged and tried to look acquiescent.

"We didn't even know this place was here until yesterday, and we only live a few miles away."

"Oh yes we did." Elsie gave Albert a slap. "Only it's never had this name."

"Must have new owners?" Jenny added helpfully.

"Either that," said Albert, "or the place has been losing money so badly they had to change the name."

"I think we're nearly there." Never had Longdon been so pleased to get to the head of a queue. His joy only lasted a moment, however, as he and Jenny were handed tickets and asked to stand in the group accumulating to the left of the entrance hall. Elsie obviously wanted to continue their conversation but Jenny was too busy staring open-mouthed at the doorway opposite, or rather, the sign above it.

"Yes I've spotted it too, Newham." Longdon was also doing his best to avoid Albert's eyeline. "However, judging from the fact that the door is shut I very much suspect that 'Dr Diabolo's Temptations Limited' is closed today. Thank goodness."

Jenny was resisting the urge to point. "That must be where he caught Charles Herman."

"Well if he's still in there, he's going to have to wait."

If Longdon planned to say anything else Jenny didn't

get to hear it, as the collective mutterings of the tour group were silenced by the main doors closing with an echoing thud.

"Ladies and Gentleman. Thank you for coming on this short guided tour of Summerisle house, and for deciding to spend part of this lovely sunny day indoors!"

Most of the crowd laughed at the young woman's words. Longdon didn't. He was too busy trying to work out if it was the same girl who had pretended to be Carola Peterson the other night.

"If you'll follow me, we'll begin our tour upstairs."

As the group moved to ascend the broad staircase, Jenny tapped Longdon's elbow.

"Isn't that Valentine's assistant?"

"Yes I'm pretty sure it is. But we're not going to make a move yet. I want to get them both, and chances are, if we arrest her now, she won't tell where Elliot is until it's too late. Let's follow the group but hang at the back."

They let everyone else shuffle past before Longdon and Jenny began to climb the stairs. By the time they got to the top they found the group had already stopped at a broad landing from which oak-panelled corridors led off left and right. The walls were adorned with numerous heavy, gloomy-looking paintings.

"Summerisle House is home to a number of art treasures," said their guide. "Only a few of them are on display here. Sadly, I'm afraid we don't have time to view them all but if I could draw your attention to this one." She pointed to a substantial work that depicted a priest fighting a horned beast. "We believe this to have been created during the reign of James III. It shows a local judge fighting off the devil. It's not clear who is winning but, if you look very carefully, you can see just a trace of blood on Satan's claw, suggesting that it is not always the forces of good that get the upper hand."

Was it Longdon's imagination or did their guide give the two of them a pointed look at that remark? Never mind, the group was being shuffled along to the next painting of interest.

"Here we have a picture of a grim, lonely, far less welcoming country house than this one. As I'm sure you are aware, all country houses have their tales of ghosts, but very few can boast haunted paintings." She moved closer to the foreboding piece of artwork. "It's said that from time to time a light appears in one of the upstairs windows, and that if you stare at it long enough you might see a figure moving within. Or hear them screaming, I can never remember which. The title of the painting is simply 'Landscape – Artist Unknown'." She smiled. "It's a shame we cannot conjure that artist out of the picture to tell us whether it really does change or not. Let's move on."

"Let's not," Longdon whispered to Jenny. "Once they turn the next corner, hang back."

The group, with Longdon and Jenny now at the back, had reached a full-length portrait of a man dressed in what looked like a blue cavalier's outfit.

"This dates from the time of King Charles II," the guide gestured to the painting. "The subject is Sir Michael Sinclair, a member of the king's court who was rumoured to consort with the devil. He vanished after penning his infamous tract 'An Experiment in Darkness' in the twenty second year of the king's reign, after which he disappeared, some say into the ghost room he speaks of in his writings. For all we know, that's where he still is now."

"Is the room in this house?" Elsie asked.

That raised a smile. "Not exactly, but who knows what someone might find if they were to look behind the wrong door?"

"Come on." Longdon laid a hand on Jenny's shoulder. "I think it's time for the *un*guided tour."

They slipped away and retraced their steps, descending the stairs to the now empty foyer.

"Where should we start?"

Longdon was already opening and closing doors. "Probably a cellar, knowing Valentine. See if you can find any steps leading further down."

Jenny was about to follow orders when a noise from outside caused them both to halt.

It came again. Two sharp blasts on a horn to silence the crowd, followed by what sounded like the rattle of a tambourine.

"Could they be starting?" Jenny whispered.

Longdon pulled on the front door handle. It was locked. As realisation gripped him he darted back upstairs, past the paintings and in the direction in which the tour group had gone, only to be confronted by another locked door. Longdon thumped it in exasperation.

"He's been watching us!" He pointed at the chandelier above them, and at the surveillance camera concealed amongst its crystal teardrops.

Outside a folk band had started playing. Jenny peered

through the window to see a procession of weird and gaily dressed characters proceeding through the massed crowd. They were led by a man in a dress and a long black wig, and their destination was obvious.

"They're headed to the wicker man!"

"Right!" Longdon looked round for something to smash the window with and settled on a Queen Anne chair upholstered in green velvet.

It was heavier than it looked.

"Give me a hand with this."

"To do what?"

Longdon nodded at the window Jenny had been looking through. "To smash the glass so we can get out of course."

"But it's probably hundreds of years old!"

"And our careers are only minutes from being over if we don't get out there, Newham. Now come and give me a hand."

Between them they lifted the chair and, after some further encouragement from the Inspector, flung it at the window. Jenny winced at the sound of splintering glass, then ran to the gaping hole they had created. She looked down.

"Looks like a twenty foot drop onto flagstones, sir."

"Already on it, Newham."

Longdon was busy using his car keys to lever up nails from far end of the red carpet runner. Once he had taken out a couple he ran his hands underneath and pulled. The carpet came free with a series of popping sounds. He gripped the free end he had lifted up, dragged it to the window, and swung it over the sill.

"Are we going to climb down that?"

"No." Longdon was breathing heavily. "I'm far too heavy. You are going to climb down it while I hold onto the other end up here. And before you say anything – that's an order."

Knowing she would only be wasting time if she delayed, Jenny bit back her reservations and climbed out of the window, holding onto the sides of the carpet and letting herself down hand over hand. When she got to the bottom she signalled for Longdon to wait, and darted out of sight.

A moment later she was back, pushing an enormous sack of grass cuttings.

"Come on!" she said. "Jump!"

Longdon checked the corridor again for anything else that might break his fall. Once he had convinced himself there was nothing, he braced himself in the window frame.

"If you miss I'll catch you!"

"Newham, you will do no such thing. Better one of us is able to stop Valentine than neither. Now clear out of the way."

He almost missed, but Jenny had no intention of telling him that with any immediacy, and certainly not as a grass-stained and breathless Longdon was getting to his feet to dust himself down.

"Something the matter, Newham?"

"No sir, nothing at all."

Longdon pointed at the procession. "Then let's get over there!"

~

By the time Longdon and Jenny caught up, the procession had reached the towering effigy erected in the centre of the amusements area. The procession encircled the wicker man, while their bewigged leader took up a position in front of it. The crowd, quietened by the drumming, and their attention now fully focused on the macabre living tableaux that was being presented to them, waited to see what would happen next.

It was unlikely anyone was expecting what actually happened.

First, the leader removed his wig and dress to reveal a tweed jacket over a yellow pullover. He then raised his hands and began to speak.

He didn't get past taking a breath.

"That's enough, Valentine!"

Inspector Jeffrey Longdon and Detective Sergeant Jenny Newham, both holding up their badges, stepped out of the crowd. Longdon's bellow cut through the pregnant silence. If anything it served to emphasise how still the audience around them now was.

Everyone waited to see what would happen next.

"Inspector!" Valentine beamed. "How very good to see you, even if you're not wearing the appropriate costume."

"You mean Punch?" Longdon sneered. "Did you really think the thought of doing that would have entered my head?"

"Of course not, and so I did not contrive to put you in the situation where you would have to. It makes no change to the outcome, anyway."

"Well, that's what we're here to change."

"Are you, Inspector? Are you really?"

"Yes." Still brandishing his badge with the one hand, Longdon took a revolver from his overcoat pocket with the other and pointed it at Valentine. "If you'd be kind enough to release Elliot Edwards from that thing behind you and then come quietly, it will save us all a lot of embarrassment."

Valentine responded with a deep-throated laugh. "There may be some embarrassment here today, Inspector, but I can assure you that none of it will be mine."

Longdon persisted. "If you'll just open that thing up we'll get Edwards out."

"You're sure, Inspector? In front of all these people, you really want me to do that?"

It was only at that moment that Longdon knew Valentine had something else planned.

"Will opening it harm anyone here?"

"None of the assembled members of the general public, Inspector. I'm not a monster, you know."

"That's a matter for debate, and I think you'll be the only one on that side of it."

Valentine took a step back. "Enough, then. I shall do as you ask."

Under Longdon's watchful eye Valentine strode to the wicker man and climbed the wooden steps that led to the construct's body. Longdon thought he could he see an inert form slumped inside.

"You're sure you wish me to open this?"

Longdon waved the gun. "Get on with it, Valentine."

"Very well."

Valentine pulled a cord of fraying rope and the door in the wicker man's torso swung open to reveal what it contained.

21

The crowd shuffled uncomfortably, not knowing whether this was meant to be the end of the performance, or even what the point of the performance was supposed to be. Was this some sort of play? The man who had been wearing the wig was beaming again, while the plain clothes policeman was staring in disbelief at what the wicker man contained. What was so special about that? What was so special about a rather floppy-looking wax dummy dressed in a white smock?

"Where's Edwards?" Longdon snarled.

"Well he's not here, obviously." Valentine sounded surprised that such a thing should ever have been the case.

Longdon looked about him. "Then why all this? Why go to all this trouble if you're not going to reproduce the end of the film?"

Still at the top of the steps, Valentine's voice boomed over the audience. "My dear Inspector, you really have missed the point, haven't you?"

"What 'point', Valentine?"

Valentine addressed Longdon as if he were a schoolboy who had made a basic mistake in his Latin sentence construction. "What happens at the end of *The Wicker Man*?"

"An innocent man is burned to death to satisfy the absurd beliefs of a bunch of pagan lunatics."

"No. Goodness me, I think you might need to go back and watch it again." Valentine began to descend, slowly, talking as he did so. "In the film *The Wicker Man* a repressed representative of a controlling establishment, wishing to impose his, and thereby his establishment's, views on an isolated island community, is tricked by that community to his very great detriment."

"Are you saying..." Longdon was having trouble keeping his temper under control "...are you saying that this has all been some elaborate trick at my expense?"

"My dear Inspector, you do take a while to catch on, don't you? How many cases of homicide have you now failed to solve? How many individuals are there left for you to protect? And yet here you are, wasting your time at some silly May Day event while your final possibility of redemption is nowhere near here. I don't think the papers are going to present you in a very favourable light, do you?" Valentine looked over Longdon's head. "I don't suppose there are any members of the press here today, are there?"

Longdon glanced behind him at the forest of hands that had gone up. When he turned to once again regard his nemesis, Valentine was holding a small silver box with a red button dead centre. His thumb was hovering over it.

"Elliot Edwards isn't here, Inspector. He isn't even in England. Why oh why would I have passed up the opportunity to put paid to that meddling egotistical film producer who thought he could exploit my very life for his profit in any other way than by reproducing, at the exact same location as the original was filmed, the fiery climax of *The Wicker Man?*" Valentine held the device aloft. "Time to say goodbye to Mr Edwards, I think. Your men will find him eventually, but of course by then it will be far too late, both for Mr Edwards, and for your career. Don't get me wrong, Inspector, this whole thing has been a delight, but I think both of us could do with a rest, don't you agree? You in eternal shame and I, well, I have other plans that no longer concern you."

Valentine's thumb came down on the red button.

For a moment there was silence.

Then Longdon began to shake his head.

Then he started to laugh.

And laugh.

He only stopped when Valentine spoke again.

"I am presuming this latest episode has caused you to lose your sanity, Inspector. For that you have my sympathy."

"You can be as sympathetic as you like, Valentine." Longdon turned to the audience, who were still trying to work out if the drama staged for them had actually finished yet. "How many of you here said you were press?" Again there was the forest of hands, in a semi-circle close to the front. Longdon nodded as he looked round them. "And how many of you here are police in disguise?"

A far greater forest of hands went up, enclosing both the press, Longdon and Jenny and, significantly, the whole of the wicker man Valentine was standing beside.

"You see, Dr Valentine, I'm afraid it's my turn to offer you sympathy. I knew you wouldn't be able to resist restaging the end of *The Wicker Man* where they shot it, just as I also knew you would want me as far away as possible, preferably being humiliated as the final act of this particular little spree of yours. Well this time I'm afraid the joke's on you."

The press were snapping pictures now. Of Longdon, of the police, and of Valentine, who still hadn't moved.

"You can let the members of the public out," Longdon instructed his colleagues. "I've got my eye on our culprit."

And so the police moved in and the public moved out. Some of them, assuming the show was over, began to applaud until they were silenced by looks from those with greater awareness of what was really going on.

Valentine gave Longdon a wistful look. "So Elliot Edwards is..."

"Alive and well, thanks to the homing device we planted on him. Or at least he should be if my colleagues north of the border have done their job."

"You're forgetting Christina..."

"...who will have been picked up as she exited the house with that tour group we were a part of. If not, you can be assured she won't get far."

"My, my, Inspector, it would seem that for once I have underestimated you." Valentine clapped his hands three times, slowly and deliberately. "I have escaped a police cordon like this before, you know."

"I know that, sir, which is why I have taken precautions against it happening again." Longdon smiled. "I have spent the last five years watching so many of your favourite films you never thought to ask me what mine was."

"I had no idea you regarded the cinema as anything

other than a passing distraction, Inspector, and now I have to say you have me genuinely curious. What is it?"

Longdon took a whistle from his pocket.

"*Zulu*. Cy Endfield. 1964," he said, and gave the whistle a mighty blow.

No-one at the Summerisle House Open Day could have predicted what happened next, but many of them told and retold the story of that day to their increasingly disinterested children, and later to their even more disinterested grandchildren, such a unique experience was it to all of them.

From over the horizon in every direction surged a sea of blue. More policemen than many of the public had dreamed ever existed marched across the countryside from all corners of the compass, a cordon that seemed to enclose the estate itself, and the Public Enemy Number One they had been instructed to ensure did not escape.

"A cordon to enclose a cordon," Valentine mused, "press coverage, my master plan thwarted. You seem to have thought of everything, Inspector."

"If you would just come quietly, sir," Longdon did his best not to sound too pleased with himself, but it was difficult, "I think that would be for the best."

"You are probably right, Inspector." Rather than coming forward, however, Valentine was making his way back up the steps. "However, if everything is to come to an end I would much prefer it to be on my terms than the British legal system's."

With that, Valentine clambered into the effigy's torso and then closed the door behind him. "I do hope you've got the fire service in hand as well as all those policemen!"

Longdon heard Valentine call from inside the wicker man.

Almost immediately there was the smell of burning.

Oh no.

"Right, keep back!" Longdon began to wave the inner cordon away. "I think he's set himself on fire in there. Keep a safe distance until the emergency services get here but on no account are you to break the cordon!"

Soon the body of the effigy was ablaze. Over the noise from a large group of increasingly distressed people who had been expecting a fun day out came the sound of a helicopter

"That was bloody fast." Longdon looked round Jenny, who was returning from checking the cordon was intact. "Did you radio for a helicopter?"

"No sir."

"Did any of you?"

Apparently not. A moment later the question became irrelevant as the helicopter in question rose from behind Summerisle house, hovered for a moment, and then began to approach the mass of flames that was the wicker man.

The length of heavy steel rope trailing beneath it had a large hook on the end.

"Oh, shit."

There was nothing they could do. The flames were already too high, the heat too intense, for anyone to approach. All Longdon and his team could do was watch, helpless, as the hook was swung through the right eye of the statue.

Then the thirty foot tall burning wicker man was lifted into the air.

Jenny peered up at the swaying, blazing figure. "He can't still be alive in there? Surely?"

Longdon was shaking his head. "I don't believe it. I just do not bloody well believe it."

They expected the helicopter to move away rapidly. Instead, it hovered for a moment, giving time for the door in the wicker torso to open and a flaming dummy to be ejected. It fell to the ground close to the wooden steps Valentine had been standing on only moments ago.

Officers were on it with fire extinguishers in a flash.

"Something pinned to it, sir!" The one who shouted brought it over. An envelope covered in what looked like tinfoil.

"Heatproof," Jenny said as Longdon tore it open. He growled acknowledgement as he took out a piece of paper.

"Looks like a message, sir"

"It does, Newham, it does." Longdon read it aloud.

My dear Inspector Longdon.

It would appear things have taken a somewhat unexpected turn, hence this rather abrupt and fiery exit of mine, for which I offer my apologies. Be assured, however, that you shall not be hearing from me again. I gather from our film producer friend that his idea to make a film of my adventures has already been copied elsewhere. Apparently those responsible reside in Italy. I therefore feel it is my solemn duty to travel to Rome and teach the gentlemen responsible a lesson. So I bid you farewell, Inspector, and thank you for all the entertainment. I cannot imagine the representatives of Interpol will be anywhere near as much fun as you.

Yours, with very best of wishes as always,
Edward Valentine MD FRCS

"How did he have time to write all that?" Jenny was still looking at the note, wide-eyed.

"Because he didn't did he?" Longdon screwed up the paper and stuffed it into his pocket. "This was his plan all along. Maybe not Elliot escaping but all the rest of it. I don't doubt for one moment it was that assistant of his in the cockpit. Our men must have missed her."

The helicopter was moving off now, its smoking burden swinging gently beneath it.

"So that's it then?" Jenny shielded her eyes from the sun as they watched the helicopter's retreat. "He's escaped again?"

"Yes." Longdon was turning a dark shade of red while grinding his fist into his palm. "Damn. Damn! Damn! Damn!"

He looked around him and spotted something close to the bouncy castle. Suddenly his entire demeanour changed. "Sergeant Newham," he turned Jenny away from the retreating helicopter and drew her attention to where he was now pointing.

"Am I mistaken, or is that by any chance an air ambulance?"

22

"Yes sir, that's right." The noise inside the cockpit was so great Longdon was having to shout into the radio. "Yes sir, we're on Valentine's tail. In fact we're right behind him. The noise is because we're in a helicopter, sir. Yes, Valentine's in a helicopter too, sir. No, not the same one. And to be precise he's not so much in the helicopter as underneath it. Yes sir. In a burning wicker man. I have no idea sir – some sort of flame retardant suit I would imagine. Yes sir, bits of the wicker man do keep dropping off. Yes the pieces could pose a risk to those on the ground. Well seeing as we have no idea where he might be going it would be difficult to predict which roads we might need to close. Right now we're..." he looked at Jenny, crammed in between himself and the pilot. She looked to her right.

"Just over Shepton Mallet," the pilot replied.

"Did you hear that, sir? Good. My guess is he's making for the coast. For all we know he's got a boat waiting. Could you arrange coverage of anywhere a boat might be moored, say from Weston super-Mare down to Watchet? Yes, yes I understand – all available forces were mobilised at my request and are currently back in Wiltshire. Yes sir I realise that leaves just myself and Sergeant Newham. Thank you sir, we'll do our best."

"On our own again are we?" Jenny asked.

Longdon nodded. "All we can do is follow him and hope when he lands we have enough time to nab them both."

Jenny pointed to the still-flaming load of the helicopter in front of them. "I can't believe there's any of that thing still left to burn."

"It wouldn't surprise me if the chamber Valentine's in is completely flame retardant." As Longdon spoke, the last pieces of burning wicker fell away, to reveal a torpedo-shaped aluminium chamber. The rope from the helicopter was hooked around a metal loop protruding from the chamber's roof. "So that explains that."

"Passing over the Mendips now, sir."

Longdon and Jenny looked down at the rolling hills the pilot had named. In the distance, a grey band divided the land from the sky.

"If we keep going in a straight line," Longdon asked the pilot, "where we will eventually end up?"

"How far do you mean, sir?"

Longdon glanced at Jenny and shrugged. "Just say the Somerset coast for now."

"If we maintain this trajectory we should reach Weston super-Mare in bit, sir, which is funny, really."

Longdon gripped the man's arm, then remembered it was connected to the hand holding the helicopter's joystick. He let it go. "Why 'funny'?"

"Oh, only because that was the other job I had the chance of doing this weekend – emergency medical service on Weston beach."

"Because of the May Day crowds, I suppose."

"Yes, sir, and because of the science fiction convention."

"The what?"

"Science fiction convention, sir. They were going to hold it indoors, but the plan was if the weather was nice to move it onto the beach. Said they had something special planned."

Longdon could barely stop himself from shaking. "I don't suppose this convention had a particular theme, did it?"

Jenny was way ahead of him. She showed him the webpage on her phone:

Weston Classic SF Weekender
This year celebrating the Greatest British
Science Fiction Films of All Time

"That's where he's bloody going! And he's going to use the crowds to stop us getting to him!" Longdon turned to Jenny. "I'm too wound up to think. Give me the names of some British science fiction films, Newham."

"Well *2001: A Space Odyssey* is probably the most famous."

"Wouldn't work on a beach, though. What else?"

"*Alien*?"

"Valentine may be nuts but he's not going to burst out of that canister dressed as an acid-bleeding monster, is he? Next?"

"*Under the Skin*'s very good," Jenny was floundering. "Scarlett Johansson's in that one."

Longdon shook his head. "Too modern."

They were so busy talking they hardly heard the pilot announce that they were coming up to Weston.

"Then I don't know." Jenny looked dejected. "It sounds silly, and besides he's already done them but for a minute I thought it might be..." she tailed off.

"Doesn't matter Newham, I'll take silly over nothing at all. Out with it."

She pointed out of the window at their quarry, and specifically at its metal burden, swinging several feet beneath. "That capsule..."

"Yes?"

"Well that's it. It looks like a space capsule, a bit like the one in *The Quatermass Experiment*. You know, the old..."

"...Hammer film," After a moment to collect his breath, Longdon got back on the radio. "Sir, I think Valentine is going to crash this capsule or whatever it is that he's in, on Weston beach, and then use the subsequent panic to make his getaway. If at all possible, and if there are any men spare, get them over to Weston beach. I don't know how he plans to do it, sir. The impact of dropping that thing from any height would kill him and—"

"Jesus Christ!" That came from the pilot. "What the fuck is THAT?"

For a split second both Longdon and Jenny were speechless as they stared at the horizon, at what was on the horizon, rising up from Weston beach. Then Longdon was back on the radio.

"Sorry, sir, but we now appear to be looking at a one hundred foot high inflatable... I don't know what it is? A grasshopper?"

"It's a Martian," said Jenny. "THE Martian, the giant one from the end of..."

"*Quatermass and the Pit!*" They both said together.

"Oh my God." Longdon let the radio drop. "He's going to fly straight into that thing just like in the film!"

"It's a crane in the film, sir."

Longdon pointed at the vast crowd that was now visible amassed on the beach. "Do you think half the people down there will be bothered about that?" He turned to the pilot. "Find somewhere to land close by."

"That'll be difficult, sir." The pilot didn't look happy. "A lot of the beach is very soft and—"

"That doesn't seem to be stopping HIM, does it?" Longdon pointed at the helicopter, now rising about the Martian demon as it planned to swing the metal cylinder with Valentine inside it into the monster.

"Sir, a small metal capsule is very different from a helicopter with the three of us in it, surely you can see that?"

What Longdon and Jenny saw at that moment was the helicopter ahead of them releasing the metal cable holding the capsule, which swung into the very heart of the Martian demon. The huge inflatable structure immediately began to fold in on itself as the momentum from the swung capsule propelled it forward.

"Get. Us. Down!" Longdon growled.

"I. Am. Trying." the pilot replied, veering them to the left.

It was hopeless. The areas of firm ground that weren't filled with parked cars were host to multitudes of people. Out on the beach, those dressed as what might kindly be described as superheroes, aliens and other well-known science fiction standbys broke into spontaneous applause as the enormous Martian demon was propelled out to sea. Some took pictures. Others were filming it on their phones. Little did they know they were creating visual records of the escape of the most diabolical and flamboyant serial killer the world had ever known.

The pilot finally got them down, not too far away and with no damage to person or property.

"Well done, son," said Longdon.

"Just go and catch him, Inspector!" The pilot was practically pushing the two of them out of the helicopter.

And then Longdon and Jenny were running along the beach, pushing aside Trekkies, people dressed Patrick McGoohan in The Village, and one particularly statuesque gentleman in a scarlet evening dress complete with feather boa and a badge that said 'Supreme Commander Servalan'.

But all they could do was watch.

Watch as the helicopter flown by Valentine's assistant made its escape.

Watch as the hundred foot tall inflatable Martian demon, slowing now, and flattening out, became a life raft complete with power motor that began to buzz its way down the Bristol Channel, no doubt headed for international waters.

Watch as their backup finally arrived, as police swarmed into the beach, police that would soon be asking "Well which one is he, then?" All Jenny and Longdon could do was point with the utmost embarrassment, frustration and sense of defeat any human being might capable of, at the rapidly vanishing figure of a monster from a classic British Hammer science fiction film of the 1960s.

Longdon looked at Jenny. "You know what?" Over her shoulder he could see the massed might of three separate police constabularies approaching. "Interpol can bloody well have him."

The End

Except...

Epilogue

The film world mourns the loss of Elliot Edwards. The head of independent production company American Enterprise Pictures, over the last twenty three years Edwards was responsible for a string of exploitation titles that received surprisingly wide distribution in the Western hemisphere thanks to Edwards' knack for publicity. Known for his abrasive attitude and frequently colourful language, Mr Edwards was in Rome to discuss completion funding of his latest project, a film version of the popular book The Nine Deaths of Dr Valentine. *It is known that the production had run into considerable difficulties during location shooting in England, and as a consequence Edwards was having trouble getting the project finished. The only surviving member of the AEP team who made that fateful journey across the Atlantic, Edwards was staying in a hotel in Rome at the time. It is thought that the poor state of repair of the building, and of the ancient elevator system in particular, contributed significantly to the events that led to his untimely death in a manner even more bizarre than that of some of his former colleagues.*

The Rome police remain baffled as to how, even with the lift being in such poor repair, Mr Edwards could have met such a fate. It is thought he must have been wearing something like a fine metal chain around his neck, which then got caught in the mechanism. There is also no word as to whether the items found at the scene are considered to be part of the ongoing investigation. The single black glove and the straight razor seem elements more suited to one of Mr Edwards' lurid projects than real life. The investigation is ongoing, and it now seems unlikely Mr Edwards' final film will ever be finished.

The Last Afterword of Dr Valentine

Or is it? Those of you who have just read the book may be wondering otherwise, and if you haven't read the book you are strongly urged (by both myself and the good doctor, who will find out if you haven't) to go and read it now. It will make this section a lot more fun. Each of the two prior volumes in this series have featured afterwords consisting of my thoughts on the films referred to in the story, notes on the creative process, and the autobiographical reminiscences I like to include at the end of all of my books as an excuse not to write a proper autobiography. As usual, what follows is not intended as a critical appraisal of the films in question but rather the effect these movies, and the people whose efforts went into making them, had on me when I was growing up.

Horror Express (1972)

Justifiably remembered with tremendous fondness by a great many film fans, I first saw this British-Spanish coproduction when I was twelve years old. It was the film's 'First Showing on British Television' (which I do remember), and the date was 2nd January 1980 (which I don't – thanks BBC Genome). It was Cushing and Lee, which meant it would be great, but I don't think even I would realise how great. *Horror Express* is crammed with elements that were pure horror gold to me at that age, and I still think a major part of why it works so well is that it's a true ensemble piece. As well as the acting from the leads, there's a plot involving a rampaging monster and a train (yes I loved travelling on trains back then, and my wife Kate, who has accompanied me many times on the Bristol Parkway train to London, will tell you I still do). The script (by Arnaud d'Usseau and Julian Zimet aka Halevy) is crackers but at the same time extraordinarily ambitious. John Cacavas gives us a great music score that, for a man who apparently preferred to avoid melody (according to an interview regarding his score to Hammer's *The Satanic Rites of Dracula*) manages some deliciously creepy variations of its main theme. As well as the above, there are the more unsung heroes. I don't think editor Bob Dearberg has ever received sufficient credit for how *Horror Express* is cut together. The pacing at the climax is a major reason why the movie works so well. Alberto de Mendoza gives a brooding performance as mad monk Pujardov but it's (presumably) Robert Rietti the 'man of a thousand voices' who dubs him so well.

Will it surprise you to learn I was very disappointed that the idea of learning and memory being engraved on the normal brain to leave a wrinkled surface was nonsense? Or that the idea of doing a post-mortem on moving train was just fabulous? So finally, here I get to do my own little tribute to that scene. Many years after watching *Horror Express* I finally got to travel the trans-Siberian railway, starting in Moscow and finishing up in Beijing. Of course, my journal entry for each day started with a quote from the film. Did I check the baggage van?

Did I wear tweeds? And if I was asked in the dining car, three days into the trip, if I was a doctor, did I suggest they "Ask me when I've finished my dinner."?

I'm sure you already know the answers.

Psychomania (1972)

The 'other' Benmar horror film, and the second (after *Horror Express*) that I added to my wish list of movies I wanted Dr Valentine to somehow emulate in this latest volume. *Psychomania* isn't exactly a good film but that doesn't stop it from still being rather wonderful. Just in case there's anyone out there who doesn't know what this film is about, or has forgotten, or more likely, isn't quite sure what they watched in the first place, the plot goes something like this.

The Living Dead motorcycle gang consists of a group of young RADA-trained actors with beautiful speaking voices trying to act evil. They are aided in this endeavour by the names given them by the script which include 'Hatchet' (played by the chubby little ginger chap from *Blood on Satan's Claw*), 'Chopped Meat' (who ends up a singing one of the strangest songs in horror film history, but more on that in a minute) and 'Jane' (Ann Michelle, keeping her clothes on this time after the copious nudity of Tigon's *Virgin Witch* a couple of years previous and soon to appear in Pete Walker's *House of Whipcord*. All these acting choices, along with Chris Boger's *Cruel Passion*, mean she is still regarded with affection by British film fanatics to this day).

Each member of the gang has their name written on their leathers, presumably in case they (or indeed the actors playing them) forget who they are. It also makes it very handy later on for the police to be able to identify the various perpetrators of any ensuing miscreant behaviour. The leader is Tom, played by Nicky Henson (Ian Ogilvy's friend from *Witchfinder General*), whose girlfriend Abby is played by Mary Larkin. Despite being pretty much the only one left alive at the end of this, as far as I'm aware Ms Larkin never went on to do anything of any significance afterwards.

The opening title sequence of this film is wonderful. John Cameron's music theme is very seventies but it's the right kind of seventies, and when this sequence is watched now it lends an even more haunting otherworldly atmosphere to the proceedings. The incongruous image of motorcycles riding around fog-wreathed standing stones in slow motion is at once outlandish and engaging, and is almost perfect in its atmospheric scene setting. The movie which follows is also going to be filled with standout moments, albeit on the whole for reasons other than what one could hesitatingly call quality.

After a little bit of road-based violence to get the film started (and to demonstrate just how nasty the bike gang is) Tom and Abby pop off to the nearest graveyard where their canoodling is interrupted by Tom's interest in a frog who has been thrown onto the set. Popping his new 'little green friend' into his pocket (!) he leaves Abby to probably seriously reconsider her position in a relationship where amphibians seem to take precedence, and drives back to the manor house where he lives with mum Beryl Reid, butler Shadwell (George Sanders) and some of the most hideous seventies wall-sculptures you will ever see. While Shadwell admires the frog (now housed beneath a transparent cover probably last used for a sponge cake) Tom brings us up to speed on how Shadwell never gets older, that the butler knows the secret of the living dead, and that the house has a room that's been locked for eighteen years. A huge baguette loaded with fillings magically appears from nowhere and Tom munches on it to provide dialogue punctuation, but not as well as Peter Cushing would probably have handled it. Brave try, though.

Needless to say, Tom's soon in the mysteriously dust-free and highly polished forbidden chamber, finding his dead dad's NHS spectacles and having visions of a big frog and then Beryl doing something suspiciously like signing Tom's soul away when he was a baby to a man with a frog ring. Tom should be okay, apparently, because he's wearing a frog pendant, which leads one to wonder if the producers spent a day in 1971 at World of Frogs buying up their unsold stock, and then got screenwriters Arnaud D'Usseau and Julian Halevy to follow-up their previous movie hit *Horror Express* with "anything (and we mean literally anything) involving frogs and motorbikes".

The 'big secret' is that if you kill yourself but believe you'll come back then you will, which if it were actually true would mean a world full of the buggers. There's probably more to it than that but I suspect the film-makers thought it would be irresponsible to divulge anything else, although somehow I imagine it involves more frog-based shenanigans.

After some very poor shopping-centre antics and a road chase, Tom drives off a bridge and into the local river, killing himself. "We'd like to bury him our way if that's ok" says Abby when she visits Beryl's house. Trusting Beryl agrees without asking any more, so it's a bit of a relief when it turns out that the gang's 'way' involves burying Tom in his leathers and sitting on his motorbike in the stone circle. Rather than anything, you know, a bit silly for when he comes back

Which he does, in one of the most memorable screen moments in all of British cinema. "Do you want him back?" says George Sanders beforehand. "Yes," says Beryl. "Yes, God help me I do." Which is the cue, ladies and gentlemen, for you to either hit the fast forward button, go and make a cup of tea, or brace yourselves for one of the most incongruous moments in movie history as this zombie biker horror picture grinds to a halt so that the gang, dressed in hippy gear, can make wreaths and other flower-based items of mourning while the song 'Riding Free' is mercilessly etched into your subconscious. Tom may indeed have 'really got it on' and may well have 'rode that sweet machine just like a bomb' but I am going to stop before I tell you the full horror of these lyrics in case there's any risk of copyright infringement.

Tom comes back and looks remarkably clean for a man who's been buried under a grave full of earth. He gets some free petrol and then proceeds to murder a pub full of people. Police inspector Robert Hardy, looking unsure as to how he's meant to be playing this, keeps a straight face as the bodies start to pile up, especially when the gang cotton on and proceed to kill themselves in a montage of suicides so ridiculously over the top that the comic moments of the film so far are in serious danger of being topped by this single three minute sequence.

Scarcely has the pathologist time to answer a call from his wife than the gang are up and about again, including Abby, who's not actually dead as her overdose failed, but not before giving her a slightly trippy dream sequence where her nightmare becomes so extreme and unpleasant that she envisions herself wearing something approaching a gaily coloured African tablecloth.

Beryl finds out from the police that Tom's told his gang the Family Secret and tells Shadwell she wishes to break her bargain. "And you know what you will be become for all eternity?" he says and she nods, figuring she might be able to get a job presenting The Muppet Show in a couple of years.

Tom finds out Abby is still living and in a showdown with the gang back at the stone circle attempts to kill her. Fortunately Beryl has completed the ritual, acquiring a distinctly croaky voice and a Kermit-like appearance in the process, and as a result Tom and his gang turn to stone. The End. Apart from black-cloaked Shadwell approaching a distraught Abby in the stone circle as John Cameron's music plays us out in another haunting moment that almost makes up for what's gone before.

Now, how was Dr Valentine going to do justice to a storyline like that? Of course there had to be a motorbike, of course there had to be 'that song', of course there had to be a frog reference somewhere, but the 'turning to stone' bit was the part I was most pleased with. It probably won't surprise you, therefore, to learn that I didn't come up with that bit at all. Instead Mrs Probert helpfully suggested it, and I am forever grateful to her for helping this chapter end on a suitably outrageous note. The terrible joke at the very end, however, is all mine.

Frightmare (1974)

I had to have a Pete Walker movie in here and it had to be this one, because I think it's the director's best film – a contemporaneous British equivalent to Tobe Hooper's *The Texas Chain Saw Massacre*.

Like Hooper's film, much of *Frightmare*'s action takes place in an isolated location in the country. Where it differs, however, is in its very British attitude towards all the madness and horror that occurs there. Dorothy Yates (Sheila Keith, whose performance I enjoy more and more every time I watch this film) is a cannibal with a predilection for brains. But when she isn't gibbering with glee drilling open people's skulls, or subjecting pretty Pamela Farbrother (who you would think would have had enough of being tortured on film after *Cry of the Banshee*) to a poker through the guts she's a kindly (and slightly pathetic) little old lady who does crochet by the fire. Her husband Edmund (Rupert Davies) knows exactly what's going on but adheres to the time honoured British traditions of Not Wanting Any Trouble and Pretending It

Doesn't Exist. Because of Keith's stellar performance, Davies' role often goes unnoticed but it's also a masterly study – this time in male impotence, never willing to take responsibility and insidiously scheming so that the blame for any upset within the family can be attributed to his daughter Jackie (Deborah Fairfax). Jackie's his daughter from his first marriage, which means she's sane. Debra (Kim Butcher) is Dorothy's daughter, which means she's not. Graham (Paul Greenwood) is a psychiatrist, which means he's going to get everything wrong with self-confident superciliousness before dying horribly – Walker and screenwriter David McGillivray do seem to have it in for the psychiatric profession in this one. Graham's boss is called Dr Lytell and he has an X-Ray upside down on the screen in his office. He gets referred to the director of the mental institution from which Edmund and Dorothy have been released. "We didn't kick them out for the fun of it you know," he says. "They're completely cured – as sane as you or I." Cut to bloodied corpse being hidden beneath straw in the barn. And if we haven't got the point by the end of the film, just as heroine Jackie is about to be meat-cleavered in the face by her stepmother we get a replay of the sentencing judge's "And let the members of the public be assured that you will remain in that institution until there can be no doubt whatsoever that you are fit and able to enter society again" from the movie's black and white prologue.

It's been said that the first three collaborations between Walker and McGillivray (*House of Whipcord*, *Frightmare* and *House of Mortal Sin*) form a trilogy in which the respective institutions of the law, the family and the Catholic church are attacked and to some extent satirised. I've found that much of the horror in Walker's films tends to stem from their implication of a lack of trust. We cannot trust our elders and self-appointed 'betters', or our doctors, or our priests, or the girl we're married to (*Schizo*) or even a kindly old couple of housekeepers (*The Comeback*). Much of the power of the cunningly constructed endings to these films lies in how believably the innocent parties are drawn to their fates. In Walker's world of horror, it's always the scheming villains who will win, and you can't get more bleak than that, except of course if they're Dr Valentine dressed up as 'Madame Dorothy'.

The World of Amicus

When I was a lad I loved everything and anything that was a British horror film from the period, but perhaps the films I loved the most were the anthology pictures made by Amicus, offering four of five short stories bound together (sometimes rather shakily, it must be said) by a framework story. The first one I ever saw was *The Vault of Horror* (1973) and it scared and thrilled me in equal measure. It was by no means their best (only the 'Midnight Mess' and 'Drawn and Quartered' episodes are good, but they're so good they're worth the price of admission). These films introduced me to the concept of EC comics (but not the actual comics themselves, because you just couldn't get hold of them easily back then) but also the work of two great short story writers, Robert Bloch and R Chetwynd-Hayes, whose stories I have loved ever since.

I also loved the Amicus anthology structure. In fact I loved it so much that the first and third books I wrote (*The Faculty of Terror* and *The Catacombs of Fear*) are put together along the same lines. It's not something you see in prose very often, although R Chetwynd-Hayes, quite possibly flushed with the success of Amicus' very own adaptation of his stories, *From Beyond the Grave* (1973), made a very creditable attempt in 1975 with his *The Monster Club*.

I thought long and hard about which Amicus anthology film to include in this volume, and as you will have already seen, in the end I couldn't decide, so I crammed in as many short story segments as I could. Hopefully the discerning Amicus fan will spot all the in-jokes. As for the films, we kick off with *Dr Terror's House of Horrors* (1965), move through *Torture Garden* (1967), *The House That Dripped Blood* (1970), *Tales from the Crypt* (1972) and end on *Asylum* (1972), where the dummy of Otto from 'The Weird Tailor' chases him back through the 'Blind Alleys' episode of *Tales from the Crypt* to end on possibly my favourite death scene from all of them, when a painter knocks a can of paint thinner over Tom Baker's portrait in the final story of *The Vault of Horror* (1973) causing his face to melt off. Lovely.

Peeping Tom (1960)

Here's a film I didn't really get on with when I first

watched it as a boy, but then that's because Michael Powell's fascinating, disturbing character study isn't for kids. Of course it wasn't for a lot of adults either at the time it was released, leading to the near cessation of the career of the man who had helped bring *The Red Shoes* (1948), *The Tales of Hoffman* (1951) and *Black Narcissus* (1947) to the screen. Never underestimate the ability of the public, critics and your peers to give you not even one break, not if you upset them enough.

Nowadays I can appreciate the film for the classic that it is. People may be surprised at my favourite scene, though, because it doesn't involve murder or insanity or a gleeful shredding of the audience's senses. Although certainly at the time there would have been a bit of that last one. You see, my favourite scene in *Peeping Tom* is the bit where Miles Malleson (as 'Elderly Gentleman Customer') goes into a newsagents to ask of the proprietor has 'any views'. It's not the views themselves, or the acting (which of course is marvellous) that endear me to this scene, but the fact that the newsagents is exactly like the one the I used to walk to with my father from about the age of eight, every Thursday evening, all year round, until at least my teens. That tiny shop in Abergavenny had a profound effect on my development. We went so my Dad could buy the Radio Times and TV Times, plus the Western Mail, the South Wales Argus and the Abergavenny Gazette, but often I would come away with something, too. I bought my first Agatha Christie novel there (*Elephants Can Remember*) and countless others, all with those superbly creative and disturbing Tom Adams covers. I bought my first pulp horror novel there (*Night of the Crabs* by Guy N Smith), as well as a series of little comic books called 'Pocket Chiller' that scared the life out of me and which are the only item from my childhood I wish I had hung onto, as they are near impossible to find nowadays.

Every now and then my eyes would stray to the top shelf.

It looked even higher when I was little, of course, but even now I suspect the shopkeeper had to use steps to get up there so he could fetch down the boxes of chocolates (Black Magic, Dairy Box, that one that was all fruit jellies). Of course behind the posh sweets were the magazines with pictures of girls on the front covers, and no front covers on the girls, to coin a phrase from Leo Marks' *Peeping Tom* script. And in between those boxes of chocolates were other boxes – small cardboard ones with more girls on. I only found out much later that these must have been 8mm loops that were still being sold into the mid-1970s.

The newsagents is gone, now – it's part of a larger shop that sells bicycles – but every time I watch *Peeping Tom*, and every time we get to meet Miles Malleson in his pursuit for 'views', I'm taken straight back to those years when I used to visit that place that's no longer there.

Night of the Demon (1957)

Arguably the best British horror film ever made had to get a look in sometime. I first saw this, like so many of my age, when it was shown as the first half of a BBC2 double bill on 28th June 1980 (the 'A' picture was the 1975 Tyburn film *The Ghoul* with Peter Cushing). The following Monday I and my classmates were busy passing runes to each other, leaving them in textbooks, and other boys' bags, and chalking them on the blackboard.

Night of the Demon was fun for a twelve year old, and as time has passed I've only grown to love it all the more. Appreciators tend to fall into one of two camps – those who like that we get to see the demon itself, and those who don't. I've always been firmly in the former camp, partly I will admit because it was stills of that very creature that made me seek out the film as a youngster in the first place. Of course, I am guilty of being extremely forgiving of the special effects in movies that are older, and those that have lower budgets, and I suppose it's possible that back in 1957 when *Night of the Demon* played cinemas that the effect looked a bit silly, but somehow I don't think so. Certainly the rest of the film allows me to suspend disbelief sufficiently that the creature works very nicely. I believe it would certainly win were it pitted against any of the giant creatures Universal and Toho were putting out there at the time.

But *Night of the Demon* did so much more for the young me than just being an entertaining monster movie. There's a wonderfully weird bit in the reading room of the British Museum that made me want to go there. I had never heard of M R James but I sought out the Penguin edition of his collected stories as a result, and caught up with the BBC's terrific *Ghost Stories For Christmas* whenever they were shown as a result.

And so, fittingly, it's M R James who has the 'last

word', as it were, in Dr Valentine's dispatching of poor old Raymond St Pearce. Bristol library isn't designed quite the way I've described it, by the way, so I hope you won't be too disappointed if you ever visit it and discover that the wall against which he meets his demise isn't there. You see, it only appears when the runes have been cast just right.

Dead of Night (1945)

From one widely acknowledged classic of British cinema to another, and the oldest film by far that Dr Valentine uses for inspiration. I think I had seen every Amicus anthology film before I finally had the chance to watch the Ealing movie that inspired Milton Subotsky to use the same structural device. I had already read E F Benson's 'The Bus Conductor' in *The Fourth Armada Ghost Book* edited by Mary Danby, because in those days it was relatively easy to pick up anthologies aimed at children that had those kinds of stories in them. It didn't scare me as much as its literary inspiration did, but for some reason Alberto Cavalcanti's 'The Christmas Party' with Sally-Ann Howes really spooked me, more so than the other stories. My favourite was Robert Hamer's 'Haunted Mirror' story (because haunted mirrors are just great) but the obvious choice to reference in this book was the much-appreciated and utterly splendid final story (also directed by Cavalcanti) in which Michael Redgrave's ventriloquist's dummy takes on a life of its own (or does it?). I do hope Dr Valentine's method of tribute meets with your approval.

The Wicker Man (1973)

My original plan was for this to be the final movie referenced, and for the climax of the book to take place on the actual Summerisle, with Longdon rushing in like Sergeant Howie does in the film. I was even going to have a burst of electric guitar being played over speakers as he attempts to rescue ghastly film producer Elliot Edwards from the burning wicker man. But the more I thought about it the more I realised it was too brief an ending, especially as this stood a good chance of being the final Dr Valentine book. Also because of that, I wanted to cram in as many British horror film in-jokes as I could, so instead the reader gets a barrage of references including *A Field in England* (2013 & the most recent film referenced in these books), *From Beyond the Grave* (1974), *Three Cases of Murder* (1955), and *Blood on Satan's Claw* (1970). Before all those, though, I hope some spotted the reference to dear old Ken Russell's *The Lair of the White Worm* (1988), which segues into *The Wicker Man*.

Yes, back to *The Wicker Man*.

My first chance to see it was in ATV's season of Christopher Lee ('Prince of Menace') movies back in the late 1970s. I would have been about ten. The week before they had shown *Scream and Scream Again* (1969) which had so traumatised me that, having read in Alan Frank's *Horror Films* book that *The Wicker Man* did not end on a happy note, inspired me to give it a miss. I don't necessarily think this was a bad thing. Whereas *Night of the Demon* still works if you watch it at a young age, I don't think *The Wicker Man* does. In fact, I was actually very glad to have been given the chance to wait until I had read the fabulous Cinefantastique special issue on the movie before watching it, so I could appreciate so much of what I might have otherwise missed. Interestingly, it wasn't until I discussed this film with Mrs Probert that I appreciated that you're not necessarily supposed to be on the side of Edward Woodward's character. But then like all great works of art it's probably a pretty good inkblot test that tells you more about yourself than you realise. Now where did I put my uniform and my set of unshakeable standards?

Quatermass and the Pit (1967)

And so we come to the final film...kind of. Something that had to top brain surgery in a train, a remote-controlled motorbike encased in concrete, Dr Valentine dressed up as Madame Dorothy, every Amicus film, and three all-time classics of cinema.

So how could I not fly a helicopter into an immense Martian grasshopper demon? *Quatermass and the Pit* remains one of my all-time favourite films and might just top my list of favourite science fiction films. I've written extensively about it elsewhere, (in Neil Snowden's *We are the Martians* Nigel Kneale book from PS Publishing) so I won't repeat myself, suffice to say it felt right to end everything at a science-fiction convention on the beach at Weston super-Mare.

And finally...

Ah, yes. Just how 'And finally...' can the Dr Valentine books ever be? Before I even started this one I had ideas about how much fun it would be to have the good doctor bumping people off in the style of some of my favourite Italian horror films, which is why there is a nod to Dario Argento's classic *Profondo Rosso* (1975) in the epilogue. Well, I could hardly let Elliot Edwards get away, could I?

Will Dr Valentine stay in Rome? Or perhaps move to France or Spain, where so many wonderful 1970s EuroHorrors were made? What if someone upsets him in Australia, a country finally being recognised for its terrific heritage of 'Ozsploitation'?

The honest answer is I cannot tell you, not right now. What I can say is that out of everything I have ever written, the Dr Valentine books have all been terrifically enjoyable experiences, from the selection of the films to the devising of the often bizarre and Heath Robinson-like methods of despatch. That's always the order, by the way – film first, then the working out of the creative death.

There are some acknowledgements on the following page, but here I would like to thank each and every one of you who has read and enjoyed these books, have come up to me and told me what a great time you had with them, and have asked me when there's going to be another. Writing the books has been brilliant, but it hasn't delighted me anywhere near as much as learning that others have had fun with them, too.

So, as always, all I have left to do now is to ask that you

all take care of yourselves, keep on being nice to each other, and I (and perhaps, just perhaps, Dr Valentine) will see you all again sometime.

John Llewellyn Probert,
Possibly planning a trip to Rome,
May 2018

Acknowledgements

My first and most heartfelt thanks have to go to Steve J Shaw of Black Shuck Books for rescuing *The Last Temptation of Dr Valentine* from the 'production hell' it had fallen into. Thanks for saying yes to this, Steve – you were my first and only choice for giving this book the love and care it needed.

In the first book I thanked all those involved in the making of the films of Vincent Price. In the second I thanked all those involved in the production of all those wonderful Hammer Films. It is only fair, then, that here I thank each and every cast and crew member of all those wonderful horror films made in the British Isles from the 1940s to the 1970s. The influence your work has had on me has been vast, the pleasure I have derived almost infinite, and the friends I have made from our shared love of these productions just the very best. Thank you all.

None of my books, nor I, would exist if it were not for the tireless efforts of my wife Kate, aka Thana Niveau, who keeps me sane, listens to my ideas (often performed loudly with lots of melodramatic gesticulations and a variety of voices, sometimes within earshot of others) and has the good grace to read and improve my manically written first drafts once I think I'm finished so I don't end up embarrassed in public. Well, not in that way, anyway. Thank you, my love – here's to many more adventures, literary and otherwise, for both of us.

About the Author

John Llewellyn Probert has been watching British-made horror films since he was ten years old, when he saw *Dr Phibes Rises Again* (1972) and *Witchfinder General* (1968) on a Vincent Price season on ATV. He was probably a bit too young for that second film, but the first influenced him to an extent that is still being felt by readers to this day, and especially readers of a book like this.

He is the recipient of the British Fantasy Award (for *The Nine Deaths of Dr Valentine*) and the Children of the Night Award (for *The Faculty of Terror*). His latest novel is *The Lovecraft Squad: All Hallows Horror* (Pegasus Books), his latest short story collection is *Made for the Dark* (Black Shuck Books) and his latest non-fiction book is a monograph on his favourite film of all time, *Theatre of Blood* (PS Publishing). There are lots of others and you can read more about them at www.johnlprobert.com

His next projects are a new novel, a new portmanteau collection in the 'Amicus' style, and more writing on film. His film review site, House of Mortal Cinema, is at www.johnlprobert.blogspot.co.uk. He is married to the writer Thana Niveau and at the moment he has no plans to hang from a helicopter and be flown to Weston super-Mare. Or anywhere else.

Printed in Great Britain
by Amazon

49571857R00307